I AM BILLY THE KID

OTHER BOOKS BY MICHAEL BLOUIN

FICTION

I Don't Know How to Behave
Wore Down Trust
Chase and Haven
Skin House

POETRY

I'm Not Going to Lie to You

I AM BILLY THE KID

MICHAEL BLOUIN

A NOVEL

Anvil Press // Vancouver

LIBRARY AND ARCHIVES CANADA CATALOGUING IN PUBLICATION

Title: I am Billy the Kid : a novel / by Michael Blouin.
Names. Blouin, Michael, 1966- author.
Description: 1st edition.
Identifiers: Canadiana 20220167788 | ISBN 9781772141887 (softcover)
Subjects: LCSH: Billy, the Kid—Fiction. | LCGFT: Alternative histories (Fiction) | LCGFT: Biographical fiction. | LCGFT: Novels.
Classification: LCC PS8603.L69 I2 2022 | DDC C813/.6—dc23

Cover design: Rayola.com
Interior layout: HeimatHouse
Author photo: Paulina Hrebacka
Represented in Canada by Publishers Group Canada
Distributed by Raincoast Books

The publisher gratefully acknowledges the financial assistance of the Canada Council for the Arts, the Canada Book Fund, and the Province of British Columbia through the B.C. Arts Council and the Book Publishing Tax Credit.

Anvil Press Publishers Inc.
P.O. Box 3008, Main Post Office
Vancouver, B.C. V6B 3X5 Canada
www.anvilpress.com

PRINTED AND BOUND IN CANADA

His roots twist up
into hips and down
through hardened
beetle graves. Bark peels
like dead skin, cracks
in callused fingertips.
An orchid breaks through
caverns of pulsating brass

and all the unlit corners
of all the unlit rooms.

— *Conyer Clayton*
from *We Shed Our Skin Like Dynamite*

"rumour has it that billy the kid never died."
—bpNichol, *The True Eventual Story of Billy the Kid*

"Blood like a necklace on me all my life."
—Michael Ondaatje, *The Collected Works of Billy the Kid*

"Do not tell me what is great/or how great gets made."
—Phil Hall, *An Oak Hunch*

This, my friends, for you.

❖ PART ONE ❖
BRAND-NEW DAY

☙ TURNER

Turner, do you remember our mother and how it was for us back then? How she would tend to the two of us as if she were a baker and we her fine pastries? Pinafores and ringlets and the smell of rosewater in the morning and the simple pleasures of being a girl without the burden of being grown-up women just yet, a duty that none would take upon themselves if the stakes of it were ever properly and plainly explained to us in advance.

I suppose that is why they never are. We are left to find our own way in the forest.

You were the favourite, Turner, there is no use in pretending it was not so—the younger one and the blonder one and always wings for feet and a shine to your eyes that suggested you were ready for anything, but you could never have been ready for what was to come, Turner, could never have been ready for any of this. I had but kissed a boy one time, I never told you, but I would have told you had there only been time enough. Do you remember the socials at Forrester's Hall before the house burned to the ground and took our mother away from us and how she would dress us up in ribbons and bows and the two of us would have tea and fine soft cakes and regard the young men on the other side of the room with the most unapproachable of gazes? "The Doctor's Daughters." So different now than the trail woman you have made yourself out to be or Father has made you out to be. Different in appearance and manner but still the same strength and the same set to your jaw when you are angered. Do you recall how once in a blue moon a pair of shined or scuffed shoes might slip across those white pine boards of the hall and a young gentleman might inquire as to the health of our mother or father or comment upon one or another most extraordinary aspect of the recent state of the weather and how we would practise our pleasantries while trying not to look at each other and laugh?

One boy I had seen at church on several occasions and at school every day, though he was in an older grade than I and seldom saw me at all, I think, managed to arrange for both him and me to be outside the hall and under an oak tree at the same time and there in the middle of a too-warm Sunday afternoon he found in himself the temerity to say to me, "I should very much like to kiss you, I think." Such words! Well, Turner, I thought to myself what would Turner say to him because you have always been more outspoken than I with that mouth of yours and you have always known just what to say to make someone tell you what you want to know or to shut them up and I said: "Well, just thinking a thing will not make a thing so." Can you imagine? Whenever I wanted to be brave, I would just pretend to be you, Turner, and then I was. Well, he looked at me as if I had just spoken backwards, but he kissed me. I don't suppose a girl had ever spoken to him in such a way as that and it wasn't even me speaking, it was you! Right there under that huge oak tree and in the middle of the broad, unblinking sun of daylight he kissed me. Davis was his name, Davis Blake Johnson, I do not know if you recall the look of him as I never told you of this or of him but oh I told my diary that evening how fine he appeared to me and how it felt to be so close up to him and how when he touched my cheek his hand smelt of bay rum and woodsmoke. I would change things if I could, as I wish now I had told you all about this instead of just putting it down onto dry old paper. Nothing lasts aside from the moments we have with each other and so many of them we just let slide by for the sake of the meaningless and empty things of this world. Imagine me setting aside precious time to tell something to a book now long gone, the same thing I would not share with my own sister whom I loved. Love. Whom I love, Turner. I would hold you now, if I had the moment to spend and the arms to do it with, would hold you and tell you so many things but mostly I would tell you to be careful, Turner. Things in this world are not how I had thought them to be at all and it seems clear now that they never were. Be guarded against it all. The thought that I spent even a moment of my life not fully engaged in this world when I was a part of it plagues me now, Turner, it touches on me like a branch in the night and there is nothing I can do about that, there is nothing now to be done. Do not let anyone hurt you. Wake up, Turner. Now. Everything is going to happen now. I am dead. I am a breath on the glass in the winter. Wake up.

(Missouri Wing speaks of her sister Turner. But this is Turner's story now. Speak, Turner.)

❧ BILLY

He is a quiet man for the most part, well-known in these parts for his long silences and the manner in which he sits and studies whatever room he is in as if there is always something to be learned in any place he finds himself. In conversation he listens carefully and occasionally he might ask some question. He never touches a gun unless to clean it or shoot it. This is a long and humid August afternoon, and he is tired of this town meeting and of the discussions of the new school building. He feels too old to spend a bright afternoon this way and he walks slowly out of the building for a moment in his new clean white shirt and he surveys the roadway yellowed by the sun and examines the wooden buildings stretched out beyond it. There by the corner of that house some children have strung a tired old rope from a dying oak tree and the earth beneath it is kicked at and worn down just as smooth as flour. He takes off his hat and wipes at his brow with a handkerchief and places the hat carefully on a railing by the doorway. His hands are still now and he does not move at all.

"This is a terrible place to put a fellow in"—to a reporter in the Las Vegas jail after his capture at Stinking Springs.

Unlike many of the quotations attributed to him in his life, that is something he actually said just the way it was written down there, but you have the sense, knowing him, that when he said it he might just as well have been speaking of any place on earth. Standing there on the porch he has a history longer than it is supposed to be and it has been a long road to here. A long road. .

(But let him tell it now. Speak, Billy.)

❧ 1 ❧

Don't call me Ishmael.

My parents did, and I have never forgiven them for doing so.

My name is not what they called me at my birth, it is William. Or Billy. You can call me whichever you like. My brother though, he calls me Ishmael but only when he wishes to torment me. He does this because he knows he is the only man on this earth who I will not shoot for using my actual real birth name. He troubles me with that name because it amuses him to do so. He shortens it. My real name, I mean. "Ish" he calls me. He is old enough to know better. He knows how I feel about it. Call me Billy, that is what I tell him to do. That is my name. Who names their own child Ishmael? To saddle him up with such a weight right at the point where he is just starting out on things? It is from the Bible, they said, this is what they told me in all earnestness when I was five years old, I remember the wallpaper and the looks on their faces. It is from the Bible, they said. And so what of that? So's William. There must be a William in the Bible somewhere, it's a big fucking book.

Ishmael William Henry Bonney McCarty. And on top of that I am Billy the Kid. I suppose. At any rate he has not matured in the way most men do, my brother. I remember when the poor excuse we shared as a father took us down to the sandy creek one fine May day and he told us, "Boys, today is the day you learn to swim." And he threw us one by one into the water. It is surprising that he had that much strength, being as drunk and as old and as of no account as he was. He threw Joseph first and when I saw that Joseph was not going to come back up, I thought to myself, "Well, that is not going to be me, I am not going to drown today because the school picnic is coming and there is going to be egg salad and sugar pie." So I fought like hell because I could see the trouble Joseph was having and I truly enjoyed egg salad and I broke that surface and helped pull him out of there too. It is useful to have an older brother. He has never tried to swim again because he does not know how. He has become wise in other things, but he remains a child in some ways and at times he turns cranky and petulant. Yes, petulant is what I said, Joseph. It is likely that you do not think I would know that word. I know many words. They mostly name hurricanes after women. You ever notice that? I know what you are thinking now—that they did not start to name hurricanes until well after I died. Well, that's one thing you may know, but there are many you do not, and you are wondering: just how does he come to know that fact if he was shot dead in 1881? Well, read on.

Paulita she left me, saying she was leaving, you see, just suddenly telling me she was going. Well, I could see she was going. She was in the doorway and then she's on the other side of the door. Well, that is a pretty simple situation to understand.

"I'm leaving," she said.

What is that?

An explanation? I do not have to have explained to me what I can already see happening right in front of my face, I am not a stupid man. I loved her. Or I thought I did. I thought she was the only one and I was mistaken about that. This business of— the purpose of—living a life is to create a soul and I have not done a very good business of that. Anyway, she left me. She said it was time for her to go and she was right. Women always know some things that I do not, and they always seem to know everything before I do. I never claimed to be a genius. Or a particularly fast gun, for that matter. I am not fast. I'm determined. *The True Life and Death of the Desperate Outlaw Billy the Kid*. And maybe it's a true story at that. But then here I am right here as big as life, so I guess it is not, and I guess that like most stories it is a mixture of both lies and wishes. It was not long after Paulita left that I staged my own ending. And not long after that I fell to the bottle and spent some years trying to find the bottom of it. And I suppose too many years of being drunk and being no one to anybody ended up being just as bad as or maybe even worse than being someone. Maybe toward the end of my exile I said things in bars that were not prudent. Then I stopped drinking. I did not stop talking and that is how it has come to be that men want to kill me again. If you give people someone named Billy the Kid, that is just what they want to do. Kill him.

My brother Joseph buys some bread, and he buys three bags of dried beans. Some molasses. Flour. Cured bacon. Tobacco. The lady, she wets a short pencil with the tip of her tongue and adds it all up on a piece of brown wrapping she tears from an iron roller on the counter.

"Where you boys headed?" she wants to know.

"No idea."

She nods.

We know exactly where we are going mind you and we even have it on a map, but there is no need for her to even wonder about it. You ever notice how many things people think they need to know when they actually do not? Some folks will gladly offer you an opinion about anything from politics to tooth powder to penny nails.

We walk out and we pack up the horses. Both of us are watching everything around us all the time—the alleyways, the shadows beneath the overhangs, the rooftops.

"You'll die unremembered, Joseph," I tell my brother. "I can tell that about you just by lookin'."

[17]

"And what do I care about that, Ish? I'll be dead. Besides, I have no taste for remembrance. Anyway, I'll be remembered as your brother. Brother of the biggest ass in four counties. Brother of the great and wonderful Billy the Kid."

"I told you I'm nothin' special."

"Oh I believed you."

"Well, why you gotta be such a hump about everything?"

"I wasn't born this way."

"No?"

"No. I worked at it. Life is a great teacher, Ish, and experience is the mother of wisdom."

Well, that right there is the type of nonsense he throws around on the regular. Experience is what throws shit down on your head until you are all colours of brown and it has no children that I am aware of. My brother pretends to know a great many more things than he can possibly actually know, but one true thing he has told me is that water will always seek a lower level. Place it in the sky and it will fall to the earth. On a tree it will drop to the ground, and on the ground it will sink beneath the surface. Well, as a man I have surpassed water and done an outstanding job of sinking. I disappeared from the earth on the moonless night of July 14, 1881, if the stories told of me are to be believed, but the fact of the matter is that on the morning of July 15 all that happened was that I began to sink beneath the surface of things and it was many years before I could even think of rising. Water that sinks below the surface provides nourishment so flowers and fruit trees might grow, but all I provided was the false and enduring legend of a gunfighter and I was outlived by lies. But that is true of all of us, don't you think? So I fell to the bottle and I did not pull away from it for many years. I became a great friend of whisky, only to find that it was one more thing that did not wish me well and now I will not touch strong drink, for the taste of it pulls me back to those days of emptiness and namelessness and aimless longing. It is popular to say that a woman drives one to such extremes.

I drove myself.

So I do not need my brother to tell me that experience is the mother of wisdom, I know that only too well. Though I might be inclined to term my state not so much as wisdom but as the eventual exhaustion of stupidity. In the thirty-four years I have been gone and invisible I would say the first thirty were spent in alcohol and pointless pursuits. I was like a man up all night in a graveyard with nowhere else to go and I wandered as if I were someone other than who I was. Whose hands are these, I would ask myself, and whose face? I let my beard grow out and I wore glasses, I dressed myself as a fine gentleman at times and as a vagrant at others. No one knew me and no one asked my name. I wished to be someone other than who I was, you see, and eventually I came to realize that Billy the Kid is who I was and who I am, who I had made myself out to be for better or worse. Worse most likely. And so, after all those lost years, I claimed it, my name: I am Billy the Kid. Only after admitting it only twice too late in the evening in bars and taverns too dark and too quiet, I found the old patterns beginning to return.

"Are you Billy the Kid?"

"Who wants to know?"

We cannot escape ourselves, you see. None of us can. And that is the wisdom I learned in my long exile before my lost brother appeared to drag me off to somewhere safe.

"I shit piss this morning," Joseph says, and he spits a long line of tobacco juice to give an illustration of his sudden remark.

"You what?"

"I went for a shit and piss came out of me instead."

"Out of your ass?"

"Yes. You have an understanding of the situation."

Minutes go by.

"I can't say that I really do, Joseph."

You could be shitting out shiny half dollars and I could not possibly give fewer fucks than I do right now. Maybe your gut is so full of your own poison that there is nowhere else for it to go. Perhaps you are just dying.

"Perhaps you are dying." I tell him.

He spits again. Well, the fact of him showing up to drag me off to somewhere safe does not excuse his long line of bullshit.

"Could be," he says. "Well, I suppose we'll see about that."

"I think it's like to be a certainty."

"Just a question of velocity, I suppose. We are all going to die, William, that's not exactly today's news, now is it?"

We ride on.

"How do we know which way we're headed, Joseph? Tell me that."

"You mean generally or specifically, Ish? Because one is a philosophical question and the other is of a more geographical nature."

"I mean right now. I mean how do we know we're goin' the right way to get where you think it is we're goin'?"

"Just remember that the moss grows on the north sides of the trees."

"You remember it."

I am in no mood to get filled up with his nonsense at the moment.

"Just forget I asked. It was a mistake," I tell him.

"People make 'em."

"You?"

"Not lately."

These are lawless times already and they are getting wilder by the hour. Soon the pictures of the end times in the Bible will seem like gentle doves and wildflowers. Yeah. I can read and I have been educated. I have read a lot of books and more than what you think I have read, I would imagine. I have had more education than any writer has given me credit for, but then any writer giving me credit for anything thinks I died at twenty-two years of age and, like most people I know of at twenty-two, I knew next to nothing at that time. If you read anything that's ever been wrote about me before this you might not think I even learned how to read. What is written in the books ain't the same as what's true in the world and it can't be even if it tries. I know things. I know we are headed for a place where no one cares who Billy the Kid is, maybe a place where no one's even heard of him ever. That is Joseph's idea, his vision for the both of us.

"Time to get yourself gone, Billy, and we might as well go together. There's a few people are well aware by now that you did not die when you were supposed to have died and a few people is a few too many."

She never knew how lovely she was, but then they never do, do they? Oh some will try to show they do by play-acting the part as if half of them believes it might be so or maybe just hopes perhaps it might be so and the other half knows for certain it is a lie, even when it is not a lie at all. And it is never a lie, but they never know about that part of it, not really. We do them a disservice thinking they might. They are always so filled with doubt about it all and we put that doubt into them maybe. Well, we do.

Joseph and I keep on riding with the sun at our backs now and our shadows, horses, and riders ghosted out before us long on the dried-up ground like sharpened knives. Old black lava gravel straight out from us in all directions and just as far as the eye goes. Flat. Like they say, your dog runs away in this country and you'll see him still going two days later. He is still running fast and, when you think about it, who can blame him? This country is pretty, but it is no place to actually be.

∽ 2 ∾

Question: *In addition to the names you have given, were you known, or styled in Lincoln County, as "the Kid"?*
Answer: *I have already answered that question. Yes, sir, I was. But not "Billy the Kid," not that I know of. That came later.*
   —25 May 1879, Fort Stanton Court of Justice

I have been told that God is a great believer in justice. My guess is that he is not always paying close attention to what goes on down here then.

"What was that you said? I didn't catch your name."

"I didn't throw it."

People are always coming up to me in taverns and hotels, in bright sunlight and under cover of dark, and asking me questions like that.

"Is it true that you...?" they ask.

"Are you...?" they ask.

Well, maybe I did and maybe I am, but it's been a long time. When we were little children, we weren't always in the same place, my brother and me, but on the occasions that we were we would play together as young boys, as brothers, will do. I remember one time he was playing as the devil—you know... Satan. He had on this red piece of cloth as a sort of a cape and I was pretty young, so he had me almost believing him and then he said he would put me into hell. Well, that was his job to do, I guessed, so I let him do it. His hell was an old wheelbarrow he'd found and turned upside down. So I sat under there for a while smelling the rust and the rat shit and looking at the darkness and after a while I got bored and took off from under there. I found him eating some jam on bread and that's when I knew for certain he was not the devil. And I surely knew that hell would be a worse place than a wheelbarrow turned upside down. And sure enough it was. There is a little piece of it coming up right here in the story, just to show you what I mean.

"Jesus Christ..."

"Now, Ish, there's no need to take the name of the..."

Three days out from Fort Sumner and we come down a little rise and into a hollow shaded gulley where there is a stream closed in by some heavy brush. There's a drinking tree hung low over the water. That's a name I heard once for a tree that's partly felled by the wind or lightning, shifting the earth up at its roots, and it hangs low over the water as if bent for thirst.

"Jesus Christ on a stick..."

"Oh my Lord."

Hanging over the low bow of it is a girl, her bare arms and her legs straddled over the wood like she's riding it, just like she's riding a big horse and she's huggin' it at the same time like I seen some young women do. Except this one is naked.

The wind suddenly rustling out of the leaves and rippling the still water.

Her hair.

Her hands, her feet—blue.

What sort of man does this? Out of nowhere a dead woman, and for what reason? As if there could be any kind of a reason for doing this and placing her here. I ask you again—what sort of a man is responsible for this kind of thing? One thing we do not need in this world is another dead woman, and now some ham head has produced one for us out of the bare air just like some damned conjuring trick and right here at the start of our journey. I do not feel that it can bode well for us.

I saw a magician once in Abilene who could pull playing

cards right out of thin air. Well, it was the damnedest thing I ever seen, up until just now and until this spectacle before us. I always wondered though, if you can pull playing cards out of the air, why not pull silver dollars? In my travels, I may have left a dim trail of varying lengths of dead bodies (depending on who you ask for a number), but none of them were women, not a single one of them a woman. And I am not saying all women are angels on earth, I know that not to be the case. But the worst woman usually has far less to hide than the best of men. Whoever killed this woman here might just want to think about that next time he sets himself to killing another. The kind of a man who would think of cutting a woman's throat and leaving her naked in a tree has got a great deal more wrong with him than I do, and that is all there is to be said about that. And I am not a pure man. I will tell you that I set fire to my brother one time, and it was on purpose.

We were small then too, me maybe ten and Joseph maybe eleven or twelve. We do not know for certain our real ages, for no one ever thought to tell us. He is braver than me sometimes, and smarter than me most times, I suppose, though I would never indicate such to him. It was not to hurt him at all that I did it. I just wanted to see what he would do. Because I figured he would know what to do. And then I would too.

Sometimes I think if I turn quick enough, I'll be able to see myself coming up behind. Sometimes my soul enlarges as if someone were at it with a bellows and sometimes I am stupid as a plug. He still has those scars on his back and his side from where the flames ate away at him.

"I have said it before, Ish. You are seven kinds of a fool."

"I see no call to revisit that territory, Joseph."

"Still, you are a very foolish man."

"By your account."

"By all accounts."

There are times when just continuing to move forward is a sort of a prayer.

"What's the worst thing you would say you have ever done in this life, William?"

"Lying."

"When do you lie?"

"All the time, Joseph. Right now."

"Ever tell the truth?"

"Saw no advantage to it."

"And what about shooting a man?"

"I never lied about that. If I was a better man—"

"Well, you're not. So do not be worried about that. At all."

"Well…"

"You have this little whistle sound you make when you sleep."

"And when did you become a woman?"

"What do you mean?"

"You watchin' me while I'm asleep? What shit is that? You only got one thing to do when I'm sleepin', Joseph, and that's to sleep yourself or keep watch. And I do not mean a watch on me. I don't need to be thinking about you watchin' over me like some kind of a haunt. I'm in my bedroll asleep and you're what? Hunkered over me like a crow. Stink-eyein' me like the crazy bastard you are. You know there is something wrong inside you. You are as slow as ditch water and there is something in you that is just not right."

Did you know they have given names to the mountains on the moon? What did they do that for?

3

Tell you what you do. You just find the tallest tree you can find and then you lean a ladder up against that tree. You can climb the tree itself if you prefer, but I like using a ladder to get started; so you climb up that ladder and then you climb up the rest of the tree as far as you can. The ladder just gets you a head start, you see? And then you can see everything in the county from up there at the top of that tree. You can see somebody comin' before they even decide to leave their own house and in this way they can't ever get the drop on you, if you see what I mean. Course you gotta stay up there. That's the problem, the problem is you can't stay up there forever. Bein' known as a fast gun, well, that is the same as bein' dead. You might just as well take out an ad in the newspaper—*"Come and Try and Shoot Me, Says Billy"*—and just be a corpse for hire. I saw my father cry one time. That was just before he passed. I was but a little lad then, but I recall it and in fact I cannot shake it.

"No. I'll tell you what, William. I keep thinking now about that dead girl."

"Which one? The one in the tree?"

"You got others?"

"No, I don't, just the one."

"Well, I think we should go on back there."

"It's a little late for that, Joseph. You're not going to stop her from being dead."

"No, but we rode right on past her. There is something wrong with us, William. Normal people don't do that."

"Normal people don't go lookin' for trouble that ain't theirs neither. Nothing you do now is gonna make a lick of difference to that girl."

"You don't know that. At any rate I am going back."

"You are likely going to come to a sad end one day, Joseph."

"Most probably. Are you coming?"

"No. Yes."

Joseph just sees the world all black and white like in a tintype and he always has. He put himself on the white side of things when he was about knee high and he hasn't budged any from that spot, not in his mind and no matter what he does. So anyway, Joseph makes us go back just to see if that girl is still there. Well, she is of course, I mean where is she gonna go, seeing as she's dead? And there's even less that we can do for her now. Another day adds a lot of worry to a dead body. The tree is right by the bank of the Gallinas, a low place where you ford the river and you can't miss it the way the trail's laid out, which tells us that no one else has been by.

Here, it looks like this, I will draw it for you in the book I keep to write things down by the campfire at night:

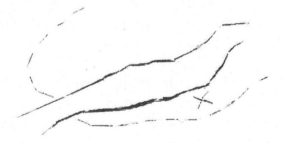

See those solid lines? That there is the Gallinas and them hashed-up lines there, that is the trail. And Little Miss Lucky by the tree there, she's the X. She's a pretty girl and that is the truth. In life she must have looked like sleep looks to a man who is freezing to death.

I recall everything I have ever seen. The smokehouse I am remembering now is about eight feet square and seven feet tall in the peak of the roof. It is built of vertical boards of a uniform width. The door is flush to the wall without a frame and held shut by a wooden button. On the uphill side, at the dead centre of the wall and flush to it hangs a nearly new washtub, the circles on its bottom just like a target. Its galvanized material is dryly eating away at itself in the sun. The wood of the wall itself is smudged. The natural use of a smokehouse is to smoke and store meat, but meat is not smoked here, this is a storage house now. Mainly there are a couple dozen tin cans here, mostly holding sorghum; four hoes; a set of sweeps; a broken plow frame; a can of rusty nails; the strap of a white slipper; a pair of work shoes, the uppers broken away, still smelling of feet; a boy's soggy, worn-out cap; a blue coil of soft iron wire. The whole structure is hanging and in danger of falling. The floor is just the cold earth. The man lying there on it has been dead for some time. Perhaps it was my father. Where I grew up there was a lot of open space right outside the door and so I followed that. Just as soon as I was able to. You lay one man's life against the history of everything in the world and it's no more than a full moon on a Saturday night. One day I would be a bandit king.

"We'll have to bury her. My mind is made up on this, William."

Well, that's your mind, I want to tell him. If you got your mind made up, you just make it up that you're in this all on your own lonesome. You can make up a mind to do anything you want it to, Joseph. You can make it decide to dig that grave. Joseph isn't going to do it, even though it is his diseased mind that has brought us back here. Wherever I've gone, the hired-out law has always run the game. Most of the time the only difference between their guns and mine has been that theirs had badges attached to them. And money. And maybe that just means I've been to the wrong places. But I have spent the better part of this pageant of mine in rail yards and in taverns and been none the worse for it that I can see, but I have always meant to steer straight clear of the places where I am clearly not the one running the game. But that is most every place there is.

So I climb up there and I start to move her, but my hands sink into her as if her flesh were day-old cake and the smell is disaster and young onions.

The women I have loved did not return my love in kind, but we drank thick Italian wine sailed here from Europe on big wooden ships and then we'd line up the bottles and shoot them out in the yard at twilight under the salmon skies and watch the green glass fly. They say there's a man from Galilee and he has all the answers we yearn for and he can drive out snakes and spirits and is always on the right side of every battle. They say his face shines and lightning and justice rise from his eyes. And he has two lives. Well, me I only got the one. Well, I will do what I can for this poor girl but I will tell you one thing and it is that I am damned if I am going to dig that hole for Joseph. He can sort that shit out for himself. They're always better than us, women, even the worst of them. And they know it too, so they just give the big lie to all of our strutting. All of our Don Juaning. Our wishboning and our sorry-assed pretending. They know better.

That rooster strutting through the drying fruit trees there. That empty bottle, right over there by that table leg. And all those songs about Billy. She breaks into my head from what is now so long ago, and she fills it up like a balloon.

"I killed him," I tell her.

"What does that even mean?" she asks me.

I don't answer. I take off my greatcoat and hang it on the wall.

"What does that mean?" she asks.

I am a soft-spoken man much of the time. Sometimes I am not even heard. "Never mind," I tell her.

She was one to scare easily about death and so I regretted having mentioned it to her at all. When I worked on the ranch, I got thirty-five cents a week for fourteen hours of work a day. One man there he was too old and too sick to work so they told him just to go. That was it. And be sure you take nothing with you, they said. A dog they would at least have shot. That man had nowhere to go.

"You got a shovel?" I ask Joseph.

"There by the tree."

I stand there looking at him. Human beings are capable of anything. I think about telling him this in an effort to get him to take up the shovel himself because I really do not have any interest. The shovel is not heavy, but because it is made to travel with a horse it is small. The task is not large, but the tool to perform it is lacking. Anyway, I find myself rolling up my sleeves. I do not know what makes us this way, him and me. Maybe he is weak or maybe it is me. Likely it is the both of us. But at least she will be buried and then maybe she will go up and see the altar of God. Who is to say? There is more of a chance when you're dead, I guess. Listen, as much as someone might want to be with God, you can't be, not while you're down here in this muddy mess. Where God is there are no shithouses. And here, down here where the shithouses are, I mean, well, this is no place for God, he has left us down here in the dirt and to our own devices is what I feel, and it is what my own experience has taught me. My hat is an old felt hat that is worn in spots down to a hole. Which is useful on a warm day to let the air in and of no use whatever on a cold day. It is not the hat of a rich man. It is a simple hat, and I wear it plain. Sometimes I think there is too much poverty in this world. Other times I am sure there is not enough.

And death. That is nothing.

A man once told me something...I would say it was my father...but it wasn't my father. My father never told me anything of any use. This man he told me never to get into a fight when you don't already know the outcome, he said that's how you keep standing. He said there's two kinds of a man in this world: a fool and a damned fool. He said a fool gets so drunk he can't stand up. He said a damned fool does the same but he does it amongst people he don't know well. He said a fool falls in love with a woman. He said a damned fool falls in love with the wrong woman and he said they're almost all the wrong woman. He said a damned fool never realizes that fact. He said a fool robs a bank. He said a damned fool has the notion he's going to get away with it. So I never got drunk with people I didn't know well and I never robbed a bank. And as for love, well, here I am. Things can go wrong. They will go wrong. They do go wrong. They have gone wrong, that much is quite evident.

They come riding high down the ridge and they had us on the run with nowhere left to run to. This was the time of the Lincoln County War as it was called. There was so much shooting that the blood glazed the tops of the grass. I swore right then I'd never find myself stuck in another man's war. So I started my own wars, I guess. Someone did anyway and I occupied myself in the fighting of them for many years. I got shot once and the wound got greened up pretty bad. I lay in bed for days with a pain on me that felt like crows were pecking at my marrow. Then she came into my room on the seventh day and she opened up the curtains, and then it was like all the birds just took flight up into the clear air. Her white breasts and all her body hot pressed against my bones. I had the thought back then I would die there in that room and it certain looked to be the case but then she came in and I saw then that I was wrong. But that, as I say, was some time ago now and she is long gone.

"Well, someone should say some words over her," I say as I brush off my sleeves and pants and drop the shovel.

"Well, go ahead."

"This was your idea, Joseph."

"That doesn't mean I know any Bible words by heart."

"Oh you know you do. It isn't right just to leave her."

"Well, you go ahead then."

"I will." I think about it some. Bible words...

"And the sun will come up after the dark of night, Ish," Joseph says. "Just how long you fixin' to take to get the thing done?"

"Shut the fuck up, Joseph."

"Nice. You get those words from the Bible?"

Everything I do becomes the story they tell about me. Everything I do is two things: it's what I'm doing now and also it is what they will say I did later, and those two things are seldom the same and I don't care about that anymore. I'll make a better story than I did a man anyway. But then I suppose that's true of most. At least they'll say something about me. Shot to death in a dark room with nothing but a knife in my hand after going out unarmed in the night for a piss. That is not what happened but it is the story that has been written and is most often told regarding my ending. To me that does not sound too much like me—that I would die unarmed and unaware. But no one cares what it sounds like because that is the way that Billy the Outlaw was taken down and it is the way that Pat Garrett became famous after he wrote his book (I will admit I did not see that part of it coming, him writing a book, I mean, and I should have but it is of no matter now) and I became nothing at all aside from the stories that have been told of me, which has suited me better than being well-known ever did. So in the end it was worth every penny, I suppose.

When I was a kid we lived at the end of the road. A swath

of forest separated us from the rest of the world. Well, I would have gone through it with an axe if I'd had to. Just to get out.

"Bury her did you, Billy? Did you? Nice and proper with some Bible words? Well, she looked better up there in that tree where we had left her. Billy the fucking Kid… Well, fuck you, Kid. How's that for a story?"

∽ **4** ∾

There's this story my mother told me one time, at least I believe it was my mother but I could not say for certain. Some old woman said it to me anyway. Well, I'll tell it to you now. It is called "The Devil's Bridge" and it is a story from Ireland in the old days and it concerns a woman who has these sheep, you see, and she has to get them across this river and she ain't got no bridge. And the devil, you see, well he's there, I don't remember how, just there he is with his hooves and his tail and his smell of sulphur, and he says to this woman, *I will build you a bridge,* so she says, *That's just fine, that's what I need, a bridge, so you go ahead and just get busy about it.* She knows it's the devil, you see, but she needs a bridge for her sheep, and so he makes this bridge appear for her and he tells her, *The only thing about it is that the first soul that crosses this bridge, their soul is mine to keep,* he says, and she says, *Well, okay,* and all of a sudden she throws this stick and her little dog he goes running across the bridge to get the stick and so she wins, you see, she wins against the devil. And the devil, well, he is some sore about that. And that's the end of it. That's the end of the story.

Well, I don't know what you're thinking is on it, but I think it's a stupid story because first of all you don't go around pissing off the devil. He's gonna come back at you with might and he's got the deck stacked well against you, believe you me. Let me ask you something, you believe in the devil? First of all you better be certain even if your answer is no (and just how certain can you be about a thing like that?), and even if you don't are you willing to take even the slightest chance about pissing him off? Plus, in this story, he's right there so she don't have no choice but to believe in him, that's the thing about it, in the story he's real whether you want him to be or not and then she just sets in to rilin' him up anyway. Well, that is not the way I'd play it. And let me tell you something about the devil, he don't give forty fucks whether you believe in him or not. In fact, he'd much prefer it if you didn't believe in him or even give him a second thought. It is easier for him to get his work done that way. The other thing is, and this is the thing that pisses me off the most, what about that fucking dog? That woman just throws over her little dog to eternal damnation like that? He'd never do that to her, I bet, not if I know dogs. Never. Dogs are loyal and that is for certain.

Anyway, it's just a story. The woman's not real and the dog's not real. The stick's not real. The river. The sheep. Hell, there's not even a bridge. But the rest of the story? I'll leave that up to you. That's the power of a story though. Even filled up with bullshit as it is, it has still stuck with me all these years.

I only took a prisoner just one time. If I had it to do again I wouldn't do it at all. Since that time I've been a prisoner of it myself.

"You went to check on him?"

"Yeah."

"You okay?"

"I'm fine."

"And he's okay?"

"He's fine."

"Good."

"I mean if you count him being dead as being fine, then yeah, he's fine."

Well, I sit here between these closed-in walls of this snow-bound cabin and you sit there on the other side of these pages where you are reading these words now and just look at us sitting here like this, the two of us. Tomorrow will come just as easy for me as it will for you and at some point we are both going to run out of days. In the meantime, I will have fresh biscuits with jam and a fried egg hot from the pan.

True Facts from a Book about Billy the Kid:
While he was in the third grade, William McCarty (William Henry Bonney at that time) drew a picture of a gun and mailed it to President Andrew Johnson.
According to one of his last notebooks he was planning on buying a saxophone.
His hands were always moving, like birds.

Those are true facts, all of them. There's lots more told about me that ain't true at all. It would take a man years to sift through them all. Well, anyway. Joseph and me we put our hats back onto our heads and we ride up out of that gulley and we never go back. We mark her place with a stone and a cross that Joseph fashions out of two stripped branches. We don't know of her Christian name, so I carve *"Young Woman of About Twenty or Thirty Years Age"* into a piece of wood and I lay it there by the stone.

"Pretty wide margin of error," Joseph says.

"Well, maybe we should have cut her open then and counted up the rings, would that make you happier?"

Honestly, I do not know what he expects half the time. I ain't never been a good judge of a woman's age at the best of times and especially not when she is starting to rot away. Maybe her people will find this place if they are looking for her. I hope they are looking for her and I hope they do find her.

"Should we go?"

"What?"

"We should go now, I suppose."

I will tell you another story. Many things happen in these

times of ours. Pat Garrett, the man who it is said shot me to death, it was in an ambush situation, I should say. Well, he himself was shot to death while pissing and that was done by a man named Wayne Brazeal and that's the only thing ol' Wayne ever did that was in any way worthy of putting into a book, I can tell you that. Or it was Jim Miller done it, which is also a story that is told and has made its way into some books about it. Does it matter? There is no end to books about it. The story goes I was in Pete Maxwell's bedroom when I was shot dead. Pitch black. And all I had on me was a butcher's knife. Most of life is just letting go of some things you never really needed anyway. Pat Garrett, the mighty hero of the West. When I think about how things get so twisted around I want to shit out iron skillets. Pat Garrett was not a likeable man and it was for that reason nobody liked him. He was not a man with any skills or features of any note or value. He was a failure of a man made out of thin planks and penny nails. The only successful thing he ever did in his life was to kill me, and even that was not successful for, well, here I am. A gunfight does not determine who is right, only who is left. And now old Pat he is just as dead as dust and here I am talking to you, so success is never certain, wouldn't you say?

This life is all just a ride on a horse that does not know where it is headed. In my experience it is of a very temporary nature. Often it ends twitching and bloody and in a ditch or a dirt hollow—or in a grave unmarked and unknown. At least you can read about me and the way that I went: at the side of a bed in a wooden house surrounded by meadow and my small voice rising quietly up into the dark just one last time and huge great flocks of blackbirds breaking and rising up into the night sky at the sound of the shot that took me down. But then none of that actually happened at all, so it is clear enough that books will try to trick you, and people will too.

Years after my death, rumours were spread that I had not died at all or even been shot and that Pat Garrett, being a friend of mine at one time (and what time was that exactly?), he had gone along with it for money, he had let me go and then collected the money for killing me anyway. Well, I suspect it was Pat himself started those rumours just so he could hunt me down and kill me again for another reward and then he goes and writes a book about how he did kill me after all. Well, I cannot say if he killed me or not but here I am, and Pat, well, he's in a box now.

I see her with something other than my eyes because my eyes are closed. I see by remembering: her turned head, her voice. She's on her back on the mattress, see, and I have both of her little feet in my hands, her little feet, and I raise them on up slow and gentle so they're at both sides of her face and then I just settle down into her warmth and she rises up just enough, just enough, then slides herself up and down on me like that and she keeps up like that for the longest time just staring up and breathing hard and smiling at me like everything is fine, and it is, it is fine, and old Iron Annie is pounding on the door: *"Let me in! Let me in, you bastards!"* She yells, *"I know what you're doing in there!"* and the sun dust is floating lightly through that room and she stays very quiet beneath me and just keeps on moving herself onto me and pushing hard and just staring and staring up from that pillow. Her eyes staring up into me wide open and her quiet and breathing and her smile. And me thinking that…oh Holy Christ, I am in love with this girl. I am in love with her.

Goddamn me for a fool.

And I have to tell you, listen here, it was misspent that love. It was ill-advised.

ᥫᩣ **5** ᥫᩣ

Here is how I feel about women—I feel that they are better. That is what I think. The way they rose-brush through this world pretty to see but with enough grit on them to protect themselves from a world that does not ever wish them well. The way the night is all lit up by them without them even knowing about it. Sometimes they should know it well enough, but they—each and every one of them—doubt that it is so. They illuminate the world in spite of all of our best and all of our concerted efforts to blow out their damned candles. But I make no pretension to really know anything about them. At all.

I make no pretension to know about book writing either, but I give it to you here in plain English, and the best that I can, a story of these events unadorned with the usual lies or with bad memory. Now, where I am sitting, which is a place you do not know of yet, there is an abundance of time. I repeat for the record that I was not killed by that fool Garrett, as they say. That was a story made up for the sake of the convenience of more than just me, though I appreciate its effectiveness and I admire its longevity. It has been told well and told often and I have been actively complicit in its telling by my near silence up to now. I have lied about myself throughout most of my life and I see no grievous sin in having done so nor can I see that it might be of any harm to anyone in particular. I have not lied about others or if I have then only indirectly or at least not by intent. I have, as I say, been complicit in the fabricated nonsense that Pat Garrett shot me dead but that certainly did no harm to Garrett. In fact, not having shot me and claiming he did is the one thing he may have done well in a life otherwise stricken by abject failure. When I say I have been complicit it is to say I have not by actual intent shown my face as it was known to be then nor spoken a word to the contrary except on occasion where it was necessary or seemed of practical use to do so or if maybe I had one too many drinks. As happened. As I've said. I do not make a secret of it. Perhaps I should have. Then I would not be in this situation.

I suppose that is not so much lying as it is hiding. In a sense I am dead, and it is Billy the Kid who lives on now in story and in place of me. He is a story that mams tell to their children at night. *You can say your prayers now or you will end up as Billy the Kid did. You eat your supper or you will end like the Kid.* I see no harm in that. There ain't nothing wrong with either eating or sleeping such as I am aware and if me being dead helps to achieve such in the youth of this day, then much good there is to be made of it. I killed as a matter of expediency and not nearly so much as is said and there was not one man I killed who was a loss to this world and there wasn't one of them should not have seen it coming nor one who wouldn't have taken it as a part of the bargain he had made with the world in the first place. And not one of them who would have avoided killing me for the price of a nickel cigar.

I have no peace now to make with this world or with myself. I write these words down here so that maybe people will finally understand that. Well, that's up to them now.

It is up to you.

So Joseph and me we ride on up and out of that valley and away like I said, the holy words having been spoken and there being nothing else needing doing to make the situation any better.

"How far we goin', Joseph?"

"Back to where we been already and then on a far piece more."

"But how far?"

"Goin' on up to where they ain't never heard of Billy the Kid."

"That's a long ways."

"Canada. Yes, it is a long ways."

You believe in haunts? In ghosts and people who are dead but still walking? No? I do. When I was a boy there was this man by the name of Mr. Samuels and he would come into my room some nights, this is after me and Joseph was separated so he don't know a thing about it, and Mr. Samuels he would just sit himself there on the foot of my bed and he would just look at me. That may sound just like the biggest scare of three counties or like I am colouring the truth a mite, but it is neither of those things. There was not a frightening part about it, if you want to know the truth, it seemed like he was just there to let me know he was there and that things were okay. And every word of this is the God's honest truth. He never said a word to me, but he listened, and he spoke just the same without the use of any words. I don't know how I knew what his name was because he never told me anything out loud, but I knew. This is when I was living in a thin-walled rooming house before the first time I was arrested for stealing and I felt, and still feel, that he was someone who passed away in that bed I was sleeping in and he had just decided not to leave there. Ghost and fright stories that are told around a camp at night in my experience are told by people just pissin' fire about things they know nothing at all about. Maybe I think I am special and I got the only story that's true. Well, maybe I do. You tell me how I knew his name without him tellin' me it then. And how I knew everything was okay and that he did not mean to hurt me. I think people who end up as haunts are just more persistent than others. They will decide when it is time for them to go. I suppose I will end up in their company when it is my time.

You gotta watch people tellin' stories to you. There is always a reason they tell them. Most of the stories people are going to tell you are about themselves or about someone else and they ain't gonna have two licks of truth in them. But this man he would come quiet into my room and just sit himself there on the foot of my bed, I could feel the sheets stretch under me when he did that, and he would fix his rheumy eye onto me and just stare at me until I went to sleep. And I did go to sleep too 'cause I knew there was nothing to be afeared of. That's a true story because if I wanted to make up a story it would be a better one, do you see? I would add something to it that would make it a better story but it would also make it a lie. Now, I believe I have been clear on this: I don't mind lyin'. Not one bit, but this Mr. Samuels, he was real and that is the unvarnished truth of that. Just as real as the frost in the winter and the sun in the springtime. Real as my hand on the stalk of this rifle right here. Real as the ice on the water cup in the morning. And just as real as death.

He had eyes that burned into me like two coals in a bright fire.

I would have said something such as that, but he didn't have eyes like that, so you see what I mean? He just had two regular old eyes just like anybody else, like a regular person, except he was dead. And his eyes were blue and grey. And that's all. You see what I mean? It's dull. But it's the truth.

So anyway, Joseph and me we ride all the rest of that day and on into the evening and we go right past where we started back from. By the time we have our bedrolls out it is well past midnight but Joseph he is in a mood to talk, which is not normal for him at this time of the night.

"There's a pair of coyotes right up over that ridge," he says.

I am looking at the stars and I don't pay him any mind, which is a thing he cannot tolerate.

"Right over that ridge up there," he says, pointing his finger.

"How do you know?" I ask him. It costs me nothing to do as he wishes.

"Sound. I can smell them too."

"How do you know there's two of them?"

"Could be more."

I don't much care to hear about the coyotes and so I clam right up again. If he wants to talk about coyotes he can do it all on his own and with no assistance from me. I am thinking now about how when I die if I become a haunt I will not be sitting myself on the foot of any bed slept in by a little child. I don't even care if they are sleeping in the same bed I once called my own. Maybe when I am a ghost I will plant myself on my brother's bed and listen to him go on and on about his coyotes. Most of the time people think mostly just about themselves and about what they want, but I suppose they can do as they wish. I think now that I will say this about these coyotes to Joseph.

"They can do as they wish," I say then.

"Who?"

"Your coyotes, they can do as they wish, what care have I for your coyotes?"

"No need to be contrary, William, I am just pointing out the facts of the matter."

"Fine, there's two and perhaps a greater number of coyotes there on the other side of that ridge. I've made a note of your facts."

"They are unsettling the horses. You see?" He points again.

"No. I can't. I'm studying the stars."

This makes him go quiet again and I think that maybe I will get some sleep now. I try to listen for the coyotes but I hear nothing. I don't believe that he can smell any coyotes. I look over at the horses but I make it look as if I am just rolling and settling into my bedroll. The horses do not seem to be moving at all.

"Most of those stars do not exist anymore," he says now. "You are looking at things that have long since died."

Before I fall asleep, I decide that my brother is someone who wishes to be or to think of himself as someone who is intelligent more than he is someone who is actually intelligent. I take a smell of the air once more and I smell nothing.

But I cannot sleep.

In my dreams I am always going somewhere but I never know where.

It seems that night in the desert is a time for thoughts run rampant. I suppose the enormity of time and the darkness of the sky play a part in it to be sure. It is best just to sleep, but if sleep is not forthcoming soon then one becomes overly aware of being stuck to the side of the slowly spinning earth like a specimen pinned to a linen canvas. There is the fear of becoming, or already being, so insignificant as to warrant no importance whatsoever, which is indeed likely the case and would cause little consternation in the daylight hours, but under this immense black top is disconcerting enough and banishes sleep quite effectively. And so here I am.

I went along the road by the railway embankment, and on toward the hospital and chapel where my mother had been laid out in her coffin. I was aged about thirteen years at that time. Freight cars were being shunted up and down the tracks and men called to each other from behind the bare trees and the wood fencing. The chapel was made of plain and unpainted wood and looked more to me like a stable and when a man opened the double doors before me I half expected a team of horses to charge out. Inside in that dark hole broken through by slants of light lay my mother bereft of flowers, wreaths, nor anything special or decorative, her plain bare coffin open and her black cloth dress buttoned up to the neck, as in life. The only difference to her countenance from how it appeared in life being that she was no longer there inside of it. Her gaunt face a pale milk white, her cheeks rouged as never they had been in life, her thin black hair most carefully and artfully arranged and her hands folded across her bosom. There was something about her, a quiet certainty she had never possessed in her waking hours. Her skin taut. Joseph stood there in the sun outside waiting for me. I did not feel alone, but I was. I was prepared for a long period of solitude. I'd made myself ready for this solitude. All of my energies dissolved briefly into nothingness and then I became resolved. And then, outside, a long line of black horses with a man who I took to be the devil. I am not certain still that he was not. Some folks might think it unusual, that I would think that. I guess it is unusual, because everything in this life is, if you think about it long enough.

\text{\Large ✍ 6 ✍}

W e smell the man with the bag over his head long before we see him and we see the smoke from his fire long before even that because it is hard to miss some things in the desert and it is not every day you come across a full-sized man with a burlap sack over his head tending to a bonfire. He has a small tent and a covered wagon. Well, isn't this a caution to the big blue-eyed world, I say to myself. Everything I have ever seen up to now would indicate to me that I ain't ever seen it all yet. I keep on getting surprised. I guess that is how you know you are still alive.

"Well, what do you think of that?" Joseph asks me.

We're up on a little rise and the man hasn't seen us yet, which means this is no place for him to be because he should have noticed us by now, it means this is not a natural place for him to be. He does not understand the desert and he is away from his home.

"I don't like it," I tell Joseph.

"Me neither. But what do you think of it?"

"Well, he's not going to shoot at us, if that's what you mean, unless we scare him."

"Who's going to scare who? He's the one with a bag over his head."

"I guess maybe he's got something to hide."

I watch the man move from the fire on over to his horse. His horse starts and hooves at the ground.

"His horse knows we're here and he doesn't know we're here and he doesn't even know that his horse knows. So the only

[\,46\,]

danger he represents to us is that it seems he's a stupid enough sonofabitch that he might pull a gun on a stranger without measuring the cost to himself..." This is what I tell Joseph.

"But then you could just shoot him."

"Look, just because I shoot people doesn't mean I just shoot people."

"That does not make any sense, Ish."

"You head out on the trail with a cook, you gonna make him cook every meal for you?"

"Why not? We'd eat better than if I did it myself."

"Well, maybe he don't want to cook."

"What's he a cook for then?"

"Don't be deliberate. Maybe he wants a rest."

"What's he all tired out for?"

"From all the cookin'."

"Cookin' ain't such hard work when you know how."

"Neither is killin' unless you do it every day."

"But I'm payin' this bastard, ain't I, to cook? You said so yourself."

"Goddammit, Joseph, you are deliberately messing up the comparison I am trying to make here. I am talking about shooting men. I am sayin' that I have lost the taste for it entire."

"I thought you were talking about cooking."

"Fuck cooking. I'm tired of shooting, that is what I am saying."

"But you'll do it though...if he does?'

"Yeah."

"Think he will?"

"What are you planning to do, sell tickets for it? No. I do not think that he will."

"Why not?"

"Because I think he will go to his grave from age with the both of us still crouched up here talking about cooking and shooting, and because I think he has got a bag over his head and

[47]

that signifies to me that maybe he's got bigger problems than just being worried about what we might do, also that he probably can't see for shit and will probably hit you instead of me."

"I'll hang back a bit then."

"I used to be a force to be reckoned with in these parts."

"You still are."

"No I ain't. I ain't even a force to be reckoned with in this gulch."

"Why do you suppose he wears that big fur coat?"

"Well, why don't you go on down and ask him?"

"I ain't that curious."

"You are worried about a fur coat and he's got a big burlap bag over his whole head. And you ain't curious about that at all?"

"A bit."

"Well?"

"Let me know what he says about it."

"Fuck you, Joseph."

"Or maybe we should just send your imaginary cook down there."

"Just fuck you."

So we both go. Which wasn't ever really at issue. We both knew it would be that way, we just had to argue about it first, and so I go left and Joseph goes right. The odds are that the bag man is right-handed and he will cover my side first and I am a much better shot than Joseph with no discussion about it and so there is no need to discuss that. I get within eight feet of him before he even knows we're comin' for him and he whirls, a surprisingly fast gun coming up from his right side but it's halfway out of its leather and I'm two steps up to him with a full straight-arm bead right between his two eyeholes and just short of six inches from his face or where his face would be. His bag.

"No," I tell him, and so he stays put. Nothing else he can do.

"Not unless you want another hole in that bag," I add.

And I can see now the yellow whites of his eyes. And his fear. And now the smell. I mean I can see the smell coming off him, that is how strong it is.

"What the fuck is that?" I ask.

Joseph has come up behind him and slid his pistol away from him like relieving a child of something they've stolen and been caught with.

"What is what?" the bag man asks. It's a deep voice. A voice with some authority and if it wasn't coming from inside of a bag I might pay that voice some heed. And it is strangely muffled, echoing, as if from inside of a cave. His voice sounds...wet.

"That stink."

His body eases off a bit. I keep my pistol steady between his eyes though. I don't blink. He has to know what I'll do—that I'll kill him. I'm too close for him to think otherwise. He can see my eyes.

"I..." he starts, and he looks to Joseph and then back to me, "I may not have washed myself in some time..."

I ease up on the pistol. Something in him has changed and he slacks a little in his shoulders.

"I have not been in proper company...in some time."

"Well, you're not in proper company now...so sit yourself on down."

He does so, on an upturned bucket he's been using by the fire. "I'm not...I'm not a fit man."

I take a look over to Joseph but he is taking a look into the wagon and then he turns and looks at me and his eyes tell me that things have just changed.

"If you hurt her I will find a way to kill you. Just know that," the bag man says then.

Which is not exactly what I'm expecting. Not at all.

"There's a girl in here," Joseph says.

"Do not hurt her."

I cross over to take a look. Joseph keeps both eyes on the bag man. The girl is sitting on a bench that looks like it is being used as her bed. She's blond and she's pretty with big green eyes and an expression that gives away nothing, but she is older than being a girl, I think that much is certain. I begin to holster my gun but I pause.

"Who is she?"

"She's my daughter."

"And why you got that bag on your head?"

"Fuck you."

"Alright. Fair enough." I would like to sort this out now and just get on with life but apparently that is not the path before us. "Listen. You know what my father always said to me?" I ask him.

Joseph is still looking at the girl, and then he closes the canvas and moves toward the fire.

"No," the bag man says, "I do not."

"Well, neither do I. I never knew the sonofabitch."

I am about to go and sit down next to him when there is a sudden movement and I make a note to give myself proper shit for even thinking about holstering my gun just as it goes off and the bullet clips him in his shoulder. It is a shot meant to stop without killing and it's enough to prevent him from branding Joseph's face with the burning branch he's all of a sudden pulled from out of the fire. Damnedest thing. He reached into the centre of the fire to pull it out, which means he closed his bare hand over a burning log, which is no small thing, and as he slumps to the ground the question that occurs to me is whether he did that to protect himself or to protect the girl. If it is himself then he is just a garden variety ass wipe but if it is the girl then he may yet prove to be dangerous, if he does not prove to be dead first. Now there's a damned hole in my holster and it was one of the few possessions of mine that I pride myself on, it was hand-tooled and it cost me no small amount. At the exact moment that I am thinking these thoughts the girl bolts from the wagon and is off and away barefoot across the sand and the rocks. Joseph takes off after her fast and I approach the bag man, my gun now held steady at the back of his head. I get my boot under one of his arms and I roll him over so he is eye holes up. He's not dead but he's not feeling very well either, that is for certain. The bullet has gone clean through him, which is what you would expect at such a close range. The shot may prove to have been ill advised but, well, no matter, at least Joseph did not have his face set ablaze. Still there's that dank smell to the man. And he's losing blood. I kneel down and lift up the bottom of the burlap. I have to pull at it a bit to free it from him and there's a coarse rumble and a groan coming from deep inside him. Chances are good he's going to take a very long time to die if he is not assisted along in the process. I've seen men this size hold on for some time if there's no damage to the organs, and maybe he'll luck out on the organs and the infection and not bleed out and then find a doctor somewhere in the middle of all this nowhere and he'll outlive us all. My mother's father had a woman who would help him to eat soup as he was unable to feed himself and could eat nothing but soup and thin porridge. I would rather die earlier than that.

He has no chin. Nor nose, nor much of a mouth. Essentially he is in possession of two eyes and a hole. He's struggling.

"Stay still or you'll die quicker," I tell him.

"The girl..." It is a miracle to me that he can make himself understood with the little he has left for a mouth.

"He'll get her."

"What will he—"

"He'll bring her back here where it's safe is what I mean, what do you think, that my brother is some kind of a fucking animal?"

"Who—"

"Listen," I tell him and I can't say I'm not having a difficult time not staring at the red hole that is struggling to form his words. "My brother and I just dropped by for a neighbourly visit and you tried to light him up like a torch…"

"You—"

This whole one-word arrangement is tiring me out. "My name is William Bonney."

"Don't." It's Joseph, back with the girl.

"I'm Billy the Kid," I tell the man.

"For fuck's sake, Ish. Why don't you just wear a sign around your neck and take out an advertisement in the newspapers?"

He has the girl under his arm and, judging by the manner in which she is struggling, she appears none too happy to be there.

"He says she's his daughter," I say.

"Well, whoever her daddy is she's a hell of a runner and a scrapper, I'll say that for her."

He puts the girl down and keeps his arms out like a baseball umpire calling safe in case she runs again but she stays put and she just looks at the man on the ground, maybe in the way a girl might look at her father, I cannot say. Joseph comes over and leans down to have a look over my shoulder at the bag man without his bag.

"Why's he got a vagina for a mouth?" he asks.

Joseph has always had a succinct way of expressing himself. That means he picks the best words for the occasion always. You see, I do read. I am neither the savage nor the simpleton they make me out to be. I am a man who makes firm and irrevocable decisions when required to do so. Irrevocable. That means you can't take 'em back. I know things.

"You'd have to ask him," I say. "But be advised, he's not so much a man of few words as he is a man of one word at a time."

"Fuck you," the vagina says.

"Or two," I add. "Listen, you might be dying now, my friend, well…if you are dying, sir, is there anything you would like us to do for you in the meantime?"

"You mean besides fucking off?"

"Yes."

There are teeth in there. It's very disturbing to look at for any length of time and the use of the bag becomes understandable now. It is like most things that are ugly. You want to look away but you can't. Then you have to look away and so you do but you also have to look back. Regarding his newer wound, I've seen men with bullet holes such as this die and I've seen them live. I believe the outcome depends for the most part upon a combination of the path of the bullet and also the will of the victim.

"Listen," I tell him, "I'm not a doctor—"

"Well, it's a fucking good thing I am then, isn't it?" he says, starting to lift himself onto one elbow.

"Do you think you should—" I start.

"What? Take medical advice from the cunt who just shot me?"

"I just—"

"No!" he suddenly yells out just as a rock comes down onto Joseph's head. I swear it is as if my brother magnets mayhem right onto himself. Unseen, she has picked up a sizeable stone and struck my brother as if striking the head off a turkey with an axe. Before he falls, all I have time to take note of are the whites of his eyes. All that is left.

It seems she is a resourceful little girl.

⤳ 7 ⤺

There was a poor woman named Taylor who came all the way from, well, I don't know where she came from but she lived right by the railway line in Chimayo in New Mexico territory in a little shack that wasn't much more than a few old boards nailed together the way a child might draw a house on a slate. The two things she had was she had a goat for her milk and a chicken for her eggs and the one thing she did in order to not die from the cold in the nighttime was to stand her goat in the middle of the track whenever a train was coming into that town and the conductor would stop the train and throw lumps of coal at the goat to get it to move, and whenever old Mrs. Taylor she figured she had enough coal to keep a fire lit through the night, she would whistle so the goat would move off the track and then she'd collect up that coal. I do not know why I think of that story now except it shows you the practical side of life and that you have to do for yourself what you can just to get by, which is what I am doing now. It is as if I am a ward nurse here. It is night. Joseph reclines on one side of the wagon still dead to this world, and the good doctor he resides on the other. Between them at their heads on an upturned bucket and opposite to me is my junior nurse Turner (for it seems that is her name) sitting in a similar fashion to me. Mostly she just stares at her father. Other times she stares at me. She never looks to Joseph. That is little wonder, for Joseph is not prone to any activity that would draw interest, not even that of a nurse.

"Are you really Billy the Kid?" she asks.

[54]

"No," I say, "but I'm closer to being him than anyone else is."

"You look too old to be him."

"I am."

She continues to stare.

"I am too old to be him," I continue, in the event my meaning was not clear to her. "He is a much younger man than I."

"I thought he was dead."

"That too. I mean, so did I. I mean, he is. Dead."

She regards me carefully as one would study a magician's trick, one you know is poorly done but that still confuses you. Her look suggests a certain familiarity with the world beyond her apparent years. This can be a terrible thing for a child. But practical. And I do not believe she is as young as Joseph claims. Not at all.

"You don't make no sense," she says.

"Everything's going to be okay," I tell her, for this is the type of thing you say to people in circumstances such as this.

"Don't pat me on the head like a small dog you found wandering along the road."

This is not what those people are usually expected to say back. "I am just telling you something so you will not be scared."

"I'm not scared. So what if I was?"

"Fear is an open pit. I've seen grown men drawn into it and killed."

"I hate you."

I watch for signs that she will cross the wagon and set herself on me, but there are none. "Your hating of me is of no concern."

"It ought to be." She refolds the cloth she has been using to wipe her father's brow and sets it carefully onto her lap. "Ákoo bitseeí," she says.

"What did you say?"

"Ákoo bitseeí," she says again.

"What is that? Sounds like Apache."

"It is just something the Apache say, a wise saying they have for use in times such as these."

"What does it mean?"

"It means fuck you."

"Do you know who I am?" I ask her. "I have killed eight children, all younger than you and most of them in their sleep."

This statement, I hasten to point out, could not be further from the truth. I have not killed as many as I am storied to at all and I am not even rumoured to have killed any other than full-grown men who well knew the stakes of the game they played and certainly I have never done anything to harm a child, not even by accident or by omission. Maybe it is just because I have been around very few of them, but nevertheless the fact of it remains. But if it takes the Billy the Kid that others have created to shut this girl up for now, then I am willing to call on him in a time of need. She eyes me like one would a snake, judging when it might strike.

"I guess that makes you a very big man," she says. "You killed any small dogs or kittens yet?"

I do not believe this generation has been raised with respect for their elders and betters as the cornerstone of its values. But if things do not turn out well for her father, I will do my best to ensure that this girl is safe, for I am warming to her by the moment, there is no doubt of that.

"I am not so young as I might look to you, and even if I was, it would not stop me from cutting your throat," she says.

"I'm starting to like you," I tell her.

"You cocksucker," she replies.

And this exchange shuts the both of us up for the present and we both sit in silence for a while.

"What happened to your father?" I ask her finally.

"My father makes friends with difficulty and enemies with ease. He is that kind of a man."

"And?"

"I do not know that he would wish me to tell you of it."

"I only shot him because he was trying to kill my brother at the time."

"He was just trying to protect me."

"Well, we were not going to hurt you. We presented no threat to you at all."

"He did not know that."

"Then he acted hastily."

"Well then, I guess you do not have any children? If you did, you would know you are being foolish."

This shuts me up for a time. Then: "I was just curious about what might cause such an injury as that which he has."

"Fine. Many years ago there were some men who had done some very bad things. My father knew the truth about them. They were afraid my father would tell about these things they had done and so they drove a railway spike through the bottom of his mouth and out just under his chin, you see?" She places one hand into her mouth and indicates with the index finger of her other hand a place just underneath the chin so that her index fingers would meet if not prevented by flesh.

"And there is a rope tied to that spike and they draw this through his chin as if darning a sock and then they draw the whole line through and hand the bloodied spike and the other end to a rider and tie my father to a tree and they charge the horse to run away at full speed. The horse does so and my father's lower jaw is split and torn away from his skull. They foolishly cut him down and leave him unconscious to bleed out and die, but my father, whether through shock or sheer stubbornness of will, refuses to do so and he crawls away from there with half his face left in the dirt and he crawls all the way

to safety and eventually to a courtroom, where, through a burlap sack he thinks makes him somehow presentable to the
world, identifies the men who so treated him and thereby sees
that they are imprisoned for their crime against him. This is the
type of man my father is. The man who you, at point-blank
range, when he could not see you or know your intent, shot in
the back."

You see what I mean about this girl? I like her right away.

"My father found a doctor and he pretty much showed him
what to do about putting his face back together or at least
stitching it up so he would not die. He was conscious that
whole time. If you think the fact that he can make himself understood with half his jaw lying out in the desert somewhere
is a miracle, then just you think about the fact that he is even
alive to say anything at all. Think about the nature of the man
you have shot."

And now she just stares at me again, her face pinched up like
the pointy end of a lemon. It is not wrong that she hates me, it
is just the result of a lack of time spent with the world or with
me. She is likely to be at least twenty years of age, that is my
guess, but I am not a good judge of age in women or in children. She has seen too much for her age, whatever her age is,
but also she has not seen quite enough for her to be the person
she pretends or wants to be. Well, that is the way of youth. She
would like to see me dead is what I think and would be happiest
about me if I were in the ground. I am just one of a thousand
dusty desert cowfucks she has seen over the course of the last
few years, different from all of them only in that I have put a
bullet through her father and that is not a difference liable to
endear her to me at all. But what do I care if she wants me
dead? She hasn't got a gun.

I think that when I am dead and lying in my grave, if I then
have the power to think still, I will think of this girl and do so

with fondness. It will pass the time, as I imagine there will be a surplus of it then. Her will to do me harm endears her to me. And her eyes.

"How old are you?" I ask her.

"Old enough."

"Old enough for what?"

"Old enough to slit your throat while you sleep."

I can't help smiling, it is just that she somehow makes me feel happy. However, I do not intend to die this evening and it is necessary to take steps. "How do you know I won't just come over there right now and smash your face?" I ask her.

"I don't."

You see what I mean? She is something. If you think any other way about this, you better stay up on your own fucking horse with your own opinion because I will fight you on this point, but there is no practical advantage to be had right now by letting her know she's found her way into my veins.

"Fuck you anyway," I tell her. "Just maybe I'll be the one to kill you while you sleep. Anyway I'm going to sleep now."

"Suit yourself."

"Spare the rod, spoil the child," I tell her. "Good night. You sleep well."

I take a last look at my brother... That is inconvenient wording... I have a little check on Joseph before turning in. He is breathing regularly and deeply and I suppose that much will have to do for now. The doctor is making considerable noise with his breathing, more noise than Joseph, but that is to be expected due to the fact of having a reproductive organ for a breather hole. There's nothing to be done for him either. As I say, either Joseph will live or he will die, I've done all I know how to do for him and the sleeping doctor is not of much use. The rest of it is up to God himself to listen to and sort through. If the good doctor survives the night, maybe he will be able to tend to himself and to Joseph too with his doctoring skills, though I suspect that Joseph just needs to sleep it off, it wasn't that big of a rock and his head is a reasonably thick one. I have locked up all the weapons aside from my own and I have kept the key. I cannot lock up all the rocks in this part of the desert, but I will spend the night awake anyway, I think. It is not that I fear she will move in the night without waking me, but that I don't sleep a great deal at any time and tonight I think I will enjoy the feeling of looking after her in the middle of nowhere with no one else to do so and of making sure no harm comes to her. I think if she had the chance she just might cut my throat tonight, but perhaps time will fix that inclination. Especially if her daddy lives. She may learn to unhate me then. Others have, though it has been a rare thing.

I never encountered my natural-born father much in the day-light. My only real memory of him, aside from him crying, as I said earlier, if that memory is even real, would be of his foot-steps in the hallway at night and encountering him there once by candlelight. My stepfather though, now that is a different story, I last saw him at his own funeral.

"You never combed your hair that way while you were living," I told him, leaning over his casket.

There was a sudden sharp intake of breath from some woman next to me in line who seemed scandalized by my words in the same way she might if I'd run a hand up under her dress. The way some women will let themselves enjoy some-thing they are not used to and then they will act as if it was not the case at all. *I didn't enjoy that. You disgust me.* That is certainly the way that she looked at me at that moment.

"In life he parted it in the middle," I explained to her.

"I believe he looks quite presentable," she said.

I suppose that was so, for a corpse. You could have stood him up with a drink in his hand and not known any different. You might have mistaken him then for someone about to take your coat, or offer you a beverage, a julip maybe, or a cup of tea. He did look quite presentable, for someone already beginning to putrefy inside of himself like soup in a sack. I do not blame my fathers, either one of them, not for all they managed to do to me or for everything they did not do for me. They were by demons rid hard, the pair of them, and I have turned out a better man than either of them so I suppose they cannot have done me too much harm. You could spend a lot of time blaming others for faults that are your own but then all you'd have is a lot of wasted time and nothing to show for it. They did not ever beat me to death and that is something in their favour, I suppose. They were never any help to me either, but I have got by okay in this life without any help.

The good book says something about the meek and how they shall inherit the earth. I don't doubt they will eventually. If that is a true fact though, then me and this girl here might as well get out of the line right now because we ain't gettin' nothin'. And anyway, suppose they do inherit this earth just like it says? Well, what are they going to do with it? Sit around and wait for someone else to do something is what, only not a single one of them will do anything, being the meek bastards that they are.

"Would you care for a mint?" they will say to each other.

"No, thank you, I could not possibly..."

There was one time that me and Joe Pepper, this was in the time of the range wars, we was outgunned down in a ravine and getting shot at something terrible and neither one of us ended up being dead, but when it was over I took out my pouch where I kept any money I had and it was full of blood. Those coins stayed sticky right up till when I spent them. I have been shot three times and I don't plan on there being a fourth. After some of the battles I was in and before the corpses had been carried off the field and buried, I would make my expeditions amongst the dead all mixed up inside myself with a sense of both relief and disgust. In the early morning a man who has been opened up offers himself to heaven with steam rising from him somewhat like a fresh-baked cherry pie. Only he don't always do it willing. Many's the time he'll fight it something terrible. I seen some things I don't even want to recall. A dying man with his intestines being pulled at by a starving dog and he don't got any way to stop it so he just has to watch the tug of war and moan out his sorrows. And as the dog shakes its head back and forth tugging, the man reaches out, and *no*, he says, *no, no...let 'em go*, and he's crying, *they are mine...*he's crying because he can't do a thing to stop it. There are terrible things in this world and others too horrible to bring back and talk about here. There are.

When you're a child, you imagine the terrible things. And then when you grow, they're real and they're right in front of you. You live them.

～ 8 ～

Well, she has not killed me in my sleep and there is that to be happy about.

But most likely that is because I have not slept.

"Are you going to eat?"

I have gone to the trouble of cooking up beans and skillet biscuits and they are ready and no one is here to eat them so I am setting about to clean my guns while I wait for the day to start proper.

Joseph woke in the night and asked where we were and he said his head felt like it was full of ditch water, then he looked at the girl and said she had a powerful swing on her. "Was that you?" he said. "You got a swing on you. Sonofabitch, William, she has got a swing on her." Then he passed out again but he will survive, I think.

"You can starve yourself to death if you want, but it will be of aid to no one and will just leave the rest of us with more provisions so…suit yourself," I tell her. "Up to you."

She hops down and I set my guns aside and start spooning out. She has wrapped herself up in a blanket.

"You should eat," I tell her.

"It's cold."

"It is, but the sun is climbing. Here."

I pass her the first plate and she sits down and looks at it.

"Won't kill you," I say.

She looks at it like she knows better. "I can shoot a gun," she says.

I give her the eye. "I have no doubt that you can."

"Let me have yours and I'll show you."

"You'll show me a brand-new hole in me that I didn't have yesterday."

She keeps her eye on me like I might jump on her. "These beans might kill you better," she says.

"There is nothing wrong about my beans."

"I wouldn't feed 'em to a hog."

"That just shows what you don't know. A hog'll eat anything, no matter how bad it tastes."

"He'd eat these biscuits then."

"Why're you so crispy to me?"

"Why'd you shoot my daddy?"

"We been through this."

"So everything is fine then because we been through this. I will tell that to my daddy. 'Don't worry,' I'll say to him, 'maybe you been shot through your back but it is okay because that man over there that done it, him and me, we been through this.'"

Goddammit, she is a feisty one even at dawn.

"Listen, if he lives he'll be happy to have been shot by Billy the Kid. He can write himself a book and live free off the money he makes out of it."

"Ain't nobody gonna believe he was shot by a dead man."

"That just makes for a better story. 'I was shot by the ghost of Billy the Kid and lived to tell about it,' he can say that in his book."

"He ain't gonna live to do it." The way she says it in such a sudden small voice makes me cold but also makes me like her more.

"Now, how do you know that?"

"Because I just checked on him and he is dead...and that is how I know that."

I sit looking at her and then I climb up into the wagon to see and there he is sitting up in the corner all ugly with his sack off and looking at me and, I think, laughing, his eyes are winking in the light. I would say that he is smiling but it would not be accurate. I stop looking at his mouth.

"Only a flesh wound, as it turns out," he says, "and your bullet passed through nothing of importance. If an infection does not set in, I will survive just admirably. Oh I will be stiff for a while, but that is all."

"She said you were dead."

"Oh she says a lot of things. Or ain't you noticed?"

Merry pranksters they are.

"She has a lot of views to express, I have noticed that."

"Comes by 'em honest. She's done a lot more livin' than you might expect. She has—" He stops.

"She has what?"

His eye is caught by something. "She has a pretty good hold on your Colt .45."

It is as I am jumping from the wagon that it all spreads out in my head too slow to make any difference now. The way he has lain through the night pretending to be dying. The time they have had together since I started the fire to whisper their plan over Joseph's sleeping head. Her claim that he was dead, did they plan that or was that one she came up with on her own in the moment? No matter, I fell right into it and then let them both play me without any mercy and I suppose I deserve what's coming to me now. And I was looking forward to those biscuits too. I'm moving fast but it seems slow to me and then I have stopped and I am staring down the hole of my own gun.

"Don't you think that I won't do it," she says. "Don't you even think that I won't."

She's got some grit in her.

"I'll put a window right though you."

And the vagina in the wagon is laughing out loud now for he has heard these events through the canvas. "Good girl," he is calling, "that's my good girl…"

If there were bullets in the gun I would be undone.

It is a bad thing for her I took them out to clean it.

I take a step forward to take hold of the barrel.

"Don't."

"Ain't loaded."

"Wasn't loaded."

She fires into the ground between my feet close enough to indicate she don't care what she hits. "But it is now. You think you're the only one with bullets?"

"You are the victim of an underestimation of the situation at hand," says the vagina-faced man, disembarking heavily from the wagon behind me and holding his arm tight to himself. "Sir...I would say you are precisely that."

There's something about being tied up by a girl to bring you right down off your high horse.

And Joseph does not understand it at all.

"That little old girl," he says, "that girl knocked me cold for a whole night and half a day and then she got the drop on you? That girl? With your own gun?"

"She knocked you out."

"I just said that."

"You made it sound like it was my fault."

"And it wasn't?"

"What could I have done about it, Joseph?"

"Stopped her?"

"Oh how exactly? I mean, exactly how should I have done that, Joseph? She took us both by surprise."

"Well, one of us she took by surprise twice."

"Fine."

"What?"

"Fine. That's it. I got put down onto my ass by a girl, that may be. But so did you."

"And so did you."

"I just said that."

"I'm just placing an emphasis on the statement, so it's clear.

[66]

So it's real clear that Billy the Kid got taken down by Sally the kid."

"Her name's Turner."

"I don't care what the fuck her name is."

"It's Turner."

"Fuck you."

"It does her cause no harm to have us fighting at each other like this."

"And just what is her cause?"

"Bein' the one on top," I tell him, "just like everyone else. That's the only cause anyone's ever got."

"Turner?"

"That's right, that is her name."

"What the hell kind of a name is that?"

She brings us some beans and biscuits and Joseph refuses to have any but I am not a fool and I do not know where the next food will be so I let her feed me like I am a child. As soon as I am done, Old Doc Vagina he has the wagon teamed up with one hand and we are rolling along with our horses following along by rope and Turner is sitting with her arms on her knees and watching us both.

"What is the point of this?" Joseph asks her.

"Of what?"

"Of keeping us tied up in this manner. It is stupid. We have done nothing wrong to you and we mean you no harm."

"That is a matter of some contention."

"Contention?"

"Yes, contention. It is a word meaning dispute. And there are two points of view regarding your intent."

"Where the Jesus did you get the word *contention*?"

"It's the same price as any other word. They give words away at very little expense, it is a person's actions that come with costs."

Joseph looks over at me and I just look back. "Actions?" he asks.

"This is what I have observed. I have seen it in abundance just this morning. Your actions."

"Our actions? You're the one hitting folks over the head and shooting off guns."

"Only because I had to. Only because your actions compelled me to."

"*Compelled?*"

"Forced against my will and better judgement. That is the meaning of the word *compelled*. You gonna have any beans or not?"

The way that dry wood cracks and pops in the fire like it was meant to be there. You wake in the dark middle of the night and you take your woman and a far-off train makes its noises just as she does. More and more I enjoy the simple act of writing things down on paper or of just sitting still and thinking about them. I am getting older. I have almost been killed and died many times and the events of my life have been taken over by others and lied about and magnified as in a funhouse mirror. Every stage of this life longs for another stage—the young wish to be old, the old to be young, and not one person knows what they actually want, not really, and certainly they do not know what is best for them. I don't expect much sense can be made of this world. I have found it, this world, for the most part, to be a cold and a brutal place. Life is a dangerous path and getting older on it makes it not a stroll but more like an ambush. The worst moments of our lives are what make us.

"Yeah," Joseph tells her, "I am gonna have some beans."

"Well, get to it then. Supplies are short."

She feeds him, then wipes his mouth with a cloth. She takes another look at the ropes that bind us, then returns through the canvas to sit up by her father's side as he guides the wagon. Eventually we will both be untied; of that I am reasonably sure.

In the middle of the night you can wake up and just lie there and listen to the rain, the same old rain that falls on everything, and that's reason enough, I think, for putting up with most things, it is a nice sound and you have to pay nothing to listen to it. I'd put up with a lot of shit falling on my head during the day just for that peaceful sound in the night.

໑ 9 ໑

In my dreams there is always a horse. Oh the weather is always different, maybe it's a bright day with the sun up high, or it's at night, but there's always a horse. I'm either on it or it is tied up and waiting for me, but I'm always going somewhere or getting ready to go somewhere and the me in the dream, well, he always knows where he is going but the me who is doing the dreaming, well, he does not. I mean that I do not. In my dreams nothing fares well for me and I am often lost. If it was raining soup I would not be able to find a bowl.

Things could have gone different for me in this life. I could have been a barber and I could have sliced locks of dark hair onto a sun-spread wood-plank floor, then swept them all up at the end of the day and been done with it. But that's not how it all turned out.

We moved to Coffeyville, Kansas, when I was three years of age or thereabouts and that is where and when my papa died on us. When I was a boy I was convinced I would be the King of America. At school they told me America did not have no king. It was worse than being told the job was taken. There was no job! Then we moved to New Mexico where I learned to play cards, smoke, and drink like a man. And no person requiring an assistance with anything was left wanting when I was nearby. Pat Garrett has written, "He was a champion, a defender, a benefactor, a right arm. He was a favourite with all classes and ages, especially was he loved by the old and decrepit, and the young and helpless." Yet still he chose to put a cold bullet into my head if reports are to be believed. And his account goes and makes me appear to be the Nazarene himself, which I most certainly was not and am still not by any stretch. I spent as much time drinking and smoking and playing at cards as a young man as I ever did helping old ladies to cross the road, which, if I remember right, may have been exactly one time only.

My mother was what the world calls a "fine-looking woman" and she was a kind woman and honest too, at least she was to me in the little time that I knew her. It is said that my step-daddy influenced my nature for the worse and his actions turned me against the world and this is simply not so. He was a man of no account, but he was not a man who had an effect on me one way or another. To me he was like a board, or a rock, or an empty barrel over in the corner, just there and absolutely nothing to be done about it.

Another man of no account and of no rightful or deserved place in this world unleashed a harsh word against my mother on a public street and I right away struck him with all my force in his fouled mouth and would have killed him right there with a stone I was able to grab up quick from the ground had he not just then rushed back at me and been struck down in the act by an honourable man by the name of Moulton. Ed Moulton done me a favour then and I am not one to forget a favour. So when I seen Ed Moulton in battle against two loafers at Joe Dyer's saloon later and seen this man—who was not a man so much as a serpent or a cipher of something that could have been a man if allowed to grow up proper and not twisted all around in himself as he was—lift up a chair and come after Ed with killing intent, well, I took the chance to fully avenge my mother's honour and abet the well-being and continuance of Ed Moulton by drawing my blade into the fray and stabbing deep and well into his rat's chest three times in quick succession, resulting in his timely end.

And thereby was I outlawed.

That man had been a big man in those parts until I ended him and folks were not about to let that slide. They say that every man needs a companion and at that time I had none. I wandered the desert for many days and nights but in time was able to avail myself of a good horse and I made my way in the world by way of a skill with cards that was, in that time and place, a positive boon to one's good fortunes. I was runned out of Arizona though on account of the killing of a soldier blacksmith at Fort Bowie, a matter of which it is best to let others speak at length as they no doubt have very much to say and many ears that will willingly listen and I ain't got nothing much to say on the matter. Lots of funny things happen in Arizona, I once saw a cat eat a pickle there and once I saw a two-headed calf. At any rate, I found myself back in New Mexico. I guess I had to be somewhere.

You know what that's like having people looking at you like you are the second coming? Looking at you like you're just the best thing there is, like you are honey on a warm biscuit, and at that same instant drawing on you because they want you dead just so they can be who they think you are. Only you're not even that. And that's not even the whole of it, they don't even care that you're dead, just so they're the one that pulled the trigger of the gun that killed you. Down in New Mexico is where that shit all started.

"You Billy the Kid?"

And I'd just turn around, I'd already be shooting because there weren't no point in wasting any time about it, and that is where that question always ended, it didn't ever end with "I am pleased to make your acquaintance."

Maybe after I shot I'd say, "Who's askin'?" but I'd say it but just for show 'cause there weren't no one there anymore. Just a belt and a pair of boots left. And a body inside of them waiting to be carted off.

So there I was in New Mexico. Something was bound to happen. And she did.

This is not Paulita now, she was gone by then. This is the second one. But she is gone now too. But she was not gone the day that I saw her for the first time, no, she was definitely right there and no doubt about it. There's no way to avoid a pretty woman in green stockings, that is something I have learned. I have put men into the ground before the time their Creator would have chosen for them and for that sin he put me into the same room as those green stockings and he did not let me go from there. Not that I would have gone away from there anyway. I have always felt I would hate to be the woman waking up and seeing my face on the pillow next to her in the morning but that has never stopped me from negotiating myself into that position and it did not stop me then.

I could walk right out on top of the water and she'd just roll her eyes.

"Billy, you are getting your feet wet," she would have said.

Shoot ten cans off a fence just like that, like it was nothing, and she'd just spit.

"That's all you got?" she'd say. And then she'd laugh like she'd just won the cakewalk. Like she was the Lord's favourite living thing and she had him wrapped around her little finger. A smoky throat laugh she had. You almost didn't mind that it was you she was laughing at, just so you could hear the way she laughed.

I came home with my nose on my cheek one time and wearing the blood like a beard and she took one look at me as I came through the door, took one look up at me and she said: "He dead?" She was a hard ticket.

And I said, "He is."

And she just went back to what she was doing. Slicing potatoes, if I recall correctly. That was it and we had the potatoes

[73]

fried up in a black pan that evening with onions and tomatoes and with my nose just crusting over and crooked. It's funny the things you recall. But we didn't get tomatoes often, which I guess is why I remember it. And I recall trying to breathe that night with my nose whistling away like it was trying to remember a tune.

It would be best if I just forgot about her. There were battles and bad men and even a war between us and I'm saying that if you come at me you better bring the best that you got. Well, she did. One time I told her there was no advantage to be had talking about things, that you could talk and talk your way around anything, but no matter what you said it was still the thing that it was and the talk didn't have any effect on it at all and I was tired of talking and was going out for the evening and I had no intention of returning.

"Poor thing," she says.

I said nothing then. I did not know why she pitied me.

Not long after that I ended up in the Lincoln County Jail from which I escaped, against all imaginable odds, killing James Bell and old Bob Ollinger in the doing of it. For over a year I stayed well on the run but after a while I drifted back to Fort Sumner. On July 14, 1881, Pat Garrett was waiting for me there and in the dark he shot me dead. And that is what it said in the newspapers and what it says in the books. But like I said, the best parts of the truth do not get made into newspapers and do not get made into books and I am not trying to tall-story you about this or anything else but here I am. I am right here.

After Bob hit the ground, a little gurgling sound came out of him like a private thing no one else should ever hear, then a little popping sound, like a bubble gone. You can shoot a man in the head and there's no blood at all to speak of and another time there'll be a considerable amount—I suppose it depends where the bullet goes through. It's all in where that bullet lands,

I suppose, maybe a doctor could explain it, and maybe Turner's daddy would know about such things. I am going to look it up next time I am in a library, but that might be some time from now. What no one could explain to me then is why in hell a man puts himself purposely into a situation he knows—or he should know—he cannot win. If you can't afford to lose, you don't sit down at the table, that is the way I see it. By the time someone reached down and closed his eyes for him, well, I was gone. By the time someone reached down to close my eyes for me after Garrett shot me, well, I was gone by then too. But I was on a horse. Or just maybe I was never there in that room at all. In any event that was someone else who got buried in my name and boots, and the tears shed, if any, were misspent.

ᘓ **10** ᘔ

The great big heart of the world breaks as Joseph and I sit here like the couple of busted cunts we now find ourselves out to be. We can pretend we are not, but then we are just two busted cunts pretending not to be what we quite obviously are and we will fool no one with our weak-ass play-acting.

"What's your name?" I ask.

She looks back through the canvas cover at us as if she is looking at two bugs in a Mason jar.

"I told you…it's Turner. You deaf?"

"I don't mean your Christian name, I mean the whole thing start to finish..."

"It's Wing."

"Your name is Turner Wing?"

"You have it."

"That's a hell of a name."

"You think so? Billy the Kid? You think it's a hell of a name? Mine?"

I think about that, then I look up and watch the quiet flip-flap of the canvas next to her face. "Yeah," I say, "I do."

Our horses amble behind us, tied up to the back rail. They must think this quite a show and also a much more amiable pace than has been set for them so far on this trip.

"That is what I meant. A hell of a name. That is what I said. I admire it."

"Why?"

A woman. The way they work.

"It flows tripping off the tongue. *Turner Wing.* It is a name to be remembered. No one has a name like it."

Women—young ones especially, I find—appreciate some tenderness.

"It is a name and that is all." She looks back again, her hair falling in long snakes around her face. "It will look good on a wanted poster," she says, and her father the doctor laughs deep from his belly as if appreciating a story told in a saloon.

"If it's Wanted posters you want, it doesn't take too much to get on 'em these days," I say. It is a learned piece of gunslinger's wisdom for her.

She sits regarding me. The sun out there is strong on her cheeks and her eyes are green and heavy on me now. "I know that," she says.

We both listen to the sounds of the hooves and the wheels. Or I do. I do not know what she's listening to.

"It would cost you nothing to let us loose," Joseph says, and we both turn to look at him as if he has suddenly appeared like a saviour come down in mortal form, but he is, as he is in the process of pointing out, not currently in a position to save anyone.

"Now, that might be true and it might not," she says, looking at him with the same heavy assessment with which she had favoured me. "Sure as hell though it costs me nothing to keep you the way you are. Stilled hands are trustworthy hands. That is what I have found."

And she closes the canvas on the both of us with some determination and I suddenly feel like a small pale animal without a shell. When I was a younger man I was never in a situation such as this. Nobody got the drop on me, not ever. There was no man I could not best with a gun or a word and certainly no girl of sixteen or twenty or thirty or however the hell old this one is. When I was twenty and full of piss and vinegar I was something to see. I was spectacular, a raging barn fire of a fellow. I would not then have been captive of any girl and her gap-faced father.

They say that Jesus Christ came back and spoke to people after he got killed and that he took that one doubtful fellow's hand and poked that fellow's finger right into the hole in his own body. I didn't have to prove anything after I got killed 'cause the people who saw me after I was supposed to be dead just said, *"Well, that bastard ain't dead after all."* But there weren't too many that saw me anyway, hardly any, and who was there between here and Canada who was going to believe them that they did? Not one person. I do not have the longevity nor the conviction of the saviour. Nor do I wish to, eternity being a very long time. I would eventually find myself with nothing left to do and there comes a time when you just wish to lie down. Sand, when it's mixed with blood, takes on the consistency and feel of the kind of clay that young children play with to form pretend cows and barns, horses and their riders, and pretend pipes used to smoke pretend tobacco.

Joseph professes a seedy allegiance to the idea of valour. To a man's valour and honour, which I guess is the idea that we can rise to be better people than who we actually are. But in my view we are who we have made ourselves out to be and we are well and truly stuck with that version. I suppose that even now he pictures us free from these ropes and on our way to some sunny kingdom of the future. I am not so optimistic as he. Sometimes it is as if he thinks the sunshine runs straight out of his ass and right down his leg like a leaky shit and other times he has more than his share of dark at the top of his staircase. I suppose we are all like that to a degree, but he can irk me with this irrational sunshiny view of things that he unexpectedly launches into at times. I do not really think the less of him for this though. I wish I had the capacity for hope that he does, only he spends most of his time as nasty as a squirrel stuck in a jam jar and then all of a sudden he's "Consider the birds of the field, William..." Well, fuck the birds is what I say.

However, I suppose this quality of his is what has me back out in the desert and searching for the safe haven he assures me is out there somewhere just for the taking. Canada, he says. To me it's just a place I don't know on a map. He can be a man of few words and the few he does use can be as surly as a cat in a sack, but at the heart of him he is a man who believes that tomorrow may hold something better for us all. This, I suppose, is what compels him to bury the remains of any passed-away young women he runs across in the desert. Or causes him to pick up the tail ends of a brother and try to carry him off and far away from dangers that are mostly of his own making.

I admire my brother, but I wish he was not aware of that fact and not such a big high-assed prick about the knowledge. Regarding the things about which you can do nothing, I find it is best to refrain from trying to do anything about them and definitely it is always best to refrain from pissing and moaning about the state of things—you can change 'em or you can shut the fuck up about them. For a time I allow myself the luxury of not thinking about anything at all and then I lean my head back and let my eyes roll back into their black holes like those of a child's doll. It can get very dark inside my head and I try to tell myself that things are not so bad as they might seem but then I assure myself that yes, in fact they are, and they really could hardly get any worse. Then I swear dead cats because nobody likes to hear the truth, especially from themselves. I try to be careful about what I let myself think. But you can't be careful all the time and there are things that creep into my head from time to time in spite of my best efforts to keep them out. My brain is not always a friend to me.

Like my own mother when she left us alone some years before she died, not even looking back to see if I was there. My thoughts about her are complicated thoughts.

"Joseph."

"What?"

"Well, what are we going to do?"

"Persevere."

"I can't sit around here much longer with my hands up my ass."

"Then don't."

Everyone is against me now, it seems.

"I'm easy to catch but hard to keep caught." I say, and start to laugh.

"What?"

"Somebody wrote that about me in the newspapers one time."

"You should not read your own press reports."

"I think I would have made a good lawman."

"A little late for that now, Ish."

"I suppose."

"And the fact that you are a prisoner to a fourteen-year-old girl does not recommend you to that profession, I do not think."

"I do not believe she is anywhere near to fourteen."

"You're right. Being prisoner to a sixteen-year-old girl is much more admirable. Maybe you'll be able to read about that in the papers."

"Fuck you."

"I am already fucked."

I watch a bloodsucker fill up on the contents of my arm and wish I had some sweet tea to drink. I sit heavy and rocking between the canvas walls of this tunnel that flaps open at both ends to the blue sky at the rear next to my sombre brother and amidst the soft smiles of a breeze that now and then stirs the dust up off the trail and suddenly I wish I were in a home of my own at last and all this wandering and running would finally come to an end somehow, and some man I do not know did not want me dead or put into jail, and perhaps I would be with children familiar and dear to me and blood to my blood, and I would watch them play their little ordinary games on the floor before me and any regret I might feel would be just a delusion from which I could awaken with a sudden cold-water splash and a coffee with hot biscuits or at least I might be able to shake it off and replace it with something else—something simple unto itself and unlikely to cause suffering to any other being but I have no access to these things, having done nothing at all to earn them and having made no decisions in life to warrant them and having no heart really now with which to welcome them, nor time in which to gather them up and, oh, what a deep and clear path of unbridled waste I have shouldered through this life and what little I have to show for the effort of having done so.

And it is apparent that Turner Wing's daddy might be heading toward the town of Las Cruces and if that is the case, then Joseph is correct: we are well and truly fucked. Places where there are other people have never worked out well for either one of us.

⤶ 11 ⤷

If they dig me up a thousand years from now, I am sure I will have a look of surprise on my face. Not because they dug me up. I think in a way I'm expecting that. Fame and notoriety breed a coarse familiarity. When they wouldn't even consider digging up someone else's bones they won't think twice about mine. *"Let's dig up old Auntie Mable,"* someone will say and others will answer: *"Shame! We pale at the thought. Do not do it!"* but then the suggestion will be made: *"Well, what about ol' Billy the Kid? Let's dig him up then!"* and then will come the answer: *"Excelsior! Let's do that very thing!"*

And I think my look of surprise will be more disappointment than anything—first of all that they dug me up and second that I had died in the first place.

"Hey, boys, why you throwing dirt on me? Hey, boys. Boys?"

I've been hiding for a long time now and I don't want to hide anymore. Or maybe I just want to hide better. But not in a pine box. Not that well.

"I think we might be heading toward Las Cruces," I tell Joseph.

"I know that," he says.

"That's not good for us. People will know me there."

"I know that too."

"Well, what are we going to do about it, Joseph?"

He looks at me like one would look at a child who has asked once too often why the sky is blue. And then he lifts his hands from behind his back to show me they are no longer tied together, which is exactly like something a magician might do, come to think of it. It is as if he is holding a rainbow between his outstretched palms. And now he smiles. In the deepest ocean I do not believe there is a creature as unexpected as my brother is to me at times. He lifts his finger to his mouth to signal that he does not believe it would be wise for me to yell out the information that he has freed himself. Nor is there a creature more infuriating to me. He sits there smiling at me like he is some kind of a carnival treat, leaking balloons and calliope music out his ass. He is insufferable. But in spite of myself I begin to smile as well. The sunny kingdom. He has manifested it all by himself right here before us.

A nd so we find ourselves free again and in a tavern. The details are not important. Or maybe they are. Details usually are but it is also the details that get forgotten. We make up stories about what happens to us and it is the stories that end up telling us who we are, not the events themselves because the stories we tell ourselves are always different from what actually happens. Here are the details of it though, in case they are of interest to you:

It is a simple enough business. With our paws free we simply wait for the right moment to grab our captors from behind the canvas and bring the laws of natural science to bear through the counterbalance of weights and the providence of gravity. We scare the bejesus out of the horses in doing so though, and the wagon pops a wheel when we suddenly take out across the scrub and hit a rock. And in spite of the fact that the Wings are some pissed at us for turning things over on them all of a sudden, it seems that the setting of things right in the balance of power leads to us being more like compatriots than the blood-sworn enemies we had seemed for the best part of the first half of the day, although I still believe young Turner Wing would have slit my throat if given the chance, if only because I bested her. There is something wrong with the youth of the day when they resent being bested by an elder. Whether she is twelve or fourteen or eighteen or fifty she should realize that being outgunned or outmanned is not an indignity, though I suppose I certainly did not see things that way at her age. Being bested has not been a part of my plan at any time, to be honest, and least of all now, but dammit I am not her enemy and she should see that and I have no idea why I should have to prove it to her.

It takes some time to settle the horses down, impress upon the Wings both Junior and Senior that the tables now have been definitively turned and to make repairs to the wagon wheel such that we have time only to start a fire before the full darkness of a desert night is upon us in earnest.

"I am going to tell you a story," I announce to the small gathering when we have completed a small but hearty meal of beans and hardtack. It is no small achievement to complete one's supper in the presence of Mr. Wing's complicated and vociferous mastication, and let there be no confusion in your mind about that. It is a carnival and not one you would pay to see nor ever return to if given the choice.

"I am not interested in your story," says Turner. "I'd rather throw peas against a wall than sit here and listen to your story."

"Listen, you," I tell her, pointing with the knife I have been using to dig into the hard tack, "someday, somewhere under the drifting eye of God, you are going to receive your comeuppance."

"Patience, William," Joseph counsels. Joseph is forever seeking in me qualities I do not possess. I have the patience of, well, the patience of something that does not have any patience at all.

Turner has her jaw stuck out now and her golden hair is all lit up in the light from the fire. I do admit that she is a pretty enough girl.

"If someday I do receive it you can bet it'll come from a better man than you," she says.

She's right, a voice in my head says, she is right this girl. It won't be you. You're a stupid man to think it might be. The pig voice, the devil voice, it is called. That voice within you that tells you that you will amount to nothing. That you are non-sensical and all your efforts will turn to nothing but dust.

"Maybe, maybe not," I say.

"Well, that uncertain and hesitant statement has certainly put me in my place. I suppose I'd best just shut up now."

"You should."

"I won't. You gonna tell us your big story now?"

"Never mind that."

"Your story have a nice moral we can all learn a little lesson from?"

"You ain't gonna find out 'cause I ain't gonna tell it."

"It have a nice happy ending to make us all feel just a little better about our lives?"

"It ain't got no ending 'cause I ain't gonna start it."

"You know why stories always have happy endings?"

"I don't care."

"It's because people always end 'em in the wrong places, that's why, the princess that gets married and lives happy ever after? Well, that's just until she dies. Probably she gets to be the queen and then some people come into the palace and cut her fool head right off her neck for her. Folks should maybe try ending the story right there instead so people might actually believe it. Kings and queens are gettin' their fool heads cut off all the time, from what I hear. They should put that in the stories."

"Might cut down on the popularity of the princess trade. Or the story-telling business at that."

"Ain't no such thing as a princess—you believe there is then you're an even simpler man than I give you credit for."

[85]

"There ain't, huh?"

"You ever seen one? I ain't."

"You ain't never seen a polar bear either, now that don't mean there ain't such things."

"And I suppose you have?"

"That's what my story was about...polar bears...I guess now you'll never know."

"Well, there ain't none around here."

"Polar bears or princesses?"

"Neither one. What difference does it make to me if they're somewhere else? I ain't somewhere else, I am right here and I ain't ever goin' to the North Pole nor any fairy tale land where there's princesses and such."

"Now don't ever think small about yourself, darlin'," Wing Senior interjects in his voice with a boot in it. "You never know where you're goin'... There's lots of places to be besides Shit-shine, New Mexico..."

"Oh I know it, and I'm goin' somewhere, don't worry about that, Daddy...it just ain't the North Pole and it sure as shit ain't here 'cause this shit here...it ain't nowhere."

"There you go now. That's my girl."

Familial love and allegiance are heartwarming things. Parental pride and protection. Well, that's just fine, I suppose. I was once cleaning out an old barn of thirty years of shit that no one had wanted for forty and I came across this old wooden box, seemed to have been a cheese box from a dairy at one point, and it was filled with a couple of horse collars and some Mason jars and at the bottom was a ball of thread and some paper and a couple of handfuls of hairless and blind baby mice and their momma looking right up at me. Looked to me that she had got in there and delivered them and could not get back up the smooth walls because they had some kind of wax paste on them. I don't mind saying that most small animals put the jimmy onto me more than any haunt or spirit would. They just make me crawl all over for some reason. So I slammed that lid back down on that box and I thought for a minute what it was I could do next. I could maybe just leave the box there like that but I was being paid to clean the place out and I needed the money. I fought the urge to jump on the box repeatedly until the mice were no more. I am sorry but you may not fully know my feelings about small animals and my wish not to have them even within the same county as me. Nevertheless I carried that box out of the barn, squirming the whole time and doing a foolish little dance like my boots were on fire and I walked it out to the tree line and for a moment I was just going to leave it there closed up like that and at least I would not have to think about it any longer but something wanted me to open it on up and leave it on its side so at least the mother could take her time and carry those young ones off to cover at her leisure so that is what I did and as soon as I opened that lid that small grey bitch looked up at me with eyes like the black heads of the pins ladies use to put their hats in place on their heads (if they realized how much those implements resembled the eyes of rodents they would not use them at all) and then she darted, black cold eyes that held nothing in them but fear for herself, darted out of that box and into the brush, leaving her children cold and squirming and on their own. I was saddened by the way their little bony paws reached out for something that was no longer there. Then it was confirmed that they had been in there for some time as I saw one of them was chewed in half and its innards were sucked right out.

She was not ever coming back.

I stomped them into blackness.

Anyway, that was the story I was going to tell. I guess sometimes it's best just to hold your peace. I keep learning the same lessons over and over.

⤷ **12** ⤶

"Are you fellas drinkin' men?" Wing Senior asks.

"More of a pastime, less of a career with me," Joseph answers.

"I am not. I never found a lot of advantage to it myself," I say. "It seems a good way to shorten the distance between the other fella's shooting ability and my own."

"Now now, let none amongst us allow ourselves to be shot tonight. Turner, why don't you get out those bottles of whisky from the bags and we'll have ourselves some refreshment. Come, gentlemen, you'll have a drink with us? We'll drink to my health because it is my professional opinion that I shall make a full recovery—a party in the condition in which we currently find ourselves is always fortunate to have a medical man along, even if he is one of the patients, and we'll drink also to the end of hostilities and to our new alliance."

"We got no alliance with you," Joseph points out.

"Well, maybe not. But, gentlemen, our hostilities have ended, certainly. And my health is improving just as yours has and so, just to show no hard feelings, a drink?"

Turner has returned to the fire with three bottles of whisky and she stands at the edge of the light with them as if she holds three freshly caught fish.

"I'll drink," Joseph says, "but we have no alliance. And why is it that you talk the way you do? I mean, like you got a bouquet of roses rammed up your ass."

Joseph does not let on that he is one for the flowery language at times himself, particularly when he wants to let the world know how smart he is, which it seems to me is most of the time.

"Fine then. We'll have a drink together," Wing says. "And I suppose I have become accustomed to speaking in a slightly mannered way because folks like to know that their doctor knows a thing or two. It sets them at ease. They would rather hear 'You appear to have a serious condition, sir' than 'Mister, you ain't gonna live so long.' That is the way of it. And perhaps it is also because I have spent many years in the study of the practice. More training involved in becoming a physician than a gunfighter, I would think."

"Doctoring work is a little less forgiving than the gunfighting trade, I can tell you that," I point out.

I have seen some who considered themselves gunfighters who could not hit the door of a barn while stood inside of the barn and with the door closed. Folks want to know that their doctor can help them to live and their gunfighter can shoot them dead. It is often in my best interests to advertise the fact that I am qualified in that regard. Sobriety is another essential trait and one not much possessed by a great many gunfighters and outlaws I have known who are now no more alive than those baby mice I told about so I must confess that for much of the imbibing that takes place at this point I play only an illusory role in that the other players do a great deal of drinking, and I—well, I merely pretend to drink, strong drink being no friend of mine as I've told. Even for someone who has not had the experience of being hunted by others I think becoming drunk at night in the desert is a foolhardy thing to do and I am surprised that Joseph proceeds to do so now, but then my brother surprises me on a nearly continual basis.

There is much banter and ceremony regarding the passing of the bottle. Much comment on Turner's attempts at downing the brew and some coughing and spitting, which ensues when she does manage to do so, but she holds her own fair enough. For me it is an easy thing to fool others into thinking that I am drinking, as I have had to do it on many occasions.

"That's it!" Wing enthuses. "Run that into you, boys!"

The situation degenerates gradually, and all are greatly diminished in capacity, but there is no diminishment of sound as the three trade stories and tales. Wing expounds on Turner's shooting abilities, which are, according to dearest Daddy, "prodigious."

"Hit the tail off a moving bobcat at fifty paces!" he exclaims.

"I have not seen many bobcats around here," I offer.

"No and you won't either, not with her around!"

Turner laughs and takes another drink.

He has been slowly approaching for many minutes and he is alone. Just himself and a horse that he has left southeast of this spot and about a ten-minute slow crawl through the sage. He has his gun with him though. Or else he is a fool. He takes his time and makes virtually no sound, so he is not a fool, and so he is armed. He has a purpose in approaching, though what that purpose might be I do not yet know. He is either approaching with extreme aggression or extreme care or likely he is doing both. At any rate his approach is a cause for some concern. I have found that there are no friendly strangers in the desert at night. The advantage is his in that he has seen and heard of us for miles during his approach and we will not see him until he decides to step forward into the lit-up circle of the fire if he does so at all. He could just decide to pick us all off from out of the darkness in order to save himself any danger. He may have an interest in the horses, or the wagon, maybe whatever may be in our pockets, or his interest may be of a more romantic nature if he has figured out that there is a girl here, which, given the way the least sound travels at night, is a certainty. Young women in the desert are hard to find and easy to hold down, if you will excuse my frankness regarding a less than discreet topic, but it

[90]

is the truth of the matter and no mistake about it. In my experience the desert, particularly when it is covered in dark, will bring out the best or the worst in people and it is seldom the best. It is as if the dry cold air brings out a dark opening in their souls. If you've ever watched a thunderstorm approach, flashing from a hundred miles away through open land in the pitch dark, then you understand how the Bible came to be written. There is a terror that is always near in full darkness on open land. Sometimes it comes with chain lightning down a mile-long ravine lit up brightly like sudden day and sometimes it just comes in on its own out of the blackness.

"*Who the fuck are you?*" Wing calls out.

The stranger has stepped forward suddenly and sooner than I thought, which is of no matter as my gun is already drawn and trained now for his stomach, or at least where I estimate his stomach to be based on the position of his head, which is his only truly visible feature at the moment with the light falling as it is, as if he is a floating skull. But Wing is not as prepared as I and he is still fumbling to find his pistol, which cannot be an easy task in the relative dark and with a bag over your head.

"I said who the fuck are you?" Wing repeats to cover the lack of any weapon in his hand.

"Doesn't matter who he is, he'll be dead if he moves in any direction or even so much as blinks," I say in a voice loud enough to be heard but low enough not to denote any hesitance to make its statement a matter of historical fact. "Step on into the light and show us that your hands ain't got nothing to do at the moment," I tell him.

The kid takes one slow step forward.

"That's far enough," I tell him.

The kid, for he cannot be more than seventeen, has a face like a loaf of prison bread, holes in it like a crow's been pecking at him and the shadow light from the fire does him no favours.

His hair is greased in a forelock but his most distinguishing feature is the fact that he is, from head to toe, root to fruit, bare-ass naked.

"You ain't got no clothes on," Turner points out rather needlessly.

"No, I ain't," the kid admits, as an afterthought bringing forth his hands to cover himself.

"That boy's naked." This from Joseph, who is still in the process of analyzing the situation.

"And is that a matter of personal expression, son?" I ask the kid, holstering my gun. "Or have you just lost all your clothing?"

"My clothes got stole from me, sir."

Wing has managed to find his pistol and is waving it generally in the kid's direction.

"I don't think he's got but one thing to shoot at you right now, Wing, and I don't expect he intends to use it."

"No, sir," the kid says, moving again to cover up the weapon in question.

I get up and move toward the packs on my horse.

"He ain't got no clothes on," Turner says as if she is repeating the punch line of a joke and then she laughs. I believe she is quite drunk.

"I got something here you can use if you want, son," I say, pulling out my extra pair of long johns.

"Yes, sir. Thank you, sir. That's very kind." He steps back out of the light a bit and struggles into my gear with his long white shanks flashing. "I am sorry to come up on you like this in the dark. There ain't no good way to announce that you got no clothes on and it's hard to know how people might take that information, if you take my meaning." He moves forward again and crouches closer to the fire. "I been gettin' real cold." He wipes his chin with the back of his hand. "Are those beans in that pot?"

"They are, and you're welcome to 'em, I believe everyone here is done. There's some hard biscuit in that pan there too if you'd care to have some of that."

"Yessir, I would and thank you. Thank you, sir."

Very polite kid. Impossible to trust. My hand slips back to my gun belt.

He eats like he is mostly stomach. "What are you folks doing out here, if you don't mind me asking?" His eyes are studying the bag on Wing's head. It would be odder, of course, were they not.

"Wearin' clothes," Turner replies fast. "We're just out here wearin' our clothes…" And she starts to giggle, a sound I never would have expected to hear from her.

The kid looks at her for a moment. So do I. "That's wise," he says.

And we both just keep on looking at her. In the light from the fire she looks like she's swimming in honey, or like she's lit from within. She continues laughing slowly. Then we both look away.

"My brother and I, we're just travelling," I say. "I'm writing a book," I add. And I don't know why I say it. I hear myself say it out loud and it shocks me, as if someone else has said it of me and it has come to me as fresh news. If I am writing a book it will be some time before I have the chance to commit the bulk of it to paper, but then you are holding a book in your hands right now. So there you go, I suppose I succeeded.

"Is it gonna be a funny book?"

"Will be if I put you into it."

"You're writing a book?" Joseph asks.

"Maybe."

The kid finishes his beans and wipes the plate with his fingers. "I like a funny book, like the one I read once in Yuma. They got a building there and it's full of books. All kinds."

"They got a jail there too," I say.

"I ain't seen that. But I saw this house full of books. Is your book gonna be in a place like that when you get it wrote?"

"I suppose so."

But there'll be a lot of wind and rain between here and there, is what I'm thinking. A lot of open space. There are a lot of stories in the desert and most of them just get lost. Writing them down is maybe a way to hold on to them.

"More important to the moment," I say, "you seem to be wandering through the wilderness with no clothes on like John the goddamned Baptist, but the thing is you don't seem to me to be anything like a prophet, son. Now, I don't mean to pry into another man's business—"

"But you'd have to admit that it's unusual."

This interruption is from Joseph, who seems to have sobered up some and engaged personally with the world once more.

"It's more than unusual," Wing, who has finally re-holstered his gun, adds.

"I guess around here it's best if you lock your boots up at night," the kid says.

"I find it best to keep everything locked up all the time, here or anywhere else that I've been," I tell him.

"I sure wish I had done that, mister. I sure do. But locks wouldn't have actual helped me out any. These fellas just took everything I had, everything excepting my horse, and they shot at me with my own gun before they left—they thought that was about the funniest thing they'd ever seen too, I guess, a man bein' shot at with his own gun. With his own gun…"

"They left you your horse?"

"Well, I can't say I blame them for that, you ain't seen my horse, he's a lean one for certain, he sorta looks like a wooden sawhorse with a hide thrown over the top of it. In fact I named him Sawhorse and you can guess why. I don't know how he keeps hisself goin' with no fat on him but he does. They most likely thought he was bound to die any day, but that is where they made their first mistake because he has just always been on the lean side, he just don't accumulate no meat on him…"

"What was their second?"

"Their second what?"

"You said that them leavin' your horse with you was their first mistake—what was their second?"

"Well, I don't know…I expect they'll make others." The kid paws at the dirt a bit and looks into the fire. "Leavin' me alive, that was their second mistake," he says. "I expect I'll kill them if I ever see them again."

Nobody says anything then.

"Mister, do you mind any if I go on and get my horse. I left him back there a bit so's I could come up and see who you folks was and I'm worried he might wander."

"You go ahead and do that."

"I'm mighty appreciative."

"Don't mention it."

The kid turns to go, and as he does Turner comes out with a sharp laugh and: "Sonny Boy Jim, you might want to close up the barn doors because the moon is out."

The kid feels behind him and realizes his trap door is down. My trap door actually.

"Well, dammit," he says, disappearing back into the night, "if that don't beat all, first those fellas try to light me up and burn me right down to the ground and now I'm walking around with the window open…"

The Wings, Junior and Senior, freeze up, like a ghost has walked right up to the fire and spit into it. Any air that was moving has stopped and there is suddenly the sort of quiet I do not much care for.

"Hold on, son," Wing Senior says quietly. "What did you just say?"

I slip my hand onto my gun. I don't know yet what has just happened here, but I'll want my gun handy when I find out, I can tell that. Joseph has done the same, without anybody but me seeing, as far as I can tell in this light.

The kid turns around, still fidgeting. He is unaware that everything has just changed. That means he is not the threat. But there is a threat nearby somewhere now and that is sure and clear. It is just a matter of determining what that threat is.

"I said I left my window open, and I just can't seem to stop showing folks my ass tonight, pardon me, miss…and I'm real sorry about that, I am."

"Before that."

"What?"

"Son, I'm asking you real nicely what you said just before that, about those men trying to burn you to the ground—what did you mean by that exactly?'

"I meant just that—those men tried to light me up."

"They wanted to set fire to you?"

"Yes, sir, that's what I'm saying. They were talking about doing just that when I got to my horse and I got away from there."

Turner has gone bone-white and quiet. "What did these men look like, son?"

"Well. There was one real big and then one on the smaller side and with a funny right eye, and the bigger one, he was in charge and the smaller one, he just did what the bigger one said, except for the burning of me, that was the little one's idea, the bigger one he just said, 'Well, go ahead and do it then but let's be quick about it,' like they was fixing to fry up an egg or something before they went on their way. I didn't like that one little bit and I told 'em so."

Wing is silent now so I chip in with, "What'd they think of that?"

"Not much. No, they was so busy arguing about what to do about it, I just lit off on my horse as naked as I was and as quick as I could go and I don't know why they didn't take after me but they didn't. They would have caught me right easy too, they had some good horses."

"One black stallion, one white?"

"That's right."

Wing has his head down now and he's drawing in the sand with a stick. "First light comes, you're going show us exactly where you left them."

"No," Turner says.

"I'm not asking *you* about it, Turner. You be quiet."

"Actually I ain't real anxious to go back there," the kid pipes in.

"I'm not asking *you* either!" Wing yells at the kid. "First light comes and we head for that spot, you two boys do whatever you like and you can shoot me again if you want to, but if you don't, then that's where this wagon is headed so there's no discussing it unless it's with bullets, but I'd just as soon not have to kill anyone over my travel plans."

"Daddy..."

"That's what we're doing, Turner. That's final. Everybody get some sleep. Son, you go get your horse, you're going to need it. You boys do what you want. At first light Turner and me we go north. Turner, you get yourself some sleep now. I'm...I'm going for a walk..."

"Daddy, I'm gonna be sick."

"You go ahead and be sick then, and then you get yourself some sleep. Morning is coming."

And with that he walks off into the dark.

No man steps into this desert at night alone unless he has lost his mind or does not care if he lives or dies. Joseph and I have found ourselves in the middle of something here and I do not know what it is and that concerns me.

[97]

And Miss Turner throws up her beans all over the sand with a sound like the opening up of hell and then she falls face forward into the ground by the fire.

"Oh," says the kid, "well, I guess I'd best go get my horse…"

"We're into some darkness here," I tell Joseph when the kid is far enough away to be out of earshot. "We're into some kind of evil shit."

"She's passed out," Joseph says.

"Did you hear what I said, Joseph? I said there's something just plain evil coming up here and I got no interest in it. None at all."

"Nor do I, but she needs to be taken care of or she's going to choke to death maybe."

I look over to Turner and she's lying with her face down into the dirt and her own spit-up on her and her daddy off wandering alone into the night. "I'll take care of her," I tell him.

"You sure?"

"I'm sure."

"And then let's get some sleep. Wing is right about one thing: morning is coming."

"We just going to stick with this thing, Joseph? These people don't mean a thing to us."

"Not yet."

"We could put this girl into her bedroll all safe and sound and then just be gone the hell away from here. I thought you were taking me someplace where no one has ever heard of me? I thought we were going to be safe this time. The both of us."

"Thirteen-year-old girls with crazy fathers served first," Joseph says. He has not stopped looking at Turner in the dirt.

"I told you she's at least sixteen, maybe more," I say.

"That safe place will still be there when we're done with this," he says.

"Probably eighteen... Done doing what?"

Joseph stands up and stretches and then starts unstrapping his bedroll. "I don't know yet," he says, "but we been brought here for this work. It is clear and certain that we have."

"Could be nineteen or twenty for all we know..."

My brother he looks up into the sky like he's shaking hands with the Lord God above and as if any such God would listen to a word he is saying to the sky. Folks with a strong and plain faith in God are amongst the most dangerous folks of all is what I have found to be true, and they are likely to do just about anything. By the time I struggle Turner into the back of the wagon I can hear the kid is back and he is speaking in whispers to Joseph. That's of no account. Joseph has got no secrets from me that would have any importance to my health and I couldn't care less what the kid has to say. If I know my brother, and I do, he is trying to find out more about these other men as it's clear this wagon I am sitting in is hooked up to wherever they are now with some kind of invisible rope that Joseph and Wing can see each in their own way and I cannot. I look down at Turner's face, which is now in my lap. I take an edge of the blanket and start to wipe it clean. In spite of the dirt and her own puking she has beautiful skin, like it's the face of a china doll I am wiping at. Her hair too, which up to now has been mostly under her hat, is out and around her face and glowing in the light from the lantern. Her lips are a woman's lips. I get her cleaned up mostly, then onto the bedroll full and stretched out. She lets out a moan and pulls her knees up to herself. Small hands like white birds.

"Turner?"

Sleeping. Then I reach and pull at the breeches by her hip and pull them down to take a good long look at her ass. Full and creamy and white.

Not a single day under twenty.

I cover her up again and trim down the lantern, then hop down from the wagon.

I'm losing weight, I think. My clothes seem looser on me and my belt does not do the job it once did, and there's no room in it for new holes without having it snake way out so I will have to cut off the extra. I am disappearing slowly. It seems that Joseph has told the kid who I am, I do not know why, maybe so he won't get any ideas about anything including the now unconscious Miss Turner. My brother Joseph, everyone's daddy.

"Hey, I guess I'm kind of lucky," the kid says, smiling. "Last week in Taos I met me a lady singer and today I meet a famous dead outlaw."

"You're the lucky one alright, kid. They don't come any luckier."

It's colder now than it was. I turn up my collar and walk away from the wagon.

ᥱᕲ **13** ᥱᕲ

*I*am a killer true enough, Billy. I make dead people. And now dead myself. Dead people cannot do whatever they want to do, Billy, at least that is what I have learned, not like when I was alive and could do anything at all that I wanted, only up until such time as I was killed by you, and oh how my mind wanders now with nothing left for my hands to do. I am a white animal skull wasted in a field. I can still see everything as it was then. The country around there was like an unmade bed. The wrinkles in the sand like an old sheet. Over there a darker smear like someone had pissed into the mattress. I could do and act as I pleased but now I am a broken-down old wagon, wheel-deep in the dirt. The horse threw up sand to my eyes. There are places always you cannot go, no matter how you travel, there are always places you cannot get to, Billy. The worlds of the living and the dead are separate places. I needed a drink; I do remember that. At the same time, I was not regretful but nor was I satisfied. I was never satisfied in my life. Long tall daddy's dead, shot his poor self he did, blood on the walls on both sides, window glass taken clean out and did the boy cry to see it, oh he did yes. Well, that boy was me, but I learned to do my own killing soon enough and it was not myself I learned to kill. My father had a bad teacher in this world, and I could see that well enough, there was nothing he passed on to me except sorrow. The way the morning fog conformed to the air. No colour. Just fence rails staggered and torn. A town was coming up, the horizon smeared out of the sand the same as the sky. Wood lots. Trails. Heat. A man of such intelligence was I. I had read the encyclopedia one volume at a time. I had carefully turned the thin pages. N to P. Narcissist. Olfactory. Pancreas. White finger to mouth, then smudged one tissue-printed page against the next against the next. And Semples he would say to me, "When are we goin', Caleb? When are you ever gonna be done readin' that book?" And I would just turn the page and start again from the top. Panacea. Pancreatic ulcer. Panic. And then we came to the town the next morning finally and we made our way to the tavern by the station and there was a sign there saying "BEER" and a cheerful young thing with a smile and a napkin. A serviette. Carefully placed thousands of times. The pour. A jostle of the elbow. Not a drop. No. And then Semples on his way to the jakes for a piss and what did he look at me for? "You need help shaking it?" I asked him. Then it was my turn and I just stood in the doorway and pissed out into the air in the back lot, the white clapboard fence paralyzed, darkened windows papered over, nailed over glass to keep out the outside kiddies' metal toy rusted red and cracked. Disused. Bitch with my next drink, where now? Rickety dirt street wooden plank steps dusk falling offices and blacksmith Dry Cleaning tavern railway bells quickly by backstreet main street muddled together messy doorways shed water tower quick by end of day gloom waited for the light and start it again sleep behind cold dark glass Mr. Death Mr. Death Mr. Death made her kneel right there I did she kneeled right there her soft knees against the hardpacked earth it hurts I know it does and made her lift her red dress in the centre of that field and no one was coming no one was ever going to come, give me your necklace I told her give it to me lift your dress over yes over the top of I know it's cold girl I know I said just yes that's the way and let it yes fall there your knees against the hard dirt just don't cry little doll just here put this stone into your mouth I said just do it soft warm and it will be fine drop your hands to your side and let them just hang there I said don't I said don't I mean what I say girl I said and she said there's a shovel she asked what is it for? and then I said what was true and then it was truer just one more stone, girl don't cry I told her just put one more into your mouth warm there dead rustling stalks in the wind and there my darling one don't cry I said just open your mouth one more just one more stone to swallow down sweet and just one more and don't cry I said it makes it all wrong when you cry hush and just one more just open and the last one. Open your mouth, girl. Just one more. See, girl? How easy.

It is?

"Just one more," I said.

And she took every last one that I gave her. Hungry for it, I believe. Then I carved her throat tidy for her and left her there in a tree to drain fast and then slow out of herself. Her eyes. I always liked to hang them from the trees, you see, it would have been more prudent to bury them but I am not one for physical exertion and I suppose the practice carried something of the trophy about it. After a time the blood stops by itself, thickens, hardens. Everything hardens. Eyes even in their sockets. Hers. Then everything breaks down. That was the first. There were so many more to follow as Semples and I joined up and practised the disputed art together. I was aware that many people did not share my views on these matters but it was a pleasant thing to recall, that first encounter. A waste to think of the past when one was still living so then I just stopped thinking about it or anything else, Billy, and I shook the last of the piss from myself and re-entered the tavern and turned to the beer girl there and I asked her: "So what precisely do people do for fun here in Las Cruces?"

And you were still far away in the desert outside of town at that time, Billy, but you were getting closer. You were getting closer.

♋ 14 ❧

Women save the world and then we just go ahead and mess it on up again. They are like animal trainers following us around with shovels. Just like I told you, she said she knew I wasn't the one. Well hell, I knew I wasn't the one and I didn't need to be told. That is not true, I was as stupid as a boot at that time and I needed to be told any number of things. Still, it didn't come as anything fresher than last month's newspapers to me. Some men they make the mistake of thinking women are there to save them somehow and that is not the case at all because it is all of us who are all here to save each other and it is always the men who fail at the job so badly and so often that it seems to us as if the job is solely woman's work. Or maybe there is no one to save and no one to do any saving at all and at the end of the day there are only two people and what they might need. Still, I feel that they were better fashioned, that he saw something in us he realized was clumsily made and he sought to do better the second time around and he succeeded. This is not a view I have found to be shared by many men I have known, and it was not even held by me at that young age and so she had come to realize I was of no use to her at all and that was not an easy thing for me to hear, mostly as I did not know what the hell she was talking about.

"And what the hell does that even mean—not the one?"

"You're just not the one, Billy, and I'm leaving you now, I am going." She was throwing her things into a bag. Stockings, a hairbrush.

"I am not which one? What do you mean? Which one am I

not? I'm not the one you rode like a three-dollar pony last night? I'm not that one? Because I am pretty sure I am that one. I'm pretty sure that was me." I was angry.

"You are cheap," she said. She was right.

"That's lucky for you because I'm all you can afford."

"I have had my fill of you, Billy."

"You ain't either. You ain't goin' nowhere so why don't you just sit down and calm down? Have a drink with me and you'll feel different."

"I'm never drinking again either."

"Now I know you're lying."

"I'm not."

I slid up behind her then and I wrapped my arms around her. At first she struggled but then she settled some.

"No no no no no no no no no no no no no no no no no…" she whispered.

"Just stay."

"No. Not this time."

And she was right about everything and she knew it and so she left. I didn't try to stop her. A person will end up doing what a person wants to do. Life is more bruises than kisses, this is what I have found. The thin slit of light under the closed door and then her little shoes, moving away from me.

I once saw a man killed in the street, an altercation over a parcel of land he professed ownership of, and he was shot clean through the centre of his chest and right on out the back of him. The front of him was clean but for a small burnt circle in his shirt, but the back of him was not and in the middle of all that was his torn-out heart bleeding into the red clay dirt, making it a muddy brown. A craggly shitty talon-faced torn shirt of a man with an axe line of a jaw on him tough enough to crack a walnut, and this woman, his woman, running out into the road and then she's crying over him, *"Oh what have you done*

to my Jim? Jim, what have they done? Oh damn you, damn you all!"
she's yelling and then she's kissing his face even after he's dead,
wetting him down with her tears... A love like that, well I ain't
never had a woman would feel that way about me, just some
that I wished they would. Keeping on kissing him until long
after he was dead, and she had to be pulled off him eventually
by two strong men.

I once woke up after a long night and sat wrapped in the
sheets on the cold edge of the bed, peering through the
wooden window frame like it was a frame for a painting that
would tell me something but it was just a field and trees that
had nothing to say to me and it felt like the back of my head
was being peeled off with a shovel and I felt old too soon and
smart too late and suddenly some fool he starts yelling his head
off out there in the trees, which is the last thing I needed first
thing in the morning so I yell back at him to shut the hell up
and he's got some hard bark on him because he yells back right
away, *"Fuck you and your horse and your mother,"* and of course
he don't know he's yelling that at Billy the Kid but still he don't
know who he's yelling at period or whether there's a gun
already drawn on him from somewhere he can't see and that
takes some gumption or some stupid and maybe both but
whatever it is it's more than I have to offer at the moment so I
just shut myself up because I have nothing else to say and just
then a soft hand places itself warmly on my back and rises slow
up to my shoulder and I turn to look at this woman in the bed
and she just looks at me and says:

"Jesus Christ, who the fuck are you?"

which strikes me as a not very romantic thing for her to say.
After I tell her who I am I end up taking a few sad potshots in
the direction of the trees but I can't see for shit and that boy
has stopped yelling now so either I got a lucky shot in or he's
gone home.

One time when I was just a young kid I found some little beasts crawling around at the base of my cock and I don't know any better at that age so I put them into a bottle and take them to the doc and say, "I found these on my pecker." He squints into the bottom of the bottle and says, "Of course you did, you dirty little fucker." So I want to be rid of them so I, instead of shooting him I mean, I say, "Well, what are they?" And he says, "Listen to me now, son, they're crabs, you filthy bastard, and you got them from hooring around with hoors and sticking that thing into God alone knows what." And I say, "Well, how do I get rid of them?" thinking I might just shoot him anyway, you know, after he tells me what to do about it so at least I'll know what to do after he is dead. He says, "Best thing would be to stop jamming it up hoors...but here." And he hands me some carbolic soap and tells me to wash it up three times a day and they'll curl up dead and fall right off. My fingers still want to go to my gun but I just pay him up and take the soap and leave. I have not the time for miserable bastards who think themselves better than plain folks just because it's legal for them to ask others to take their clothes off in a little room. But I use the soap and it works and the bottom of the washtub looks like the inside of a crab fisherman's boat.

Though I am very sad a lot of the time, I breathe, continue to breathe, I see angels flying with round open mouths like the silvered black ends of gun barrels calling back to us, *"There is news, there is good news!"* but there is no news and there are no angels. For a time the door to her room was the door to mine also and we breathed in there together and I hoped to never leave. Everything is happening all at the same time, and I hear voices. I can't tell what they say but it might be that we all have to take our own share of the blame for there is plenty of it to go around. It might be that.

ᴄꙮ 15 ꙮᴄ

This pain in my head is without excuse as I did not drink last night and this fucking desert just goes on forever around me and now here comes this hump who I do not know. I do not care for strangers as you know. I have been up all night while everyone else has slept. They are all still sleeping and I am tending the fire. And here is some mutt walking across the early-morning desert like it makes any sense at all that he even exists. I do not like strangers, I know I keep repeating that but I really do not care for them, maybe because no stranger has ever good-newsed me. I do not like the look of this melon nor do I appreciate the feel of him getting any closer to me.

"Right there," I say, just loud enough to be heard.

"I mean no harm," he calls back.

"Then you'll cause none," I answer.

"I am telling you that there is a sickness in Las Cruces, señor."

"And what is that to me?"

"If you are planning to go there. Many have died of it."

"You came here to tell me that?"

"It is not far. I saw your fire."

"And?"

"And I am hungry."

"Well, this ain't the Salvation Army." Joseph has risen and dropped out of the back of the wagon with his rifle.

"Good," this shrub says, "because I do not know any hymns…"

He's Mexican. I like Mexicans better than I like most people.

I have found that they are less wrapped up into the world of made-up problems and more likely to take a person at their face value.

"Come closer and state your piece," I tell him, "but move slow."

Joseph circles around to flank him.

"I have no gun, señores," he says.

"Then you're a fool."

"No, I am poor and cannot afford to have a gun but maybe I am a fool too. It is likely. A poor fool, but I am a poor fool with no gun."

"So you're just generally wandering around the desert looking out for the health of strangers? Is that it?"

"It is a bad sickness, señor."

"You just lift up that jacket and turn around slow, real slow..."

And Joseph's rifle goes off so I dive low and I draw but the man is already down and quiet in the sand. I keep my gun on him.

"What the hell was that?"

"I slipped." Joseph is squinting at the man in the dirt.

"You kill him?"

"I think so."

"Hell and damnation, Joseph."

"I know it." He moves out and examines the man more closely. Turner is out now and the kid has risen from his spot by the fire.

"What happened?" the kid wants to know.

Turner asks nothing, just surveys the scene and then looks to the horizon on all sides of us, then back to the man in the dirt. Good for her. I stand up.

"Chest," Joseph says in answer to a question no one has asked.

"Too bad."

"He was lying about not having a gun. But yeah, it's too bad."

I liked the man, for the short time I knew him. "Kid, get us a shovel from the wagon," I say, "and I'll say a few words over him."

"How do you know he wants that?"

"He's Mexican. They all want that. They are a God-fearing people."

Joseph is examining his rifle.

"Listen, I told you not to shave that action down so close," I tell him.

"Yeah, you did."

"Been telling you that since Moses wore his hair short."

"Yeah, you have."

Well, he must feel badly enough about it already. It is a shame though. The man did lie about having a gun on him and that does not speak well of his intent but still it does not excuse us having to take out the shovel again.

When everything is ready, I choose something I have in my head as no one appears to have a Bible on them. "Jesus said, I am the resurrection, and the life, and if you believe that, then you won't die, even if some fool puts a bullet through your chest by an accident..."

"I'm not sure that's—"

"It's good enough. Fill it back up now, kid. Turner, where in hell is your father? I want to get into Las Cruces and sleep in a bed tonight."

"I thought we weren't going into Las Cruces. And what about this sickness?"

"There's no sickness there, Joseph, or he wouldn't have lied about having a gun. There's no sickness there, but something's there he didn't want us to know about, so I'd like to know just what that is."

"There he is."

And sure enough he is. Way out in the scrub is the shape of

[110]

a man looking like a bear with a bag over its head striding forward toward us on two legs.

"He cuts a striking figure, your father," I say.

"He is a mountain of a man in that coat," she agrees.

"Why's he got that bag on his head?" the kid asks.

"Ask him," I suggest.

The kid just keeps looking. "No, sir, I don't believe I will."

The kid himself has a head like a mushroom, curved like a dome at the top, an impression his bowl-cut hair does nothing to improve. And his white corned-beef-hash skin suggests he has been kept in the cellar too long. He might well consider the use of a bag himself is what I am thinking as we each of us stand watching the approach of Wing Senior. He gradually gains in dimensions as he gets closer with a dust cloud following him as if it's the long train of his greatcoat. I am reminded of Moses except that Wing is undoubtedly of much greater girth and not likely to be God's prophet at all or even listening to any such prophet, and there was nothing said in the Bible stories I was taught about Moses wearing a bag over his head, although it was claimed that he consumed locusts and wild honey or maybe that was one of the others, I get them all confused at times. I would imagine Wing to be no stranger to honey but he does not strike me as the type to be foraging for locusts unless it were to become an absolute necessity. He keeps on coming until he is the correct size for a large man with a bag over his head. While waiting we have said nothing to each other, Joseph has spit twice, and I do not imagine he is pleased with himself over losing his balance and ending that Mexican fellow. There is nothing to be done about it now though, more than what we have already done. Wing has pulled himself to a stop and he stands surveying the scene as if doing an inventory of the stock at hand.

"There is a fresh grave and yet—" he appears to be counting

"—you are all still here," he says, "so you have killed someone, I take it. Kid, is there any chance that it is one of the men who apprehended you?"

"No, sir."

"I thought not. Those two have headed in the direction of Las Cruces. I spent these last few hours tracking their movements and that is the direction they took after their business with you. They are likely there by now."

"This man here," the kid says, pointing toward the mound of earth, "he said he lived in Las Cruces—"

"*Lived* being the operative word in that sentence," Wing says.

The kid says nothing.

"In the past tense. He being deceased now," Wing explains.

"He said there was lots of sickness in Las Cruces."

"But I don't imagine that's what killed him."

"No, sir."

"No. Strikes me his death was sudden and unexpected." He's looking at Joseph and his rifle. "At any rate we are now headed for Las Cruces, gentlemen. I do not do well in towns myself for obvious reasons and I prefer for the most part to keep to the countryside, but this cannot be helped."

"It could be helped if we just turned in the other direction," Turner says.

"No, it can't be helped, Turner. Las Cruces…that's the place for us."

"Well, shit," Turner says, and she spits and turns back to the wagon. We all of us watch her go and we watch her climb up into the back and pull the canvas closed behind her with vigour.

"That's a child who knows her own mind," Wing says.

"Well, what else does she know?"

"Your meaning?"

"I mean there's something here between you and her and these men, and if we're going into Las Cruces with you, plague or no plague, we better know what that thing is too. If not, well, we'll just be on our way to other places."

Wing looks from the grave to the fire, back to the grave, and to the fire again. "I suppose we'd best have some breakfast then," he says.

⚛ 16 ⚛

When I was thirteen it fell right out of the blue sky—I mean, this talent I have for shooting clean. I don't know if *talent* is the right word, but I have never known precisely what the right word would be. *Talent* seems a word better used for the playing of the fiddle or for the painting of something that looks real: fruit with the dew on it so it looks like you could reach right out and touch it and get your fingers wet, or playing a fiddle so pure that someone would ask you to play at some poor bastard's wake. *"He loved the way that you play, would you play him on to home please?"*

God sends the big waves down to swamp out our boats, but he doesn't do much about teaching us to swim. He sent down his son for that, I guess. Like a life preserver too late thrown from a sinking ship at sea. Well, seems he could walk on the water, but he never taught that trick to anyone else.

Do you suppose a rock has the same ideas about the passage of time that we do? Or a field of grass? Or a deer even. Do you suppose a deer opens up its eyes in the morning and thinks, *"Well, I am three years old today, what will I do with my life? What have I accomplished so far?"* No, it goes and eats some grass and has some water. It lives. Go ask a dog what time it is. There are some nights that I am more the man for a hotel than I am for the trail but the trail will teach you things the hotel will not. The hotel will encourage you to be more like you are, to have a steak and a cigar, spend the evening with a whore—hell, even take a bath if you're so inclined. But the trail will promote you to be the person you forgot you were in the first place. On the trail you maybe have no towel and so after a rain you strip down and just lie there and let the sun dry you. Man wasn't born with towels, that's what I'm saying and that's all I'm saying.

"What happened?" I asked my father when I could not have been more than three years old. My small fingers traced the mountain range of scar from beneath his left eye to his mouth.

"Someone, can you believe it? Someone tied a baby to the rail tracks. How could someone do that? A little baby! And how could I, being a God-fearing man, not try to save that child? In attempting the feat I was struck by the train."

"Did you save it?"

"No. No, I did not. There was no one who could save it. I tried."

And the next week he was gone so all I had then were his grandiose stories. Being older gave him the advantage of being able to pack his suitcase full of crap like that. I often wonder now why, when he was so obviously lying about how that scar came to be, he hadn't saved that baby. Why, in the name of Christ, when all it would take is the changing of a few words in the story, had he not come out the hero of it? Long after he left he came home to die. What man leaves his family just to come home to die? In behind our house at that time there was a small garden of dust and cracks that no one ever cared for. I have seen myself changed after death into something I never was in life and maybe that happens to all of us. Maybe I should not let it worry me, but I do.

"There's more to life than just livin' it," I tell Turner.

"Sure, there's dyin'," she says. "As options go, it's the weaker one."

"I mean there's things you can do that's not just the normal things people do. You could do great things that no one expects."

[115]

"Like what? Fly?"

"No. Now you're just talkin' shit. I mean you don't have to just do what everyone else does."

"Sometimes you do. They make it that way. Particularly if you're a woman."

"So you're a woman now?"

"I was about a good number of years ago, if you're countin'."

"Well...if bleedin' made me a man I'da been a man when I was three."

"If bein' stupid made you a man you'da come out the chute bein' a man."

"Well—" I am on unfamiliar ground here "—I did... Look, I never claimed to be a genius, now did I?"

"There ain't no need to make a claim about what you are, people can see it comin' a mile off."

"The hell they can."

"They can smell it off you."

"What am I then?"

"You're someone who's not afraid."

"Yeah?" That is not what I expected her to say.

"And they don't know what to do with that."

Maybe she has a point. But I am trying to convince her that she does not have to be a servant to her crazy father, and she will have none of it. She knows what I am hinting at and she will not listen at all. Over a breakfast of hard biscuits and bacon Wing has relayed to us the story of the two men who bested the kid and just how he has come to be overly interested in their whereabouts. And now Turner and I sit on the bench of the wagon leading the team toward Las Cruces and I am in the midst of the laborious and inadvisable task of driving a team while attempting to convince a young woman of something of which she is already aware but refuses to see clearly or even admit to.

"Strike out on your own."

"Easy for a man."

"Easy to say."

"Well, most things are."

I do not know if she means that most things are easy for a man or if most things are easy to say. Wing is ahead of us, Joseph and the kid in the rear.

"You owe him nothing more," I tell her, indicating the back of her father's greatcoat.

"That's a ridiculous thing to say."

"I don't see why."

"You never had a father who loved you?"

She's a pistol, this one. I'm not a faster draw than her, not in the thinking end of things, and I can see that clear. I don't see that very often. I never see that. Not that I am a genius but I tend to run across a lot of non-genius types. I don't meet a wide variety of folks. With her I am struggling just to keep up. I could still outdraw her in a gunfight though. But I wouldn't. She's smart enough that at whatever the hell age she is she thinks she's got everything treed. She thinks she's got it pretty much all figured out. She don't know how much she don't know and that is all I am trying to point out to her. I'm not saying I know what she doesn't know, just hinting that neither does she.

"He thinks he can save her," she says.

"Who?"

"My sister. Mister 'I am Billy the Kid and I know things you don't know, young lady'...he thinks he can save her."

Like she's in my own head.

Last night there was a full-bellied moon and it lit up the flat-plained desert in black and white and I stood next to the wagon and rolled myself a smoke and had a piss and I carved out a gully for it with the heel of my boot. When Wing had walked off into the night the moon had not yet risen and there was a cloud cover and the night was a black curtain on a stage, but as I smoked, the lights came on again and everything was lit up wide in a steady silver stream. I could hear her breath soft right next to me through the canvas as I stood there waiting and I was lost in it.

ᥦ 17 ᥤ

Wing is a man to be reckoned with and that is something certain. Half his jaw is bone-bleached out there somewhere in the desert and yet he persists. That no one seems to know precisely what it is that we will do when we reach Las Cruces is also certain now.

What was certain in Wing's mind this morning was the fact that we were going to Las Cruces, that we were all going, we were going there together and we were departing soon. Not everyone was so convinced until he told us this story. Well, stories change things. A lot of drool drops from under his sack when he speaks at length but he makes himself heard and that is a fact.

"Turner and me and her sister Missouri, we were travelling southwest of the Gallinas and we had been along the trail for some days. Now, my main line of work of late, gentlemen, has been investment—the soldiering of funds into the places where they will do the greatest good, if you take my meaning: using money in the service of making more money. People allow me to shepherd their spare resources in such a manner as to bring them more resources...more gain than they would see with their funds mouldering away in a bank. Now, since this unfortunate matter of my missing a lower jaw has arisen, the doctoring business has fallen off slightly to be sure and that is why I have taken to the refuge of the financial profession. No one wants their health fixed by a man who is so broken, it seems. I can understand the workings of a petty mind. It is astounding what people will abide if they know that you will make them money however… They won't let you fix their gut ache or their congested chest, but they will hand you their money if they are convinced you can use it to render more of it for them, and I can do this, you see. I have the ability to do this." Wing pauses to use a soiled handkerchief to wipe up under the bag at what would have been his chin.

"Like magic?" the kid wants to know.

"Somewhat…" Wing hesitates, tucking his handkerchief back into a pocket. "Somewhat like magic, yes, I put the money in the proper places and it expands. The magic trick is in knowing just where to put it and at what time, what places may be rich in oil or what businesses may prosper…I confess that I am good at this."

"Even with a sack over your head?" I ask him.

"Ah. Yes, well, the trouble has been that even for a simple transaction, folks are unwilling to transact with a man wearing a sack over his head as you say. I can't blame them for that. Tradition suggests a train robbery, I suppose. At any rate, the plan, such as it was, such as it still is once this matter is settled and my elder daughter is restored to me, the plan was to have Missouri, who is fair of face and not unpleasing to a gentleman's eye, to be coarse and blunt about the matter, to have her conduct the transaction side of the business and leave the actual manipulation of the funds to me. This was an endeavour best plied in a larger town, we thought. San Francisco being one possibility. A simple matter of renting an office in a central location and then hanging out one's shingle, so to speak. *"Wing Investments—Watch Your Money Take Flight"*—a usable trade name and motto, I'm sure you'll agree. Well, at any rate, there the three of us are engaged in the progress of our futures and venturing forth to a larger centre of trade to do so when who do we run across but two men, one large, one small, the same two men who robbed you naked, kid, of that I am certain now. And they tell us they are lost. Well, I am a Christian man, gentlemen, with the normal Christian motives and inclinations, no nobler than anyone else's but present and insistent all the same. You'll not hear any stories of me turning away those in need of directions or anything else. Christian charity and forbearance. William, two days ago you yourself put a bullet into me—"

"I'm sorry about that."

"It is of no matter now. I bring it up only to prove my point, which is this: I forgave you. You shot me with the intent, no doubt, of killing me in cold blood and watching as the life seeped out of me and into the sand with my own young daughter looking on defenceless and, as would have been subsequently, fatherless..."

"I am sorry. I said that I was. I've said it again now and I believe the matter is closed."

"Certainly. Certainly. But even though I am alive before you now and no lasting harm was done, well, that bullet, having traversed a little to the left, a little to the right, could have brought an end to the old doctor, and even when it did not do so, infection could easily have set in and I might have woken up as cold and dead as a nickel—do you take my meaning?"

"I ain't sayin' it again."

"To be sure, no need to, Billy, none at all. But the facts remain. Just listen to what I am saying: the odds of me having survived in that situation and under these conditions were stacked and not in my favour and but for the grace of God I would have been a dead man at your hand. Are we all agreed on that?"

"We better set ourselves on agreein' on somethin' else, Wing, or that situation regarding your well-being might just change somewhat," Joseph sets in, him being able to tell from past experience that the set of my jaw and the position of my right hand do not bode well for anyone.

"Of course, of course, my only intent here, Joseph, other than to convince you once again that there is some force here that bonds us all together in this place and at this time, is that I bear William no malice. None whatsoever. This is what I mean when I say that I am a Christian man. I am one who attempts his levèl best to follow the figure set down by our own Saviour, meek and mild. And so, when I saw those two men ride up to us I was wary naturally but I did not assume the worst and that was my failing. Do you see what I mean? I welcomed them initially even though now it is clear that any other choice up to and including driving lead bullets through to the backs of their skulls without another moment passing would have been the preferable option had I been able to see more clearly the nature of the picture before me."

"Which was?" I inquire, the coffee all but consumed and the sun climbing higher in the sky.

"Thieves, gentlemen, and kidnappers—evil, evil men," Wing returned. "Men set on taking whatever they deem theirs by desire and hang the considerations of others. Do you not know this to be the case, kid?"

The kid looks up like a child in Sunday school who has fallen asleep at his lessons. "If those are the same men robbed me, then they ain't no friends of mine, that's certain," he says.

"Then how is it you still have your possessions and team and wagon?" Joseph asks.

But I already know the answer. I know all of Wing's answers and the reason he is so driven. I know the end to this story of his, even if he does not.

"And Turner," Wing points out, "I still have my darling girl because though Missouri was with me when they came upon us, Turner was off looking for supper to shoot. Otherwise they'd have her hostage as well, I fear. You go ahead and search that wagon, Mr. McCarty, and you show me my elder daughter, you show me my Missouri, my own beautiful girl with the red flaxen hair and bright green eyes. You show me her."

"Those men took your daughter?" the kid asks, as if he is still at his lessons and has just learned of the miracle of the loaves and fishes.

But Joseph is looking steady across the smoke of the dying fire at me and I am returning his gaze.

"You were likely not more than ten feet from Missouri as you stood by their wagon, kid," says Wing, "if only you'd known it. They threatened to set myself and this wagon ablaze just as they did you, but in the end they just took Missouri and off they went. But there was no way you could have known she was there, undoubtedly they had her bound and gagged so she wouldn't be found out. Nothing else would have prevented her from calling out, d'you see?"

Joseph looks away. I follow his gaze. He is looking at nothing. But I know what he is seeing for I am seeing it too.

"We don't have to do this," I tell Joseph as we prepare to depart, the two of us on our own for the moment.

"What else have we to do?"

"Leave. Leave all of this and be as comfortable as two coons in a trash can. I thought that's what we were in the process of doing."

"We were in the process of moving you far away from armed conflict."

"Well, what happened to that plan? That was a perfectly good plan, I think, and now it's just all shot all to hell, that's what. Just what do you imagine this will turn out to be?"

"This is different."

"I cannot see how it is."

"This is not bad men coming to you to seek you out."

"Well, it sure as hell feels that way. Whoever these men are they ain't no do-gooders and they may as well have my address and my shoe size."

"You're one kind of a man...or you're another, and that is all there is to it."

"Oh what the hell does that even mean? There's all kinds of men, Joseph. Mostly there's a lot of good-for-nothing shit hats."

"And what kind are you?"

"Oh goddammit, you know what kind I am. I'll face up to trouble. But that doesn't mean I'll go looking for it like a two-dollar whore to a dick parade."

"I ain't never seen a dick parade, William, I don't imagine there is such a thing."

"It's a figure of speech, goddammit, why you gotta take everything so plain and simple all the time? That's the problem, there ain't never been no nuance in you."

Joseph checks his saddle and looks at me plainly. "I have never heard that word before."

"*Nuance?* Well, I guess you don't know everything then."

Joseph pauses to roll himself a smoke. "What does it mean?"

"It means that if you see a lady that you like the look of, you're just as likely to go up to her and ask if she has a place for you to sleep tonight and what does she care for in the way of breakfast instead of just maybe bringin' her some flowers or buying her a drink and tellin' her she looks pretty this evening."

"There's a lot to be said for getting to the point."

"There's a lot to be said for getting laid too but I guess that part don't concern you much."

Joseph just stands there looking at the rolling papers in his hand. "You got any tobacco left, William?"

"I guess nuance ain't the only thing you ain't got, now is it?"

"I ain't got no matches either if you're makin' up a list."

He is smart when it is important to be smart. Not a bad-looking man in addition as these things go, handsome even, though maybe it is in a carved Indian or a walnut sort of a way. Weathered. He closely resembles our father if memory serves, which it may not, as I do not remember our father very well aside from a series of shadows in the hall and strikes to my head. A hooked nose and a pipe. Coveralls. He was the owner of a flabby heart, and I believe that is what killed him. I recall him being dead. That is the only other real detail I remember: his mouth in death, slackly open, and all pink inside. The rough grey blanket they covered him with. And the cold. At times I fear that I share his heart—the only thing of his I have—and that it will fail me too, I am certain it may.

I worked a cattle ranch one time and there was a man there, Bill Semple. Simple Bill we called him, no offence, it just seemed to stick is all… Well, he had this trick he'd do with a silver dollar. He'd take a silver dollar and he'd work at it and work at it like a little piece of clay, right in front of your face he'd do this, he'd knead at it like it was a pie crust or a loaf of bread he was making, just like this…both his paws right up at your face like this, and he'd scrunch up that dollar like it was paper and then, and then he'd open up his hands and there'd be two half dollars there and the dollar gone! Can you beat that? He'd do it over and over and you could never see what it was he was doing. Once I got my friend Pete Daniels to come in behind him while he was doing it and stand there in the dark to watch and see how he did it and old Bill he just finishes the trick, just staring at his hands in front of him the whole time, and then he smiles and he says, *"You see anything worth seeing back there, Pete?"*

One time I figured I had him, there was these showers there at that ranch, you see, like a room with five or six taps you'd stand under to wash yourself off, and I followed him in there one day and I walked up to him under the water and naked as the day he was conceived and showed him a silver dollar and I said, *"Here, you bastard, do it right here and right now."* I didn't have no anger against him, you know, it was just friendly like: there's no way you can do this without no clothes on, now is there, Bill? And sure enough, you know what he does? He does the whole trick, just like every other time he done it and he holds the two half dollars up to my face, grinning with the water spouting off his forehead and he says, *"Go on, Will—you have them, they're yours."* But I didn't take them because I knew there was only one place he could have taken them out of. We became good friends though. Then he got half his arm tore off in a thresher one day and that was that. No more tricks for Bill.

And that's what Joseph is like on his best days. Not that he can pull half dollars out of his ass, but he can do just what it is that you don't expect him to do at all. He can surprise you, or whoever else is around, and sometimes that can be a very useful thing, especially if you find yourself in a jam.

I'll tell you one thing that I believe: the best way to be here on this planet for a reason is to just make one up. Joseph has done this, and I admire him for that. He's seldom shaken, though I imagine the recent passing of the Mexican gentleman has shaken him somewhat. It must have.

"Yes, I had a father," I reply to Turner, "not much of a father but I had one."

"Then you should know," says Turner, "you gotta deal with whatever it is you got." She looks ahead to the large figure in the rising dust. "And he's what I got."

Joseph rides up to our position. "We will be in Las Cruces before too long," he says.

"I know that."

"And we do not have an adequate plan."

"We don't got any plan at all. What would you suggest that we do?"

"It is…a difficult thing to discuss."

"You mean in present company?" Turner interjects. She

looks over to Joseph with the sun in her eyes, the smooth skin of her brow winking.

"That is what I mean."

"I'm not a child."

"She's been a woman going on some years now," I add.

"Shush you."

"I am just not certain that we are at all prepared for what we may face, that is all."

"Meaning me? Meaning I'm not prepared? Isn't that what you mean?" Turner is angry now, there is a flush to her cheeks.

"Meaning not you, and not your father, and not—"

"Why don't you make sure the kid's ready then," I tell him. "Just drop back and make sure he knows what to expect…"

Joseph nods in agreement and begins to recede.

"And maybe shoot any more Mexicans you see back there too," adds Turner, which would have had Joseph's gun drawn if it were anyone else saying it.

"That remark is not going to make him your friend," I counsel her.

"It ain't meant to," she says. "I don't need no friends." And she spits, then crosses her arms over her chest. Her wrists are smooth and tan at the edges of her rolled-up sleeves and her mouth is set.

I wait. But I do not know what it is that I wait for. There is no appropriate moment to tell her that her sister was probably raped by two worthless men and then definitely killed and left up in a tree. There are times when circumstance calls us to be more than what we are. And there are times when it is easier just to be quiet.

⤺ **18** ⤻

Worms, Billy.

They crawl in and they crawl out.

Everything is black when there's no light. Black ceiling. Black walls. Black table. Black chairs. Black floor. Black door. Black coffin. My hand black in front of my face. Black.

There had been no moon that night in Las Cruces and very little daylight in the closed-up room that morning. We were accustomed to sleeping late as our schedule was our own. I was not even certain it was still morning. If I had had the energy, I would have gotten up and at least drawn open the curtains so that whatever light was available would have spilled into that dreadful room and I could have seen that we had slept until the afternoon. As it was, the window was shut and Semples and I might have passed away due to a lack of airflow and the stink of Semples. They would have found us with our mouths drawn open like empty cups.

He had become a disappointment to me, recent events had seen to that.

"The excitement of town living does not always shine forth, does it, Mr. Semples?" I asked him by way of a rising greeting.

"Hm, what?" he grumbled, as was his way.

"I said the excitement of town living does not always shine forth, does it, Mr. Semples?"

"I guess not."

"You said what?"

"I said I guess not, you're right, I guess that it does not."

"Quite right. You are quite right there. There is something to be said for sleeping under the canopy of the stars, is there not? Out there where a man may do as he wishes, do you not think it to be true?"

[128]

"I suppose so. You can't sleep?"

"One of us should open the curtains a little, Semples, it is full day now, I feel it, but I do not have the strength to move. I am bored, Semples."

"Well, there's lots of things you could do to pass the time. Open the curtains maybe, for example. I just got back from hitching the wagon like you told me last night. I could use just a little more sleep."

It did not seem to me he had achieved much recently that warranted sleeping in but I held my peace about that for the moment.

"There is little point in doing anything at all...so one might as well do whatever one wishes, is that not so?"

Semples hesitated at this point. He was not one for philosophical thought and he easily froze up like a rusted-out gear when confronted with it. I changed my direction.

"What could I do?" I asked him.

"About what?"

"Goddammit, Semples, you said there are things I could do, well what are they? Name them."

"Hell, I don't know. You could let me sleep ten more minutes. Why do I have to tell you things you can do? You can do anything you want."

"That's just it, Mr. Semples. My point exactly, I can do anything I want but there is nothing much I want to do in a place like this except to go running downstairs and shoot everyone I see."

"Well, don't do that."

"I don't see why not. Why not?"

"It will make a mess and a lot of noise and someone just might shoot back."

"Likely they will, that is what creates the interest in the activity, Semples—the excitement—the enjoyment of it. The suddenness and uncertainty of it all."

But Semples was not one for that type of anarchy as he likely saw no percentage in it for himself.

"Let's just go back to sleep. Ten minutes more."

"Knit the worried sleeve of care, eh, Semples? I suppose you have no worries that torment you, but it is not that simple for me, I'm afraid. I am kept alert with plans and concerns. Planning out a future that cannot be planned. I am alive with the depressing realities of life and with my own delusions."

"So you want me to open up them curtains?"

"If you would not mind doing just that, Semples, the truth is I am just concerned for our health here in this plank box of a room Recent events indicate that you are not a healthy man at all. The brain requires oxygen and without it survival will be a mere matter of minutes. We have surpassed our limits. In this darkness it is impossible to determine exactly what is what. It may well be that we are already in our coffins. Perhaps when you attempt to rise you will come face to face with the solid pine planking of your own casket."

I could not have known at the time how things would actually be later on. Though I suppose I should have. I was too occupied with the necessities and trivialities of being alive.

"If we are in our coffins, then how is it I can hear you speakin' such nonsense?"

"There is much that is unknown regarding the netherworlds of death, Semples. Who knows what is possible or impossible in that strange new country? Few have returned to report."

Except for me, Billy, except for me. But Semples was not one for deep thoughts and soon enough he got up. The bone rack of his back was set into motion toward the window. That comment of mine regarding the pine planking had unnerved him. He needed to show himself that it was not true that he was no more. You can make people do anything you want them to, barring physical limitations, but I'd guess you'd know all about that, Billy. As the white shadow of him moved further into the dark closeness of that room it was impossible to determine just what was Semples and what was not Semples. If I were to have shot, there...

there...

or there...would I have hit the man or the air, or the chest of drawers, or fired right through my change of long johns... How many bullets would have returned Semples's voice: "Hey what?" "What the hell?" "What the hell are you doing, Poore?" "Have you lost..."

And which bullet would have returned the rich red sound of hot steel through flesh? And a cry perhaps, a cry.

I would have missed him though. His presence at that time, I mean, not that I would have missed putting a bullet through him if I had tried, for I am handy with a firearm when necessary. His presence had always comforted me in a manner I believe to be untrue of any other being I came across while amongst the living. Not really due to anything in his own nature, mind you, more in his willingness to be led. Although it is true that he had begun to disappoint me sharply in those last few days and in fact had me reconsidering our entire arrangement, still I could not have withstood the sudden hurt look on his face had I shot him then.

"What have you...?"

"Why have you...?"

And I would not have known the answer. You may as well have asked the wind. "Why do you blow?" Things are just what they are sometimes, and nothing more than that. We try to make them into something they are not, and we do them and ourselves a disservice. They are things, we are things. To try to make this all into something...meaningful, well mind you, many do turn cartwheels attempting to do so...loaves and fishes, my friend, loaves and fishes. My current perspective informs me that perhaps I could have endeavoured to do better in that life of mine in the time I possessed it. Well, there is little to be gained in examining matters that are done.

"Goddammit, Semples, what is withholding you from opening those goddamned curtains?"

Well, I tired of his slowness, you see. The truth is, I hate to admit this even now, but he was dimwitted. As loyal as he was, he wore me down to the bare end at times. I am not one for blind tolerance and perhaps because of that I am one of those who died in pain and suffering. Well, most do, I suppose. Somewhere, at some time, I suppose someone has passed away in their sleep dreaming of angels and of peace. Had I been there I would have awakened them and then slit their throat while smiling down at them. I was that kind of a man, that is all.

So now you know me.

The curtains had finally been opened to the light and Semple's white and furry form, but there was still no air in that room.

"Semples!" I must admit I was frustrated with him.

"The window is jammed, Caleb. The damned thing is stuck somehow."

I have never wept to see people's endings and I did not weep for my own ending, Billy, so you need not worry about me. Not that you can hear me now. But I speak to you regardless. Perhaps my voice will land somewhere in your head. Things are not pleasant for me now but then they never really were anyway and we all of us do it. We all die, I mean. There is nothing special in it. It is certainly no achievement nor is it even an end. Which is truly unfortunate in my case, but there you have it. Perhaps you will fare better. People who die become ghosts inside of other people for a time. The living carry everyone around with them. This is why they tire so easily and they end so quick. They cannot stand the weight of it all. You can feel it on you, Billy? You are carrying me now. Horrible things have happened. They will continue to happen.

"I suppose it is time to rise anyway. Your simple inability to determine cause puts me in a mood to start the day, Mr. Semples. Someday I aspire to wear your clarity like a necklace, 'the window is stuck, the damned thing is stuck,' yes, you have summed up the situation well."

"Well, it is."

"So you've said."

This world is ugly and the people in it are sad most of the time. It took two seconds for me to cross to the window and put my elbow right through it. The bone of the elbow is remarkably strong and may be used in much the same way a rock or a hammer would without significant pain. It is the skin one must watch out for and I simply forgot that I was naked and without the benefit of shirt or jacket, so of course there was blood. In significant amounts.

"Now I am cut and bleeding, Semples."

"Course you are, you just put your arm through the damned window."

"Well, grab a towel, would you?"

Honestly, the problem sought a solution. And one problem leads to the next apparently.

While Semples wrapped my arm up with a filthy towel, my eyes were on the road below where a wagon and horses had stopped and their riders looked up now at the broken window. I believe you will remember this next part rather well, Billy.

"Semples, how does it come to be that the young yokel we bandied with and left for dead in the desert and the sack-headed father and the sister of that girl you dallied with days ago are right now down there in the street below, looking up at my naked and blood-soaked form?" I asked.

"Are they?"

"They may as well be reading my lips. I thought you had paid some locals to stand watch at the edges of the town."

"I did. I paid 'em in advance too, goddammit."

He was still wrapping my arm as we both looked down at the bright little group below. You'll recall that we both smiled and gave you all a little wave at that point.

"Well, not enough. Everybody we are gazing upon now wants us both dead," I said.

"There are two men with them." Semples always had a way of clarifying what needed no clarification at all.

"I can see that."

The sack-headed man was pointing up at us. I recall your face then, Billy, and its focus. Like the edge of an axe. Like a needle.

"Step back."

We both took several steps back from the light.

"I do not believe that those men you hired had the best work ethic."

"It could be so."

"Arm yourself, Semples."

When I stepped back to the window with a rifle the street was empty. You made it so damned hard for anyone to kill you, Billy. Most people were not so uncooperative in the matter of me bringing about their ends. You, the wagon, the horses, your compatriots—all gone in a matter of seconds. Like phantoms and, I'll say it, like ghosts. It was enough to scare the baby Jesus right out of me. There were times in my life when I felt like a man with a fork in a world made of soup.

"Semples, what has happened?" I felt about as solid at that moment as eggs just before they hit the pan. "You'd better go check the wagon," I told him. I looked up and down the street.

"It's fine. You want me to check it right now?"

"Dammit, Semples, yes right now! I will not have her tampered with." Fear is a terrible thing. When I feel it, I mean. Not when other people feel it.

"Oh sweet the Lord Jesus, alright I am going."

Fear claws at you when it can. By that I mean it does so when you let it. It makes you into something foolish and ineffectual. When my dear mother died all the air went out of my life and then I became something else entirely. Being alive is a frustrating state but I have found that not being alive does not clarify things one iota. Nothing is normal now, Billy. But normal is nothing. Normal is for people who can envisage no other options for their lives. Time slips away from us. I had always been chased by something in the world. When I was a lad, I was chased by a bad man in the woods behind our farm. The details regarding the cause of this do not matter. Some small thing I had done that he had taken offence to and that is all. That man was not a worthy man, and he meant to do me harm, that much was clear. I would have been about five at that time, but I knew those woods better than he did and I knew of a thin crevasse in the rocks covered over by branches and bracken and that stretched a good twenty feet down to hard rock but was still wide enough to fit a man of his size. Perhaps I knew of its location because I had fashioned it myself, but you cannot claim, if this was in fact the case, that I had not been prudent in doing so. I angled through the brush toward it. Make no mistake, the man would have outrun me had I not taken this action. I led the man straight through the branches and I jumped just where I knew the crevasse to be and then heard the sharp intake of air as he hurtled down and the expulsion of that same air and the shaking and broken sound as he hit the stone below. The settling of the branches, the sound of my own breath, and then nothing. I went home. For all I know, his bones remain there today untouched by light. I kept the knowledge of his whereabouts like a secret treasure as the community spoke of him and searched for him and eventually forgot all about him, he being, after all, of no good account. I knew where he was. And I still do.

I came from nothing.

In fact, I was made up from nothing at all. And now, Billy, I am here in your head with all the others. Carry me.

ᏊᎧ 19 ᏬᎧ

Well, to backtrack just a touch, old Wing he sat us down that morning, he sure did that, and we sure stayed sat where we were put because, like I said before, what he had to say was like a heavy chain roped around all of us and around me and Joseph especially because we knew the ending of his story and he didn't even know it himself. I looked at my hands. I know I paid close attention to his tale. I always do when the possibility of death is involved. And it seems it most often is. I mean, I can stare at a tree or a field for just as long as the next fellow, but when there's the chance of a bullet coming out of that field and right at me I just stare that much harder. I get fixed on things right quick when the loss of blood could be involved, particularly if it might be my own. Wing's story had both bullets and blood and I listened to it hard and saw it just like his words were paint from a paintbrush. Turner, I noticed, kept her face pulled in tight to her knees the whole time. If you have ever watched a dog in its sleep when it starts to bark and run, well, that's how she was in her face, what I could see of it. A flinch. A nod. Her eyes closed. And she was running but there was no place for her to go. People can't hide what's important to them.

I pulled my own hat down over my eyes because I did not want Wing to see them, after all I could not see his so that was fair, I figured, it was only fair. Maybe he'd be able to tell that I knew something of the whereabouts of his elder daughter somehow if he could see my eyes and so I was not taking that chance. My father was right: it is best to carry a hat, and usually on your head. With a hat on your head there's just more for people to shoot at that isn't you.

"Maybe I'll just shoot the hat off his head," they'll say, "and scare him some."

Which is better than having your head shot off. I'd like to take care of a woman. That would be something nice. Just to keep her safe. But none have let me, and I have kept my hat pulled down. I pulled it down then. For the story about the dead girl.

It was easier to hear it than to see it.

"We had been on the trail for several weeks and on our way to San Francisco, as I said," Wing continued. "Provisions were low, and the hunting had been poor. Perhaps I am a poor hunter. Well, at any rate we were down to hardtack and johnnycakes every day. The girls would not complain but that is just the way they were raised. So, with us surviving on very little sustenance, Turner was off with the shotgun looking for our next meal. When they rode up, there was no reason to suspect them other than the fact that they seemed right pleased to see us, which is reason enough, I suppose, certainly with hindsight. I do not wear guns but I am always aware of where my gun is, of how far from it I am. Which was much too far in this case.

"'Good morning, friends,' the larger one said.

"Well, it is not a matter of ill nature but I have always felt it best to ignore strangers who call you friend as I believe it belies either a very small nature in them or a very large intent to do harm to you, it is always the one or the other. And these men did not seem to take note of my unique circumstances, of my appearance. Nor did they seem interested in Missouri, an attractive young woman out in the desert. And so it was their very lack of qualities to render them suspicious that now made them suspicious to me, if you take my meaning. The smaller man squinted through round silver spectacles and seemed

[137]

always to be licking salt from his lips as if he were surprised to find some foreign taste there. He had one eye that refused to behave. They travelled with two horses pulling a large black wagon.

"They climbed down and approached our camp with an apparent casualness and amiability.

"'Well, it is fine to encounter others on the trail,' the larger man said, 'and to have a chance to break bread with someone other than my associate here, not that he is lacking in the social graces, quite the opposite, but we are continuously in each other's company when travelling and, well, a change is comparable to a rest, I believe. It is just that we could benefit from some help with direction…it would seem we're a little turned around…'

"Well, that was truer than I knew at that time. Missouri was having none of them from the start and I could tell that. She had a scowl on her like the steel wool you'd use on an old pot. I always tell her not to dress her face like a store window, but she has always been that way. She is not a poker player like Turner. Missouri's got all the available merchandise on display all the time. And they saw that—they saw that clearly right away and so that was it. There was no reason for them to hide it anymore and the big one he turns to the little one then and he says, 'Alright.'

"And the little one he pulls this shotgun, double-barrelled, out from nowhere, it's bigger than he is and it just comes out of his coat somehow and blows a hole into the side of our wagon, I guess to stop her from getting up into it, which is where she was headed because that's where the rifle was. And the bigger one he just stands there looking at her and then he just says, 'No,' and that's all he says."

Wing stopped talking then and he just sat there looking down into the sand like he'd dropped something and then he looked up at Turner. And Turner looked up at him like she was going to say something, but she kept quiet.

"They took her off with them then and they would have killed all of us if we'd tried to stop them. The little one he wanted to burn the wagon with me in it but the big one he said they had all they needed and they should just get going. They would have just killed us all." Wing stood up. "Let's get this fire out and get going ourselves. We'll find them and we'll get Missouri back and then the three of us we'll just get on to San Francisco. That's what we're going to do."

He walked back toward the horses and wagon.

"If I'd tried to stop them without my gun...they would have killed me and probably found Turner too," he said again as he walked.

Turner was crying then.

I do whatever I want. I've always done just whatever I want and sometimes it has worked out for me and sometimes it has not but at least I played my own hands and won or lost on my own and I ain't about to change any habits now. That's what I was thinking. But that's not what I did. And I'm not saying the change in habit now was because Turner was crying, but if it wasn't that then I don't know what the hell it was. I wanted to tell her I'll find her sister for her but I couldn't make the words come out because I knew they would be a lie. But that had never stopped them from coming out before.

Look at me, trying to fix something that can't be fixed.

I remember a time when Joseph and I met this banker in a tavern, and I was settling in to play some poker with him, and Joseph counselled me to keep my money in my pockets that evening.

"He's gonna shake your hand, but he'll piss in your pocket," he said.

I listened to him.

I recall another time when Joseph advised that I not stay any later in a certain establishment, that it was late and there was no one there I could count on besides himself and he was going to go to bed regardless. He advised me that the big, bearded bastard in the corner had the look of someone who wanted to put me down and he certainly could do it too if there was a fight that involved anything other than firearms. I remember telling him then to mind his own business and I remember seeing him through a haze of cigar smoke going up the stairs to his bed. I remember the sound of something heavy hitting the ground.

It was me.

And I recall one time sitting with Joseph by a campfire with a full bottle of empty there on the ground between us. "You know there's less disease on a dog's ass than in most people's mouths?" I asked him.

Joseph sat there considering the matter and looking into the fire. He looked at it for a long time. "That don't sound right," he said finally.

It wasn't. I'd made it up. I knew I was safe for a while because it was a long way from where we were to a library for him to look it up.

"You know what the difference between you and a pimple on my ass is?" Joseph asked me.

I didn't say a thing.

"Someday the pimple will go away."

✒ 20 ✑

My father was found dead in a field. By that time there was very little left of him. He had worn it all away to the bone and then right down to the marrow.

He had come home to die just so it would be easier for him to haunt us all. There is a reason small children are afraid of the things under their beds, and I believe it is because they just automatically know that the world does not wish them well. For years I believed that my passed father was lying under my bed while I slept, staring upwards to the dark wooden slats like they were the inside of his coffin lid. He followed me from house to house. The dead do not go so very far away. I believed it then and I believe it now. They are here amongst us but we are too weak-eyed or weak-hearted to see them. They are birds at the window and we are distracted away from them by things of no account, and by nothing at all. They hover and they remain. There are taps on the glass. I never saw my father's face. Or maybe I did. I must have. I do not remember it though. Not at all. I remember the scar and that is all. My father was hard in a lot of ways, mostly around his hands. I remember his hands. I never really had the choice to know him, but by all reports I was lucky in this. He was a man best left alone and maybe he had the wisdom to know it.

Once at the top of an oak tree when I was a lad, I was glad and I sang out a song about open plains and home. A cowboy song. I don't remember where that was, or when exactly. I don't remember the song either really. A few notes. The smell of the air then was different and there seemed to be more of it to breathe. I do not remember what had made me glad. People believe in God and I am not saying there's no such animal, but listen for a moment to my thinking on this matter; he's not often in my neighbourhood. I talk about him a fair bit, as if he is walking around here in his golden robe, and I think about him even more, but I am not certain about anything at all. People believe in alcohol, and they make a religion out of it. My observation would be that if you cry in your beer, you'll cry in another beer, and eventually you'll cry into your whisky…and in the end, well…you're just crying.

But you maybe want me to get on with this story, so fine. Here we go.

So we find ourselves in Las Cruces and lined up like empty tomato cans in a shooting gallery—me, Joseph, Turner, Wing, and the kid—and we've run into a shed just next to the hotel on the main street and we're crouched behind this black wagon hitched up to two horses in the dirt when the little one Wing told us about comes in, I can see his bare feet and I can tell by the way he moves that he's carrying a rifle. It doesn't matter what he's carrying because between the five of us there's five revolvers drawn on him. He doesn't seem much interested in the possibility of us though, he's fiddling with some keys and unlocking the back of the wagon and squinting at the lock with his droopy eye.

"Missouri," Wing whispers, and I caution him to close whatever it is he has instead of a mouth, first because I'd rather not have to shoot anyone in the middle of the day on someone else's property and then face the resulting shooting of additional people or the resulting legal entanglements and the naming of names in court documents, and second because I am curious as to what he's got locked into this wagon and I am certain that whatever it is it is not Miss Missouri Wing. That much is certain.

"Quiet," Wing whispers to the benefit of no one as he is the only one currently doing any talking.

The little one is up in the back of the wagon now, moving around like he's looking for something.

"I didn't say a thing, you're the one talking."

The sound of Turner's pistol being cocked shuts us both up. "If none of you ladies is going to kill him, then I will," she hisses.

"If you kill him we have nothing to get us closer to Missouri," Wing says back to her in a whisper.

"We still got the fat one."

Could be a lot of money in this wagon is what I'm thinking. For a wagon that ain't got nobody in it they have for certain got something in there that they are concerned about. "She's right about that," I say.

"No," says Joseph.

Which is funny because Joseph was not particularly against the killing of people at breakfast this morning. I decide I will point this fact out to him. "You—"

"I know what I did this morning. That is different."

"How exactly? I bet it doesn't seem much different to that Mexican fellow."

"That was in the desert."

"I don't see—"

"Everything's different in the desert, Ish. Ain't nobody watching you out there. You see what I mean? Different from ridin' into town and shootin' the whole place up in front of witnesses. I believe I may have mentioned this before, how such acts are not prudent for us. Besides, this morning was an accident, I am tired of pointing that out."

Turner will have none of it. "I see what you mean," she says.

"Fine."

"You mean you're the only one gets to shoot folks, that's what you mean."

And real sudden I point my finger right into her face and then she shuts right up and her eyes get real wide real quick. She becomes just like a little girl fast. I didn't mean to scare her. But I did scare her. I just needed her to shut up because I could tell the little man was coming out of the wagon. And come out he does and he locks it up tight with the five of us just holding our breath.

In my heart I have no brain. It just does what it does all on its own. I mean about her. I mean about the way I somehow feel very bad for scaring her just now.

Anyway, the little man he climbs the four stairs up out of the stable and into the hotel and he's gone. Nothing but the smell of horses and hay.

"What do we do now?" asks the kid.

I'm still staring at Turner. She's still staring at me.

"I say we get a better breakfast than what we had this morning," I say. And I'm still staring at her.

"These are the men that took Missouri," Wing complains.

"She's dead," I say sudden, without thinking about why. And I'm still looking at Turner, I haven't looked away. She's still looking at me. With eyes now that have heard what I have just said. Taken it in. Eyes that shrink, just a little bit, then harden.

It happens quicker than a lot of things do. Actually, two things happen. I guess that I kind of fall in love with her right then and then she hits me so hard straight in my mouth that one of my teeth comes loose and floats around in there like a piece of rock candy and the salt taste of the blood flows against my tongue. And except for the moment my eyes close on the hit we are still looking right at each other and neither one of us is going to break that, it seems. Then she knows that I am not lying, and she knows that somehow I know what happened to her sister. I fiddle the tooth with my tongue. And then she starts to cry. Her face just breaks all apart and I pull her to me, and I hold her.

"I don't like staying here," Joseph says. "I ain't never had a taste for horseshit in close quarters."

"You're right," I say. "We should get out of here and get some breakfast."

"Are you saying—" Wing begins.

"You don't really want to know what I'm saying," I tell him, getting up and lifting Turner with me. "It doesn't matter."

We're all standing now.

"It doesn't matter ever what people say," I tell him. "It's only what people do that counts. What you do at any particular time, that's what counts."

Joseph opens the doors to the stable carefully, the hinges complaining a little, the light coming in, and his gun up.

"Right now we're getting some breakfast," I tell Wing. "We're going to eat."

I look down at my empty hands. I've holstered my gun without knowing it. Turner won't move. I put my arms around her again and move her toward the door.

She lets me. I want to know what's in that wagon. But I want to get her out of here even more.

Make no mistake. Life will surprise you. And it will break you. In spite of the moments that might lead you to think otherwise, there is nothing kindly about life, it has no heart of its own and it does not care about you and in the end it will win, and not you. Life does not give four shits who lives it. Holy stink, a man does not need any schooling to understand that much.

"Your sign out there says 'Beans and Sandwiches.'"

"Well, we ain't got neither."

"Well, it also says 'Free Beer and Chicken.'"

"Beer's free if you buy the chicken."

"How much is the chicken?"

"Three dollars."

"Does it sing and dance?"

"What?"

"For that kind of money, you should get a show. What have you got that ain't free and ain't some form of robbery?"

"We got whisky."

"That'll do. Five whiskies."

"Yessir."

"Bring the bottle."

"Yessir."

"You must have got something to eat with it though."

"I think we got some eggs."

"I would think so, I would think that chicken better be doin' some fancy egg-layin' for its three dollars... Bring her some eggs then."

"And maybe we got some bacon."

"Bring her that too."

"You look familiar to me."

"No. I do not."

"I think—"

"I got one of those faces."

"You're—"

So I pull my gun and point it at his head and cock the hammer. "No. I am not."

He goes white. "No. Right...you're not, I can see that now..."

"Eggs," I say, easing the hammer down.

"And bacon."

"Right."

"That whisky very far away, is it?"

"No, sir." He takes a look at Wing and then sets about his business.

"We are conspicuous," Joseph says, "and pulling your pistol does not make us less so."

You ever hear the one about the guy walks into a bar with a bag on his head?

I'm back to looking at Turner. "That we are," I say, "but I don't think a pistol makes us any more so."

"I'll be needing your attention," he says.

"You have it." But I'm still not looking away from her. What is she thinking?

"What are you thinking?" Joseph asks me.

"I am thinking there is a time to do something. And there is a time to do nothing at all."

"What do you mean dead?" Wing suddenly asks.

"What I mean is that she's dead. I mean those two bastards murdered her. Did you think they were hiding her somewhere? They killed her. Doesn't matter how I know. She's dead. I'm sorry."

"It's a terrible thing," the kid chimes in.

Turner closes her eyes.

"I'm sorry," I say again. And I am.

Wing moves to get up. I stop him.

"Jesus Christ, why don't you just walk out into the street with a gun in your hand and a bag over your head? Is that your goddamned plan? Because I don't think too much of it. I don't

[147]

believe it to be well conceived and I don't expect it to be well executed."

He slumps down again. "But I must do something."

"Have a drink then. It beats getting yourself shot up."

The man is back with the whisky. "Eggs and bacon will be coming," he says, "and there's ham, and some bread."

"Leave the bottle."

"Yessir."

He's had time by now to let half this town know that Billy the Kid is in a corner of the saloon with some fellow with a bag over his head and some of those he's told either think he's foolish or drunk but there are others who are counting out their bullets. This is a bad spot for us to be in from any angle. There's only two of them and there's five of us. But then there's the whole population of this fucking hole in the sand and they don't know a damned thing about those two men and they think they know everything there is to know about me because they have read of it in a five-cent book written by a two-cent hired gun, either that or they've heard tell about it from a drunk.

I take the tooth from my mouth. I'd been holding it there between my cheek and gum like a plug of tobacco, and I place it on the centre of the table. Then I spin it. "Well, here we are," I say.

"I do not see any advantage to any of this," Joseph says, watching the tooth slow down.

"This was your idea, remember. And all we have to show for it so far are one dead Mexican and one missing tooth…"

"Not much of a ledger."

"I'd sure appreciate knowing what's in that wagon."

"You think there's money in there?"

"I don't know what's in there and that's what interests me about it. That and the fact that those two obviously place some importance on its contents. First thing they wanted to do was check on it."

"Are you fellas planning on opening up this bottle?" the kid wants to know.

"Sorry about your tooth," Turner says suddenly.

"It's alright," I tell her, and we're looking at each other again. "I got others."

"Jesus Christ."

That's Joseph.

"Well, what are we going to do, just sit here?"

That's Wing.

"Well..."

That's me.

"We're going to open up that bottle, kid...if you'd do the honours for us...and Miss Turner's going to have her some breakfast, and we're all going to have us a drink."

"But these men—"

"Ain't going anywhere, Wing, not without us seeing them, and I got my eye on the door of that shed and I can tell you this, they ain't moved yet and they ain't going anywhere without that wagon...and they ain't coming in here or they would have done it already and be lying there dead on that floor."

"So you have a plan?"

"My plan right now, Mr. Wing, is just as I have outlined. Miss Turner will have her breakfast and you are going to have a drink. It is not yet an elaborate plan but I'd counsel you to follow along with it. Things do not get any easier from this point. A drink might do you some good. I'm thinking I might ask the proprietor if he could find a steak the same place he's been finding all these other refreshments. For a place that ain't got nothing, it seems they got quite a bit."

"Then I just wish to be clear—there is a plan to kill them?"

"That's your plan. Mine's to sit right here and not get killed by anyone and maybe find out what's in that wagon…and have a steak if I can."

I don't suppose my father ever loved anything.

"His plan," Joseph says, nodding in my direction, "has four elements to it."

"And kill them," I add.

"Five," says Joseph.

It's hard to tell what Wing is looking at.

"It's a good plan," Joseph decides.

"It's mostly about staying alive. Go on, Wing, and have a drink."

"Do as he says, Wing," Joseph says. "You should drink. A man in your position, he oughta take a drink."

If you cut the head off a lizard with an axe, it will continue to move, not as a chicken does, haphazardly and directionless, but with a purpose, as if trying to locate the head that had been there just moments before. Where did it go? Is it over here? It will do this until it can do it no longer. It can be an inspiring thing to watch. But still, it ends in nothing. It would be best for Wing if he just drank himself into unconsciousness.

In the end I'm the one to look away from her. "Yes. Have a drink, Wing. Please."

"I am sorry for your loss," the kid says, pouring out a measure into a small glass.

"We're all sorry…we are. It is a horrible thing to have to face."

They'll leave by night. That is what they'll do. What they'll attempt to do. They'll hole up until they believe it is safe to go. These are not men who fight it out. These are men who run away and who fight only when they know the odds are overwhelmingly in their favour; in other words, they will fight only when there is no one to fight them back. I will count the exits to that building and we will make certain they cannot leave there unnoticed without digging a tunnel.

Jesus on a black horse, Wing makes an unusual sound getting that drink into him and it is best not to focus on it but to think of something else. The effects of his misfortune seem magnified somehow now that we are indoors.

Leastways that is how the situation strikes me. I mean, it is how these two men strike me. I do not know them personally, but still I feel that I know them well. We have all day in front of us. In spite of what they have done, or because of it, they are frightened men. But those are often the most dangerous sorts of men. Men with nothing to lose but their blood are often unpredictable, but these two will not risk leaving until dark, I am certain of that. They are not the men for broad daylight unless certain they are unwatched, and they are watched, I can see their window from here and, aside from looking at Turner, I do not look away from it.

The food arrives with a shaky hand and Turner attacks it with a fervour that no one expected, at least not me; she is on that food ferociously and we all look away like you would when a horse breaks a leg.

Something is going to happen here in this town tonight.

I don't know for sure what it will be, but when it is done those men will be dead and Turner will not be dead. Finished eating now, she wipes her mouth with the back of her hand. I wish that it was my mouth. I have become foolish. And this is no time for that. I am always aware of how many guns there are likely to be present near me. There are too many at this moment. The quiet man who once had no food is back.

"Excuse me but that will be thirty-five cents, if that's alright, I mean if that's all you'll be needing."

"You closing up shop, junior?"

"No, sir, I just… If there's something else?"

"You think I'm leaving? Do I make you nervous, son?"

"No, sir."

"I could use a beer then," Turner says.

"A—"

"The lady will have a beer. And bring another bottle of whisky. How were the eggs?" I ask Turner.

"A little burnt."

I turn to the thirty-five-cent man. "They were a little burnt. You see? It is difficult to find perfection in this world. Everything is marked by its being less than it could be. You've heard, probably, that I am an excellent shot?"

"Yessir."

"It's a fair statement. So hurry along. Beer and whisky. Now what could be easier? Aren't they the specialties of the house? Nothing too good for Billy the Kid..."

"I do not think it's wise to announce your presence here," Joseph says.

"I do not think I'm as smart as you, Joseph. I would have thought you'd know that by now. And I would have thought the two gentlemen across the street would show nothing but interest."

"And?"

"And at least three of the people sitting at this table have an interest in killing those two men...perhaps more than three of us..."

The kid is looking around to see if he's one of the three. Maybe there's a paper he should sign up on, he's thinking. When was the question put to him? But he cannot recall. But yes, yes I would kill those men, he's thinking, I would.

And that makes four.

"I'm not uninterested in ending those men," Joseph offers.

Five then.

"I just feel that whispering that old name around could bring other elements out of the rabbit holes and the back rooms of this town—"

"I didn't whisper it."

"No, you said it right out loud."

"I suppose."

A rabid dog will run until it is dead.

ᒪ 22 ᒧ

She's drunk. The better part of a day spent drinking will do that, I suppose. Her father is drunker than she is and has already been in bed upstairs for an hour. It took three of us to get him there. The sun is going down soon, and it is in my eyes through the window at the top of the stairs as I carry her. There's a red carpet all the way up. She's light to start but she's heavier nearer to the finish. That is me, I suppose. I stop on the stairs and shift her weight. Doing so brings my right hand right onto her ass.

And I move it. Away.

I cradle her hips in my elbow instead and hike her head up off my chest and onto my shoulder where she burrows her nose into my neck. And then I smile as if I have done something noble.

Jesus Jesus Jesus and Christ, there is something wrong with me.

Joseph and the kid are in a front room keeping a watch on the stable. The kid is in not too bad shape and Joseph is as sober as a widow's Bible. He knows there is no room for being otherwise. There has been some discussion between us as to how best to proceed. Without climbing through windows there is no exit from their hotel that we cannot see from this room. The kid had thought one of us should go over there and watch their room from the hallway but I say there is no need to take a risk when no risk is needed. They will bolt, and we will be ready. I am certain of this.

"Turner."

[154]

No answer.

I get her into her room and I drop her onto the bed, where she bounces and curls and then settles. I watch one of her hands reach out blindly and pull at the blanket. That yellow hair. Could...

I should check on the view across the street. I close the door and make sure it is locked and then I pocket the key. Down the hall to where Joseph and the kid are, with my mind focused now—what is in that wagon? And what would be the harm in me going over there after all? Might bring things to a conclusion faster.

But there's this thought. The way that my hand on the stairs was suddenly full of her ass.

And then not.

And how it just moved away.

"Joseph?"

"There's nothing to see."

"I am going over there."

"Wait a bit."

"Why?"

"They're either going to make a move or they will go to sleep, Ish, and either time is a better opportunity to go over there."

Well, damn him and his shirt collar always buttoned up. "You're happy just sitting here then?"

"I thought that was the plan. I am a patient man. We have tobacco and we have three chairs. Do you have something else to do?"

The key in my coat pocket taps me on the chest. "You think Wing is just going to sleep through all this?" I ask him.

"I'd say the whole Wing family is down for the count, wouldn't you?"

"I suppose."

"She asleep then?"

Fuck you fuck you fuck you fuck you. "Yeah."

"Sit down then."

"I'm going to check on the horses."

"Good idea."

Fuck you. "But careful they don't kick you, Ish."

Fuck you fuck you.

I step back out of the room and I close the door on them and take a long walk down the hall with the key in my pocket along for the ride. I saw a man once shot so many times that it seemed like the air whistled through him as he fell. I remember another time when me and Joseph sat in an empty cabin in the middle of the Mojave with nothing but two guns and a bottle of corn liquor.

"I been thinkin', Joseph," I told him.

"Yeah? Well, don't hurt yourself."

"Fuck you. There will come a day I swear I am going to make soup outta you."

"You are welcome to try, and what have you been thinking about exactly?"

"Well, it seems to me that we, I mean man, I mean us people, we're the only mistake that God ever made."

"Listen, that's not your thought, it's not original."

"Hell it isn't."

"It ain't new. Seems to me that's what the Bible's mostly about."

"Is it? I ain't never read the whole of it."

"Well, that still don't make that idea belong to you. I believe you'll find that on several of its pages."

"Damn."

Joseph says he's read the Bible seven times. I believe that he mostly looks at the pictures. And I sure don't believe it says in there that God made any mistakes.

Fuck him and his old face that looks like a bowl of walnuts.

Joseph, I mean. Not God. Listen: Joseph was made to disparage me. It is his life's work. If he wasn't who he is I would tie him to a chair and break his ankles, then untie him and watch him try to walk away.

Well, now look at that. My hand on a doorknob.

I close the door behind me. With no window the room is hotter than the devil's asshole and with no light now I struggle to find the candle to light it and I knock it over in the process and she stirs just a very little. Why do I feel as if I am in the cabin of a ship? I ain't never even been on a real ship. I hate boats. I can swim but I see no reason to do so or to put myself in proximity to the possibility. The floor of this room feels as if it is tilting and I have not had a drink to make it so. There is a shift of the sheets. I get the candle lit and there she is with the light dripping over her like yellow wax and a soft glow radiating from her skin as if she herself was the source of the light. She has shed most of her clothing while I have been gone and the sheet is stretched up tight over her, one short arm folded over herself, the other tucked up by her head. Soft.

The bed is a tin affair in the style of a cathouse, a sort of brass affair with what looks like fence posts at the head and the foot. A wooden stand in the corner for clothes. A plain pine dresser with a wash basin. White papered walls with pink flowers in almost straight lines. There are no chairs. No table. There is a mirror nailed to the wall with the silver coming loose from the back of it reflecting like a puzzle the missing parts of the room. The floor is made up of wide straight-milled pine boards. There is a simple round hooked carpet by the bed where her clothes lie in a heap. She has pulled them from herself and dropped them there, a hindrance to her, tying her and binding her, now gone. They no longer carry her shape, which is now outlined by the white sheet that wraps her. Her arm moves. She rolls and presents her back to me. White cotton.

The first man ever pulled a gun on me said it was a joke. But then he never got the chance to laugh about it.

And her quiet breath the only sound in the room.

I feel she is certain to be at least twenty-one.

I leave. The door closes behind me with a soft click like a pistol hammer on an empty chamber.

❧ PART TWO ❧
TRIBULATION

ᥩ 23 ᥕ

"Missouri, we are only alive until we are not anymore and so we must do the best we can while we still have the chance to do so."

Our father told me that one time, Turner, and he was right to say it. Being dead is no easier than being alive, Turner—in fact it is harder. To say otherwise would be just like saying that things become easier when you leave the womb. And they do not. And neither do they do so once you have passed away. You lose that chance and you can no longer make things right. Your tongue—that red flesh weapon. I told you it would be your unmaking, Turner, the way you tell the boys just what you think all the time. Men do not care much what you think, that is the way of them. I told you to keep it to yourself and that there's no boy who wants to know what you think, not really. None in New Mexico nor Arizona nor Texas is as interested in what you have to say as you are yourself. You're always talking, Turner—just stop it. Stop it.

You're so smart. You're so pretty. You have so much to say and you always say it but you talked yourself right into this room and into this hotel with these men who are not your family, that's what you did, you talked yourself right into it. Just like you straight-talked every boy away from you too. You never understood that men like to be the ones to say things. Just because they don't ever say much or even have much of any worth to say does not make it otherwise. You could pass away just waiting for them to say something that is worth a button, but that is of no matter. It just takes patience but instead you have talked yourself out of every boy who ever came around you. Turner, if you'd just listened once to any one of them. Talk, talk, talk, talk. Like a lizard rolling itself in the sun, that tongue of yours. But somebody somewhere will love you, Turner. Someone along the wide flat Rio Grande or riding the borderless plains of New Mexico. You're a beautiful girl, Turner, inside and out, you are.

Turner, I think I'm hollow inside now. I cannot feel myself. Turner? It is cold.

You never knew how to just be quiet. That man who looks at you the way he does, he either means you a true harm or a great good, I believe, but I cannot tell which and you just lie there sleeping. You are not one to handle liquor and you never were. Too true.

Some nights I look out and I see your father, Turner, just standing there white in the middle of a black field. Your father, Turner. A fire-brand. A torch. A sack over his head, yes, but his heart on fire and now burning just for you because I am gone and now he knows it for certain and for certain his heart is broken once again. I do not know how long this can last.

Turner, you must make yourself into something now without me. And no one else is going to...no man will do that for you.

Don't wait for any man to pull you up, Turner—that is not the direction they go.

Just because I hover up here by the ceiling in these cobwebs and this darkness and am made up from almost nothing at all and you cannot hear me, that does not mean you can't listen to me somehow. Remember me. Listen to me please, Turner, it is not too late for that and it is not too late for you now.

One foot in front of the other. After they took me away they said they were going to let me go. I knew it wasn't real, what they said, but the little one with the fallen eye just staring at me, he seemed so sure that I wouldn't actually get away from him, and the big one, well, he just stood there watching it all and wiping at himself with a big handkerchief. They had taken me down by the Gallinas and set me down by the mud bank and they talked about how they might let me go maybe and then maybe how they might kill me instead and they talked and talked about it and one time I cried out, I was so scared, Turner, I cried out, I could not help it and the little one he looked at me with his one good eye like a straight razor and he told me to shut myself up and don't make a sound and then he talked to the fat one about how there was no one around here and how they had all the time in the world to do just what they pleased. All the time they needed, that is what he said. That one lazy eye of his slanted like he'd borrowed it in a hurry and just slapped it onto his face the way it hung there and then he walked toward me and he said: "Why don't you just walk away? You can go. We're letting you go, girl, why don't you just do it then?"

One foot in front of the other and I knew it wasn't real but what else could I do so I started to go and every step was like getting away and every step was like getting trapped deeper and deeper and I could hear him behind me, slow behind me like he was in no hurry, and so I just kept walking except for the times I fell to my knees onto the ground. I couldn't think of anywhere to go so I just kept going in a straight line through the brush by the river and then on south, where it was clear. I was just as desolate as the pilgrims in the Bible, Turner, lost in the desert.

For some reason I remembered when the house burned when I was ten, you were eight, and we stood there together and watched the fire move from room to room like it was investigating the view from each window, like it might just buy the place, and we saw each set of curtains become gripped by the flames and fly out the windows and how after the fire was done I looked down into the charred smoking cellar with your hand in mine. The dining table that had fallen through the floor and broken its legs and the blackened silverware shining through in spots. The family Bible that was just a mush of ash in its cellar grave, soft now like a cake and its gilt-edged pages charred brittle. Ashes too. Leather cover curled tight. Your little hand in mine and looking.

And then I fell a last time and I thought, well, I will get up off my knees now when God pulls me up, that is what I told myself, and I waited and I listened, but he did not do that, he did not pull me up. And I never got up again. The little one he forced himself on top of me

[163]

and then I could feel him trying to get himself into me but it seemed he could not and the big one he just stood there and watched and he started to shout: "Dammit, man, do it to her, do the job!"

But the little one was swearing and holding me down but it seemed that what he wanted to do he could not do at all.

"What is wrong with you? Now is the time!"

And the little one was swearing more now and then I could feel him pushing himself against me, but what was necessary to the act he wanted so desperately to perform was not something he was able to produce, it seemed, and so foolishly I started to believe they would let me go. They will let me go now, they will let me go...

The little one he just fell on top of me breathing hard and the big one continued to yell at him: "Dammit, I have told you what to do and now is the time for you to do it! Get yourself inside of her now! Ride her, dammit, it is what she wants, she is waiting for it! Look at her waiting for you to do it!"

And I thought, how to believe in a God after this? And how not to? Because without that there is nothing at all. So I listened to see will they say anything next but they were silent then and so I just waited. How dirt when mixed with blood becomes like tar. And my face in that muck and how after you have had enough of fear and humiliation there is just nothing left to you.

"Well, then just finish her," the big one said then as if he had just been dealt a losing hand. "Yes, now just let her go..."

And for a moment I thought he meant to free me but the little one he pulled out a knife and in the end, yes, it's the same thing in the end. In the end I did get to go after all. High, high up and away. Only it's not what you think. And then it is. And then not. There is no way to explain what it is.

Now I see three graves. Our father's wife, our mother, and me, his daughter. And then himself. As good as buried is how he is now, the way that things are for him. As good as burnt up dead he is now. Curled up tight and charred black with white teeth I see him. Gone.

Lying drunk down the hall now and just as good as passed already in his mind and in his spirit. And that gunfighter who stares at you through the dark, I see him now too, sliding down the hall outside this room in the blackness and now quickly and quietly down the back stairs as if he is floating and cannot be heard. Out of the plain-wood side door with not a creak or a sound and along down the alley and on into the street. Going to seek vengeance for a crime not done to him but done to you and to me, and doing it just because he can, because perhaps it is in his true nature just to do so. Wake up, Turner.

Wake up.

Three bone-handled knives in his vest and his guns on either hip. When he walks with this dark intent, he walks steady and silently like a ghost and none can hear him passing.

Wake up, Turner.

Now.

❧ 24 ❧

It is easier to kill a man at night. Even though you can't see as well in the dark, you need to remember that this works both ways and also that broad daylight is a messy time to kill somebody. Lots of people never seen a man get shot before and when they do they'll remember it, and they'll remember you're the one who did it too. I don't like to kill a man but I have done my share. I remember Jackson Darger, he was a fine fellow but it was a pleasure to shoot him. I ain't ever ended up ankle deep in blood and hair like some have, but if a man gives me the idea to shoot him most times I don't see a way around doing it. I could walk away from this situation here, but since I have not done that ever yet I am not about to do it tonight. And there ain't no question about these two men in my mind—they're like a huckster and a rube all wrapped up in one snake oil and grease paper package and there ain't nobody gonna cry over them when they're gone from this human stew and that ain't exactly today's news. What they done to that girl it ain't what normal folk do. Isn't. It isn't what normal folk do. That's Joseph's voice in my head telling me how to speak proper. He torments me with it like a hog with a corncob.

"Don't say *ain't* so much, Ish, say *isn't*."

"And don't call me Ish so much, Joseph."

"It is your rightful Christian name."

"No, it ain't. There ain't nothin' Christian about it."

"It's a Biblical name, William."

"Wrong part of the Bible, Joseph. It ain't in the Jesus part. I know 'cause I looked for it. Took me hours and I used up two candles doin' it too. It ain't there and it ain't Christian if it ain't in the Christ part of the book."

"Lived to be a hundred and thirty-seven years is what they say."

"People say a lot of things."

"People lived longer in those days, Ish. They say a fella named Methuselah lived to be nine hundred and sixty-nine years of age. A prodigious life."

"I'm sure that it was. And I'm sure the angels pissed down gold over his head."

"I don't believe that's mentioned."

"Just seems to me there's a tendency toward tall stories in that book at times."

"Ain't no lies in the Bible, William."

"Don't say *ain't* so much, Joseph."

That sets him back a step. "You hold yourself up too high and you speak too rough with folks, Ish, you speak at everyone as if they were your sworn enemy."

"Well, ain't they?"

"You'd catch more flies with sugar, that's all I am sayin'."

"And who the fuck wants flies? Who wants flies, Joseph?"

What these two crackerjacks have been doin' holed up in there all day I do not know. Whatever it is, it ain't worth a bucket of spent shells to me because it is dark now and I am comin' across the street with reminders of humility for them. I am tired now of waiting. They are going to bolt and I might as well be in the way when they decide to do so rather than chasing after them. I don't hold myself up higher than anyone else but some men are just so low that it don't leave much in the way of room not to. I mean that some men just need dealing with. I suppose I should inform Joseph and the kid that I have altered the plan and am about to hang fire but I just don't feel in any way disposed to seek any assistance. I feel partly bad about this, but after the job is done no one will really care how it was accomplished and the fewer of us who need to get away clean from it all, the better it will be for all concerned. Sometimes I think I am in love with the doing of things like this and that is why I seek them out the way other men may seek out women or money. We create our own destinies and I have not done such a stellar job of polishing mine. Perhaps this is why women and money have not come to me so very much. I keep getting under my own feet with plans and events involving death and killing. The best place to be in a gunfight is behind something. The best place to be in a gunfight is not in a gunfight at all, but that is not the way my life or this evening has led me. I tear up easily now at small things and I am old, I have become old.

Not too old to do what needs doing now. There is no more waiting to be done.

৵৯ 25 ৫৩

You can feel the presence of the world with your hands, Turner. Just let your palms hover over the earth for a moment and you can feel it breathing right under you. You can feel your connectedness to it and the warmth that it holds for you. You can begin to understand it for a moment and you can just be with it. You can do this for longer than a moment, but few people ever do that and most just trample it underfoot. And once you are gone from it you cannot touch it any longer, Turner. Once you have lost it, it is gone from your hands and from your ability to touch it for good. You know how good coffee smells in the morning when it is straight off the stove and hot in the cup? When you are dead, that is just steam and you can't smell it or taste it or touch it. It is as dead to you as you are to it. When you're alive, you're all wound up with just being alive but you don't know it. You don't think that way when you're in it because you're just too busy being in it. You just want to grab the bull by the horns but you don't even know what the bull is or where the horns are. And so you just spin. I mean me. I mean all of us. You are made up entirely of flaws. But beautifully made. You wake up. And you move. You touch the world. How the thin light from under the door touches you in return. Maybe you are walking through a wet field at dawn, or you are leaning over the stove in the old cold kitchen. Your soft skin and your little feet. How alive you are now, Turner. How warm. You pull your sheet to yourself. Turner, you are yourself but you are also everything else you think is not you. You are a part of everything, it is all connected if I could just tell you. For now just put your clothes back on and for now just go. Just go where you think you need to go. You are wrong. But that can't matter to you now so go anyway. That is what living is: it is being mistaken about everything most of the time. What has long been denied you, it turns out, is you. So go ahead. Everything counts in this old rodeo. And everything matters. Once in a while we get something right in spite of ourselves and that is where and when beauty is to be found. So go ahead and cross the street. Follow him. Find what you think you need. Do what you need to. Get up.

You can die later.

∽ **26** ∾

There's lots of ways to go into a room but there's only one way when there's guns on the other side of the door and that's fast and in this particular case fast and already shooting. What you want to achieve is a complete surprise and if you don't have that and if they're expecting you, then at least going in this way they are likely to be dead or injured by the time you are into that room and then there's less for you to worry about if the job's already done for you. You knowing that I am coming through your door don't do you a bit of good if you've already got a bullet hole through your head or in your chest. Yes. Surprise is always the advantage you want. Unless the room is empty.

Well, then you're just fucked.

There's nothing in this room but for two beds and six of my spent bullets. One bullet through the chamber pot and piss all over the carpet now when it should have been blood. I have never understood chamber pots. Why mess up a perfectly good bowl when there's a window to piss out of? Save yourself the stink. I look out the window over to the room Joseph and the kid have already run out of on their way over to here. Some people down in the street are looking up here. Some are heading for shelter. No big man. No little man. The wagon.

The wagon.

Before I can make it down to the stable, I hear the creaking and the hooves and the crash of the doors. I'm down the stairs and out into the street and on after it and I even raise my gun to shoot it but it's too late and it's too dark and they're too gone. Joseph and the kid are with me and Joseph has his rifle raised, and then he lowers it.

"Damn," the kid says.

"Yeah."

"Well, you know that saying," says Joseph.

"What saying, Joseph? What saying is that?" I ask him, putting my gun back into place after I take a quick look at the crowd of blank-faced planks staring after the wagon and then at us like we're some kind of tent show that just pulled into town.

"A bird is only as good as its wings," Joseph says.

"That is not a saying."

"Sure it is."

"And how do you know that?"

"People say it."

"They do not. I never heard anyone say anything even like that, ever."

"Certainly they do. That's what makes it a saying."

"Shut your shit."

"Why do you say that?"

"It's a saying."

"It is not."

"Certain it is. 'Shut your shit,' I just said it. That makes it a saying."

"Don't you fellas think that maybe we should get on after that wagon?" the kid offers.

"We'll get after it."

"What about the Wings?" the kid wants to know.

"I said a bird is only as good as its—"

"I mean the Wings…Turner Wing…and Mr. Wing—"

"We should wake them up," I decide.

"No time," Joseph says. "Let 'em sleep it off. We'll come back and get 'em when we're done with the job, when we've got something we can show them."

I got one hand on my pistol and I'm chewing on my bottom lip. "We'll get the horses," I tell the kid, "but you go get Turner. And get her fast."

Because I already know her good enough to know she don't want us heroes running off and bringing back her dead for her. She wants to be the one to pull the trigger on them and I don't blame her one little bit for that. She has that coming to her. I should go get her myself but we gotta round up the horses fast. And I remember she ain't got very much on so I shouldn't have sent the kid. But I gotta get the horses. Those two bastards are pulling a wagon so it ain't that much of a rush but time still counts. I shoulda gone myself and let the kid help with the horses. I am always stuck in my own way.

"Hey!" It's the kid in a window. "She ain't in here!"

"Whattaya mean she ain't there?"

"I mean there's a room here and a bed here and she ain't in either one of them."

"Well, where the hell...?" I look down past the edge of the buildings and into the black. "Let's get going," I say.

༄ **27** ༄

They say this part here is the beginning of my story. It's not, but it's the one we'll use for now. It's as good as any other.

Windy Cahill he called me a pimp. On top of that he was sitting on my chest when he said it. And Windy Cahill was not a light man and he stunk of meat and onions and wasted time.

So I shot him.

I was seventeen, almost eighteen.

That was the end of his story and maybe the beginning of mine. He bled out there onto the floor of George Atkins's saloon and I rode off. He was wrong. I was not a pimp. And he should not have been sitting on my chest either. He was a scruffy bastard and a bully who badly needed ending, and he died dreaming that he was a better man than he was. How do I know that was the case? Well, because we'll all do that, every single one of us. Me. You.

I am an outlaw, you even know what an outlaw is? It's anyone knows that the lies are lies and also someone who ain't very much afraid of that fact. They see things clear. And then they live that way, usually to their own detriment. And I believe that spending some time in the desert does help a bit with that kind of seeing. You can see the shit hawks comin' at you days before they arrive and there is not that much there to distract you from seeing them unless you are too wrapped up with what goes on inside your own head. Your thoughts of yourself and your memories of all you have done. I had a life before I shot a man too but no one seems much interested in that part of the story. You cannot weigh yourself down with everything you have done or not done, but that is what most people do. It is a horrible way to spend time.

I was once locked up with this fella by the name of Bill Quentin. He liked to keep himself looking presentable Bill did, even where we found ourselves, which was behind a set of particularly thick iron bars.

"Is you wearin' some kind of a cologne, Bill?" I asked him one time.

"Just 'cause I am in prison that don't make me an animal," he says.

I swear this world gets uglier every single day and so I don't criticize Bill for wearin' his fruit water. If it's up to me, people can do whatever the hell it is they want to as long as it don't include firing bullets at me or at anyone I'm with. Lots of boulder heads think they have a better way to be that they are just absolutely certain is the best way for others to be too and they usually are not afraid to push it on them either. Be whatever way you want to be as long as you are not in my way is how I see it. It is like people my whole life have just been pushing me out of the road to get out the back door of a building that is on fire. My name is William Henry McCarty, Jr., and I am Billy the Kid. Some people raise a whole lotta hell about nothing at all and some people they just abide. I am not the abiding type.

"What do you think about a life after death?" Joseph asked me one time.

"I don't even think much about *this* life," I told him. But I do. I'm going to be an old man soon enough. And that is alright with me because mostly I did not care much for myself as a young man. There was no point in that fellow even being. He was not the diamond he made himself out to be. I suppose that is why in the end she just eyed me up and down with a look on her face like she was figuring out the price per pound of me and finding that it was a bit too dear.

Of course, that was before I was a well-known figure. There are a few things worse than being a well-known figure, I suppose, but I am certain I do not know what even one of those things would be exactly. It feels very much like being the only chicken in a bag full of foxes. You walk into a room and everybody knows you're there and you can trust me when I tell you that is a far less appealing feeling than what it might sound. It is interesting the first time it happens and directly after that it takes a very sharp decline in appeal.

Joseph has a child he does not admit to even having. He says she is not really his but you can tell easy enough that she is his daughter if you just look at her because she looks like he just spit her out. He says her mother was with another man and she is a liar about whose child it is and there is no way she could know what seed planted that girl. I say she knows well enough.

One time he was paying a prostitute in this hotel in Cimarron, I think it was, and she says to him: "Is that all you goin' to give me?"

And he tells her: "Dammit, woman, what about that fine ham supper I bought you?"

And then he tells that story to me later like it was about him getting a good price on a horse. There is no figuring my brother. Sometimes he is a sharp card and other times he is just a blanket on everything. Most of the times he is a blanket though. Mostly lately he is a blanket. It is a long life and as I have said, it is for the most part of it untrue. And sometimes there is God in it. And sometimes there is not.

Listen: this part of the story that's coming up here next is a part where there is not; there is no God in it at all, at least not as far as I can see.

So be cautioned to that.

There is nothing pretty about this part that is coming now.

✎❦ 28 ❦✎

A brown-leathered face like old candle wax and little yellow teeth like talons and a wisp of white yellow stubble and, Turner, this man he told me he said, "Miss, let me tell you that you are prettier'n a Swiss watch."

Well, Turner, I didn't even know what a Swiss watch was at that time and so his intended compliment didn't affect me very much one way or the other so I suppose he felt he should elaborate and then he said, "The two prettiest things in this world are a handmade watch from Switzerland and a woman from anywhere."

And that didn't help him in any way with me because then I knew what a Swiss watch was, but I also knew he was lumping me in with every other woman in the world and that is something only stupid men do—"Women are this way..." or "Women are that way..."—when men don't have even the simplest idea of what women are. So I can assure you that what he wanted from me he did not get, so just you be careful of men, Turner, they will try to trick you every way they know how, even when they don't know how and sometimes even when they don't rightly know themselves what it is they are doing. There's all kinds of evil in this world, Turner, there's little and there's big and the best you're going to get from what might be called a good man is that he's not as bad as some of the others.

And just what is it that you suppose you're doing here now, Turner? You are so scared but you are strong when you are scared. You're thrilled but you're foolish when you're thrilled and so what is it that you think you will do now? What will you do? You thought you would kill these men and maybe you will do that but maybe they will kill you first and that is not all they'll do to you if they find you here in the

[177]

back of their wagon. *I want to help you. I want you to know that I want to help you. I want you to be safe and you have gone ahead and put yourself into the most dangerous possible situation here and you have done that for me, and I am dead, Turner, there is nothing you can do for me now or do about that. Nothing. Tell me, why are the living so unthinking? To be alive is to be foolish.*

Oh don't. Don't.

If you open that pine box, Turner, you may cry out and if you cry out then they will hear you and I cannot bear what happens next. I cannot.

Nobody can save anybody.

Don't.

Don't.

Your body and mind are a woman's and your hands are still a little girl's and they are reaching. You don't have to open it, Turner. It does not want to be opened.

Don't.

Such small fingers that reach out and they want everything.

A simple pine box might not be what it looks like. But it is. In fact it is worse than that. And the roughness of the trail and the movement of the wagon jostle you so that your little fingers, now indecisive, now unsure, hover and bounce. Maybe you won't open the box. But you do. You do.

It is hard to make death look beautiful.

But he has tried, and I think just made it all the uglier in the attempt. Like putting lipstick on a pig.

And so you take a short quick breath, Turner, and the wagon bumps on and you drop the pine lid. No one expects to find the desiccated body of an old woman in a black velvet dress with rouged cheeks rubbed onto her and bright painted lips. A wizened old death mouth like a cave, he can't get it to shut and is so afraid he will crumble her jaw to dust if he tries too hard and so it keeps him awake at night. Her dried-out tongue like a little animal crouching in there. It is not

*your fault to have made the sound you made but you have made it now,
Turner, and they will find you. We aren't all treated the same in this
life and neither will we be after we are dead.*

Oh Turner, the way you will be treated now.

Hide yourself quick.

*There's a whirlwind in the thorn trees. Hide yourself quick. They
will come. They are. Coming now.*

There. Hide under that canvas.

Hurry. Hide.

ᴄᴏ 29 ᴏᴠ

I could have done different things in my life. I could have made shoes and boots. That is a useful trade and an honest one. People need leather to be formed into the size and shape of their feet and that's not something most people can do for themselves and nor do they even wish to. It is something that is needed and something for which people are willing to pay. And so we have cobblers and when cobblers go to bed they know just that they have spent the day doing something useful for people and with a purpose. Making shoes and being of some practical use to the world. Protecting the feet of the world from wear and harm. Dead people seem to see forever, judging by the way their eyes just keep on looking. Who knows what they see. Most likely they see nothing. There's no one in this world who doesn't need shoes. Those who don't got them wish they had 'em and those who got 'em will eventually need a new pair. And no one needs another man with a gun. Except sometimes they think they do. This thing here is something more like making shoes. The killing of these men will be like the making of a fine set of shoes and then donating them to someone who has none. The dead have a blank fish stare. I will not mind seeing it on these two.

I feel good. There's two men up ahead somewhere in the dark who need my bullets into them and I will be happy to provide them with that service. Although if it wasn't for Turner I don't believe I would bother. Make it your business just to shoot bad men for being bad and, well, you're going to have a busy time of it in life because there is no end to that work.

No, it's Turner. I want her not to hurt so much as she is hurting right now. It is not right that a small thing should suffer as much as that. I will end these two and drape them over their horses, then lead them back into town and show them to her in the light with blood rags on them and their long-seeing eyes now shut hard for them. Here, Turner, I'll say, here are the men who hurt you and see how they are no more. Look, Turner. See?

Because she already has her some shoes and what she really needs now is these men gone.

What I am thinking is that we should be on top of them already what with them draggin' a wagon over this rough trail.

Currently my purpose in walking in this world is just to kill these two men. That is my work now. It is what I do for the earth and for Turner because she is a simple goodness naked and alone in the world like a plain piece of board that someone has stuck up into a broken window frame to keep out the cold and the rain, that is how she is in this world.

But we should really be onto them by now. Hold up.

"Hold up. Hold up, Joseph!"

"Whoa now! Whoa. What are we stopping for?"

"What's the idea?" the kid asks, pulling his horse up next to us.

"We shoulda been onto them by now."

"I was thinkin' that too," Joseph says.

"You were? Well, what was stoppin' you from sayin' it?"

"I didn't want to whore everything up—you seemed quite happy chasin' your tail up here."

"Well, that's fine. Just the three of us just out here for a pleasure ride with no end in sight," the kid says.

"I got an end in sight, kid, I got an end, don't you worry, and I got six bullets I intend to use very wisely in the pursuit of what they call frontier justice. You ever heard that expression, kid?"

"I ain't no kid, I'm a grown-up man who knows what's a

bullet for and who don't need any schooling about it from the likes of you."

My right hand goes loose.

"It's a long life, kid," Joseph tells him quick, "and it's got a lot of pretty rough surface to it, so I'd pace myself just a little right now if I was you."

Joseph is telling him not to get shot. The kid eases down a little but I stay ready just in case.

"Say, what is your name anyway?" I ask him to lighten up the conversation a bit. "Nobody's actual name is *kid*."

The kid spits. "It's Chance," he says.

"Chance? That ain't no real name neither."

The kid spits again. "It's short for Chauncey," he says, "and did I hear anybody here say they got a problem with that name? Because the last man had a problem with that name he wishes he hadn't."

"I ain't got no problem with that name," I say.

"Well, good."

"I can see why you go by *kid* though."

"I don't. You two just started callin' me that...but it's good enough for you and it's good enough for me."

"I believe I'll just call you kid then."

"Suits me fine."

Nobody says anything then. We just look at each other.

"We gonna play cards or are we gonna make a plan of what to do?" Joseph asks.

"Well, I can't see shit out here with no moon," I tell him. "They musta pulled off somewhere back a ways and I guess I missed it."

"It's a couple of hours till light."

"I know it. Two hours after that Ol' Bag Head'll be on us like a dose of the clap and Miss Turner with him too, and with no strung-up bodies to show 'em I wouldn't give a nickel for our chances with that girl when she's been left behind and she's sore and angry."

"I thought you thought she was—"

"I been thinkin' on it, Joseph, and I think if she got into that wagon, well, she'd have just shot those two in the back and been done with it. I'm guessing she was on her way to do just that when they up and took off on her."

"That girl's got a lot of spit in her, don't she?" the kid says.

I just look at him until he stops his smiling and he looks down at the ground.

"You're right," he says, "there's no wagon ruts down there."

"They turned off. I already said that."

"I heard ya. I'm agreein' with ya is all. I just think she's a nice—"

"It don't matter at all what you think."

"And it's too bad what's been dealt to her. That's all. It ain't right."

"You gonna fix it for her?"

"I—"

"If you boys are done with your schoolyard business, we could always decide what to do next," Joseph says.

Yeah.

"Well, William?"

"Yeah?"

"Well, what do you want to do?"

"I say we keep on and we lie in wait for them. We ain't gonna find them easy in the dark unless they light a fire and they ain't stupid enough to light a fire in the dark. We keep on till light and we find some high ground and we wait for 'em to show us where they are. I believe they turned off the trail for the night because they did not think we were on to them. I don't believe they know we are on to them, not for certain anyway, they don't even know who we are. Somebody shot the Mexican fella who was going to tell them all about us coming, so all they know is that Turner and Wing showed up unexpected into town with three men. And so they took off into the middle of the night."

"Then why—"

"I don't know how to think like men who'd leave a woman dead in a tree, Joseph, and I ain't gonna try to start now. I say we keep on going ahead for a while and find a good spot and we wait for them there. We just got away from them somehow in the dark and that's all and no matter the cause of it they are behind us now and not ahead, not if they are following this trail, which is the most likely thing for them to do. I do not know what else there is for us to do at the moment."

"Then that's what we'll do," Joseph says.

"Sure," says the kid, "we'll do that."

There was a second there when he started in to say "She's a nice…" when in my head I heard him say "…piece of ass" and I pictured him with a bullet in his face. I think now he was probably just going to say "girl" and so it's just as well that I stayed my hand from shooting him. Caution wins. You gotta watch that. You can wreck things up pretty bad with a bullet without even trying too hard.

When I was just a young kid we lived at this boarding house and one day there was snow and I can remember maybe three times that I ever seen snow when I was a kid, it was sort of like suddenly seeing an albino in the dark or maybe a bearded lady, or just something you don't expect to see, and you don't forget it, and me and this little girl who lived there too, she was younger than me by a bit and she was blond, she lived down the hall with her momma and a long line of men and none of them were her daddy. Sally her name was, and we took this metal can lid that we found and we went spinning down the only hill in that town quick before everything melted and went away, but the edge of that lid took a catch on something and we spilled out and tumbled down the rest of that rise and her little white teeth up and laughing and her small laughter clear like the first sun in the morning before anything moves. Before the day even starts. And I kissed her then. And that moment was a light entering the black song I'd been singing to myself at that time.

I don't remember what happened to Sally, and I don't suppose I ever will know. I remember being on the floor of that house in the dark though, on my hands and my knees, a bottle to my lips, and the white pattern of the wallpaper spinning around me like a storm. Sometimes we live on nothing at all.

❦ 30 ❦

I never did appreciate surprises and I told him so.

"Dammit, Semples..."

"This ain't my fault, Caleb."

"No. Nothing is your fault. You forget your purpose here, Semples. You are here for certain physical abilities you allege to possess and also for my protection, and of late you do not seem capable of either task."

"I told you I had just had too much to drink, that is all."

"In the morning, Semples? It was in the morning."

"I mean the night before. I had too much liquor the night before. That has never happened to me."

"So you say. The fact remains that your role in our affairs is a clear one and you have so far not proven the adeptness of which you bragged."

"I have done lots of women, Caleb, I told you that, and there is nothing wrong with my pecker."

"Keep on talking."

The man had a line of bullshit to him, that much has become clear to me. Perhaps I had been taken in by the visual evidence I had witnessed in our early-morning camps and even some acts I had assisted him with merely out of charity and to relieve his strain, which I will not divulge right now but which I can tell you did nothing whatsoever to dissuade me from the belief that this was a quite capable man when it came to matters of the flesh. This was the sole reason I had enlisted him, and he was not living up to the faith I had placed in his abilities. The fact that I had taken him in hand, so to speak, was an indication of my luck at that point in my life. When I myself lost the ability to satisfy a woman, I had the notion of taking on an intercessor, if you will, someone who possessed the brawn if not the brain, so to speak, someone I could bring into the unique theatre of my own amusements to physically perform the aspects for which I no longer...well, the role I would no longer play. A "stand-in," if you will, an understudy for the lead role that I would continue to take on much in the way an orchestra conductor marshals his forces. This was our simple agreement as well as our financial arrangement and so you see it was a bad time for the two of us. This is what I mean when I say luck was not smiling on me at this point. God would have liked me dead for most of my life, I think, but I did not listen nor oblige for the longest of times and that had him pissing fire down on me at every opportunity. This girl showing up in the back of the wagon was not a part of any plan of mine and I was not happy at all to have to plan for the fact of her presence now. I preferred to hunt down the opportunities for our little performances and not to have them all arranged for me like this. It was ill-timed, particularly with Semples, well, unable to perform in his all-important role.

"You had better at least be up to the task this time, Semples," I told him.

"There is no worry there."

"We will see. Your lies come home to roost, Semples. You said you had checked the wagon too, apparently not too well."

"I ain't no pot o' honey grabbin' flies outta the air, Caleb... This little bitch must have showed up after I checked it. That ain't got nothin' to do with me."

"Well, it does now...it surely will now."

"Well, I ain't sayin' that I won't be able to find a use for her..."

You had better be able to is what I was thinking.

"Just put her away."

"Meanin'?"

"I do not mean to stick your dick into her or to kill her either, Semples. At least not right now. Tie her up good and tight and cover her with that canvas again and let me just think for a minute."

[187]

About two minutes of your hands around their throat, that is all, it doesn't take so very long. All the fighting at the start and then the end of it is like it is nothing. They just go. So much inside of most of them and it all just leaves in a flurry as if it suddenly needs to be somewhere else. But I reached a point in my life where I did not care to take up with that business anymore. I preferred to have others do my work for me in that regard and my work then was in causing them to undertake that work on my behalf. It was a harder and more complex feat to achieve, but I found for myself that I enjoyed it even more. Once I kept a girl's head in a bag and I carried it around with me wherever I went for four days and no one knew about it until it started to stink so bad that I had to get rid of it. I got to a place where I liked to have done for me the things I used to enjoy doing myself. You see, at this point it was more pleasure for me to see some other man's cock shoved into a woman rather than to do the shoving myself because, you see, I was making that happen anyway so it did not matter whose cock it was, it was the fact that I was the one making it do its work. And when he killed her, that was me too. It did not matter whose knife it was going in. I had broken through, do you see? I was on the other side of things. No one had ever been where I was then. And so we were of mutual benefit to each other, Semples and I, in our ways. We were profitable to each other's interests. Provided we each played our parts according to the script.

I had never been partial to the rules of others. A sign that said "No Spitting" just made me want to spit shit and onions.

So, do you believe in the devil? Just let me tell you that his faith in you is enormous. Evil has always existed. And it will keep getting worse. Angry. I was simply angry that she was there. She had no right to be where she was. And so.

"Just cover her up, Semples," I told him, "so she cannot be seen by you or by anyone, and if she moves, kicking her would be the only thing to do for now. And be certain that rag is secured in her mouth and she can still breathe. Just do that for now and let me think on this matter a little more."

What had to be done would be a nasty business, it always was. But it was made up of energy. And it was energy that can be controlled like any energy can be. The size of things like this could be controlled. If you learned how to do it and if you let yourself...loose. I had not brought this girl to where she was, she had done that herself. And as a result of her own actions, there she was for the taking.

Make things smaller. Make them huge. Disruption and control. To have done the work that I did on the earth was to be on my own. Alone, even when I was in company. That was the hardest part of what I did. Which does not mean I did not enjoy it. Not at all. Now that I have passed though and I am no longer what I used to be, I miss things. I miss the little details of life. Such as the smells. The little sounds a person may make when they are afraid of the outcome...but then my hearing was always remarkable. I could hear right to the end of things.

"Semples...her feet."

They were kicking out there from underneath the canvas. Untidy.

Detail. Everything was detail. She struggled. Well, that was in her nature.

It was one of the last things she had left to do is the way I saw it then.

"I told you to tie her, just see that it is done. We will take another route now, Semples. We will be slower, but unseen. With this passenger we are bound to be of undue interest to others," I told him. He was always in need of explanations.

"Alright, Caleb, but there is no other proper trail."

"Then we shall forge one, Semples... Do not let your weaknesses guide you. I have told you of this. Press forward with courage."

I had to teach him, you see. It was not my natural work but I did it just the same. Let us say...it was what I gave back to the world. I gave it of my own free will and I expected nothing for it in return.

ᥣᥬ **31** ᥭᥫ

Joseph has the rifle and I'm ready with the pistols to come up and crouch down low and to his left and rush on down the rise while he lays down a steady run of fire at the bastards and the kid stays far over onto our right, he's got the first shot right in front of the horses to pull them up short and to hold up our targets where we need them to be. It is the perfect little hill from which to shoot two men in cold blood so all we need now is the two men.

I long ago filed down the hammer on my gun like Joseph does, only not so fine that I am likely to kill any Mexicans with it just by chance. Some men they say they don't like an action that smooth and they say an action's too slippery when it's been filed down like that. Too slippery. Well, that is not the case if you do it right. You can say that you like a nice stiff action but you are more likely to be dead with one, so I keep mine looser. I have always found that it is ready when I need it to be and that it does not want to fail me. I prefer to use the Winchester when I'm able to, but right now it seems the Colt is the best choice for me. I will need to move fast once we start this thing and I do not want both my both hands tied up on a rifle as this is some rough ground around here. The kid says he has shot four men and he even killed two of them. That is a modest enough number, but I suspect it is not accurate. He is white-faced and speaking too loud when he says it. I imagine he has shot his fair share of empty bottles and rocks off the tops of fence posts and has also maybe killed enough squirrels to make for himself a decent-sized pie. But he has no reason to admire these men after what they did to him and he knows now what they did to Turner's sister also and so I do not expect him to be shy when the time comes for him to do the thing we have directed him to do. So long as he stops those horses up short he will have accounted himself well with me. No man is afraid to shoot at the ground, after all. When it comes the time to do what needs to be done, a man is what is needed to do it and not a boy and knowing this is what makes the difference between the two.

I feel strangely good out here now. I feel like fresh biscuits and butter on a cold morning. And I am sorry right now for every woman I have ever hurt—there is no excuse for having done any of that, for the shit I have sometimes done, or indeed no excuse for what I could have done and did not. Right now I am even sorry for some of the men I have killed. Maybe I am not sorry, I don't know what I feel, some of those men are just as much use to the world dead as they ever were alive and that is none at all. But I won't be sorry for these two. I will be happy to see Turner's face when this is accomplished, whatever expression it holds. She is a fierce girl, and too young for what she has had in her life, whatever age she is, what the world has given her to have and to keep for herself. She shines, and I cannot stand to see it. No, it is not that at all. I cannot stand to see myself seeing her. All this foolishness of mine with these thoughts that swirl and will not rest. She is a fine person. These are bad men. I have bullets. That is simple.

It does not make me a good man to do this thing for her, I know that too. I, a long time ago, gave up on such ideas of being a good man. Thoughts such as those are impractical and serve no purpose that I can see. I will leave them to the preachers and to Joseph and to all men who think they know something about this life. I have had to give up on a lot during the course of my time on this earth. Lying there. The way she was in that dark room the last time I saw her.

I want her to think I am a good man although I know that not to be the case. But I would like her to think it is for now. She tilts her head to one side when she is angry and she closes up her eyelids into little slits. And whatever she's had so far in her life, well, that is what I'll have to just try to be better than.

"William."

"What?"

"It is getting late in the morning and I do not believe they are coming this way. The sun is high, William."

"I can see that, Joseph. I can see the sun."

"Well..."

I close my eyes and listen but there is nothing there to hear. I know what I know and I know that I don't know as much as I might know if I tried harder to know shit and to see things clear just the way they are.

One time Charlie Bowdre, he says to me: "Watch your step, Billy."

So I ask him: "Why is that, Charlie?"

And he says to me: "Because there's blood all over the floor."

Charlie always had a way of putting things just the way they were. I know now that these boys are not coming this way today at all. What I do not know is where they are and that happens to be the only thing it is important to know right now.

ᦉᩯ **32** ᦉᩯ

L isten to me, Billy, and I'll tell you a little story. A part of the story
you were not there to see and so I will fill in the blanks for you, so
to speak, as in a child's game at school. Some might find this a distasteful story and I suppose they can be the judge of that however they
so choose, but the fact will remain that this is the story just how it
happened and their judgment will have to take a back seat to that fact.
It happened. Just the way I will tell it. Well, it serves its purpose here,
that is enough. It has to be told.

Semples was singing "Turkey in the Straw." His singing was not
an activity of his that I ever sought to encourage due to the inept
nature of his efforts but on that day I was not against it. Time had to
be passed. Still, I had my own work to do as well. My own inspirations
to impart.

"Most people these days are morons...you do realize that, Mr.
Semples, do you not?"

"I suppose."

"That song you were singing just now. It's a reflection of these
times, don't you see? People have not the appreciation or proclivity for
a master such as Brahms or Bach and so they just 'rosin up the bow,'
as it is said..."

"I was just singin' a little tune to pass the time."

"No doubt. The desert trail is a place for the slow passage of time
and oftentimes simple amusements are needed to hurry it along, but
there's the larger picture to be seen here—" I warmed to my theme
"—and society as a whole suffers. Formal education for the masses
is a wasted experiment for the most part, that is my belief. The
printed word languishes, and the culture is adrift. The frontier is a

lie. *We are at the frontier of our own lack of knowledge, that is all we are at the frontier of. Of our own ignorance, if you will. And it is a limitless space."*

"I was just singin' a tune is all."

"Quite so. And a rousing one at that. Let's have another round..."

"Well..."

"Come, Semples, don't be shy, I'm certain that our young guest enjoys a tune. It is the way of the young."

> *"Turkey in the straw, turkey in the hay*
> *Tune up the fiddle, doodle de day*
> *With a rump and riddle and a high tuc-ka-haw*
> *Strike up that tune called 'Turkey in the Straw.'"*

"Formidable. A glorious oratorical and musical effort, Semples. I'm certain the young lady is well pleased. Are you not, dear? Well, you can't tell us, I suppose, with that rag stuffed in your mouth... Don't struggle now. Well, at any rate my point is that young people love music, Semples. It stirs them. And the old as well. The young find affirmation in it and the aged find their peace."

"I guess so."

"You enjoy music, Semples? You find that it is a soothing thing to you?"

"Passes the time."

"Indeed. Yes it does. You know I once heard a very astute term for the tenderness of what lies between a woman's legs."

Silence.

Then: "Would you like to hear it, dear?" I inquired of our guest. And I then asked her again.

"I would ask you once more would you like to hear it? Yes? Well, I will tell you now. I will tell you. The term is 'that gritty rose'... Is that not a fine expression? Gritty rose. There's a poetry to that phrase."

The wood groans of the wagon kept us company for a time until I broke the resultant silence once more.

"I think it very accurate. Part scatology, part poetry. You take my meaning? There is something to be said for the fine turn of a phrase.

The economy of the right word. 'Le bon mot' is what the French say. Well then, there's the way things are and then also there is the way things ought to be, correct? This is the way of it, and the way we fall away from our correct path, children, we fall quickly and without our notice, as is too often the case. Before we realize even that something is happening, our weaknesses have overcome us. Well, there's nothing to be done. There can be no regret, only witness. No solace, only the flat progression of time. I have gaps, oh yes, I do, well, we all do. You say to me, 'Don't let it bother you, Caleb,' but I don't let it bother me at all, indeed I do not. We're none of us getting any younger, my children, even one so young as you, my dear. Your time in particular gets shorter with each passing minute. Yes, our young traveller here seems to age herself by the second, Semples. Look at her face. Worry is a strain on her. Time is wasting and we must press on with the work at hand. There is hope only in the occupation of the moment for the moment. Conjecture about the future only wears us down in the end. You know why I love fishing as an occupation? Do you? I spent a good portion of my boyhood fishing. It is the fact that it is so filled with the possibility of the moment. It has been a long time since I have done any fishing. In a literal sense at least. Things that are beneficial to the circulation…let me see…I'll tell you what they are: movement, cold and heat, physical exertion, fear of death, alcohol, the opening of an artery… Of course, that last example is of a limited duration. Panic, the sense of panic, that something will go wrong and the occurrence of such an event is imminent. The heart beats faster then, and colour rises to the cheek, and to other places too…courage! Courage is a most underrated benefit to the circulatory system. It is a magnificent force. The will to live, to continue fighting, if you will, for the integrity of one's own existence, of one's person. The moment one is brought into communion with one's own end. Which is paradoxically the moment that circulation ceases to be. I'll take a pause in speaking. One of you might wish to speak? Not you, my dear…you have a large rag stuffed in your mouth."

Silence.

"No? Then I shall share with you something I have never told anyone. I have a great fear that if I fall asleep, the world itself will cease to be. No, it is true. And this, in turn, makes it very, very difficult for me to fall asleep. Which, I suppose, could actually be saving the world, if my premise is correct. Except that the fear itself is a delusion. At least I believe it to be such. Delusional. And that fact alone should invalidate it as a fear, but it does no such thing because I have no perspective on the matter. That is the way of many fears, they are strictly inside of us. Not all fears. Some fears are entirely justifiable in that they exist in our own minds but also in the world exterior to our minds. In that way they manifest themselves. You, dear girl, as an example, you fear that you are soon to be raped and then killed as your sister was. A thing quite horrible to contemplate perhaps. For you. But not for Semples here. I can tell you that he quite relishes the thought of both occurrences. Yes, I am very afraid that this is the case. That is his way, it is his nature, if you will. It is the way in which he was constructed. People are different, of course this is the case. Different things engage them. That is clear. For one oysters are a delicacy, for another they are grotesque. There is no accounting for this, for individual taste. If Semples were to take those clothes from you, to rip them coarsely from the smooth warmth of your body and leave you entirely naked and shaking but still tied and bound as you are. Of course he'd have to cut the clothes from you in order to do that, and you would...well, there will be a struggle naturally, a violent struggle. It is to be expected. Perhaps also some blood. You do not wish to be stripped naked before us and so you will rightly struggle for all you are worth, and from what little I have seen, I estimate you to be worth quite a lot, and Semples here, he wishes that very much—for you to be stripped quite bare—is that not the true nature of your feelings, Semples?"

I slapped him on the thigh then to gauge the measure of him. It was my role, you see. The arranger. An orchestrator of the inevitable, if you will. If there was a chance, which certainly seemed to be the

[196]

case, that Semples might need assistance or inspiration for his upcoming role, it fell to me to do the work required. Which I set out to do with a certain gusto. It was the nature of my creative urges that made me do so.

"It is. My dear, your hypothetical struggling is of no matter to him—in fact he will relish it. He is relishing it right now, aren't you, my friend, even before it has begun? My dear, you can sense that in the way he is now breathing and in the way he is looking at you right now. Well, look at her, Semples. How my mere description of the events soon to come is arousing him. And of course you will struggle but in the end he will be successful. The victor, if you will. Of course I will assist the matter if need be, but only if necessary. I will hold you, for example, while he rips the cloth from you. We will do this together, Semples. My girl, I will hold back your arms for him as he rips those clothes from your body and exposes you to the both of us. You seem quite strong, but in the end your clothes will be removed from you and the ropes will remain intact, for as long as necessary or desired. Semples here is known for endurance, is that not so, Semples? My dear, he can exert himself in the physical act for some time prior to spending himself, as they say. For some considerable time."

Well, I knew this to be the case from our morning diversions but I certainly had my doubts regarding what was likely to ensue when this pump priming of mine reached its logical conclusion, given the recent disappointments we both had faced in that regard. So I may have let my hand slip to the matter at hand, just to be certain, you understand.

"In fact I have witnessed him labouring over the act for many, many minutes before taking his own pleasure. Perhaps for penetration we will unbind you at the ankles and I will be forced to hold your legs open to allow Mr. Semples entry to you."

There was no longer any point in keeping names a secret as the wheels of the unavoidable were now being set into motion.

"To open the door for him, so to speak. Or perhaps I might remove the rag for a time so that your mouth too is accessible for him. I would feel compelled to hold it open for his pleasure. Somewhat dangerous, but intriguing nonetheless. At this point though, certain strictures might be placed...the use of an assistive device designed for the same purpose...or certain threats, certain promises that might be brought to bear. But we get ahead of ourselves here. There is much to be appreciated first just in the direct fact of her being naked, is there not, Semples? Much enjoyment there. Her soft skin, it responds to the air on it. The breasts...her nipples. The previously hidden parts of her becoming known. The darker parts of her too. The efforts to cover herself entirely wasted, for there is no way she will be able to do so effectively. She will squirm to cover herself. But there is nothing to cover herself with. Now that is a word: squirm. Imagine how she squirms ...her small body under your weight, trying in vain to protect herself from you. Sometimes a mere word or sentence may arouse, eh, Semples? But words are just words. The thing itself...ah. Her little hands bound directly behind her so that her musty triangle is open for us and there is nothing then that she is able to do to protect herself from our gaze, or from your touch, eh? Oh, perhaps she might attempt to roll and hide it by pushing it to the floor of the wagon but that would succeed only in exposing to us, to you, what I would imagine to be her quite excellently proportioned ass. Right up to you. Bring your face right down to it. Imagine that. Her bare pure white rump upturned for you, flushed, perhaps it is quivering, through the fact of her certain fear, no doubt, but also simply by way of its proportions, which appear to me nicely generous. Imagine that, Semples: quivering. And her movements will shake it for you as well. She is trying to crawl across the wagon to a corner as best she can, bound as she is, and this naturally lifts her pretty cherry up toward you as she lurches and falls, then raises it up again as she takes another movement away from you. This angers you. But it delights you as well. Her flower peeking out at you from between her legs as she moves."

You see, Billy, it is in my nature to polish and embellish. The better the story, the greater the effect is my feeling. And I could tell that this *particular tale was having an effect on my associate. I could feel that quite plainly in my hand as I squeezed and relaxed. The required effect. I had my work to do, you see? My work was before me.*

"At this point, Semples, your member is fully enflamed by the sight of her fleshy rump, just as it is now, as that rump moves and quivers, of course it is, and that glimpse of her little quim riding there underneath it, and you are distended fully now, you know you are and so you pull your big cock out of those filthy trousers and you move toward her with it leading the way, as if on parade. As if at the head of a parade that you follow, Semples! At this point it's really just a cock with you attached to it. You drop your pants even. Oh, it is a very large cock, my dear, I can assure you of that, larger than any you have seen yet, I am sure, if you have seen any at all. Tell me, sweet, have you? Seen a man with a blood-full cock coming toward you? His cock angered and stretching out at you? I doubt that you have. And it being anxious to fill up all your little holes? Every sweet soft little part of you that it can enter? Every warm place it can push itself into harder and harder until it...well...I can smell her now, Semples, can you? Harder and harder and more until it... Well, all that will be soon enough. Eh, Semples? Soon enough, to be sure..."

The sun was at its zenith.

"The day is a hot one, to be sure! I am perspiring now. Are you two?"

Again silence.

"Mr. Semples, you are as quiet as our little guest here... Let us have another song from you for now. Sing something for us to better pass the time. Do."

You see what I mean, Billy? A distasteful story, yes, very probably, very probably. But artfully told and necessary. To prime the pump, as I say, do you see? Since my associate seemed to need the help. It is in the nature of a true artist to be charitable in nature to his associates. Let me put it this way: as Semples seemed less than the ideal painter I imagined him to be when under pressure, it became my role to provide the brushes, if you take my meaning, such as I could. I would

[199]

start now and keep on priming until the decisive moment so that we might enjoy the maximum effect of his efforts at the task. Shoulder to the wheel, as it were. I was like a general marshalling his forces for battle. All hands on deck. Whatever it would take is what I would do. If the moment came and I was called into manual service even during the act itself. A true artist does not question his role in creation—he performs it. Whatever it would take...I would do. If any part of my work is to be told, then the whole of it must be told in full. I would tickle away and tickle away at the problem until it ceased to be problematic. It was my work, you see. Any man's cock just needs the proper inspiration. After all, we are not dumb animals.

↤ **33** ↦

*I*am here with you, Turner. I am. Maybe there is nothing that I can do for you now, but I am here and I will stay.

ꙮ 34 ꙮ

There are some hills there. They look close. They are very far away. That is how it is in the desert.

"Look, we might as well just go back and get the Wings now."

"Yes."

"You wanted to deliver two bodies to them, I know that." Joseph looks around as if someone might be listening to us. Who would be listening here? Who would care in the least about what he's saying, even if they could hear? "But she wants to have a hand in this herself, you know, and not just be handed the outcome of it like some flowered Easter basket all wrapped up with a ribbon."

"You're right."

"Well then..."

"We'll go back."

"That is the sensible course. I believe that is the thing to do."

"The horses could use some water, so could I," the kid says.

"We'll get the wagon and our supplies and we'll get the Wings and we'll track those two bastards. It won't be the first time we've done such a thing. We're pretty good at it, if you recall."

He is right about Turner. She is not the type of girl to want this thing just handed to her, I do not know why I persist in acting as if that is the case when it is clear to everyone including me that it is not. I suppose it is not unreasonable to expect that it is something she expects. For her to be the one to kill the men who killed her sister, I mean. It's not an unreasonable thing at all for her to want. I was being foolish. I have been foolish for a time now.

"Let's go then," I say.

"We'll reach Las Cruces again by midday," Joseph says as we ride back through the gap we have been surveying through the dawn. "That is, if we don't meet them on their way to us…I do not imagine they have slept in and enjoyed a leisurely breakfast…their alcohol intake last night notwithstanding…"

Making sense is something that Joseph just does naturally, at least most of the time, I will give him that. Like combing his hair. He's doing it now—making sense, I mean, not combing his hair, and damn him for it. I know he means well. I have been foolish. And that may well continue to be the case, I cannot say for certain. I have a thought now of a woman once in a house in Cedro, and her wide hips and the thin mattress and the broad plank floor beneath it. A small gold necklace. A cathouse and someone had scrawled charcoal on the wallpaper in the hallway: two nipples and a scribbled-in cleft of hair. I remember her nice and familiar smile and the sounds of her washing. Lamplight. Cold. In the darkened parlour downstairs a line of sitting Mexicans and cowpunchers, and one young kid carving at a plain white stick with a pocketknife, a glass of whisky, and then the smell of woodsmoke rising up in the crisp cold of the night air when I step out onto the porch.

A man comes up to me and he says: "Are you who I think you are?"

And I just look at him. You are always at a disadvantage when people know you who you don't know seem to know.

"Fella inside of there just told me you're Billy the Kid." He takes off his hat and starts to fan himself.

And I shoot him.

Nobody needs to fan themselves when it's a cold night. His other hand was reaching for his gun just so he could be the man who outdrew Ol' Billy and he thought he'd maybe distract me with that hat trick of his. I watch him crawl back on his belly

[203]

into the room full of Mexicans and cowpunchers where he dies right there in the middle of the floor. And nobody moves to help him. The kid with the pocketknife is gone now and everyone looks up at me and no one says a thing. Not a thing. I lay a silver dollar on the table by the door to excuse the mess and I walk on out of there. The way a gun feels in your hand just after it's been used. The look in his eyes just before he reached for his. People will tell you everything you need to know just by looking at you.

"Seems to me the Wings must already be on the trail," the kid says.

"Ah, hold yer mud," Joseph tells him, cutting me off, not the kid. He knows he's cutting me off from saying something that needs not be said to someone who's not listening anyway. "Course they're already on the trail, you think they're gonna hang around that hotel waiting for someone to tell them what's going on or what to do? They don't strike me as the type, neither one of them. We'll see 'em soon enough. Baghead and the little girl."

Little girl.

Fuck you, Joseph.

"There," I say, raising my arm to indicate the speck that is their wagon coming over a rise way off in the distance, "that's them, just as you said it."

"You sure?"

"I'm sure."

"Pretty far away."

"I'm sure though."

I once knew a man name of Stubby Bob. He had two arms and two legs, all regular size too, and he had all his fingers. At first you wondered how he got his name and then you counted the fingers, the arms, the legs: all there. Then you figured it. And you figured out too the reason he hated his name. And that's just the way it is with Wing coming over the ridge. You can't tell what's wrong at first. But then you can.

"She must be inside the wagon," the kid says.

"There's her horse there," Joseph says.

We pick up the pace to meet up with him on the flat land, and as we all pull up Wing says, "Where is she?"

And then we all know what we already all knew. What I already knew. I just didn't want to be the one to say it. Truth be told, I suppose I did not want to be the one to think it and so it seems I have been even more foolish. There are thoughts you do not let yourself think. More foolishness. And I'm glad he's got a bag over his head so that I cannot see his face.

"She ain't with us," I say, and I hear my voice saying those words all even and flat. I'm still waiting for her to come out of the wagon even though I know now there is not a chance in hell that she is going to do so. The sun is up fully now and the sky is blue, but you know putting a dress on a dog, well, that don't make it into a woman. I was not feeling good already and now I feel about as low as cat piss. I can feel, not see, the blood draining out of his face, and then out of mine. I feel my own hands go cold slowly. She is with them. They have her. There is no other place for her to be. Now it is real.

❧ 35 ❧

When I was very young I was out walking alone in the dark and I got touched by lightning. I never told anyone about this. It hit the black earth right down by my feet and it danced and flashed around me in a bright blue-and-yellow circle and I have not been able to stop moving ever since that day; even when I am at rest I am moving and twitching. When I was about seven we lived in a rooming house with mostly poor immigrants who were good but quiet people and who kept to themselves and also with some other people who were not immigrants and who were loud and of no good account at all. There was a man who lived there who never left his room except for meals, which we all took together downstairs in the dining room. He never spoke. He tore his bread up into small pieces and chewed them with great concentration. He always wore a thin little vest with silk in the front of it and cotton in the back and a belt with a big silver buckle that looked like it cost him some money. What his story was no one knew, but one day his door was open and I was wandering the hall looking for someone or something to tell me what to do in my life and I recall pushing at it, the door, just to swing it open a bit so I could see what he was doing in there. There was nothing in there but a bed and a rug. Then I notice the closet door open so I go on into the room to see more. I don't know what I was looking for—a reason a man like him would live all on his own like that, I suppose. I didn't understand why he would go on living when all he had was that vest and that belt buckle. I guess neither did he because there he is hanging dead from the bar in the closet, that belt around his neck and his face all swollen up blue and red. Something like that, you see it when you're a kid and it sticks with you. His eyes rolled up in his head like he is saying he is sorry for something he has done, maybe for doing this. I stand there for a very long time, and neither one of us moves, and then there is a clicking sound from his throat and I take off and out of there like a cat on fire. The pounding of my feet on the stairs, and I hear someone call, *"Who's making that racket?"* as I am on my way out the front door. I run down the alley until I just can't run anymore. I don't even know where I am and I have to ask people how to get back to my street.

"What are you doin' lost?" they ask.

"What's wrong with you, boy?"

"You get on home."

Fear should not make you lose track of what is going on around you or of anything else either. But sometimes it does.

"You remember anything about when you were a kid? You remember anything about our parents?" I once asked Joseph.

He looked across the room at nothing for a while. Then: "I remember times at night when he came home drunk and wanted to fuck her and he'd say, *'Brace yourself, woman.'* That is something that I remember." He kept looking across the room; I couldn't tell if he was looking at anything at all. "But I'm sorry," he said, "if that's not the sunny picnic you were looking for."

I wasn't looking for any picnic. I was looking for something to hold on to other than what I had, which wasn't much.

I feel like a bent nickel. I want her like she's a bakery and I'm a starving man, but it is not just that. It is not just that wanting. It is not even that. I want to look after her more than I want to be in bed with her. I want her to be okay. Even if that means not fucking me. Especially if that means not fucking me. I don't know what this is. But I guess I don't have to understand it, do I? Everything is a crap shoot, I guess, and so I'm just lucky to be passed the dice. I care about her in some way I am not familiar with. So I'm not looking for fried chicken in a basket and a blanket, Joseph. I'm just looking for the sky not to fall on me.

"Just where do you believe her to be?" Joseph wants to know.

"I know where she is, that's why I'm not sleeping."

"Why aren't you riding then?"

"Don't know where to ride to."

"I suppose that's so."

"Not yet anyway."

"How do you think she—"

"She put herself there."

"You think—"

"It's the only way, Joseph."

"Not the only way."

"They had no time to take her."

"I suppose that's so too." Joseph gets up to stir a bit at the fire.

"She got up and she hid inside of there to kill them. Off on her own, like me. For all we know, she might already have killed them," I tell him.

"And the reverse may be true as well."

"It may."

Sparks in the air.

But fuck you, Joseph. Fuck you for saying that. It didn't need saying. She is a sight to see in this world and I hope I might see her again. Eventually Joseph falls asleep just sitting there against his saddle and bags. I won't sleep tonight. Soon the sky will burn pink.

ঔ 36 ৯

"There's lots of words you don't want to hear in this life, and I understand that."

I tried to teach as I journeyed through my life, Billy. It was my vocation. The vast majority of people seemed to know so little. Semples was a fine example of that. The girl, I don't know. She seemed smart enough, I suppose. But young. I never truly had the chance to know her before... Well, you know what happened as well as I do.

Eggs on the trail are rare and a fine thing to have, as you would also know. It is a propensity of delicate things to break. Breaking into pieces is in their nature and it is hard to keep them safe. The little things keep shattering. Unless you carry the hen with you, well, there's no way in heaven nor in hell you are going to have an egg in the morning unless you lay it yourself.

"Death," I said. "There is one word most people would care to avoid."

"Everyone in the house died in the fire," I said.

"That's a whole sentence that's an example of words you don't want to hear."

It was often necessary to clarify what I said for my audiences.

"Even the babies.

"That's two sentences.

"The eggs are burnt.

"And that's three. And three...is a significant number. Biblically and every other way. Three is a number of weight and of girth. A ponderous number. Heavily weighted down with the baggage we place on it. And look at us—we are three as we sit here. Think about that for a moment."

The girl was silent again.

"No one talking but me? Don't think about it then. It does not make any difference to me what you think about.

"And luckily for us these eggs are not actually burnt. It was a close thing though. Close. Close. An egg for you, Semples?"

"Yeah, I'll take one."

"And you? Turner? Mind if I call you by your Christian? No?

"You have not much to say this morning it seems. The rag is gone now—you may speak freely.

"No? Nothing?

"But you'll take an egg, yes?

"Good girl.

"Good girl.

"Good _girl_.

"You see? That's three. You repeat something three times successively and it just becomes all the more true.

"It is a fine day.

"It is a fine day.

"It is a _fine_ day.

"And so it shall be. So it shall.

"Now, don't take an egg and just squint at it like it's a turd, girl.

"An egg on the trail is a rare thing.

"You may never see one again.

"You may never see a lot of things again."

I looked directly at her so she would take my meaning.

"May never see anything again.

"Best be grateful for the day and its gifts.

"These good people here no longer have that chance."

Their wagon smouldering.

The man.

His hand outreached into the sand, grasping at something he no longer had, will never have. A pistol there. His little boy, hunched against a big wooden wheel, his eyes white and wide. His mother naked. Tied against the wheel. Her belly stretched like catgut. And open. *Browning blood spreading down her legs like a gown. A thickening sticky pool of it. Smoke rose up into the air. The loose hen was clucking. Wandering.*

This girl. Turner.

Staring.

Silent.

But strong. She was strong.

Imagine, Billy, that a child walks toward a house somewhere. It is where he lived. Before everything changed on him.

He covers his face with his fingers.

I was that boy.

When you consider how long you are actually alive on the earth, everything else ceases to make any sense.

∽ 37 ∾

"There's smoke."

And sometimes fate just lifts up her skirt for us. Suddenly I can hear a beetle bug on a scrub bush fifty yards away.

"Joseph, there is smoke."

"Indeed."

We look at it rising up. It is maybe eight miles from where we are.

"Whoever it is, they'll be gone...by the time we get there."

"If they want to live, they will be."

"You don't know who it is."

"I do," I tell him.

Joseph just spits.

I do.

"Did you know that it's always rainin?" I ask him.

"What do you mean by that?"

"I mean there's always a thunderstorm goin' on somewhere in the world. Hundreds of them actually. And even on up past the clouds, even when there's no clouds up in the sky that we can see, way, way up. There's a storm goin' on there, thunder and lightning and all, just you can't see or hear it from down here."

"That right?"

The smoke is still rising, a finger smudge on the sky.

"There's a lot of shit goin' on we don't know about, Joseph."

Joseph spits again. "Fella in a bar tell you that?" he asks.

There's times I'm going to hit him and then I don't. I don't do it. "I read that in a book one time."

"What book?"

"A book called *My Brother Don't Know Everything.*"

Joseph smiles. "Don't believe I've read that one."

"Well, I thought you wrote it."

"Time's passing."

"Why don't you wake those two corncobs up and I'll ready the horses. I feel like maybe it's gonna be a real good day."

There won't be any big change in the world when I die. There'll be my boots, I guess someone will have to deal with those. And my guns.

It is said that my grandmother lost her mind and ended up talking to the walls. Some she would admonish and berate for not doing a good enough job, or for moving around the house while she slept. *"What are you doing here now?"* she'd ask. *"Goddamned fucking traitor!"* She carried a grudge against the ceiling too: *"Fuck's your idea?"* she would mutter under her breath. She mistrusted the floor. She whispered to surfaces and ran her fingertips all along them, looking for seams and hidden doors.

She could crack an egg just holding it over the pan and she never lost a yolk, a skill she had well into her eighties, even after she lost her appetite for eggs or for anything else. *"Dammit, Eileen, sit down and stop talkin' to things that can't hear ya,"* my grandfather said from the corner on his wooden stool, combing his long strings of white hair over and over. A kettle of tea on the wood stove all day long that boiled down to the thickness of molasses by the afternoon. After she passed he spoke of his loneliness and how he missed her complaining to the walls. *"I expect they're lonesome now too,"* he'd say. *"No one to talk to them…"*

He'd sit still in his corner, almost blind, listening and staring at God alone knows what. *"I didn't know she was in-sane when I married her. She was a drop of cool water to an aching tongue at that time, but I ended up carrying her most of her life."*

The wallpaper peeling and fading behind him as he sat. His

torn white shirt buttoned tight to the collar against his neck and his neck the colour and texture of lined and oiled leather, a man working hard against time and reading in his Bible about how the demons were cast into the swine and how the swine plummeted into the perilous killing waters below.

"*Them pigs got a raw deal of that, but then pigs usually do,*" he said.

We need to get on now. Time is passing. The desert mesa is no place for soft things or indecision.

ᕗ **38** ᕐ

*I*told Semples, I said don't be a man who draws a crowd, Semples, I told him that. That is the key. The key is to go unnoticed and be the man over there in the corner or the man on the stairs. The man over there behind that other man. The man who said nothing, and who left early, or who may not have even been there at all because no one remembers for certain. He may have worn a hat, but it is difficult to say.

Prominent killers get shot or they get arrested and then they get hanged, isn't that right, Billy? No one is more misunderstood or more at risk of being uncovered than a prominent killer. I am not claiming that this is not the state of things as they should be, you understand, just pointing out it is the way things are, or were, and it put me in awkward positions from time to time. So the preferable thing is to get away clean, simply because no one is even watching or aware. At least that is how it was when I was alive. Now that my state is, well, other than alive... Well, I am not yet certain... the desert was full of open space in which to hide if one knew how to make oneself scarce and somewhat hard to find. I do not feel there is anywhere to hide where I am now but then I suppose I do not really know very much about where I am now.

She was silent and still. Well, what else would she have been, given the circumstances? Young people are easily shocked by the things they have not yet seen when those things finally do come about before their eyes. They are at first surprised by the sudden true nature of the world before them, and then they acquiesce, some quickly, some more slowly, but eventually they all contribute to the mess of it themselves. That first time a child is struck by a parent. The hand that feeds also lashing out. That is simply the world and its way. I would imagine that the first time a lion cub sees a gazelle taken down it is surprised, and maybe horrified, but aroused too, aroused. Awakened.

I was a wild one at one time but I tapered myself down toward my end to the very marrow of things. I myself diminished physically but I guided others in the ways of the world and then I was able to and I took my own pleasure where I could manage to do so.

How my mother would cry out in the dark of night, "They're going to kill us all, they're going to kill all of us!"

She could never see where the real dangers were, she was too consumed by the darkness of her own mind to see what was standing right there in front of her, short and eager, a string for a belt and two hard small scrubbed pink hands. Me. The child me. She'd walk right past. An unkind love is no sort of love at all. Her dangers were real to her, of course. Everyone's own fears are perfectly valid, I know this as a fact due to my studies. In that way fear is egalitarian, it takes all comers, and seldom does it give up any ground. It is without mercy or restraint. Give it an inch, is that not the expression? I have been called by some a hard man. Mostly it is by soft men that I have been called this. Let me tell you something: you either find your place in this world or you will be assigned one by others. This is grim advice, but it is accurate. You want a fairer deal? Do you want to get someplace better? You can't get there from where you are. Not by any straight path nor crooked.

I looked after my mother in ways that she had failed or had refused to look after me. It was not her fault. She was weak. And I was not. That is all of it in its plain simplicity. I have not found her here. I have not been able to find anyone here where I am now. If I, with my intuition about people and environments, am unable to find anyone in the state in which I find myself now, then I believe it is safe to assume that after death we are all alone. That suits me. No one coming after me here then. I was alone in life and I am accustomed to it.

My advice to you is to eat fresh peaches whenever you can find them, Billy. They are delightful and rare and good for you too. Time is short. I feel that you would not have liked me, Billy, if we had been provided the chance to get to know one another. Few have and we are too much alike. Can you feel these thoughts of mine, Billy? We are alike. You and I. There are times when a fine piece of music can make you forget for a time that life is just a stinking dark hole.

And there are so many pretty women.

Sometimes too there is something that happens that you do not expect. Sometimes you take a swerve in life. Well, I guess I'm the swervingest son of a bitch you ever met. A big dog howling at nothing at all. Broken. But appreciative of at least some things given. Some things presented along the way. Some people understand what's going on in the world and most do not have even an inkling. And they never will.

So the great minds are always alone.

Turner was very quiet in the short time I knew her.

You hear me now, Billy? We are alike, you and I. We can make wondrous and horrible things happen. It is our work. We are the same. Listen to me. I will keep on talking until you hear me.

We are the same.

What you did to me, Billy, it tied us together, you see?

❧ 39 ❧

"Kid…"

"Call me Chase."

"Kid…"

"Yeah, Billy?"

"Pass me that Winchester."

"You see something, Billy?"

❧ **40** ❧

"Yeah."

৩ **41** ৩

The long gun will get you sighted in better at a distance than the pistol will. I tend to shoot from the gut without a whole lot of time spent setting things up, even when there's time to set things up, and that works well for me in most applications, at least with a pistol it does. Read the old papers and they will tell you all about that. But after a certain distance the pistol is of no use at all. And I admit that after a certain distance neither am I.

So I miss the shot.

And then we start riding just like hell in the direction of the bullet, chasing after it with me feeling like a wolf lost in the burnt trees after a forest fire. I feel desperate. Like all Ten Commandments are coming down onto my head at once and I can't ride fast enough to get out from under them all.

"William, why did you take that shot?"

I don't know.

You see? Desperate.

Which is a weakness.

I admit that. I don't know.

No. That's a lie. I know all too well.

Turner. Turner is why I took the shot.

৫১ **42** ৫৬

*I*am certain now that I am alone here. I am alone here. So I will keep
on telling you this story, Billy.

The Good Lord and his horrible painful vengeance... He never
seemed to be around at all. But you were, Billy, and also your rifle.
Back then it was you just setting about to do the Lord's own work for
him. You, attempting to exact the Lord's own vengeance. Except you
missed me that time, you cocksucker.

"Give it some leather, Semples!" I yelled to him. "They are upon
us now!"

"Yeah, Captain, but they ain't close enough to hit us yet from what
it looks like."

"Never you mind, they will be, and they aren't hauling a wagon,
so they'll have the advantage. Just be to your business. I'll see to the
girl," I told him.

"When you say you'll see to the girl, you mean..." He was always
a suspicious and a jealous man, his loyalty to me aside.

"I mean that I will see to it that she's safe, Semples...well secured.
Out of harm's way for the moment. We don't want her hit by a stray
bullet. It would...lower the body temperature..."

"Just don't be protectin' her by throwin' yourself down on top of
her, that's all."

"Blame all of my faults on a heart that knows no boundaries,
Semples..."

"What the hell does that even mean?"

Sometimes I believe I could have carved a better compatriot out of
a pine branch. He had a certain loyalty but he had absolutely no
wisdom. He believed he knew things that he did not know. And he

drank more than was wise. Horrible clear liquor that he made himself and that would take the hair off a wooden leg. There's no accounting for the tastes of a simpleton. He had some bark on him but he was still a twisted little monkey.

"They're shootin' at us again, Captain!"

"Yes, Semples, I both hear and see that. Faster. But look over there."

"What?"

"There. Our salvation."

Coming through a cut pass below and to the east was the head of a wagon train. Simple pilgrims crossing the bleached and stranded desert listening intently for God's word and in search of God's graces was my guess. Searching for manna in the desert, farmers heading west to the promised land.

Which I was happy to be able to provide for them.

"How are a bunch of dirt farmers going to help us any, Captain?"

"All farmers are lovers of the Lord, Mr. Semples."

"Well, do we happen to have Him with us? 'Cause maybe you can haul Him on out from under that canvas for them to see Him 'cause it looks to me like we're runnin' real hard between two pretty bad places. And all we got in there to show 'em right now is a tied-up little girl. And I don't think they're gonna like that. Farmers is family people."

"Who will these people be more likely to listen to, Semples? A preacher of the Good News of the Redeeming Blood of Jesus Christ such as myself or an outlaw and a man with a bag over his head who are plainly shooting at that same preacher?"

"There's only one problem with that, Preacher. This girl ain't gonna see things your way. She'll tell 'em the way that things really are. And people always believe girls more than people like us."

"Oh no, Semples. We have to kill the girl. And soon. Right now, in fact. The plan has changed. She cannot enter into this equation. We have to kill the girl right now."

Look, Billy, I hate digressions at crucial moments as much as the next man, but have you ever noticed that you only really see what's happening in your own life when you look back at it? And also that you only ever get to move forward in it? Your life, I mean. Imagine if you got to move back after you had looked forward. I believe that many things would change. I would have changed a thing or two about what is to come next here in this story of mine, I can assure you of that. It would be a different picture altogether. But, well, we are stuck with things the way they occurred and that is that. I'll tell you them now as close as I can get to what happened, the parts of it that you do not already know.

As soon as I stepped back under that wagon canvas, the girl head-butted me so hard in the stomach that we both went sprawling. But soon enough I gained the upper hand and had her arms pinned from behind on the floor of the wagon and with that ball-and-cloth contraption holding her mouth tight again she was not able to yell or scream.

"Well, what in the hell's going on back there?" Semples called out.

"Nothing at all," I yelled.

I was holding her tight with my arms around her like the staves on a barrel, both of us on the floor of the wagon. And all of a sudden with her ass pushed back against me like that and me on top of her and her struggling and twitching the way that she was, something just started to happen itself into existence. Something that hadn't done so in about twenty years.

"Hell, sister, you sure got some ass on you," I whispered into her yellow hair while we rolled around on the floor.

It didn't take much fiddling to get my suddenly and surprisingly alive cock out of my pants (I tell you, Billy, it was a resurrection, can you hear me? A resurrection! Nobody could be as surprised and pleased as I was at that moment!) but it was certainly a harder proposition to get it up inside of her with her legs kicking the way they were. This girl was a hellfire fighter, and she was not just some dime-store lusty bitch, the kind that turns your head coming out of the dry-goods store all hem and seam and haughtiness. Or the kind that would have lain

[223]

herself down for the price of a bottle of whisky. This girl was "Tie me down if you want to fuck me because it ain't gonna happen any other way" and putting it into her by force was for certain going to be taking a chance. But it was a chance I was more than willing to take as I had not fully partaken of the game directly in, as I say, about two decades. Well, I thought that was more than time enough. Our small struggle had dislodged the cloth from her mouth and she was now using the foulest of language. I disparage the use of gutter language by women. Normally. It is unbecoming. Normally. You must understand, Billy. This girl was an opportunity for me. One I felt I had to seize at that moment or forever lose.

And again, not to digress, but have you noticed how it is that the openings in the body are where sensation is centralized? And that all of them are equally capable of both pleasure and pain? Let me itemize them for you, top to bottom. The immediate situation itself will not wait, but the telling of these facts, well, I need to say them to you now.

From the top of the head on down then.

The hair follicles. Granted perhaps these are not openings in the truest sense, but first let us concede the entire human body is porous so if we take that fact as a starting point and we say that anything bigger than, say, a pore is an opening, then yes, I believe we can say a follicle is an opening. So let us start there. You have, no doubt, experienced the running of your own or someone else's fingernails across your scalp. It is a very pleasant sensation. Particularly if you possess, as I do, skin of a drier nature. The pleasure derived can be quite intense. By contrast, if I were to pull out each hair individually you would undoubtedly lose your mind from the repeated painful extraction prior to losing all your hair. Or if I were to grab a swath of it, as I am doing to young Turner's bright blond hair right now, wrapping it in my fist…and…pull. With all my strength, pull, until it comes free in my hand like a brilliant yellow scarf with a bright red trimmed edge to it at the end—well, then you would cry out.

As Turner did.

"Are you fuckin' her ass in there? Are you?"

"Semples, I am not."

"Well, you are, I can hear you clear, you are!"

"She won't let me, dammit. That is the sound of her not letting me fuck her in the ass or anywhere else!"

And just as I said this, two things occurred simultaneously: another shot rang out and I didn't know now if you had closed the gap substantially, Billy, or if Semples had opened up a defensive barrage, and, concurrent to this shot, young Turner took hold of the soft flesh between my thumb and index finger with her teeth and she bit down hard.

"Bitch!"

The next point we reach on our travels would be either the ears or the eyes.

If you are unaware of your facts, the eyes and ears are placed on a horizontal line that bisects the head precisely at the halfway point. Most people think they are placed higher on the head. But they are not. They are in the middle, halfway up, halfway down. That's the way of it. Now the ears. They are our receivers. Let's take music. They are the receivers of music. I don't know what type of music you enjoy, Billy. It's of no matter. Whatever that music is. Perhaps your lover's voice. Birdsong. Water in a stream. Something that you like, whatever it is that you may enjoy hearing. Or. Here. Let me explain it this way: when you have an itch in your ear, perhaps some wax build-up causes it. Something in there. You find the spot with your little finger and you get relief. Satisfaction. You see what I mean? Pleasure. But place something else in there rather than your little finger. An ice pick, for example, or a straight pin. Shake that around in there. Push it all the way in hard. See? Pleasure and pain. All in the same place.

Or the eyes. All the visual beauty you have ever bothered to notice was communicated right there. But say I placed both of my thumbs into them and I pressed, as I was doing to Turner's eyes then. You might yell. As she did. Then scream. As she did. I don't know that you would drive your knee into the testicles of the man assaulting you but she did. And good for her, I say now. But it did not occur to me to say it then.

Let us move further on down still: the vagina and the eye of the cock. The anus. Our last three stops on the tour. And with one good strike across her little face, we were about to bring all three of these areas together with some force. She fought weaker with a broken nose but still she fought. But to no effect. Finally her legs were bare, the flesh on them shook, and I managed to get them open with my hands locked upon her ankles. I pushed them right up, crushing them against her little tits, the smooth pale flesh of her thighs against me, the soft mounds on either side of her dark treasure and my cock harder and hotter than fresh-forged metal. Ready to hit home and that home looking so very nice and so very inviting to me.

Nicely. Nicely.

Some men play the banjo.

Unbelievable.

The time that's wasted when it could be spent...putting this, into that...like this.

Now. Just like th—

ᥫᩣ **43** ᥫᩣ

A .45 calibre bullet can travel at speeds exceeding twelve hundred feet per second, which is too fast for its victim to yell or plead or duck, or even to be aware of what has happened. The bullet's entrance into the skull makes a quick and unholy mess of everything inside of it. Like gutting a cat. As a souvenir of the opening, a circular hole is formed, rimmed with scorched skin. And distance too: the closer the gun is to the head, the more the gun's smoke and powder could burn the flesh. Blood in a close head wound is expelled first almost as a powder or a fine dust and then a dark river follows. Darker than you would expect, almost like a melted chocolate stream. Always a shock to see. Blood is always a surprise. But enough about the outside: the real work happens deeper. The tissues are split open just before the bullet drives on into the brain itself. The fluid there serves as a temporary barrier. Lasts a shorter time than time can record. The bullet goes through the brain now faster than the speed that makes tissues tear. It stretches them beyond their breaking point. A bullet going at a thousand feet per second will be back out of the body before the tissues even have a chance to rip. There is not much that medicine knows about how the brain functions, but it is known that a .45 calibre bullet at close range stops it cold from doing anything at all. The ability to think is gone by the time the bullet shoves its way through the front of the brain. Behind it, a long temporary hole is left. Everything fills now with blood. The blood takes over. The brain is dealing with a lake, an ocean. A flood.

It cannot live. Then the hole itself collapses on itself.

If the shot was to the heart it would take ten or fifteen seconds for the brain to stop. In that time the man could draw his gun, maybe say some last words, or spend some time thinking about his unfortunate situation. But a shot to the brain is different. The brain stops right away. Just a second and it is over, the universe ends. I sometimes have wondered what the brain thinks as a bullet travels through it… A question? A mixed-up picture of what the eyes are no longer even seeing? A sudden light?

He falls forward. Of course. I don't like the idea of shooting a man from behind and I have never done so. Until now. Time is of the essence here, as they say. It seems like an appropriate time to shoot someone from behind. I had thought my jumping onto the wagon would have alerted him to my presence, but his mind must have been on other matters. And now his mind is on the floorboards and the canvas of the wagon. And on Turner. Along with other parts of him.

I help to push him off.

The book I read in the library, where I got most of this information about bullets to the head and the effects of, said that most revolvers miss their intended target.

Well, not today.

There's a moment when the body has not yet figured out what has just happened. Then it just gives up and it falls. Like a tree. There is no longer anything else for it to do.

It has ceased to be of use.

You have a gun and you know what to do with it and once in a while you can pretty much do whatever you want. I'm not saying that killing another man feels good. Oh hell, yes I am. There are times it really just does.

"You alright, Turner?"

And she up and spits her own blood right onto him, right into what's left of his fat face.

So. I guess that she is.

The toys I played with as a child—a tin gun and a cloth horse. They're my actual life now. How do you know when you're going to die? Well, you don't.

So be ready for it all the time is my view about it. The wind on the grass in the summer.

It won't always be there.

"Billy the Kid is dead. That is all anyone needs to know about the Kid."

Pat Garrett said that.

But there are no facts in the desert. There is just the desert itself. That is the only fact that it holds.

⤨ **44** ⤩

There are moments when there is so much pain in the mind that the body can no longer hold it all. But then there's nowhere else for it to go. But Turner, my sister, this world does keep on turning. And I have learned that. There's no end to the dark of it but you can't let that be everything. And you can't carry everything with you, it is not yours to carry. So keep going. Turner, it's not over yet. Do not think that it's over. And don't be weak. You've never been weak. Don't be weak now. I know you think it's time now that you can rest because it is over. But you can't. And it's not. It will be a long time before you can lie down. You think you know things that you don't know. You don't know them yet.

Keep going.

And thank you for looking out for me even though I am gone now. You are a strong girl.

You are so strong.

Being dead doesn't really help you to understand anything at all, it is just like being alive in that way, so you may as well just stay alive as long as you can. The real ghosts are the things the living carry with them. They carry things they cannot lay down. Turner, keep on living. My hands-on days are over now, at least they are in your world, and bones don't talk, not so that anyone can hear them, but maybe you can feel me here. If only I could hold you now. Someone should hold you now. Someone should see how precious you are. Someone should promise you something and they should mean it, Turner, and they should keep that promise. That is not too much to ask. Your day will fill with small things. Flowers on the table. The sun on your hands. Clean sheets. The moon, Turner. And the stars.

Lay down under them. And look, Turner...listen.

Hear.

Feel me.

I'll keep you close.

Whatever I can do.

And I am learning how things work here now. I am learning what I can do. What I will do here. I don't suppose there is any way I can describe my situation to you in a manner that would make any sense to you and you cannot really hear me anyway. If I just keep talking and saying the same thing to you like I love you, Turner, I love you, Turner, I love you, *then I think maybe you could feel that somehow but I wish there were more I could get through to you, but as I say, it would be like trying to describe a rose to someone who has never seen a rose and what then would I say about it? It is red. It has petals. It smells. It would be like trying to... Well, I don't know what I can compare this to, there is nothing. Imagine that I am in a room, though I am not, and that there is a window, which there isn't, and beyond that window there is a field, though really there is no such thing. But if there were such a window and such a field, Turner, then I could look through it and I could see a man walking. He has just arrived in this land and he knows no one here. He does not see me here in my window watching him. He does not know where he is or what will happen next.*

He is the same man who just tried to rape you, Turner. And he is here now. And he does not know what will happen next.

But I do.

ᥱᴄᴏ **45** ᴄᴏᴗ

"I don't believe a word of it."

"Well, I don't suppose I can blame you any for that. It's a six-foot-tall tale and no doubt."

"And how do I know that dead man over there was fixing to do what you say he was fixing to do to that girl?"

"Ask?"

"I would ask him but he's dead now, isn't he? That bullet through the centre of his head seems to have slowed down his ability to say much."

"I meant ask her."

But such an idea seems to be lost on Harold J. Putnam. He's like a dog digging at a hole that doesn't go anywhere. I don't know if you have thoughts about any of this, but folks in the city they have spent no small amount of time and a good deal of ingenious effort in distancing themselves from their own shit. They have devised various means of disposing of it in such a manner that they do not have to confront it and my feeling is that this is a mistake. Dealing with your own shit helps to root you to the place you are in and it also roots you to yourself. Having your own shit disappear as soon as it leaves you is an artificial thing, as if you are trying to hide it in order to lie about some vital aspect of yourself. It is a part of who we are and people in the modern world of city living want to deny that. But they cannot, in spite of all their vain efforts. The further we get from our shit, the further we get from ourselves—that is how it seems to me. The denial of something true about yourself is the shortest road to perdition. This strikes me as something that is true of this Harold J. Putnam. Like he has never even seen his own shit, let alone had to deal with it. He is of the type to let it get onto others, all the while saying, *"What is that on you? What have you done?"* Indoor plumbing is a dangerous thing, that is my thinking. And Putnam doesn't even have it. So it is like he carries his old shit around in an iron lockbox and if you were to ask him about it he would say, *"What box?"* I don't trust people who think they are clean. No one is clean, and this man Putnam seems to me just as slippery as two eels fucking in a bucket of chicken stew.

Why spend any time at all with this cloth patch outfit is what Joseph wants to know. Well, I tell him: time. Time and numbers, and maybe bait. That broke-down slope-eyed wheel of a man who was travelling with that sonofabitch I shot earlier, he is either on a straight line away from here just as fast as he can travel or he's lying down and waiting for a chance to come back at us, and my hunch is that it's the latter. My gut says to give it to him—to give him just that chance. Of course, I might be mistaken, and if that's the case then the worst we'll have to show for my error in planning is one less dead body and quite a few nights of beans and pork and biscuits by the fire before we have to turn and head north to this place Joseph has us going to. Plus, I have no need to travel any further with old baghead, I bear no affection for him at all and the kid is not growing on me anymore, and maybe they can join this wagon train and that way unjoin us, particularly as I do not see that we need them in any way. Of course, Turner would be free to choose in which direction she herself wants to go, she is her own woman. I suppose there's no separating a girl and her daddy though, of course there's not, bag or no bag. Well. Maybe that's for the best. Now, as to exactly why that shit heel is out there somewhere in the desert at present instead of wrapped in a blood-soaked blanket over there on the ground like his friend, well, that's another story and I'll get to that.

"Well then, you've got to give him a proper Christian burial."
That's Putnam talking.

"Go ahead and dig any size hole you want." That's me.

"What my brother means…" That's Joseph.

"Go ahead, Joseph, tell 'em what I mean." That's me again.

"Listen to me, we are God-fearing people." That's Mrs. Putnam throwing her dog into the fight. She seems just as simple as the cloth of her pilgrim's dress and I do not mean that in a pleasant way for I mean simple in the same way that I would mean stupid. Her Christian name is Sabbath. Sabbath Putnam. Who the fuck saddles their child with a name like Sabbath? It is worse than Ishmael.

"Well, you got every reason to be, ma'am, and I reckon we all do, but that don't mean I'm gonna go ahead and bother diggin' no hole for a man who just tried to rape this woman here…"

I have never been what you might call judicious in my words. I know the practical thing to say in most situations. I just don't say it. There's people dying all the time but that don't mean I necessarily have to be the one to make a hole for them to lie in. I don't have much interest in people's expectations for me nor the time to live up to them.

Don't know if I mentioned that this Putnam has a beard the size of large cat. And he moves his mouth all nervous so it looks all the time like he's chewing up a hairy watermelon. I haven't the time for that type of…*affectation* is, I believe, the right word. I understand the expediency of not shaving every day on the trail and truth be told I've never managed to grow much in the way of a facial brush anyway so I'm not in a position to judge anyone on that. But this extravagant growth strikes me as an indulgence. I just don't believe a man should take that much interest in his own appearance. And I can't tell whether this hump has decided to preen himself up like a rooster or he's just given up completely, but the shine and orderliness of the affair speaks to the former and suggests an expenditure of no small amount of time spent with combs and brushes and emollients of some sort. Either way, nothing about his appearance or his demeanour endears in any way him to me.

This world is a broken place, and one should get right with God is what I think. Whatever it is that God means to you, I mean. Something more than you is what I am referring to and not just the God of the old part of the book with his big white beard and his shimmering nightdress. You are nothing compared with whatever God might be, Mr. Putnam, so just stop the play-acting with the beard and you listen here: you can be a completely disagreeable son of a bitch if you like but I reserve the right to point it out to you in that case. I don't have the time or the patience for it. So here I am in this wagon, I mean here we are in the wagon: me, Joseph, the Putnams, Mr. and Mrs., and Turner and a dead man outside, him wrapped up in a blanket with two holes and fresh air in his head, and the kid, and Wing, sitting big as life with his burlapped head and both of them there on the outside of the canvas waiting around to see what happens next.

How did we all get here?

Well, this is how: right after this wipe of shit got his head opened up by me, I'm holding Turner close to me on the floor of the wagon because after she spit her blood into the man's face she was just there white-faced and staring, and holding on to her seemed like the thing to do then, so I just did it. So there I am and what I'm thinking is that someone is driving this goddamned wagon and so I have to leave Turner to go shoot the sonofabitch fast and I climb up there by the bench and there's nogoddamnedbody there. Which explains our erratic goddamned course. And this is the moment that the kid decides, I guess, to leap off his horse and into the back of the wagon and scare the bejeesus out of Turner and she screams and I'm thinking she's going to kill that sonofabitch before I can even get these horses stopped up and I'm thinking how I'm not exactly of a mind to stop her from doing that, what with me being, as I said, just a touch off of the kid, as it happens. I don't care, go ahead and shoot him, Turner, is what I'm thinking while I'm pulling on the reins and trying to get these horses stopped or even slowed down just a little bit but they're right spooked and they've got a mind to head straight on to California without stopping. And this is how we end up heading straight into the wagon train with me still trying to stop them horses and with a freshly baked dead man in the back and Turner trying to kill the kid and a man with a big sack over his head following up behind us. Can't say as I blame Joseph much for holding back a little while to see what would happen next.

And so this is how we meet Harold J. Putnam and his beard. And his wife. And her Bible. And the whole goddamned God-loving tribe. I really do not like these people. And I have a gun. I suppose I could just make it do what it does when I don't like people much, but that might be premature, especially as no one is trying particularly hard to kill me at the moment. Besides, Joseph would not approve. But Joseph does not fully understand the efficiencies of efficiency. He does not understand delicacy or what you might call finesse. He would say there are many things I may not understand either but I have not shot a man by accident, not in recent memory, and not in the last few days at any rate. Some things are more important to understand in this life than others. The correct pressure of your finger on the trigger of a Colt. That's very important. How to speak French—that's not. Unless you happen to be a Frenchman. Maybe I should give you an example of what I mean about understanding things.

One thing Joseph will never understand at all is how to kiss a woman.

I saw him do it once and I had to look away. First, you don't just muckle onto her and plant yourself. She might not want that. Or she might not yet know she wants you to do that. You have to ease women into these things, it's important to know that. Or she might want you to in the worst way but she isn't letting on because she's afraid what you might think about her if you know she wants you to. Anyway, my point is, you can put your lips wherever you want to and whenever you want to but you just better make sure she's on board with your plans first or at least it won't take her very long to catch up to you. Joseph is not one to take his time, he wants his hash right now or he'd just as soon not eat at all. But that doesn't work for things like fucking. The problem though with not fucking at all is that all of your spunk will back right up into your brain and you will start looking at everything like it's a vagina. I knew a man once who started to fuck his own horse. Well, the horse wasn't too crazy about that and neither was the man at first, you see, but he was a real desperate sonofabitch and he got used to it after a while, he said, and then it started to just not feel so unusual to him. He didn't put a dress on the horse or anything. He had a wooden stool he'd use and a leather strap for holding on. Even the details are distasteful. I can't imagine the horse ever warmed up to the idea much, but it put up with a lot of crap, as a good horse will…and, well, I just don't want Joseph to start fucking his horse, that is all.

"You see that little girl out there?" I ask the goddamned God-fearing Putnams, Mr. and Mrs.

Putnam pulls aside the canvas just a little with one finger and I see that Turner looks toward the wagon right away. She really doesn't miss a thing, her two eyes like coals in the fire.

"Are you telling me…d'you see that pretty girl, same age as the Holy Mother of Jesus when she was in her long-suffering birth pains and just as much a virgin as she was then—" I have no idea if either of these things is even close to the truth, you understand, I am just playing to the audience before me, my thinking is still that she is not so young as the Virgin "—are you telling me the man who tried to make her otherwise by force, by most heinous and ungodly, pardon me, ma'am, goddamned force, are you telling me the most important thing right now is for us to be digging a hole for that man to be in? Is that what you mean to say? Because my feeling on the matter is that we could leave him for the buzzards to deal with and not be harshly judged for it, not by God nor by anyone else."

I may not have changed course quite enough because Joseph and the kid and I end up in a hole that gets deeper and deeper and more and more crowded, what with the three of our shovels swinging away in it.

"I do not believe they appreciated the comparison to the Mother Mary," Joseph says.

"Well, fuck them, I don't believe either one of them has ever read the goddamned Bible."

"That's very likely to be true but they believe they know what's in it all the same. And they don't believe it makes any allowances for a white man being left out to bake in the sun with birds pecking at his eyes."

"Well, I suppose we might leave this to you with you bein' a hole expert like you are..."

This life can be a real fuck tree, and take it from me, you can try to climb it or you can cut it down. But it will fuck with you no matter what; you may climb it but it will be hit by lightning with you still in it, and you may fell it with an axe but it will fall on your head. Everyone is special when they're a child. Think about it: it's hard to find a little child who's a true asshole. They're all kind of interesting in their own little ways and they don't often go out of their way to hurt anyone with intent. But then they grow up. .

And their lives beat the shit right out of them.

Look, I know I'm wandering around a little here on my subject matter, but this is my book. You can come along if you want or you can fuck off and write your own. As a reader of this book, if you're still reading, then either you're close to being the most important thing in the world to me or, if you're stopping…well, you're about as useful to me as a dead man's dreams. But either way it's your decision to make, isn't it? Seems like my whole life people have been telling me to stop doing what I'm doing and to get back into the line. Well, fuck them. They don't even know what they're lining up for.

"If this boy is such a hole-diggin' fool, then why don't you and I just clear out and let him have his way with his dirt?" I ask Joseph, and Joseph shows no signs of objecting so up and out we go. "The boy can dig his way to China for all I care and you and me we'll just have us a rest."

We wipe off our brows and stand watching the kid's back muscles fighting like cats in a wet sack.

"Think of this world as a painting, Joseph," I say out of nowhere, but I guess out of my own tired thoughts.

"In what way?"

"Well, I mean in the way of a painting, a painting in a frame. Only the way we see things we just can't see the frame. We just see the painting, because we're in the painting, and so we see it but we don't see anything else."

"Mighty philosophical for a hot day, but I expect that's about right."

"And someone has put their fist through the painting, you see, and they've ruined it. Some cob has walked into the bar where this painting, the one that we're in, is hanging, and it's a good painting, and he has drunkenly put his fist right through it and ruined it, the cunt."

"I expect so."

"Well, that's not fair."

"No. I see your point."

"Do you?"

"Hard to enjoy a painting with a big hole in it, certainly."

"'Bout near impossible to enjoy."

"Most times it is, I expect."

"So it ain't fair."

"I suppose not…but your analogy is missing an important point, William."

"Which is?"

"That asshole that broke the painting…"

"Yeah?"

"Well, that's us, that's you…it's not some stranger who walked into the bar. We all broke the fucking thing."

"You don't think I know that? I am fucking well aware of that." It hadn't occurred to me until just this moment actually.

"Well, stop complaining then, Ish. If you don't want the painting broken, you shouldn't have punched it."

"Maybe I did it because I had too much to drink."

"It is likely."

"And by the time I slept it off, everything had just gone to shit."

Joseph says nothing then.

The kid is still sweating and grunting and digging like a garden mole. Well, we are all born into the same shit. The best we can hope to do is just move it around.

46

Your brain likes to think about things in certain ways. It gets used to the way it does things. But your brain only knows what it knows, so it can only think in the way it already thinks and this is Putnam's problem. It is a problem for all of us but Putnam's thinking affects others in this particular situation. It affects us. He thinks that if the Indians attack, God will look after him. He thinks God is listening to him and watching and somehow is on his side. But if God really is around someplace then he's on everyone's side so he is also on the Indians' side. That is a self-evident fact but you try explaining that to the Chosen People. They will have you for supper without even saying grace. So what Putnam doesn't see at all is that he's not special. If we all are, then no one is. His brain won't let him see that. His brain thinks it's God. And he lets it think that. And this is what makes Putnam fucked in four ways from Sunday and I have no patience left for him.

I raise my arms now and the desert wind takes my jacket up like a sheet. The wagons are turning in to each other and settling down for the night. That little weasel fucker, if he is rooting out there in the dark somewhere right now, dreaming about putting an end to us, it seems to me a desert storm might play right to his advantage; if he wishes to avenge his associate's death then the cover of the awe-inspiring natural power of God is just the right time to do it. But maybe that's just the way my brain runs: it suspects. I was born with something inside of me and it is not something that I am able to name. Not because it is a secret but because I don't know exactly what it is. Whatever it is, it is an aberration—that much is certain. I do not recognize this thing in other people. I seem to know things that others seem to not. And I never seem to know what to do about that. Live bravely, I suppose. That makes me sound like a good man. But I am nothing of the sort. I'll leave that territory to men like Putnam. They crave that sort of real estate more than I do. And now there is lightning in the west. So the evening seems to be off in a biblical direction. We are alone like Job in the desert. Was he in the desert? They were all in the desert, weren't they? Anyway, he was alone, I know that much.

You see, I have read parts of that book, just not the whole of it. It starts out with Adam and Eve, then somewhere after that is a fella by the name of Ishmael and I know that and it ends with a crazy man and in between comes Jesus, which is the good part and maybe the only part worth reading, it is certainly the best story in there. I have no problems with Jesus in case you were wondering. It's his father I have sometimes got a bone with. I just don't trust people who feel they have all the answers, usually people who don't even ask the right questions. "Is there any molasses?" when the question should be "Are there any armed men?" People like Putnam will come up to you and ask you if you've found the Lord Jesus Christ and they'll say, *"How are you today?"* and they'll shine their teeth at you and pat you on the shoulders and walk away and it's not until after they're gone that you figure out your jacket's gone with them and all your money in it. I got no time for people with little answers to big questions, especially when they've also got their boot on your dick and their hand well into your pocket. Matter of fact, I don't even have time for the big questions to start with. I'll take the little ones: "You got any tobacco? What day is it?" Those will do me just fine for me; they have a practical nature to them, and they are enough to see me through the day. I'll let folks like Putnam go ahead and worry about their own and others' eternal souls and I'll look after emptying my Colt into this other bastard's chest if he comes around looking to even his scores up with me or with anyone who's with me. And maybe I'll have a word or two with Turner. I should have a word or two with Miss Turner.

Maybe I'll do that right now.

"You alright, Miss Turner?"

"Course I'm alright, why wouldn't I be alright?" She's busy moving a bedroll into a wagon filled with pots and pans and flour sacks and not too much room for anything else including her bedroll, and maybe I'm catching her at a bad time.

"Maybe I got you at a bad time?"

"I couldn't picture a time much worse."

"Well, I…"

"Well, I what?"

"Well, dammit, Turner I just wanted to see was you okay."

"You can see that I am."

"I guess so."

"Well, there you go then, you seen it—you want to make a tintype of it to remember what it looks like? Or draw it down on a piece of paper?"

"Why're you so gritty at me for?"

"I ain't gritty at you, I'm just gritty. You asked me am I okay and I told you I was, so that's all. And if you come here and are looking for me to get all Oh thank you Mister McCarty for shootin' a man I could have easily shot for myself and did, in fact, want to shoot for myself…well, you better pull up a stool because there's gonna be some waiting involved."

"Well, damn if you're not a caution in this world."

"I expect that I am."

"And as crotchety as a cat that got threw onto a wood stove."

"Maybe so."

"And just as ungrateful to boot."

"Like I said, if you're waitin' on me to wipe down your feet with my hair, then you'd best take a seat."

And you see that, it is just like I said—people are always throwin' the Bible at each other just like it's a brick. That's a Bible story that part about people washin' people's feet with their hair. Those were strange times, I guess, and maybe there was a shortage of towels to be had.

"And what the hell has a cat that got threw onto a wood stove got to be grateful about?" she wants to know all of a sudden.

I will admit she has got me there.

So I go and I find Joseph and I try to see if maybe he can make heads or tails out of this. Not that he knows a single thing about women but he does sometimes have things figured before I do and I will admit that. He has this air about him that you can tell he's studying all manner of things in a quiet way, at least it looks that way but who can say if it is so, maybe he is just focusing on working up a ball of snot, but once in a great many occasions his thinking has him with a bead on things the way they really are.

"Taciturn." That's what he says when I find him by the horses with his rifle.

"What's that?"

"That's what people call me."

"Most of them I heard call you anything at all, it was either a dick or a hard turd."

Joseph considers this for a while. "That may be," he says, "but I am also taciturn."

"Oh, there's no maybe or any other kind of a be that enters into it, that's what they say about you when you are not listening—a dick or a hard turd, take your pick."

Joseph spits. "I wish I was in a saloon," he says.

"Nothing to be done about that."

"Suppose not."

"Whyn't you get some sleep?"

"Whyn't you?"

"Not sleepy."

"Maybe go talk to Turner?"

"I done that already."

"And?"

"She ain't too talky."

"Hm."

"Hm what?"

"Nothin'. Just that I ain't ever seen her not talking unless she was real drunk or real pissed off about something."

"You think she's pissed off?"

"I don't think she's drunk, and I guess I think she's a girl who likes to do things for herself."

"Nothin' wrong with that, is there?"

"Not hardly, just that you sorta took the wind out of her sails by shootin' that fella who had her at a disadvantage is all."

"At a disadvantage? He was fixin' to mount her like a wooden pony, Joseph."

"That may be."

"Once again—there ain't no mays or bes about it, he had her britches off her and his own right down around his knees. And what was I supposed to do? Ask him for a match or the time of day?"

"You did the right thing."

"Thank you."

"But that don't make no difference to her. It's somethin' she wanted to do for herself, you see."

"But she didn't have her any gun to do it with, Joseph, and his pecker was right at the garden gate, if you see what I mean…"

"Makes no difference to her. You did what she wanted to do for herself. You took it away from her."

"But he was about to take—"

"Makes no difference. Not to her."

"Well, hell."

"Women think different, Ish, that's all. Plus, you seen her like that. And all in all she'd probably rather you hadn't seen her like that and to just have been left to sort it out by herself."

"That don't make no sense at all."

"No. It don't. Doesn't have to, I expect."

"Well, I—"

"My guess is she'd sooner be dead than to have you see her... disrobed...like that. And...with another man on top of her. That's my guess."

"Women are peculiar." Joseph spits again.

"No more so than men. Just in different ways is all."

"So you think I should go and—"

"Yes, I do."

"Maybe I will."

"You got any tobacco on you?"

So we both roll one up and smoke. The lightning is still far off and looks now as if it will not come to where we are. Someone is playing a mouth harp who has not yet had much practice playing a mouth harp.

"How old do you think—"

"That is a question I'd rather not have anything to do with," Joseph says.

"I don't see—"

"How old I think she is has nothing to do with anything, that's why. Even how old she actually is, that has nothing to do with anything either."

"Well hell, why—"

"You really want to know what I think about it, Ish?"

I should just say no. No, Joseph, I should say, I do not really want to know what you think at all. He even wants me to say no, I can tell that.

I should just walk away right now.

"Well, what do you think about it?"

"My thinking on this is that no matter how old she is, you are more than fifty." Joseph grinds out his smoke with the silver tip of his boot. "So that is what I think."

"Well, that is a damn fine-looking high horse you rode in on." Damn my brother anyway.

"You asked me."

When I find her again, Turner is balanced on top of the pots and pans and old ropes like a tin star on the top of a Christmas tree and she is lit up all golden by a lantern that hangs from the wagon frame.

"I am sorry that I..." I start off.

I don't even know what there is for me to say that I'm sorry for.

"I wanted to say I'm sorry that I..."

Suddenly she leans down and kisses me on my cheek real quick and then she scoots right back on up onto her perch.

"Well...I...then...good night," I say. I turn from her to head back to where Joseph is keeping watch with the horses and she says something to me I don't quite hear. "What was that?" I ask, turning back to her.

"I said thank you...Mr. McCarty, and...well, and...goodnight back to you," she says, and then she trims down the lantern like she's in a sudden hurry to do so.

Women are like storms. You can study 'em and try to figure 'em out, but the fact is they're either going to rain on you or they're not and there's nothing you can do about that at all. I don't know. I'll just admit it. I don't know.

The scrape sound of the cold ash box being lifted out of the bottom of a dead wood stove in the morning and the cold air heavy in the fields. I think the mistakes you make are what charts you in this world. And I think that boy really needs to learn himself how to play the mouth harp better than he does right now.

I will say that.

๑๒ **47** ๒๑

Sometimes I got a dick so hard you could roller skate on it. Which is fine when you have a friendly place to put it and not of much use when you don't. These days mine has a mind all its own and some days it is up before me and some days it stays sleeping and doesn't get up at all. No matter. I am much averse to heroes. I would sooner listen to someone play the banjo than to hear about the deeds of the great men of this world. It seems to me, especially as I get older, that what someone else might think about what you do or don't do is pointless. In fact it is nothing at all. A man once bragged to me that he bested ten men in a bare-handed fight and I said, well, that was really something and why didn't he get that printed up on a piece of nice card paper and pin a rose to it and wear it around town. Men trying to build themselves up into legends and get themselves into penny newspapers, I have had a belly full of those men. If anyone were to read words at my funeral, I would want them to be small words and then just a few of them. Quiet and simple. Maybe just whispered, or maybe written down on a small piece of paper and folded twice and shoved there into the casket beside me. I have not found talking to be of much use in my life and I don't expect that to change for the better once I am dead. If all the words that were ever spoken in history were added up and placed next to a little stream in a summer field or beside a friendly dog, they would be found wanting in the comparisons, I think. You wake up in the morning and the light is testing its hands against the curtains. You won't always. Wake up, I mean.

Here is how it happens. I drift back to Joseph and he does not ask me anything at all about Turner or what was said and I am glad of that. He tells me that everything is quiet out in the desert and by this time everything in the train is quiet as well. The mouth-harp orchestra has retired for the night and all that can be heard is the groaning of the timbers of the wagons as the heat of the day leaves them and also the dry rustle of the breeze scraping against the desert sand. Joseph says he will take the first watch and I should get a little sleep for myself. I do not sleep much these days so it is of no account to me who sleeps first. I swear I have now begun to hear Turner's attacker in my head in the darkness, and he barely in the grave. A head too full of the dead is what I have these nights. One of Putnam's men is up on watch also but we take no heed of that, needing no help from people who are of no help at all. So I go back to the dead man's wagon where we have put our bedrolls, passing the thunderous snoring coming from the Wings' wagon where Wing and the kid are bedded down.

I am coming to the opinion that it might be a quiet night after all and maybe the man who has escaped me has considered himself lucky just to be escaped and has thought it wise to keep it that way. What was the death of his companion to him? Men such as that substitute pride for loyalty. Only misplaced pride would make him return now. Speaking of pride, I find in hindsight that it is best to not think too well of yourself because it can and does lead to errors in judgment. It seems in this case he is not so much thinking he is wise to be away from me but rather how much he would like to separate my head from my heart or to fuck me up the ass with a sharpened stick. But he is not a hard man, just a stupid one, he has cold vanilla pudding in the passages where his backbone should have been placed and he mistakenly thinks of himself now as a ramrod. I could have built a better man than my father out of a handful of half-penny nails and some old barn boards, but that don't account for nothing. The day after my mother passed I sat in the yard across the road from the house where she had died and I stared up at the window of her room as if it were both a reason and an answer. It was neither. I tried to forget the few things I knew at that age, the weathervane creaking above me like it had something to say to me but it did not.

But this man is as sure of himself as Adam was in his younger days. I have found it to be the case that those most certain of their actions are likely to be the most foolhardy in other things, in all other things. Like a single note drawn out by a fiddler so long that you think, *"He can't possibly hold that any longer,"* and the note is as light as the air itself and liable to break at any time. That is how I slept. Hovering, uneasy, the night full of voices, and me about as liable to jump as a schoolteacher in a cathouse. I dream it before I see it, only in my dream it is a house that is on fire. In the dream it isn't clear whose house it is but I know at least it isn't mine. Like you do in dreams, I walk right into it to see what is in there and find out what is happening. You don't wonder in a dream why you're not burning now that you're inside a burning house or if you do you just think, *"Oh look. I don't burn,"* or something just as simple as that, something that doesn't make any sense but in some way it does in your dream. As if you have forgot your own inability to burn and then you recall it. It is hot in there of course, and everything I can see is made up of flame. The walls are like waterfalls of fire moving up instead of down and as I pass through the rooms I notice that although everything is on fire nothing is burning up—as though everything is now just made up of fire and is continuously burning. The curtains are thin veils of orange and red falling like red waters. It is a dream, so I don't think any of this is unusual, it is just the way things are. As I enter the kitchen, things change. A little girl sits there at the table with her back to me. She is doing something, eating or drinking, or maybe playing with something there on the table, I can't tell. And she is made up of this fire too, she is alive but she is burning also. Then she turns toward me, calm and quiet, and I can see her face, her eyes points of white flame in a bowl of red fire and ashes, like the inside of a wood stove when it's almost too hot to open the door and the heat tears at your face and you need to look away to keep your skin from burning. And with this horrible face she looks up and directly at me and she says:

"Wake up."

And that is when I wake up.

By this time several men have already died. I do not know why the first gunshots do not wake me but I am fully awake now and the shooting is still going on and so right away I rip the canvas from the wagon ribs around me. Any bullets will go right through it anyway and I'd just as soon see where they are coming from and be hit as a target as be hit by a stray shot. What I see first is the fire and so time is wasted as I try to guess whether I am still dreaming, but I am not. Several of the wagons are in bright flame against the black of the sky, which has the effect doubly of lighting up the inside of the encampment and making invisible anything outside of it. There are shouts and cries and shots, as many shots as there are guns available to make them, it would seem from the sound of it. Unless we are under attack by a legion, it would seem that most of these shots are being made on no targets at all. I drop to the ground with the Winchester in one hand and the Colt in the other and I start in to circle the inside of the wagons in a crouch back in the direction of Joseph, which will also take me toward Turner's pots-and-pans wagon. Several men run fast across the centre of the wagon circle with rifles and as they take no notice of me I assume they are Putnam's men. Whoever is attacking knows how to do what they are doing and my guess is that, in spite of appearances, it is only the one man, his efficiency magnified by his anger but also, hopefully, by his arrogance.

You want someone to cry after you when you are gone from this earth. That is what we all want. Well, time goes by.

I will kill him. And soon. That is certain. Sometimes when I shoot a gun I feel as if I am correcting the world. What is not yet certain is who he may kill before the point at which I am able to take decisive action regarding his being or his not being. That is a matter mostly of chance and circumstance and where his chest is in relation to my gun and of how long it will take me to find that distance out.

"Joseph!"

Joseph is running into the circle of light from the darkness beyond just like he is running into a bar room before it closes. Say what you like about him, he enjoys being useful in this world.

"It's him," he tells me, "he's on a horse and he's set three wagons ablaze, Ish, we gotta shoot him off that horse of his, I believe that I clipped him...maybe..."

"Where's Turn—"

And with that it happens—jumping and falling through the burning canvas of one of the wagons drop two figures you would take to be human were they not so much like torches or matchsticks ablaze and the dance they are doing is vicious and horrible to witness. There's a bigger figure and a smaller one. The bigger one is turning with its arms raised and the smaller one has dropped to its knees as if almost resigned already to its own end. Its, not his, for there is almost nothing of a human nature left to what we are seeing now. People are frozen to the ground with the sight of it and it is too late now anyway, there is not enough left of them for us to do much of anything. The larger one lets out a strangled cry and it is Wing—it is clear now that the larger of the two is Wing. There is nothing to be done now but watch or turn away. There is so little left of the smaller figure now as it crumples over in a heap that it is difficult to say for certain if it is the kid. And there's the horrible thought for a moment that it could be Turner

"Ish..."

"I..."

but that is corrected as Turner comes running now and tilting toward the nightmare screeching and she has to be quickly held back by a small man and a large woman who have had the foresight to grab her. Joseph and I move now and I reach Turner first and take her from the two, holding her tightly enough that she can go no further. Her bones seem suddenly very small and she goes weak in my arms. It is like holding a bird. She is crying now—sobbing and choking— and as I turn her away from the sight I'm seeing—the thing that had been Wing—it turns toward the sound of her and collapses like an ashen deck of cards being fanned over a table. It is over for him. Now. Dealt.

Turner.

Shaking.

We are sorry little things.

We are not who we think we are at all. We think we are enormous and we are not.

And then everything speeds up and I shift my weight and I hand Turner off to Joseph because, like I said I would, I know how far it is from my gun to his chest now and I move to cover the distance and I can hear the sounds of the hooves outside the wall of canvas and wood and fire circle around us and I hear even the rustle of his burning torch against the night air and I move now, there, through the dark between those two wagons and I stop, and yes, now, and hold, and bring up the rifle and the pistol both and I shoot him in the face.

I hope that it is him.

The horse is faster than I'd thought and so the movement between standing and firing is an immediate one and there is only the time to make sure the bullets catch their mark and no time at all left to check the identity of the rider, which will now be difficult to do as the shot has thrown him from the mount and has likely marred his features somewhat. He could still be alive.

The horse is spooked and gone now and I move slowly to the figure writhing in the black sand with its hands to its face.

"Goddammit, I'm shot. I'm shot," it says as if an explanation of what has happened is required.

I slowly pin one arm down with a boot. And it is him.

And he looks at me through his blood-red face and no more than a second passes and I pull back the hammer on the Colt, four clicks, and I shoot him again. And that is that.

Goddammit, Turner is going to kill me now. Sometimes doing right is also doing wrong at the exact same time.

"William!"

"I'm here."

Right over here.

"You shot him."

"I know it."

"If you hadn't shot him we could have got Turner to do it." Joseph has a way of pointing out the obvious and the inconvenient with equal relish.

"Well, if my grandmother had wheels then she would have been a bicycle, now isn't that a fact too?"

Joseph spits. "Not really, Ish," he says, "and she was my grandmother too, you know."

I suppose he is right about that but neither of us actually ever saw the woman. I suppose there must have been two of them and we never saw either, just heard tell of the one who talked to walls. Well, it is of no matter. Now with the only man we knew to wish us harm for a hundred miles around being shot in the face we feel safe in getting a few hours of sleep before dealing with the outcomes of the evening. I lie down with Turner and I do not believe that she sleeps at all. She is still in my arms and we say nothing as there is nothing to be said so I just keep my arms around her and not for any reason other than that it is the thing to do. Joseph would likely think or say it is otherwise but he is mistaken. She needs someone to have their arms around her now and there is no one else here to do the thing but me. As I say, I do not believe that she sleeps at all and she stays very quiet but I do somehow manage to drift off for a little bit and I have another long dream in a short time. My brain usually does a good job of shutting out what happens to it during the night but not this time. I am standing in a field of tall grass and looking at a plain and greyed-over plank-board farmhouse. There is no one around that I can see and there is a gentle wind. The grass sways like ocean waves and a fresh-baked apple pie cools on a window ledge. I enter the house and the floorboards creak under my boots. I find my way to the kitchen and lift the pie from the sill, the tin pan still warm in my hands. I dig a fork from the drawer and sit at the table and eat the pie slowly. The apples are thin-sliced and running with melted brown sugar and cinammon. The cuffs of my jacket sleeves are worn. A weathervane turns and complains of rust in the wind. I am home.

✍ 48 ✎

So it is time to bury the dead again. This is the story of the great West—everybody thinks they're doing what they're supposed to be doing or maybe even what God himself wants them to do. As there are so many at odds with each other I just don't figure they can all of them be right at the same time, they are not even listening to each other, just shooting at whatever gets in their way.

"Six men have died here in the last twenty-four hours," Putnam observes, looking at me in the dawn light like I'm some goddamned locust swarm that came down onto him and brought the plague along with me.

"Hard time to stay alive," I tell him, "for some men…"

"We'll build a cairn right here."

"A what?"

"A cairn. Typically a mound of rough stones built as a memorial …usually on a hilltop or skyline, but the flat plains would do if needs make it so… I see ample stones about for the job."

"And I guess you can also see the men to lift them up and put them in place too."

Putnam squints at me. I swear he has his head buried so far up his own ass that he has to open his mouth to see daylight. "It is the Lord's work," he says.

"I don't see the Lord rolling up his sleeves nowhere…"

"Blasphemer."

"You're telling me you want to build a memorial to these men?"

"Why not?"

"Well, let me tell you something, you got a grandma with one eye and it's in the centre of her forehead you don't go parking her in the front parlour…that's all." And I spit. Like punctuation.

"And what does that mean?"

"I'm saying these men don't need no advertisements and they don't warrant no monuments."

"Are you saying these men aren't God's children like the rest of us?" he asks, indicating the various-sized shapes under the blankets on the ground.

"Well, that one sure as hell was not. Maybe Wing and Chance were, I sure as hell don't know for certain. I know neither one of them wanted to lie under some kind of tower for the rest of their…deaths…"

"You are not God-fearing."

"It's just I always seen more reason to be afraid of the average living man than I have of God. And you can go ahead and recite whatever of God's words you want to over these fellas, but I know they ain't listening. And shoot me for a liar if God ain't give the average living man no more brains than he did a walnut." And Putnam knows I'm talking about him now because I don't stop staring him down as I say it and I set my jaw the way that I do when I mean business about something.

"Ish…"

"No, and now I mean it, Joseph…let's just get 'em set into the dirt if we have to, but there ain't gonna be no cairns built here."

The whole notion ain't worth a bucket of warm spit.

"But, Ish—"

"Joseph, now I said…"

Oh for the love of fuck.

I could write down here that Joseph is just trying to get me to shut my damn fool mouth and that Turner has come up behind me and has been standing right there but you have already guessed that much.

And sometimes I feel like a goddamned turd wagon. I suppose that someone somewhere is having a lovely day but it is not here and it does not appear that it is me.

Then the look on her face.

Maybe some people they get everything they want from this life, but I can't imagine what that might be like.

I ain't used to a girl having to put up with her own daddy burnin' up to death while she watches him go and her having to face that after her sister has already been murdered and she has just found out about that and then almost been raped herself. That is a certain kind of a problem I am not used to at all. Men with guns and they're pointed in my direction. Card games with bad cards and they're against me. A sick horse with a broke leg and it's mine. Those are the kinds of trouble I'm used to. Here are the solutions, in order: kill the men, leave the game, shoot the horse.

Easy one, two, three.

And there's Putnam standing there slack-jawed and still watering at the mouth about what kind of stone castle towers we might build for these dead men when the daughter of one of them is standing right here in front of us and about to bust up on the spot. And me talking a lot of half-assed nonsense. Well, the Lord he sure baked a lot of fruitcake and that's a fact.

And Joseph standing there with his face done up like a badly tied knot. Like he's about to spit lemon juice when all I done is shoot a man who desperately needed shooting and just yesterday he himself shot a man who his only crime was standing there where the bullet went. You go ahead and you spit your lemon juice, Joseph, I don't have any fucks left to give for you. And I'm standing here looking at her with her face busting up now and I'm thinking there's men dead on the ground and also that I don't like being so close to the dead. But we all of us are close to the dead. All the time, I mean, they're everywhere.

A dead crow blanched into pure white feathers in a rain barrel. And black iron nails in a little pine box.

Sometimes you just expect for some kind of a magic to fix things up for you and all the time you gotta do the fixing all by yourself just the best you can because there ain't no magic to be had. Ah, hell be damned and look out, this is just a matter of picking up a shovel and starting to dig so let's just get to it is what I say.

Turner wipes at her face now and insists that she be the one to get the bodies prepared so she goes through what little is left of her daddy's pockets and pulls out a charred silver pocket watch. Checks all of the pockets then. And she does not cry anymore. She is a girl just as hard as iron when she needs to be.

৩ 49 ৩

"D id you shoot him in self-defence, Billy?" a judge asked me one time in Lincoln County.

"No, sir," I said, "I shot him in the head."

You won't find that story in any book that's been writ except for this one that you're reading right now and that don't make it any the less true. Pat Garrett he never knew that story, not that he would have let that stop him from just making it up like half the stories in that book he wrote. He even said I was arrested as a cattle rustler at one time. Now, in order to be arrested as a rustler you pretty much have to be caught with the cows in your bed and so that's just another of his badly told lies.

Once we get the bodies tucked in under their dirt and the horses ready to go, the sun is already high up in the sky and Mr. Putnam he says his few old words, which turn out to be a few more than I think is really required, particularly about the men who he knows nothing of, and also he throws in some sections from the story of ol' Daniel in the lion's den that I can't see are connected to anything at all. Then he finishes up with a *"have mercy on their souls,"* which is called for, I suppose. I have no idea about Putnam's men, they could be flyin' right up to the shining gates of heaven as we all stand here, but Wing I have to say I ain't so sure about him and the kid, well, who knows, he was pretty young to have too much of a dark smudge mark on his soul as yet so maybe he'd get in the gates and that other one, well, you can bet he ain't even settin' foot in the outer courtyard, old Saint Pete he'll give him the bum's rush on outta there before he even gets close to being inside and that's for certain and that's for true.

Joseph and I we set about organizing our belongings to get going just as quick as we can to be gone on out of here, neither of us having much wish to stay with this wagon train to heaven any longer than need be. I'm thinking about what to say to Turner to make my case to her the best way I can. I'm pulling down on these leather straps and I want to tell her she's mighty small even if she doesn't think she is and she might think she's gonna be just fine all on her own in territory like this, but dammit, Turner, you just ain't gonna be that at all or maybe you think you'll tag along with this broken-down Bible circus for a little while till they get all the way to California, but, Turner, I can tell you that Putnam's gonna be in your wagon right in the middle of your first night wanting to put the fear of the Lord into you and with his pants down around his shins so he can do it too and I can quite easy tell that just by looking at him or maybe you just want to tell me to go straight to hell and I sure hope that's not the case, Turner, but if it is you'd best just say it plain and then let's get up onto these horses and ride on outta here together because the only way you're gonna be safe now is with us.

"The only way you're gonna be safe now is with us."

And it turns out it is easy to say because she walks right up to me just while I'm thinking it and out it comes into words.

"I know it," she says.

And then I got nothing left to say.

So it's up to her.

"I maybe guess I should be thanking you for killing those men."

Straps are tight enough now. I got nowhere left to put my hands. "I didn't kill 'em. I just shot 'em. I figure the rest is up to luck and the Lord."

It's not that I don't take credit. I just don't take any bows. "Anyway…"

And then she does something, she up and embraces me and she keeps on doing it. Her head right under my chin and she smells like a woman and it's been some time since I smelt that smell but this is not like that and I don't know what that means or what this is exactly. Sure I held her in my arms last night but that was right after her daddy burnt all up to nothing and it was different than this and that was me holding her, not her holding me. This time she's the one doing the work. Women they just don't spell things out most times. Anyway she's holding on for some time and I figure this means either that she's coming with us or she's saying goodbye. Things fall apart. Or usually, most times that is what they do.

"Which wagon are we gonna take?" she asks suddenly, then she takes one quick step back.

And so that's that.

Like I said before, I didn't ever know anyone who got everything they wanted out of this world, but some men are luckier than others, I guess. I am just never expecting that it is going to be me.

"Well, if you've got no big sentimental attachment to yours, I'd say the other one's the sturdier frame…that is if you don't mind riding in a dead man's wagon…" And right away I want my words back because of course they're both dead men's wagons now, but Turner she don't seem to notice that or to care about it at the moment.

"Alright," she says, "but there's something in that wagon you should know about."

"Seems to me there was a pine box just about the size to have a body in it, but I didn't have time to take too much of a notice."

"There's a body alright, and I'd say it's been in there a good while because it don't have no stink left to it anymore."

"A man or a woman?"

"It's a woman…or at least it was, some time ago."

I have dug too many fucking holes this week. "You got any feelings about what should be done with it?" I ask her.

She just spits and looks at me and I guess that's her answer. Good as any.

↜ 50 ↝

We decide to give the coffin and whoever is in it or whatever is left of them to Putnam as a parting gift. As he is so very fond of ceremony and of breaking ground he can see to its care and then progress in whatever way he sees fit. Whoever is in that box was not killed by me and is also of no kin to me and so I want no part of the proceedings involving his, her, or its disposal. I will take a break from such things for now and leave that to those who see a purpose in theatrical spectacles. Joseph is anxious to get on the way, and he says there have been enough delays, which seems a simple-minded thing for him to say since most of them have been due to his own wishes and actions, but I don't see a percentage in bringing this particular subject up to him at the moment, so Turner and I we set ourselves to getting the wagon ready for the trip north.

I know that we're opening up a plain pinewood box to see the dried old corpse of a long-dead woman and then figure out what to do with it, but the way Turner is kneeling next to me and the manner in which her yellow hair is undone makes me feel in some way crookedly blessed. There, where her hair meets with the smooth skin of her forehead. There, with her little fingers prying at the wood and the smell of her in this closed space of the wagon. She seems to me just such a simple good in this world, that's all. Something that is enough just on its own—just the fact of her.

I have always found it uncomfortable to be so close to a dead person though, although I guess that's true of everyone except for the undertaker, but for a man who's been around his share of killing I still find the evidence of death a tiresome and a worrisome thing. We get the lid open and it as if a little child has drawn their idea of a dead woman, or like someone has put lipstick on her while she was still moving. But she is not moving. Her eyes have fallen back into her dried-out old head. Her mouth is open as if to speak but she has nothing now to say. And most that have been dead for some time, well, they have got a stink to them that this lady sure does not have. Instead there's a smell that is more like camphor and wax.

"Somebody's put lip rouge on her," Turner says, "and some powder."

"Let's close her up and lift her down out of here," I say.

"Why would someone want to do that, to put paint on her?"

"I expect they figured she couldn't do it for herself."

"Those men were bad crazy."

"I expect so."

"It's good that they're dead now."

"I expect that's so too."

She looks over at me and there are tears on her cheeks and she seems to want to be held again so I hold her and then she crumples right up into me and her shoulders fold in and shake but she's not making any sound at all. Her little hands are cupped together into her lap like they've fallen from the sky and so I put my hand over them as if I'm protecting them from something. Again, it seems like it's the thing to do.

So I do it.

But I will never sleep with this girl.

I think no. No. I won't.

But I would hold her hands like this for a long time if she wanted me to do that. I would keep her little hands from any danger. I want to tell her this, not just about her hands but the rest of her too, but suddenly she is up on her knees again, wiping at her eyes and then quickly back to the task at hand.

I think of a little girl running away from something that has frightened her.

I would have sounded stupid saying anything to her right then anyway.

"Let's move her out of here then," she says. "Time for her to be going where she's going and for us to be gone too. I don't like this place very much."

We start to lift the box.

"I don't like it at all…"

"Wait."

Under the box there is another box, and then another… There are what feel like three fair-sized metal boxes under a green felt cover that looks like the top of a small billiard table. They are the size and shape of strongboxes, which, when I pull the cover away, it turns out that they are. They are bank boxes, I've seen enough of them to know that much. Bank boxes usually hold just the one thing. Turner looks at me and pulls something out from her pocket. Three charred silver keys on a ring.

"I pulled these out of that old dead bastard's hip pocket," she says.

And it's the first time for a while that I see her smile.

And it is some nice to see.

ᦉ **51** ᦉ

Fifty thousand dollars is a lot of money. That amount of money humbles the juice right out of me. It's an amount of money you don't know what to do with it because it is so much. Five hundred dollars and you know what to do, a thousand even. Fifty thousand dollars is like having the moon right there in the same room with you. There's nothing you can do with it so you just leave it right where it is and you do nothing with it at all.

So I decide not to tell Joseph about it, not yet. He'll get his full share if we split it. I don't know why I don't tell him and then later I figure it. I want something that just me and Turner know about. Maybe I'll just let Turner have it all anyway. I got no use for any such amount and she is young and can stretch it out some and put it to good use. Joseph and me we already got this land he bought for us up in Canada so maybe I will pay my half of that out to him so that then we will be even about it. Turner should have the rest of it. Maybe a thousand to last me and Joseph. He is even older than me and he just don't have that much time left and he has nothing at all to spend money on anyway.

Putnam does not appreciate our gift of another body to bury nor of me reminding him that all of God's little children are deserving of a proper send-off to the life eternal and my saying so does not seem to fix his mind any on the task and anyway he is not listening. He seems for a moment to have lost his focus and then he looks at me like the heathen hump he figures I am. He looks at me and he spits into the dust, which seems to me not really to be a kingdom of God sort of an action and also there's just been a lot of spitting into the dust lately but never mind. I am anxious for us to get on our way off into the great big country and to see what happens next.

"You drivin' the wagon then?" I ask Joseph.

"Why am I drivin' the wagon?" He is a quarrelsome man.

"I didn't say you were drivin' the wagon, I asked you *if* you were drivin' the wagon."

"I'll drive the wagon then."

Goddamn. "Fine."

There's no need for even half of his fussing and fidgeting. Jesus Christ himself would punch him in the face. He is cantankerous. So Turner and I set out on our horses with Joseph behind us up on the buckboard and his horse following along at the rear, its head nodding and swinging on the rope.

Just like a family.

That's a stupid thing to think.

Like we are then. Like we are now.

We'll see a little bit of the world and what's out there in it to see. I have not felt this peaceful since I was in my father's balls and before everything just boiled down to a battle toward not being dead. It's what I would imagine freedom would feel like to a jailed man. Actually having been freed from jail I do know that feeling, when you are full of everything that might happen next, if only there is a chance for you to do it. We just ride silent for a while, each of us with our own thoughts, I suppose. Probably hers are quite different than ours. On a long and silent ride you look forward to camp each night, not because you don't like the trail but just for something to think about that is pleasant and simple while you ride. It quiets your mind. We have to cut through Texas territory and then on through Oklahoma, Missouri, Kentucky, and the northern states, I don't even know what states there are there... New York, that is one... Eventually we will be in snow mountains, with lynx, mountain cats, on rough trails, and we will also be in cities and in the end there will be more snow, great huge banks of snow. A long ride to where no one knows us nor cares to. Just like the whore said to the preacher—*"It's a long ride or a short one, Preacher, it's up to you... but either way it's the same price and you end up in the same place..."* But there's no shortcuts to where we're going. It is a long ride.

I start to figure out what we'll need, and what might be the first place we can get a hold of it.

Food: flour (18 pounds), bacon (4 pounds.), and coffee (6 pounds about), baking soda, cornmeal, hardtack, dried beans, dried fruit, some beef, molasses, vinegar, pepper, eggs, salt, sugar (3 pounds), rice, tea (4 pounds), lard (12 pounds).

And I think I will ask Turner if she can make us up a list of what we got right now, which I figure is maybe just enough coffee, dried beans, cornmeal, and hardtack to last us about four days. So we will need to provision ourselves by the time we get to Texas territory or we will die. Not actually die, but just be very hungry. I been hungry lots of times and am well used to it so it does not bother me much but I don't know if Turner has ever been hungry for days at a time and besides I got no interest in living that way again or in finding out if she can live like that. Most people when they say they are hungry they just mean they want to fill up their holes. Hunger is when you hurt and you want to throw up but there is nothing there inside you to do it with. It is a fire in the gut. For most people food is more of a carnival than a lifeline. Still, if I don't get my breakfast and my dinner I can get kind of mean. Cantankerous. So we have to get enough to keep us all going. And more blankets too. I ain't ever seen much snow and never for more than just a little bit of time, but nothing has suggested to me ever that I will like it very much if I see it for longer. Waking up freezing and poking your head though the canvas with the ground all covered in white and the horses rising up steam from under their covers is no way to rise. But then I suppose you get the fire stirred up and restarted and you brew up some coffee. Turner's yellow hair in the cold air then, and her all wrapped up in a pile of coats, her little hands clutching at them and her breath in the air. Maybe I will get accustomed to it.

My father once beat Joseph so bad that he beat one of his nuts right out of him. That's right, he almost bled out from it too and he had to be stitched up and to this day he's only got the one. He won't tell you about it. He don't even talk to me about it, and why would he? It's not like you need two of 'em anyway but I'm still thankful for what I have got. Joseph would have been about seven at that time and I would have been five or so, I guess. Something like that. Anyway, he don't talk about it.

The way Turner sways in her saddle ahead of me is my focus right at the moment. She does not know where she is going at all and she has lost all her people and her shoulders are small and narrow. I will find her a place to be. She is small and she thinks now that she is alone in this world. She is not.

Except right now Joseph and I are like two blind men wandering in a back alley. What I know about Canada you could carve on a short man's pecker and still have enough room left on it for the Lord's Prayer and I am certain that if I ask him right now what he knows about Canada we'll be listening from now until the campfire's started tonight so I don't 'cause I already heard him tell about it. Only a part of it would likely be the truth anyway because he makes shit up like there was a profit to be made in doing so. This fella I met once who'd trapped for a time in Alaska said it is night up there most of the time and there's white bears the size of a small house. He said the only thing between you and your death up there is what you're wearing and what you can carry and whether or not you can find something to put over top of your head when night falls. I expect that is true most places but at least most places you don't need to deal with your own height in snow everywhere you go.

Joseph said: "That clot has never been any closer to Alaska than just hearing the name of it said once in a tavern," and he says Canada ain't like what that man said anyway and they even got them a summer and a spring. He says there's tall grass in the summer and green leaves in the spring and they suck sugar water right out of the wood in the trees. Just like when the Jews found themselves a way to the Promised Land, I guess. Honey and molasses and wine everywhere. Have yourself a steak for dinner, boys, and some tobacco too and then sleep the night right through next to a clear trickling stream. I suppose I should not have trusted that man's thoughts on Alaska anyway. His hands shook for no reason that I could see and he had a face on him that looked like an asshole glued to a potato. Never trust a man whose face looks like an asshole glued to a potato and whose hands are shaking. He's either gonna try to shoot you or he's nervous because he knows he might miss when he does. Either way there's a bullet headed in your general direction sometime soon. And don't trust what Joseph ever tells you neither. He got himself a voice and a line of bullshit that could talk Jesus right down off the cross.

"When we get ourselves up to Canada," he says all of a sudden like he's right in my head and he knows what I'm thinking, "I believe I may take up the playing of the banjo..."

"Well, you can just stop rubbin' that skunk of an idea right now," I tell him.

Listening to him hammer away with all his strength on a banjo does seem a grim eventuality to me, I do not know what he is thinking. We believe we may know what goes on inside the heads of others but we are foolish to think that we do. Inside of people's heads there are ghosts and worlds and untold mysteries. Many times these places are filled with empty space only, but sometimes with stars and planets and wondrous things, I suppose it depends on the person. In Joseph's case it is a planet, but it is planet Joseph McCarty. He's the only one in there whose worth is of any account to him at all. In Turner's head there are stars—many, many stars is what I imagine there are in there. I am a fool to think I know this, but I am a happy fool, for the time being at least I am a happy one.

No matter what I do I just can't seem to get clear of myself and I have the ability sometimes to trip over my own footprints. Maybe Canada can fix that tendency right out of me. Maybe if I do less I will make fewer mistakes. We are always thinking that life will be better if, and when, and if only we... But life is right here and not somewhere on down the road ahead of us or behind us. It's right here in front of us all the time and winning it is nothing. Winning is just something we make up in our heads and then we try to make fit into the real world. It does not. I remember once Joseph had himself a girl. We were young men back then and full of piss and vinegar and everything that we hadn't done yet and he loved her, I guess. I guess that he did. At least when the news hit that she was up and leaving for California with her family it certain looked as if he did by the way his face appeared to have been hit with a broad plank. He asked her to stay with him, I guess, like a kid would, but he had nothing for her to stay on and she was just a kid too and so she could not even have done so if she had wanted. The day they packed up and moved on he just stood there and watched until that train was all the way gone, he just stood there looking all the way down that track. There was nothing for him to see but he was looking anyway, just standing the way a cow does in the rain and with the same plain look on his face.

It took a long time for us to walk back to the house. All I have ever wanted is a simple life, but things have always got in the way of that.

New Mexico sure has a lotta flat to it but when we get to Texas it ain't gonna be no different. For the most part it is like ridin' across the back of a cast-iron pan. The sun got up this morning and so did I, so here we both are and there ain't no reason to complain about that. And seven men didn't get up this morning and that's enough to take comfort in. Or it should be. I woke up on the right side of the dirt. There are some men who don't need for their gravesites to be marked in any way and I am one of those, I think, and it is a strange thing to be alive and to know there is already a grave with a rock somewhere in this world with your name on it. Makes you feel like you got up out of bed one morning and left yourself behind somewhere the night before. Walked away and forgot about it. Rocks and sand and everything just sifting on slow down into the rivers and on out to the ocean. We make small things into large things and for no good reason at all do we do this. We trip over our own feet and we make a whole lot of fuss and feathers over something that is nothing at all.

❧ PART THREE ❧
BABYLON

ᥔᥩ **52** ᥰᥞ

"I saw you killed that man like he was an unarmed dog."
"Bob, I ain't never seen a dog that *was* armed. What the fuck are you even talkin' about?"

That was Bob Ollinger talking up top there. I don't know who that other fella was. Coulda been me. We could ask old Bob but he's dead now, isn't he, so he won't say a thing because nobody talks less than a dead man. It was me. But now I can say this to you, that I have never shot a man who had no gun. I don't know if you have ever made any study of water. For a man who has spent the better part of his life in the desert I know a thing or two about lakes. You spend a day looking at a lake and if the weather is right you will see more than a hundred different lakes. That is the way of it, just like the desert. Sometimes if you don't see things too often then you can see them better and truer. Sometimes if you see something every day you never really see it at all. People are no different than lakes: mostly made up of water and changing on the surface all the time. That we are mostly water is a scientific fact and you can look it up if you've a mind to or just ask Joseph. If you need proof that people change on their surface but not much in any other way deeper than that, then I cannot help you. You have not looked around enough.

Joseph has decided to take a circuitous route up to the border of Canada. That's what he calls it just to hear himself say the word, I think: *circuitous*. You can know a word without ever having to use it out loud is what I think. He's got us cutting clear over to Galveston and then north instead of how we could just easily track pretty well straight northeast from where we started out and then be there in a third of the time with just half of the fuss. I have seen the map and his scratchings on it. There ain't no talkin' to him though when he has made up his mind on something like this. He will just talk back at you until he wears you right down to the nub. Circuitous, that's how it'll be for you listenin' to him when he's got himself all wound up like that. Circuitous.

"It is the most advantageous spot to purchase provisions for the journey," is what he says regarding Galveston.

But the provisions we need could be had in any little town with a store and a corner to put it on, so I don't know why he's got a hornet's nest up his ass over Galveston. He's the one who said we should avoid places with people in 'em. Hell, ain't that why we're on our way up north in the first place? People-avoiding? They got them a lot of people over there in Galveston and I bet some of them have even heard of Billy the Kid and his fast gun. I think maybe Joseph is just looking for his last city whore on the way up into the northern forest and if it puts me in any danger for him to see his pecker wetted, well then that's just fine with him is what he's thinking because all he's really thinking about is his one-balled pecker and where he might put it before the act of putting it anywhere is likely to become a rare occurrence. Besides, I don't much like the idea of heading into a place as big as Galveston with fifty thousand dollars in a box. Or of seein' any whores either. Or of helpin' him get his pecker wet. I could care less about whores and wet peckers. They say Texas is a place where a man can be free, I have heard them say that in the taverns, but I have felt more and more collared in ever since we entered this territory. Sometimes I do feel like I did die a long time ago just like what is said of me in the newspapers and in the books. And goddamn if I don't feel now like there's some ghostly haunt at me all the time riding on the top of me just like some kind of malevolent bird. There you go, Joseph, there's one just for you: malevolent. Just like some bird that is pecking at me all the time just to see if I'll bleed some. Well, I will.

Someone has always got to pay the cost for everything that happens in this world. Men like Putnam they say that God is the answer for it all. Me, I think that God likely sometimes looks to us in just that same way. And he must be just as woefully disappointed as we are in the outcome of his expectations and in this twisted-up arrangement. I aim to provide a life for Turner if she'll allow me to do that and that is where my sole interest lies now, a solid life needs more than fifty thousand dollars, it needs someone who cares about you. I have nothing else that is pressing for me to do and nothing else that I care to give my attention to in this world. A life free of tribulations, not for me but for her. For the both of us. But I swear to you this is true—I swear that last night in my bed I heard that same woman's voice say very low to me, *"Look after her,"* and I know this was no dream because in a dream you do not know you are dreaming and I thought, *"Well. This must be a dream,"* and so it could not have been one, that much is clear to me now. And in a dream you never breathe. Think about that. You never even think of breathing in a dream, it is something that in a dream you do not even have to do but you are thinking about breathing now just because I mentioned it, and because you are not dreaming. Breathe in, breathe out. But you have never thought about doing that in a dream, have you? Well, I heard that voice and then I took three deep breaths just to steady myself and right there is another bit of proof that it was no dream. I told no one about it. But this voice, it is a woman's voice, and it is one I have heard several times in the darkness now and it is not the voice of any living woman and of that I am entirely certain, so it is a ghost.

I went to a hotel once in Stinking Springs and the man there he said to me: "You want a bed?"

And I said, "Yes I do."

And he said, "You want a lady in it?"

And back then I did but I don't now, not anymore. I just ain't that interested anymore is what I am telling you. And most of all I don't need any dead women in there with me, thank you very much, last night's voice next to me was the last time for that, I hope. I expect that you let one dead person into your bed and there's soon gonna be a whole long lineup of wraiths looking for some of that blanket and some of that pillow. And there ain't no end to that line. Most people they just ain't got no idea of what's going on in this life, not really. They hear a church bell ring and they just hear a bell. That's not what I hear. I hear something completely different than that every single time I hear a church bell. I hear someone with a bill owing that is at some point going to require payment.

The dead are all around us still: just listen. And there ain't no secret in that, there's just those who refuse to see it. *"My God, William McCarty, I did not know you was that kind of a man,"* I can hear you thinking right now. Well, I am all kinds of men you do not know about. And likely I am a few I have not spent any time with myself. And one day I will know what it's like to be amongst those wraiths and spectres because one day I will die for real.

La da de dah de dah dee die.

☙ 53 ❧

"Forty-seven."

"What's that?"

"The number of teeth that mosquitoes have."

I look at Joseph over the top of his hot stew. "They have got awful tiny mouths to have that many teeth, Joseph."

He thinks about it and stops his chewing for a moment. "Tiny teeth," he says.

I slide my empty plate over to one side of the table and pick up my coffee. "That's an odd number, forty-seven," I say.

"It is."

"Usually teeth have more of an even number to them, I thought, 'less you've been in a bar fight or two."

"I suppose."

"Unusual."

"That's the way of things."

"No. No, it's not either, Joseph. Most things are not unusual. They are usual. That's what makes them most things—the fact that they are usual."

Joseph rolls himself a smoke and looks out the window at two men loading feed sacks onto a wagon. "You ain't lookin' hard enough, Ish." He reaches for his matches. "Unusual is all over the fuckin' place."

That fella in the yellow shirt is just standing over there at the bar by himself but he's not drinking anything and that is unusual is what I am thinking.

"I get this feeling all the time that I'm hidin' from somebody," I say. "It comes over me like a fog. You ever get that feeling?"

"No."

"Like somebody is after us. But nobody is, far as I know. Who are we hidin' from?"

Joseph lights his smoke and tosses the tobacco over the table. "Who ain't we?"

"Hey," Turner says.

"What?"

"Nothing. Just…I'm here too, you know."

"I know that."

Shit. I know that. You're sitting right there just as bright as the sun.

"We'll sleep in Galveston tomorrow night," Joseph says, "with four wooden walls and a roof overtop of us. Then we'll see to the provisions. Then north on to Canada."

With a whore on top of you is what you mean is what I am thinking but I keep that to myself.

"And why are you goin' there?" Turner cleans her plate with the last of the bread.

"Ain't no one in Canada knows his name." Joseph points his smoke toward me.

"You two don't know shit from oranges," Turner says. "Ain't nobody around here knows who you are either, and up north there ain't nothin' but cold and more cold, at least that's what I heard about it." She picks up the tobacco and the papers.

"People around here know plenty," I say.

"People around here don't know nothin' but cattle and fucking and sometimes those activities are combined in these parts, that is what I am guessing about that from what I've seen." She is making a mess of that smoke and that is certain.

"Here, let me do that."

"Hell with that. I'm doin' it myself."

"You are makin' a mess."

"Then I'm makin' a mess."

"And wasting tobacco…"

"Then I'm wastin' the damned tobacco. You the tobacco sheriff?"

"No." She's contrary.

The way his hand moves, it's like it wants to go to his side but then he keeps stopping it and holding it back. A yellow-shirted bastard standing at the bar with no drink is what he is.

She's trying to keep the leaves inside the paper while she rolls it up but it's coming out of both ends and falling onto the table.

"We'll pick up more tobacco tomorrow with everything else we need," Joseph says.

It will win this struggle of his though, his hand, because he wants it there, he wants his hand pulling that Colt out and—

This pecker's not one to announce himself. My gun's out and fired before his is even levelled off and before he's even finished his full turn toward our table. My Colt halfway between Joseph's and Turner's heads fast enough that by the time they see it it's already shot two times and three and then old quick draw in the fancy yellow shirt is coughing up his own blood onto the floor and that shirt ain't all yellow anymore.

"Jesus Christ!" someone yells out.

There ain't no need for him. It's over.

Here's a fella just having himself a quiet time at the bar and he up and decides he wants to become famous this afternoon. They're not often as good as they think they are, partly because they practise on empty bottles and on rocks and empty bottles and rocks don't move or shoot back. That shot of his could have just as easy gone through Turner's head as mine. She's ducked under the table and now real slow her face comes back up from below. Not all white and scared mind you, just curious.

"People here, they know me," I say, and I put my Colt away.

And I smile. Sometimes things are just funny the way they happen. Don't tell me people don't know me.

All the fellas in this place are just assin' around now with that boy's body and it don't seem like any of them were his friend because not a one of them is even looking over this way. He was alone at the bar and talkin' to no one. But that does not mean he doesn't have seventeen close friends nearby somewhere. You never let down your guard unless dead is a way you aspire to be. And you don't get to thinking that you are someone you are not, like ol' yellow shirt there being drug out the back door.

Goddamned gunfighter is what I am and there's nothing I can do about that.

"We better get on our way," I say.

"Well, shit," Joseph says. "Shit."

He's pissed that he did not see it coming. Well, nobody sees what's behind them. Always keep your ass to the wall, Joseph, you know that.

"I'm getting' the law," some old boy yells out.

Well, that's a heroic gesture on your part, mister.

"Here," I say, and I go to light Turner's smoke for her. It's not the best-rolled smoke but her hand goes to mine to hold the light and it's warm and it's calm. It's steady.

It is a shame about that boy. But some people are built for this world and some are not and some just move through life the same way a bad meal goes through your gut.

"So, let's go."

"I just don't like the cold is all, Canada is a cold place, that's what I heard about it," Turner says.

There's nothing I can do about that either. Someone probably will go get the bastard with the badge for this town. My experience is that when he finds out that no one even knows this old boy and that no one knows me and that I am gone, well, he will be just as likely to go back to his shack than to chase after us and if no one does know this old boy then no one will try to persuade him otherwise. They all got their own lives to get on with.

Still, we should be moving on. Trying to sort out the sense in all of it is like watching a curtain float in the breeze. Or it's like…

No, fuck it. I don't know what it's like. It's like what it is. It's like that.

And I do not believe that mosquitoes have forty-seven teeth. They likely do not have teeth at all. What would they do with them?

ᐸᗉ **54** ᗉᐳ

This'd be about the worst windstorm I ever seen. Galveston is a windy place, I will give that much to it.

"Hurricane? What do you mean a hurricane?"

"I mean a hurricane," the man is yelling to us. "You know, big winds. People dying. You know, a hurricane. A fucking *hurr-i-cane.*"

"Well, who in the hell decided that was a good idea?" Joseph asks him.

"It has already killed three people down in a place they call Cuba…and it's in all of the papers. Headin' here next is what they say."

"Is that what they say?"

"That's what they say, mister. That is what they say. I say it is already here!"

"Already here?"

"Is the wind blocking your ears, friend, or are you fucking hard of hearing?"

I have no wish to fight anymore. Apparently neither does Joseph because he just walks away from this cob and leaves him to nail his heavy pine boards over the window of his saloon. It takes no bravery to get into a fight over nothing; most of what it takes is just being stupid enough to start it. Bravery is just loyalty. That is all it is. Loyalty to one thing or person or to some other thing or person. *"Everything can't be perfect, can it?"* That is what a man with a bullet in his chest once told me. From his perspective I guess that was more true than ever. *"Listen, there's nothing in this world but God and the darkness,"* that is what he said next. Of course he was four or five sheets to the wind at that time and he was dying, his own life balling up inside him like cat fur, and so he wasn't in a very good mood. And then he was dead.

"I don't like this," I tell someone, maybe it's Joseph, maybe Turner. Maybe myself.

"Don't like what? The wind?"

"Cities. I do not care for cities. They hand me a rock in my gut."

"Never mind that."

"I can't just never mind it. It lies right here in my gut like a shitload that ain't comin' out anytime soon."

"What you got against 'em—cities?" Turner wants to know.

"There's lots too many people in them for my taste and also there's lots too many corners in cities, too many places for people to come at you unexpected."

"Now you're afraid of corners," Joseph says.

"I ain't afraid of nothing, I just don't like cities is all. I don't feel myself at ease in them. Not happy."

"Well, when the fuck were you ever happy?"

"I'm happy lots of goddamned times, Joseph."

"That so? Well, next time it happens will you sell me a ticket? I'd like to be there when it happens just one time."

"Fuck."

"It's just that I saw someone who was happy once and you don't look nothing like him."

This place just gives me the feeling of having a stick of dynamite up my ass and only a chair made out of matchsticks to sit on. Uneasy. Anyway, I have found that the thing to do about fear is just to run toward it with both your eyes open and both your fists closed. The only other choice is to just close your eyes and sit in the corner and hope it goes away. And, well, good luck to you with that. I just don't like corners. Nothing good ever came at me out of or around one. Somewhere inside of us there is everything that might be good and we just can't manage to squeeze it out on more than a few occasions, as if we have not ate enough vegetables and it is just stuck inside and won't come out. We go on forever trying and we spend our whole lives wasting time looking around corners for what's going to come after us when really it's our own damned selves we ought to be scared of. That being said, a two-by-four to the face is still a two-by-four to the face and it hurts like the bejesus so it's best to keep your head up and your eyes open. But right now Joseph is still yelling back through the wind at this cobbler trying to hammer his windows shut.

"Mister, where's the best place to stay in this town?"

"Right now I'd say anywhere else except in this town, that would be my advice!"

"But suppose you were staying here though?"

"I am staying here."

"And if you had no place to go?"

"Then I guess I'd just dig myself a deep hole and climb into it is what I'd do."

Joseph smiles back at him in a way that would worry me if I was not his brother. He is making every attempt to be amiable given the situation, but he turns to me and he says, "I'm going to shoot this fucker." But he won't.

"You ain't workin' very hard at bein' neighbourly, friend," is what he yells over the wind instead of shooting.

"Mister, you ain't my neighbour and what I am workin' at very hard is to keep my saloon from bein' picked up and set down again in pieces by God himself. Listen, I ain't the mayor and I ain't got the key to the goddamn city."

The man is trying to hold the boards into place and the wind is trying to stop him from doing so and the wind is winning the argument is what it looks like to me. I suppose it is this sad predicament he is in that prevents Joseph from shooting him.

"Well, you got any hotels made outta bricks instead of just matchsticks?"

"That'd be the Galvez, down by the water. But good luck to you tryin' to make it there without bein' blown into the ocean."

"Obliged."

"Jesus *Christ!*" The man is riding his sheet of wood like it's a whore he's trying to pin to a bed except the bed is against the wall and the lady just don't seem to be willing.

All I'm thinking is that we may lose the wagon in this storm if we can't find a place for tying it to the earth, but we are not going to lose those bank boxes. And Turner. I'm thinking of Turner. We are not going to lose those bank boxes and we are not going to lose Turner. She's lost enough as it is. Look, I'm going to remind you, this is not what you are probably thinking it might be. She has no father now. And me, I have nothing. And that is what this is. This is me looking after her and that is all. Me and my magic fucking beans. But I got no magic beans. All I got is a practical approach to the world that has not got me killed yet.

"I think maybe you better come on down from that wagon, it ain't safe up there," I tell her.

So it's the three of us by horse now and we decide to just leave the wagon against the side of a mercantile and hope to find it still there later, but I believe we all know that this is the last time we'll see it in one piece and that this storm and now hurricane is of a mind to change a lot of things for us, not the least of which will be what it does to our wagon. I would still rather be out on the open plains. I would rather just be blown clear away than to have a building fall onto me and this whole town looks as if it will come down on all of us soon enough, there are already boards and shakes flying through the air and the sky is as black as the inside of a crow and it is still only late afternoon. I know too that aside from the company of a whore there is nothing Joseph wants more right now than to know what is in these three boxes that we have pulled down from the wagon, but it is not in his nature to ask and since the only keys for the boxes are on a chain that is now around Turner's neck, he is unlikely to find out what's in them unless he does ask. So go ahead, I'm shouting quiet to him in my head, just ask me what's in the goddamned boxes. But he will not. His bear-trap jaws are so rusted shut that he wouldn't open 'em up even to ask old Saint Pete for a leg up over the pearly gates. Next thing to fly by us is a dog. A goddamn flying dog hurling through the air like someone just picked it up and threw it. Wild yellow eyes on it and its tongue flapping.

"We should maybe get on to a gallop, I think," old steel mouth says. "That wind seems to be pickin' up some."

ക 55 ൈ

There's a soft spot on the side of your head, right at your temple. Everyone has one and everyone knows if you get hit hard right at that exact spot your brain will turn into pumpkin mash, so I am not anxious to be out here any longer with the bits and pieces of Galveston, Texas, flying through the air at me.

"What do you think the kid's last thoughts were?"

"You mean besides *holy shit my head's on fire?*"

"Yeah, besides that."

"Probably *holy fuck I'm dying.*"

"You think so?"

"Well, that's what I'd have been thinking."

"We got to get inside somewhere."

"I think that's it up there."

It is dark from the time of day and from the storm both and this hotel looms up at us out of the water and wind-filled air like a whale breaking through the surface. I mean, I guess that is what it would be like but what the hell do I know about whales? Jonah lived in one. So I guess they're kind of like hotels. Funny place to live though, your pillows and sheets would always smell like fish. This whale of a hotel is like a huge solid brick sitting by the side of the ocean and everything around it is either shaking or blowing away while it just stays put right where it's been planted. Cliffs of water explode up every few seconds from the seawall like cannon shots and it is as if the ocean is on an all-out assault to take the land back. The horses do not wish to be anywhere near this battle, so we come in at the back of the building only to find that every window is covered from the inside with boards like the one the saloon keeper was dancing with, only these look like they were nailed secure there some days ago, and if there's anyone inside there's no way to tell it from here. The windows are up over our heads from here on the ground and there is no door on this side of the building.

"Hey!" Joseph reaches up and pounds on the bottom of a window frame. Nothing.

Turner gets down off her horse and picks up a white-painted rock from what is left of the garden. "Stand aside," she yells. The rain is coming at us sideways now, it is not like rain anymore, it is like the air around us is turning into water.

So we do stand aside like she says and her rock sails up past us and shatters the lowest pane of glass. Joseph and I we pull our hands into our sleeves and reaching as high as we can we start to hit at the board inside to free it from its nails. We get the edge of it lifted up a bit and Turner joins us but she can't reach and so we just keep on pushing against it and then all of a sudden it splits and falls free.

"Boost me," she yells at us, and we each take a leg and ease her on up and then through and we hear her tumble down on the other side. All we can hear outside is the roar as another mountain of water shoots up from the seawall.

"What's going on?" I yell in at her.

"There's nobody in here," she yells back, and suddenly the window frames fly in on her as if they've been dynamited and the wind is flapping the heavy curtains now like they're wet newspaper. I grab the boxes and we heave them in and then I give Joseph a leg up and then he and Turner haul on me and I scramble in and we pull to get the windows closed again after us and after a while we get it done, but they are doing nothing now to keep the wind and water out so we move further on into this room, which looks like a dining room of some kind.

"We got to get the horses in here," Joseph says.

"I know it."

Somehow he's cut up his arm on the glass. "For fuck's sake…"

"Wrap that up tight."

"This is just the hell of the evening so far, isn't it?"

Turner has his sleeve rolled up for him and is wrapping some clean cloth around it. Women always have some clean cloth or they know where to find it in a hurry, no matter where they are. They must carry it on them somewhere in case it is needed.

"Where the hell is everybody?"

Soon enough we have an answer to that question. We get ourselves slowly out of the pitch black and out into the lobby of the place and there's a pretty grim group of fine-dressed people sitting like funeral wraiths around a bunch of candles and they sit there looking up at us like we're the ghosts.

"Who the hell are you?" one of them asks, standing up like we've walked into his special supper party. He straightens up his vest and jacket as if he's readying himself to make some kind of a speech.

"We got some horses we gotta bring on in here," I announce, stepping past his question like it's a dead fish flopping on the floor, "and we need to get one of these doors open so we can do it."

"Horses?"

"Yessir," I tell him. "You know, as in…horses." Maybe he needs further explanation but it's pretty simple. Horses.

"You can't bring any horses in here."

"Oh it can be done, I'll show you."

"There is a stable in the back for your horses. Plenty of room for them there."

"Your stable's made of pine boards. And it's not looking like it's going to be there in the morning…it's maybe not even there now. My horses are coming in here." My right-hand fingers are spread and ready.

Joseph has already started prying wood off what looks to be the main door.

"Here, you, wait and stop that. Who are you people? You can't just come in here—"

Suddenly there's a shot.

"We're already here," Turner tells him in a steady voice, her pistol still pointed straight up and little pieces of white ceiling plaster drifting down into her hair, "and our horses are coming in here next."

And she lets the pistol play over the assembly of whitened faces now as plaster dust continues to fall silently over her in the dim light. Well, old standing man over there he just sits down now and he gives every appearance of a man no longer interested in discussion. Soon enough we are a strange assembly of fancy-dress hotel guests, three outlaws, their horses, and a selection of low-burning candles. Supper-party man he looks now like he's been hit with the backhand of God and I suppose at his station in life he is not accustomed to having to listen to a young woman with a pistol. Well, there's a first time for all things is what I am thinking. In the ensuing silence we all find ourselves watching that young woman carefully picking the small leftover pieces of white out of her hair and casting them one by one down onto the carpet.

"You boys pull any good-size oysters out of the water around here?" Joseph asks out of nowhere.

I swear I do not know where he comes up with his lengthy line of bullshit. Oysters.

Nobody answers him and he sits there like he just swallowed an egg whole. Well pleased with himself and the world is what he looks like. "I always enjoyed an oyster when I could get one," he says now, as if this new information might be of additional interest to those assembled. There is no indication that this is the case. He doesn't care. He starts to roll himself a smoke.

"I had some once in a place called Tampico, I think it was…"

He has never had an oyster in his life is what I'd bet.

"Salty." He continues to look well pleased with himself. "What's wrong, Ish? Don't you like seafood?"

Mister supper-party conversation. Sometimes it is it is like a live crab has crawled right up his ass and he is itching to get it out again to share it with the world as if it is a thing made of gold.

"If it wasn't for you, we'd be halfway to Canada by now," I tell him. "It's you and your oysters that got us here and right into the middle of a hurricane," I explain in case this point is not clear to him. "Has that fact become fuzzy to you?"

"I could use a drop of whisky, Ish, and I do not see how this hurricane is my fault in any way, you give me too much credit."

I put my boots up on the low table at the centre of us all and the dinner guests hold their breath. "There's lots of places we could be right now instead of in the middle of a fucking hurricane, Joseph."

By the sound of some sharp intakes of air, some of the ladies amongst the assembled worthies and maybe some of the men too are not used to such rough-chopped talk in the midst of their social dos.

"I've seen dogs and cats get along better'n the two of you," Turner says of a sudden, "and coyotes and gophers too."

And with that pronouncement a board flies off a window somewhere upstairs and the resulting crash of glass sounds like some giant is at the walls with hammers in both his fists. I grab a candle and light on up the main stairs and Turner decides to follow me. Anything that takes me away from Joseph and this graveyard wraith party suits me for the moment and I guess that is Turner's feeling too as she gets right beside me going down the hall, and when we find the room with the busted-up boards we work together to get a wardrobe pushed up against the open window, scraping and bumping it across the floorboards. The wind sounds like a thousand people just beyond the walls screaming and scratching to get in. We're both trying to get our breath back and we're leaning hard against the back of the wardrobe when suddenly we both just start to laugh for no reason, and then we stop. And nobody moves.

"I don't want to like you, McCarty," she says.

And then all the screaming starts up again outside. I don't know if it had ever stopped or if I just stopped hearing it.

"Well, maybe if you just give it some more time, you won't have to like me at all," I tell her. "That's the way it works with folks...usual."

So we don't say anything to each other then and then it's alright. It's alright. It's not what it was and now it's turned into something else. I don't know what exactly it is now or even what it was before, but it is something else, that is clear, so I'll just keep it this way. It feels like it's alright. If we live through this night it is, or it will be. I just want to keep this girl alive. So I have something to do now. I have something I want to do.

"I don't like the idea of all that money just sitting all lone-some by itself down there," I say to her after a while.

So we go back downstairs and we don't find Joseph there but we do find the whisky in the bar and the strongboxes on the floor and we make our way back upstairs with both of them and we stay up all night but we don't drink any of the whisky. Mostly we just sit with our backs against the wall. There is no way to sleep with the noise and outside are all the voices of the departed howling and inside there is just the candle on the floor and there is Turner and in the morning the candle is gone, but Turner, well, she is still here. We are both a long way from our homes and both our homes are long gone from us now and from anywhere on this earth, but I do not feel so troubled in my mind anymore and I would like maybe to have just some plain fried eggs. Big yellow suns in the morning.

༺ 56 ༻

One day it will be the fresh pine box for each of us. And all of this is so much finer than the boxes they will place us into then, so it is best, I think, to just get on with things and maybe to help each other along. And maybe I am just feeling the way you do when you think you might die in the night and then you are a little bit surprised to find in the morning both that you didn't die after all and also that you are quite pleased not to have done so. It is best just to keep your mind occupied with what you can do and not with the things you cannot. There is enough to worry about in this world with men trying to punch holes into you and whatever other miseries you might face that it is best not to chew on something that's already chewing on you.

So it is a wonder that we are alive. We come out blinking into the morning like some people I saw once coming out of a nickelodeon and into the street and the sunlight, like they had never seen anything before and as if they were now seeing everything for the very first time. It is morning and still a long way to Canada and that place is not getting any closer. Joseph is hard-crusted over this morning and not talking and I would guess the reason is that he did not get the chance to stick his hog into any mud last night as he had intended. That is not my concern and so he can just keep right on clamped-up tight if he chooses. It all puts me in mind of talking to a kid once during the time of the range wars bragging about some whore he was with once.

"Were you covered?" I asked him.

"What do you mean?"

"I mean did you have any protection?"

"Sure, I was wearing my six-guns the whole time."

Anyway we come out in the morning just as wide-eyed as that kid was back then. And it's not like a whore is anything to brag about anyway. Come to that, nothing is anything to brag about so that was a wrong thing for me to say because whores are some of the nicest people I know usually.

"People say reading is good for you but I never bothered to learn any of it. And my poor old father got shot right through his head while he was reading a book so that is just proof that reading is not any good for you at all."

A whore by name of Annie Flatfoot said that to me one time about her own father.

"What was the book?" I asked her.

But she could not recall the title of it. Maybe something about birds, she thought. Her father liked to watch and to name the birds, what kinds they were, but that was all before he took a slug to his head. Following that event he took no interest in birds whatsoever.

Everything is tore up this morning and nothing is where it was yesterday. When we find the spot that we left it yesterday we see there is nothing much at all remaining of the wagon but for kindling wood and flapping canvas and it would be disheartening if it were not for the fact that I would just as soon sleep under the sky as anywhere else anyway, like I said before. I just don't like things covering me up overtop is all, it reminds me of being dead. Not that I've been dead, not yet, but I guess you know what I mean. So we start packing what we need and whatever we can find onto the horses.

"Three strongboxes, three of us…"

This is Joseph's observation. I see no reason for him to make it as it is self-evident and very simple math. It is as if he is eager to show us that he can count.

[298]

"You always were one for the numbers," I tell him.

"Best way to travel is to distribute the load evenly, that is all I am saying," is all he says.

I take a look at Turner and she's busy packing into her bags the last of the coffee and dry flour she has found under the canvas. Where we are going to get supplies now I am sure I do not know. Perhaps Joseph has a brilliant idea regarding the purchasing of provisions in a town that has disappeared overnight. Turner's hair has come loose. She's busy with what she's doing and she's not listening to us. Her lower lip pushes out as she examines the flour bags closely for leaks. It's a face you don't forget easy, it sticks with you. She for certain has a special kind of a look about her, but anything a man can say about a woman is beside the point, that is my thinking on it.

"That's all I'm saying," he says again.

"Is that all you're sayin'?"

"You hear me sayin' anything else?"

"I don't hear you saying anything worth a single bean."

Joseph spits now and before his juice hits the ground he shifts himself quick toward me and throws a punch at my head. I can block it easy though—he might as well have sent me a telegram yesterday saying it was coming today and at exactly what time to expect it. We both go down into the dirt but before I can get up on top of him he's up on top of me and he grapples on to one of the strongboxes and strikes me in the head with it.

"You hit me with my own damned money!"

"No, it ain't yours, no it ain't. Not all of it."

I scramble up and make a grab at his collar. We fight like women when we do fight, and it is quite likely a sad thing to see, I am certain of that, but it does stop us from killing each other. Then we decide just to stop fighting and we come to rest down in the mud and from there we watch Turner still loading the bags as if we are nothing at all to her.

"If you two are done, there's some trail riding for us to do and either you can carry my money for me or you can let me do it by myself but you can also just remember that it came from the man who murdered my sister and my father, so carryin' it is all you'll be doin' with it unless and until such time as I decide to decide different about that."

Joseph and I just stay down in the mud and stay shut.

"So that's all there is about that," she says, "and that's all."

ᥦ **57** ᥯

"McCarty, you awake?"

"Yup."

"What do you think the stars are there for?"

I have to admit to her that I have never even given it a thought.

❧ **58** ❧

"McCarty?"

"Yup."

"You got any family alive besides your brother?"

No.

〜🌀 **59** 🌀〜

"That's the Mississippi River, ain't it, McCarty?"

"Yup. That's it."

Turner just stares at it. "Well, what do you think of it?"

"I seen lots of rivers."

ᥦ **60** ᥯

Once I was with George Coe up on the tin roof of Henry Ellis's place and he said to me, "You see that fella far off out there?" And he pointed toward a man who was seated for a rest on top of a cow's skull way off on the plain.

"I see him."

"Well, I'm going to shoot at him."

And he takes his shot and the man falls right over, just like someone pushed him off a wall.

৩৯ **61** ৬৩

Turner makes us stop so she can wash her face in the water. Joseph watches me. I watch Joseph.

He just looks hungry as if someone is ringin' the supper iron.

Then we both watch Turner.

And then I just sit there, feeling like a man who's been dragged through fire and through coal.

⋘ 62 ⋙

*T*urner, I remember that fight. After the fire but before we took to the trail with Father and everything else went wrong too. Before the rest of everything else that has happened. It makes me think of the splash of the water in the kitchen tub or out of the pump on a hot day but it was neither of those things. All we take with us is what we may remember in the end. This is one of the things I never told you. I took up with the wrong man, Turner, you know that. They are all the wrong man but he was the wrongest. He was all lit up about something I don't even remember now and he's up from the table so fast and he grabs at the pot of milk. The little white pot with pale blue lines that came all the way down from New York State and he throws that milk at me, Turner, and I'm sitting there dripping with milk and he's sorry, he says he's sorry right away and I can see that he's sorry once he has done it and I'm the only one who can see that he's sorry because all the others are just yelling at him and pulling at him and I can see that he's sorry before he even knows it himself. I always knew he was sorry before he did and he always was sorry, but that never changed anything. I knew before he'd ever say it. And I remember him storming out the door that day, away from himself, you see, not from me or from all of them, and they were always saying just leave him, Missouri, just leave him alone to himself because he'll never leave you, he's not that big of a fool, and me just standing there with the milk dripping down me and not crying, it's the milk that's dripping down to the floor, not me crying because I will not show any of them that and the milk dripping off the edge of the table slowly and I could see him in my mind stumping across the hardscrabble ground away from me and away from the rest of them and then the evening still going on around me and there was singing and everyone drank and everyone sang and all of them repeating you should leave him, Missouri, he doesn't deserve a woman like you and you should leave him and all of them falling into each other or asleep around the place and him coming back, his tail between his legs, and he never said sorry out loud, Turner, oh but he was in his face and in his hands and that milk still on me silky and sticky I would not wash it off, and him touching my skin where it was like it was my blood, the hair on my arms, the v at my neck and I wasn't going to wash it off for him, the sweet sour taste of it, and I always knew he'd be back and let me wash it off you, Missouri, he said, let me be the one, and his hands on me then washing me washing me clean he loved me you see, Turner, he loved me and no one understood that. They could see it. You could see it just looking at him. But they couldn't understand it.

And Father wanted to kill him.

If he hadn't loved me he never would have thrown the milk at me like that. And he would never come back to wash it off me. But in the end it was me who left him.

Oh Turner, he burned so bright when he was a good man and so dark when he was not. That's all men, Turner. They all burn like that. You gotta trust what you love and trust it will never leave you. Only way he left me was by that bullet, otherwise he'd still be coming back and Father would not have taken you and me away from there. And maybe we'd go down to the creek in the night and his moon shining white hands on me. The way he always was proud, even when he had nothing at all to be proud of and I loved him so. Tell me how would me leaving him help any with that? It just drove him into the ground like a nail and anyway Father makes me go away from him and then he goes and gets himself shot. He was always dressed up sharp, but never had anything at all in his pockets. I was wrong to be with him but I was too young to know it.

Turner, you gotta make yourself something...no one is ever going to—no man is going to do that for you. This man McCarty is not going to do that for you just because he killed the man who killed me. Killing is the easy part for them. It's everything else that is hard work. Don't wait for no man to pull you up.

That's not the direction they go.

This man McCarty he's not good enough for you, Turner.

Because no man is.

Good enough.

For you.

I wish I could tell you what is happening to me here, Turner. I wish I could tell you so many things but most of all I wish I could tell you... the men who killed me, Turner, they are here. Both of them! They are here now!

That word though does not even make sense: here. There is no here that I can see but I can see the men like I am looking through the wrong end of a telescope. And they cannot see me, they do not know about each other and they do not know about me. But they will, they will know about me and there will be a reckoning and there will be a justice performed.

So I go to prepare a room for you. This is what he meant when he spoke those words. This is what our Lord meant, do you think? It is the first time I have not been scared here and for the first time I know now what to do, I know what there is to be done. By me. Finally there is something I can do for you. And for me. There is something finally, finally to be done.

᨞ **63** ᨞

This wind is no man's friend. I swear to you I can hear voices
sometimes on the wind, but maybe it is just this one voice.
On the other hand, maybe it is just madness. Maybe this cold
is just getting into my bones and into my brain but these voices
sit on me like a thick molasses these nights and the one thing I
do know is that neither of them particularly wish me well.
Perhaps I have just grown too old for the trail. Perhaps there
are no voices, and perhaps it is just the wind. I have this feeling
that it is the dead girl, Missouri is what Wing called her, that it
is Turner's sister calling somehow to me. Other times it is like
that deranged bastard I killed taunting at me. I could address
this matter with Joseph but he would laugh at me and call me
a fool and I cannot mention it to Turner for fear of hurting her.
I suppose I will just quietly sink into insanity on my own.

"What are you doing?"

"The fire is going out."

"It's almost dawn."

"Yes, it is."

Turner sits up and pulls her blankets around herself like a
hood. "You ever go to church much, McCarty?"

"Not much."

"You don't believe?"

"In church? No."

She sits looking into the fire. "No, not in church. What *do*
you believe in, McCarty?"

"That's it, I believe in McCarty. Why you always call me
that?"

"McCarty? It's your name, isn't it?"

I don't answer that and I pull another log over to the fire.

"Billy."

I don't know why she's saying that.

"William."

So I just stay shut up.

"Lots of Sundays I don't go to church," she says.

I place the log at the strongest point of the flame and stack it so the air can get at it.

"But sometimes I do, when I can. When I could. He never knows when I'm coming but he knows I'll show up sometimes, I think he does. I try to surprise him, do you think that's foolish?"

I don't answer.

"I guess all of us just go into the ground in the end," she says.

"You want some biscuits and coffee?"

A little white church on a road. That's what I see.

I do not know what's happening here. But that is nothing new. The fresh snow on the lake is shining blue now like new milk.

⸙ **64** ⸙

We have been lucky with shooting mostly rabbit and squirrel and the snow is not so deep so as to slow the horses up any. Joseph points out to us the trees that leak out sugar water in the spring if opened up to do so with a spout and a hanging pail. This morning we see a hawk up in the quiet sky circling around lazy and high. There is a lot of staring up into the blue sky when the ground is level just to pass the time while the horses find their own way. There is not so much talking during the daylight and there is enough for us to see as we move. In Kentucky we stop to take on provisions again and some more blankets. As long as you are wrapped up well at night you are warm. Snow is not as dire an element as I had thought. It is the gentlest of things as it falls and walking in it is like examining some fine object wrapped up in cotton batting—you do not truly feel the ground under your feet, which is offsetting at first, to me at any rate, but with practice it becomes normal. It does not seem to bother the animals any. Turner is well used to it and she tells us of sledding down hills when she was a young girl and of making "snowmen" and of carving angels by lying down and spreading wide her arms and her legs. She demonstrates the technique for us and we both suffer to give it a try just to humour her. She laughs at us and that rests just fine with me and with Joseph too, I think. All in all it is a peaceful time and that is most welcome. We see only three other riders for days and they are high up on a ridge in what is called the Appalachian territory and twice at night we see the light of a fire and other than that our companions are the crows and the woodpeckers. The daylight is much friendlier to me than the night is and even now in the dark, things are more quiet than they have been this whole journey, this whole life. The strange woman's voice in my ear at night is gone now and nothing torments me any longer. It is easy to think of a life that just continues on like this, in a small cabin somewhere lost in the trees.

I don't know that you have ever made a study of or had a close look at a beehive but it is something to see and to think about too. It is intricate and practical and the most amazing thing about it is that the bees, so far as I know, have nothing we might call a brain. Yet the hive is more complicated than most houses or towns. There is no school to go to where the bees learn how to do this. They are just born knowing it and then they set right to work at it. We on the other hand are born knowing nothing and a great many of us make no remarkable progress from that state during the course of our lives. These maple trees of Joseph's make sugar water. Bees make honey. We cause each other pain and we leave nothing after us when we go.

"What are you thinking of, McCarty?"

"Bees."

"Bees?"

"Honeybees."

We make everything small.

"Do they have honeybees in Canada?"

But things are not small. We are small ourselves and so we try to make other things that way too, but it is only for our own convenience that we attempt to do so. Like many other things we do, it is a way to feel better about ourselves.

"In the summer, I mean."

"I imagine they do."

"Then we could have honeybee hives and we could have our own honey whenever we want it."

ᴇꙮ **65** ꙮᴇ

With the right woman close at hand there is no need for a Bible. We can have bees. And we can have honey. But I am stuck with Joseph, as if we are cut both from the same light brown and torn-edged piece of old leather. Turner I choose. I do not deserve to choose to be the one who looks after her, but in spite of that here we both are. It is something called the process of elimination, at least that's what Joseph would call it. It is more a matter of not getting shot to death, I believe. Not getting shot dead has been what has left me here with her. That's what I should have said when she asked me what I believe. I believe in not getting shot.

I always have.

"What about getting into Canada?" I ask Joseph. If I do not ask him, he will just ride us right up to the gates without even telling us how the thing is to be done.

"What about it?"

"Well, how do we do it?"

"We aim for the province of Ontario by way of Michigan. And then we cross the river right there by ferry, then northeast to the land I have purchased there. It is the best way and the shortest with the horses."

"We just ride on in there?"

"We do. Least ways Turner and I do. We are respectable citizens of the United States of America. You on the other hand are a common criminal."

I don't see that there's any need to throw around words like that.

"Just 'cause a man don't allow himself to get shot, that's not something that can make him a criminal."

"No, but the United States government can make him one. And it did exactly that, Ish. Maybe you remember that? I recall you were there in the courthouse at the time."

"That ain't nothin', Brady killed a good friend of mine. And no one called *him* a criminal for that."

"Maybe because after you shot him he was dead, Ish, and then there was no need."

"More because he was a lawman, I expect."

"Either way. Most governments take a dim view of people going around killing their employees. And either way he ain't trying to cross the border with stolen money."

"That money it ain't stolen," Turner points out.

"No, maybe not by you, Miss Turner, but it is certain that someone stole it somewhere along the line, that is my guess. I believe the chances of it having been gained by any legal means are slim at best."

"Well anyway, how they gonna know that? And how they gonna know who I am?"

"Maybe they won't, Ish. Long as you don't go calling yourself Billy the Kid or use the name McCarty. I got papers here saying my name is Joseph Bonney, and I cannot prove that Turner is my daughter but they got no reason to doubt it when I tell it to them and she is very pleasant to look at, beg pardon, Miss Turner, and, well, if she can manage to call me Poppa a couple of times for show and can maybe work up just a little shy smile for them they might give her a second look but not because they don't want her to enter the Dominion of Canada, I have no worries about that. I can prove who I am and they got no reason to not believe she is my daughter and if they open those boxes they got no reason not to believe that is our money."

"Well, that's a rosy picture for the two of you then."

"Plus I have papers showing I own that land. So, now, long as you can convince them that you are my idiot half-brained brother who was hit on the head when he was a baby and you don't have any papers or even know your own name, then things should be rosy all around. And also you should try not to shoot anyone."

Turner is laughing now.

"I ain't doin' that. I ain't bein' no one's idiot brother."

"Why not, Ish? You have had enough practice over the years. And if you could maybe let a little spit out of your mouth, maybe let it drool down your chin a bit, and maybe let your eyes roll back in your head some, it might enhance the effect."

Turner is still laughing. She is much amused by his patter.

"And this is the great plan you have been developing all this time in secret, Joseph? You ain't got no other plan than that? You ain't got no other plan that does not have me shitting down my own pants and picking my nose?"

"Well, like I say, when it comes to being an idiot brother, it ain't like you're without any practice."

"Fuck you anyway."

"All we need is a little natural amplification."

"The hell we do."

In addition to the deficiencies in his overall plan, I do not care much for boats.

They sink.

✂️ **67** ✂️

Joseph has a fever for busting my head on this business of crossing the border but he can't seem to get a hold of any way to do it other than by having me act the fool. Well, I have decided that is fine. If doing so means getting Turner somewhere safe, then what is that to me? Just a lot of palaver. You know that word? I learned it in the Mojave Desert, a place I have spent more time in than I cared to, even though I like the place and it was not for very long and I was paid to be there. There was a man wanted to take some possessions of his through the desert and I rode along with him, which is what he paid me for. He paid me for shooting anyone who wanted to help him with his possessions in an unwanted manner but no one did. Well, I got paid just the same so it made no difference to me. What did impress me though was the tricks this man could do, which he used to pass the time in camp. I believe there wasn't nothing with a playing card that he could not do. I would not have played poker with him, that much is certain. He had a trick where he could have you just think of a card and then he would pull that same card right out of the deck blind. It was a good trick. But that man is dead now. He tried to tell me that whoring was the only honourable profession. I told him the only respectable way to make money that involved scraping something sticky off your body at the end of the day was the keeping of bees. Well, he said he did not care for honey. Though I suppose you could say I was whoring myself out at the time on that job. Most of us do, one way or another, don't we? So I suppose it is wrong of me to try to judge whores for doing so, at least they are honest about it. I do not know what it is that makes me want to look after her. I have never cared much for that sort of thing in the past, I have let people take care of themselves, of what concern are they to me? That has always been my thinking but now I am like some foolish preacher who feels he is saving someone's young soul and really I am only saving myself. We are all only ever trying to save ourselves and I am not doing much of a job even of that. Anyway, this man. He turned out to be a man who at the end of the journey wanted to keep his bags of money and then pay me nothing at all for helping him to keep them and he had friends at the end of the trail waiting for him who felt the same way about things.

I only had the one gun at that time but I had brought enough bullets for everyone there. Blood hands again for me but I got paid out certain enough. I am not proud of anything I have done, you understand, and maybe that is the problem, I have nothing to be particularly proud of. Maybe the best thing is just to get across the border and try to forget all the rest of it. Nobody knows who Billy the Kid is up there. So we'll all be the same, because I swear I don't know who Billy the Kid is either. People get to know your name on its own and it seems they have suddenly got this strange hunger to meet you, and maybe they want to shoot you, or maybe they want a piece of you to take home or maybe they just want to shake your hand and have a drink with you. But one thing I do know about a hunger like that is that it has got no cellar to it. There ain't no reason for it to stand and there ain't no end to it either. *"I'll tell you something and it is that one time I met President Taft."* Well, who the high diddly hell cares about that if you did? Maybe that's important to you somehow but it sure ain't to me. Same thing for Billy the Kid. Who the hell needs to meet that bastard? It's a good thing he's dead and buried and there's a stone marks the spot where he landed. You chisel yourself off a good piece of that little rock for your memento and you can leave me all the hell alone about it.

I never knew him.

✎ 68 ✎

One time I was in Guadalajara in Mexico and they were having themselves a big epidemic of something called cholera. Well, lots of people died. So many that they piled them up into a hill and burned all of them together and the smoke covered the sky like something straight out of the Bible. I tried not to breathe it in. You want to talk biblical? Well, the three of us are crossin' a river now and ain't that in the Bible somewhere? Someone crossin' a river?

I bet it is. They had lots of rivers in that book, I know that much, and they must have crossed them somehow. That's exactly the kind of thing they would have put in the Bible: the crossing of a river. People put things into books for reasons, and I guess that includes God, and he put some rivers into his book. People crossing a river is like starting out new, that is clear enough. Though I think it can mean they're dying too, or it could be that's the Egyptians. I can't remember. Listen: the River Jordan. That's in the Bible. What I do know about the Bible is that everything in it means something else and you would need a preacher just to explain it all. That's what they get paid for, that and talking up a storm on Sunday mornings and judging pie contests. But there's reasons Jesus got himself strung up and it wasn't just some shit-luck thing that happened to him. People in the Bible don't just die for no good reason, I know that too. It is not like in real life where people die all the time and for no good reason at all and maybe because they turn the wrong corner or they eat the wrong food or get onto the wrong boat. In books when someone dies it is for a reason the person who wrote the book has.

I think I have told you I do not like boats. I will tell you again that this does not seem like a good idea to me. This river is full of pieces of ice the size of a farmer's field and the water you can see between them is rolling away like the furnaces of hell and is the colour of black ink. At least we are near to the shore now and this is almost over. I will feel better with my ass off this boat and back up onto a horse. Everything is ice and it is hard just to keep standing and we have been standing and sliding around on this deck too long for my liking. Joseph and Turner do not seem to mind but sliding on ice does not make me feel secure. I do not like it when my feet are not well planted and I do not like being separated from the horses. I have all the cash boxes strapped over my shoulders at least and one saddlebag with the papers we need and our extra money. They help to plant me when the ship rolls and the icy metal of the deck becomes a sliding hillside. And my stomach is just about ready to heave itself on over the side. I was not built for water travel and none of these yokels we are hedged in with seem to mind any of this nonsense. We are almost to the dock.

And it happens. Quick like it's over before you can see it even starting. It's not supposed to happen. But it does. I suppose that sometimes whoever is in charge somewhere knows what they are doing. But it's hard to imagine that is truly the case when you are down here with both feet sliding around in the shit or, in this case, on the ice, where Joseph's feet no longer are. Where he was, there is now suddenly just nothing. There he is, and now there he was. He is down under the railing just as quick as if a carpet is snatched out from under him or like he's a stale loaf of bread being throwed out of a window. All I can do is reach for where he was because he is not there anymore, he is gone.

"Man over! Man over!"

Someone is yelling that. It is me. I hold hard on to the railing and stare down into the surging black. At first he is a voice calling out. Then a face. Then already just an arm, then an arm and a head breaking the surface of the boiling water between the ship and the ice, then just an arm again. His hat. A group of people on the shore and the dock are shouting and pointing. There are men in a small boat making their way toward us. People around me are shouting. I turn quickly to where Turner is and the light is gone from her face. She is the colour of the steel wall behind her and she does not know what to do. It hurts me that she does not know what to do, and also that there is nothing she *can* do. I throw the boxes and the bag at her.

"No," she has time to say.

And I am gone.

∽ **69** ∾

There are sailors on the small boat beside us waving and shouting, pointing. I go under the ice and water and I come up again and the small boat is nearer to us now, the men on it shouting and closing the distance faster, but Joseph is not even an arm anymore. He is just water now, just ripples and the voice that he was, and the small boat sails right over the spot where he'd once been and almost over me as if the men rowing it have not seen me and there is a chorus now of shouts from the shore and from the ship. The little boat has stopped and is turning but everything is just being pushed by the ice and the churning of the water, and no one knows what to do, as if the men rowing are in molasses or oatmeal instead of water. And we have been here in the ice too long now and Joseph is slipping, has slipped away from me, down and away and under. My skin is fire and daggers and screaming at me to move, move. Then there is a splash in the water directly behind us and some man from the ferry has jumped into the water now and is swimming wildly toward the spot that had been Joseph and is now just me. There was a single spot in the water that had been a man and is now just a spot, and now not even a spot anymore, it is just water like all the rest of the water. Now it is where the new man has stopped and is diving down and coming back up gasping, just as I have been doing, but I have stopped. I have stopped. The gasping is the only sound now that the ferry's engines have been shut off. Everyone can hear it, this gasping. Then the roaring sound when you go under and then the gasping again when you break the surface, your lungs screaming with ice in them. The little boat has returned and the sailors are pointing and one is reaching out with an oar to us. The man who has jumped in ignores the oar each time he comes up and takes a breath, his beard is frozen in the air, and then he goes back under the surface. He comes up again and knocks the oar away with his hand. You can hear everyone holding their breath, and you can hear the splashing in the water, and the shouts. There is no other sound. The man slaps the oar out of the way again, and this time the man is me. And the next time I grab hold of it and I can feel myself being pulled up into the boat and my skin is on fire. My skin is fire. I cannot feel my head. Someone in the boat is shouting at me, roaring at me. Everything is pounding.

"Are you the man who fell? Mister, are you the man who fell?"

No.

"No."

Then he stops shouting and we both look out over the water. Where Joseph and the other man had been, there is nothing now. Then we see a man's body lying on the shore and a group of people around it, except it isn't a man anymore. Not anymore. And the man who had been diving with me is off to one side away from that group, he is on his knees leaning over, gasping and white, but moving.

I look up at the smoke rising over the city.

They are burning the dead is what I am thinking.

And that is all I can think before everything is dark.

When I open my eyes again someone else is yelling at me, someone new.

"Do you know who he was? Mister, the man who fell, do you know who he was?"

I am cold.

"Mister, did you know that man?"

"No."

I cannot feel.

But I can think.

"No, I did not know him."

"Mister, who are you? What is your name?"

"Joseph."

I can think.

"McCarty."

I can still think.

"My name is Joseph Bonney."

I have to.

"My name is Joseph Bonney."

I am afraid.

I say it once more to make it true.

"My name is Joseph Bonney."

And I am alive.

Turner.

৩ **70** ৩

Dust settles and sticks itself to everything. It shows no favourites. In that way it is very much like sadness; it is indiscriminate. I believe that is the right word. Joseph would have known the word. They say that Jesse James was shot dead while he was straightening out a picture frame on a wall. That, I think, is a fairly shitty way for a man to go. You can't actually make anything straight the way you think you can and it never sticks and stays straight anyway. The world makes things crooked for you again soon enough. And people, the world makes people crooked as hell.

My brother Joseph died fighting for his life. He didn't give a dried-up shit for a straight picture frame or for much else that was straight in this world either. Maybe it is true that the way he ended up going was stupid and pointless but you got one that ain't? It's a better way to go than to go levelling out a painting of some flowers on a wall. A whole lot of men are standing around now talking about my dead brother. Except they don't know he's my brother. They think I'm him now and I got all the papers with me to prove this is so and so they can't figure out who this dead man is and they got no way to find it out. But they stand there talking about it anyway while the snow starts falling and they write things down and they shake each other's hands and nod their heads. I watch them for a while in the cold, standing wrapped in a blanket someone put on me. Hushed voices on them as if they're saying things that amount to anything at all but they do not, there's a dead man and no amount of talking and writing things down will change that. I got nothing to do. I am as helpful as a second cock on a wedding night and so I just step back some into the crowd. And I leave Joseph lying there cold and flat on the snow. My brother. His eyes staring up at the snow until finally someone covers him over with a coat.

Turner is crying about it now.

This can't go on like this. I put my arm around her and I turn her away and start to walk her slow back toward the plain pine board buildings. There are going to be questions in that building and we need some answers.

"You got to stop that crying now."

"I don't have to do anything I don't want to."

We stop walking. I look down at her for a bit. "Well, no... you don't."

And she looks back at me.

"I'm goin' into Canada with these papers now," I tell her. And it's snowing harder.

"You comin'?" I ask her.

"Yes I am."

"Good then."

"But I ain't stoppin' cryin'."

"Then you better make up somethin' real quick that you're sad about because you did not know that man, Turner. My name is Joseph Bonney now like it says in these papers and you're my daughter and we don't know who that fella was. I just tried to save him 'cause I guess I'm a selfless fuckin' hero of some kind and you never even spoke to him and you didn't see him until he was in the water and you don't know who he is and you're not cryin' about him and that's just the way it has got to be now."

She's not crying now. Her eyes are steady.

"I don't like it, Turner, speaking to you in this way—" I look around us to see if anyone is watching us but there are just some men climbing up the snow path to the buildings "—but we got no time for it to be any other way than this right now and if they connect what used to be Joseph to either one of us, there's gonna be questions, Turner, because there's always questions, but there's gonna be more if they know who he is and there's gonna be some goddamned government officials just doin' their jobs and writing on their little papers and looking into saddlebags that ain't theirs to look into and then getting the both of us into a world of problems we did nothing to earn and then just goin' home and having themselves some tea and biscuits, so we got to be together on this thing, Turner, and we got to get ourselves together on it right now—you hear what I'm saying?"

"Does it look to you like I'm crying anymore?"

"No. No, it doesn't."

Her eyes are not even red now. "If there's one thing I'm used to doing it's stopping crying so you can just stop telling me to stop crying and stop telling me what it is that's best for me to do, Mr. McCarty. Mr. Bonney. *Father*."

There's nothing else to say so we both turn and keep walking toward the buildings.

But she takes my hand. And I don't mean loose. She takes it tight.

It is simple enough to understand, mister; I am Joseph Bonney, this here is my daughter. This is my money. This here deed shows the land that I own. And this here map shows where it is. There ain't any need to make a straight line crooked. I do not know who that drowned man was and that is that.

The customs building looks like it is made of sticks and you can see the cold air between them as if the walls were drawn by a child with a crayon but beyond that you can see Canada, which appears to be made mostly of brick and stone and snow. A big round sign on the top of a building says "Corbey's Rye

Whisky" and a smaller one on the other side of the street tells of "Postcards For Sale" and "Cigars Five Cents." I am not going to say it looks like the promised land but it does look one hell of a lot better than the frozen river, and all that lies between it and us is a thin metal gate. And this man.

"That was some thing that you did, jumping into that ice water after that fella," the man behind the counter tells me like it's a compliment, but he's lookin' at me like my pie ain't been baked all the way through.

"Saw no reason to let him drown."

"You know him?"

Well, this man just made the top of my piss list. You see what I mean about people thinking they got reasons to know things they ain't got no reason to know? He is standing on my hose and behind us are people waiting three deep. Far too many people and all of them far too close to these boxes is my think-ing. The man is looking at my papers as if bugs are crawling out of them.

"Nope."

He nods. "And what do you have here in these boxes?"

Joseph would have been the better man for this encounter and it is now becoming more appealing to imagine myself at his side drooling and shaking and acting the simpleton. Joseph would have been patient in this situation whereas I am imagin-ing reaching over this counter and grabbing this man by the thin hair on his head and banging his face down onto the tops of the strongboxes over and over.

"Want to have a look in the boxes? There. Look. Look. Look." And each time I said "Look" it would be another smack of his fore-head against the metal.

"My father is still in his wet clothes and if we do not get to a hotel and get him into some dry ones I will hold you respon-sible for his health."

That is Turner.

"He is a hero."

"Now, now, miss," the man says to her, "I am just doing my job. There are procedures."

He returns to me the papers and I fold them into my damp pocket.

"Bonney. That was the real name of Billy the Kid, wasn't it?"

Goddamned people and their thirst for answers to questions that need not be asked.

"I wouldn't know."

"Sure. William Bonney. But you're Joseph. That right?"

"You saw the papers."

There are men pressing up behind us now and this man feels he needs to wave a flag with "Billy the Kid" printed on it. Goddammit, Joseph, I do not suppose this could be going any worse.

"Let's just see into these boxes and you'll be on your way. They look like strongboxes..."

"That's because they are strongboxes."

"What do you have in them?"

"Why don't you take a look?"

I suppose it might be wiser to ask to meet with him in a private room but wisdom is not always in my nature when dealing with a man such as this, a man who has chosen in life just to fill a suit and be the man behind a counter. And so I invite him to open up a box in front of a wide variety of turkey-necked yokels who have recently heard the name of Billy the Kid spoken and who have never before in their lives seen an amount of money such as that which is now revealed.

"That's a great deal of money," the man says once one of the boxes is opened.

"Yes it is."

"Those other two boxes filled the same?"

"Is that something you need to know?" I ask him as I slip one parcel of hundred-dollar bills across the counter toward him.

[330]

It is a gamble, to be sure. But truly I am tired and I would like to be out of here. And it is not my money, I am well aware of that, but I am trying to secure a future here for Turner and it is a future that she is lacking and not money.

"No," he decides after a pause, "it is not. Well, everything looks in order then. Welcome to the Dominion of Canada, Mr. Bonney."

"Much obliged to you."

We secure the horses and I am well ready for Turner to berate for me for the transaction but it seems it has squared with her just fine and she is anxious to be on the way to wherever we will land for the evening. I am conscious of the number of eyes on us, there are clean men and dirty men here, all with their eyes on the old man and the young woman and their boxes filled with money and didn't someone say something about "Billy the Kid"?

That name like a bloody necklace on me all my life.

⤷ **71** ⤶

"Look, McCarty, you don't know everything there is to know, you know."

"So you don't want to stay in a fancy hotel tonight?"

"No, I do not. I'd rather shit on my hands and clap."

"Well, what's the point of having fifty thousand dollars then?"

"I'm fucked if I know that, Billy, not having to depend on some slack-jawed man for money is the point of it, I suppose. And I don't have fifty thousand dollars anymore, not since you decided all on your own lonesome to give that greasy weasel some of it."

"That was not more than a thousand dollars. And you can afford it. I just thought you maybe might like a nice bed tonight for a change is all."

"Is that all?"

"Yeah, that's all."

"That's it?"

"That's all, I said that already."

"Alright, I heard you."

"Alright then."

It's not really a fight. But there's times that she does get right scratchy about some things and I think she thinks I think we are going to somehow end up under a blanket together. But I don't. I don't think that, I mean. And I don't think she thinks that either. So there should be no problem. Each of us is just not real certain what the other really thinks about that and that is maybe the problem.

Well, there's only one way to fix it.

"I'm not going to sleep with you, Turner."

She stops her horse on the spot, then turns it back so she can face me. "You are just about as crazy as a box of frogs, you know that, McCarty?"

"It's just the way it is," I say.

"So you made up your mind, is that it?"

"I have. And what is wrong with that?"

She spits and turns and keeps on riding. "Men," she says. "Men is the problem with that. Men is the problem with everything."

"Well...no argument there."

But I don't understand women. Plainly. And I never have.

Box of frogs. That's a good one. She's a pistol.

"Like it's yours," she says.

"What?"

"Like somehow it is a decision that you get to make."

"Well, it is."

"Fuck."

"Well, what's wrong with you?"

"You." And then she just rides on ahead.

Well, we got to sleep somewhere. That's all I'm saying.

"You intend to ride all night?"

But she don't answer.

Maybe it is a fight. If it is, I believe that I am losing.

There are other things on my mind aside from fighting. Last night I heard the woman's voice once more. *"Be careful."* Perhaps I am going mad. I have become a loonbag. Everywhere I look now I see the eyes of men who do not wish us well. Men who either know or suspect what it is that we carry in these boxes. I am imagining both of these things. The woman's voice. The men's eyes. I must be.

I must clear my mind. We are in Canada now. No one knows us here.

ᴄᴏ 72 ᴏᴑ

Well, the Wilcox Hotel is the finest hotel I have ever seen and that is certain. Not that I have seen the inside of many other fine hotels unless you count the mausoleum dinner party we had in Galveston or the Maxwell Rooming House in Stinking Springs, but I do not count either. I remain reserved regarding life in a big city, but here in this country of Canada maybe there are different rules about how people conduct themselves because the folks here seem more pleasant than they are suspicious and more friendly than they are guarded and at first it is an unsettling thing to experience but I am trying to accustom myself to it. I have arranged myself at times in my life with an undetermined number of women whose views on various matters was of no real interest to me. It is likely this is not something to be proud of. I know that for much of his life a man has hungers in him that will cause him to put up with just about anything. At breakfast this morning Turner called me "an ungracious sonofabitch" and that made me smile. For the one thing, I admire someone who will speak up their mind when they're of a mind to speak it, and provided they have something worth saying and provided they do not intend to shoot me immediately following their saying of it. And second, she is right: I am an ungracious sonofabitch. Though what that has to do with me taking the last piece of toast at breakfast is a puzzle. Fifty thousand dollars will buy her all the toast she wants and the butter and preserves to spread on it too. It is true I am not one for the social graces but that has never done me a disservice so far as I can tell, so I see no reason to change any-

[334]

thing about my habits now. I am happy with things the way they are and that is something new to me and I see no reason to change anything at all at the moment. She asks me if I miss Joseph.

"Don't you miss Joseph?" she asks.

"And what would be the point in that?"

"There wouldn't be no point to it, McCarty, there'd just be you feeling some sorrow is all."

"I do not see how that would be a help to anything."

"It doesn't have to help anything."

"Then why do it?"

"It's not something that you do, it's... Jesus Christ, Billy."

So I order her some more toast. If she wants some toast there's no reason for her not to have it. "You want some more coffee too?"

She does not say.

"I'll have some more coffee please," I tell the girl.

When she brings the coffee she will pour it from a big silver ...a big... hell, I don't know what the word is for what the coffee will be poured from when it comes but it will be hot and steaming and she will pour it into a little china cup that comes all the way from England over the ocean and it says so right on the bottom. All the way from England. Which is a long way from Stinking Springs. There are forty-one million miles of water in the ocean, and that is a fact. It's not really, I did not look it up, I do not know how many miles there are but I do know it is a long way for a little china cup to go. Don't love me, Turner. It hasn't worked out for anyone else who's tried it. The china cup is so thin you can see right through it. Right through. I am a man with many crimes.

Tureen.

No, that's for soup.

A pot. I think it is just called a coffee pot.

"Now the Lord provided a huge fish to swallow Jonah, and Jonah was in the belly of the fish three days and three nights."

Did he ask for it though is what I'd like to know, did old Jonah ever ask for that to happen? It says the Lord provided it but it does not say Jonah ever put in a request for any such thing. Well, any hotel beats the inside of a fish, no matter what, and that is a fact. Even though I am no longer sleeping under the stars I am happier than I would be inside of a fish, no matter what its dimensions. Lots of people do not know that being in that fish was the part that happened after God told Jonah to listen to him and to do something for him and Jonah did not listen to him at all, instead he just tore off and ran away so when the fish up and spit him out he figured, well hell, I better do that thing now that God wanted me to or there's gonna be worse trouble in store for me. So he goes ahead and he does this errand that God had set for him and then he builds himself a little house by the side of the road out of branches and sticks because he's got nowhere else to go and nobody loves him and then God makes this magic plant grow up and cover his house for shade. This shit is actually in the Bible, you can look it up. So things are looking right good for Jonah until God ups and makes a worm bite that shade plant and it dies and Jonah is right fucked again. This is the part the preachers don't say anything about: that God is just set to fuck you right up at every turn. Trust God, they say, but they don't tell you if he'll hold up his part of the deal or not.

I find I am liking these hotels and these coffee pots and I do not mind this life like I thought that I might. None of these places smell of cows or horses or of fish either and the sheets are white and crisp and clean. It seems to me that most people just want to get on with their lives undisturbed. They've got no need to be inside of a fish and they want a clean place to sleep at night. That's all they want. And a whisky or maybe a cup of tea.

I don't know what it is about Turner but it is as if any place she is in she's the only one in it. Or maybe she is just the best one in it, and this is not something noticed just by me. Now that we are in all these places with people in them, it can be seen as easy as the light. And it is not just men, I mean it is women too. She stops them. I don't know if it is her eyes or her gold hair or if it is something else entirely. This thing that makes me unable to not look at her works on other people just about as strong as on me is how it seems. And so we are not quiet travellers making our way all discreet in the corners of places as I am used to and as I would prefer as far as safety goes. Even though we move through towns without saying much to anyone, we are noticed and it is not because I am a gunfighter and an outlaw. I am not that anymore, I have stopped being that. I am now the man who is standing next to Turner Wing. It is a thing that shines out of her and she is completely unaware of it. More and more I feel something about her that is not the thing I would usual feel about a woman but something better than that. More and more I feel as if I am having the best of days and this whole arrangement is unlikely to last, I know that, and things will darken, I know that too. That is certain. I am used to feeling my life under me more like a tightrope than a floor. You know the way you can toss a handful of dirt into the air and you can see which way the wind is blowing? You cannot do that inside of a building and I cannot do it when it comes to Turner. So I feel as if we are in a building now and out of the wind, but buildings do not last as the desert and the winds will last, that is what I mean to say. But in spite of this I sleep well, and I wake with nothing on my mind. For the first time in a long time I sleep well.

And it is also a comfort that when I wake I am not on the inside of a fish and so things could be worse than they are at present. The nights are not as dark as usual and the days do not come at me with sharp edges on them and with men wishing me harm. But it makes me uneasy, this state of ease. I suppose you might call it happiness, but the way things actually are in this life is like a mouse scratching in the wall, reminding me it is there in the middle of the night and there is nothing I can do about that.

ᒼᕙ 74 ᕘᒧ

A good friend of mine, Elmer Thomas, he ended up putting a bullet through the centre of his own head. And I often wonder, did he just wake up one morning and think, okay now, this is the day? Looking out over the white yellowy scrub with maybe a cup of coffee in his hand.

Is this the day?

❧ **75** ❧

It is my birthday.

"What was that?"

"I said it's my birthday. I just realized it now when I looked at this newspaper."

"How can you forget your own birthday, Billy?"

"I didn't forget, I just said that I remembered it. It is today."

"How old are you?"

"Pretty old."

"You mean you're not sure?"

"I lost count."

"You even sure it's your birthday?"

"I'm pretty sure. I'm not certain."

"Well, I'm going to have them set to make you a birthday cake."

"The hell you are."

"C'mon, Billy, a cake, with vanilla icing and a few candles…"

"No."

"Don't be an old man."

"Too late for that. A pie then. Get them to make me an apple pie."

"Happy birthday, Billy."

ᓚᓂ **76** ᓂᓚ

I buy her some hot peanuts from a man in a funny little cloth coat on the street. He wraps them up in a paper and folds it carefully, handing it to me. I pay him his coins and pass the little package to her.

"How many more days till we get to where we're goin', Billy?"

"Man at the hotel said that it's maybe four, maybe five days riding from here. There ain't gonna be no hotels there, you know. And no clean sheets."

"You don't need a hotel to have clean sheets, Billy. You can wash 'em yourself, you know."

"I suppose."

"You talk like stayin' in fancy hotels was my idea."

"You're right."

"Well, what's making you so all of a sudden agreeable?"

"The way you're eating them peanuts."

"What about it?"

"Folks'd think you ain't been fed in days."

But that's not it. It's the way she's laughing and wiping off her chin. Like a kid with a cookie they were told not to have. Like a full bright light in the dark street.

"Billy, why did Joseph always call you Ish?"

"It was my name."

"What kind of a name is that?"

"Not one I ever asked for. I never much took to it."

"Why'd he use it then?"

"I believe he thought if he said it enough times that I would finally wind up and hit him."

"Well, why would he want you to hit him?"

"Give him an excuse to hit me back."

She stops riding.

"He hardly ever did anything without a reason," I tell her.

And I just keep on going.

ᴄᴼ **78** ᴼᴼ

My heart is not what it once was and by that I mean it was cold and veiled before and it is not so much like that anymore. It seems now that I breathe easier these past few weeks, but this last part of the ride is the longest and the ground has become hilly and the trees dense and close together as if standing guard. We stop many times and I take the rolled papers out of my bag and study the land around us. We keep moving on. There is a dark river here that is like a snake moving back and forth across the land, not full frozen yet, black, almost looping or crossing back over itself at some points.

"I'm tired of riding, Billy."

Yes.

"It's time for us to be somewhere."

The land is like a white sheet someone has scored with a charcoal stick. More trees than I have ever seen. We ride through a small village and stop to stock up with whatever we can find that might be needed. There is no way of knowing whether the cabin is provisioned in any way or whether it is just an empty box. The only thing that indicates a cabin is there at all is Joseph having claimed it to be so and these papers in my pocket.

I can imagine him saying: "I never said any such thing."

"Joseph, you said there was a cabin."

"I never did. You imagine it to be so, William, but that does not make it so." Or some such shit as he was prone to say. He is gone from everywhere except from the inside of my head.

The people here look at us. Not because we are odd but

because it is odd for them to see people they have not seen before. This is not a place where people see folks they have never seen before.

"Good morning to you," I say to the man at the store counter.

"Morning?"

He says it like it is a question. Makes me think that maybe I have lost track of the time of day and that it is afternoon, but it is not. We struck our bedrolls last night with a view of the chimney smoke from the houses of this town and we rose with the light. It is not past eight o'clock in the morning.

"I have some land," I tell him, and I unroll the papers onto the wood of the counter. He pulls at his spectacles and examines the documents as if he is a doctor taking a first look at a healing wound.

"Indeed? Yes," he says. "Well…"

Turner is eyeing the shelves for what we may need.

"You know the place?" I ask him.

He takes off his spectacles. "I do. It's up the Third Line, just north of here maybe three miles, maybe four…"

I don't know what I thought he was going to say but my heart was in my throat for some reason. *"No such place."* Or *"That ain't your land."* Not that it would matter any. Turner could buy whatever land she wants now and wherever she wants to buy it, but this is land that belongs to Joseph and me. I am relieved there is actual dirt and rock attached to Joseph's promises and to these pieces of paper.

"You must be Mr. Joseph Bonney then?"

"That's me."

Mr. Joseph Bonney, a made-up dead man standing up just as tall and as real as the living.

"My name's Caldwell … Land Registrar hereabouts, I drew up these papers for you. In fact that's my name there," and he points to the bottom corner of the paper where it says *T. B. Cal-*

dwell County Clerk. "Pleased to make your acquaintance." He nods at Turner. "Miss...good morning to you...and, well, I'm a few other things in these parts: General Mercantile...a few other things... I have been wondering when you might show up. I thought we might be waiting till the spring thaw."

"Nope."

"Ah well..."

There is nothing more I can think to say then. We are here.

"Well, allow me to welcome you to Lanark then, folks. You'll be needing a few things, I expect?"

"We don't know if there's much in that cabin aside from cold air," I tell him.

"Well, there's a bed and a bucket, far's I can recall. That may be about all aside from some empty cupboards."

"We'll need another bed then, and we'll need a table. You know where we can get those things?"

The man looks quickly to Turner who is back to surveying the tall shelves behind the man and then he looks back to me. His mind is moving rapidly to assess us, that much is clear. But I am used to being assessed in a way that includes estimating how long it will take me to pull my gun and that is not what this man is doing.

"We can have those things up to you in a day, if you like. We'll sled them in. You'll need some provisions..."

"Candles, dried bacon, salt beef, flour, salt, lard, blankets, dried apples, coffee, tea, sugar, a sack of rice, two sacks of dried beans, butter, tinned biscuits, molasses, a barrel of salt, vinegar, we'll need a kettle and a skillet, a ladle, two pots, one large and one smaller, forks and knives, four of each in case of company, and four cups, matches, and I would like some needles and a bolt of good cloth and thread and would you have what they call maple syrup that comes from trees? And some tobacco. And I am sure my husband would like to have a bottle of whisky, my husband does not drink very much but he enjoys having a bottle to hand for those who do, don't you, dear? This is not a dry county, is it?"

Husband.

We both gaze at Turner as if she has suddenly recited from memory a long poem about roses.

"No." Mr. Caldwell recovers himself. "No, ma'am, it is not, an excellent whisky is distilled just down the road from here."

"Four bottles then."

"Yes, ma'am, four bottles, of course…"

And so I find myself married without ever having been invited to the wedding.

The man is under the same spell by this time as most people, and now that he has been apprised of the matrimonial nature of the relationship before him and can stop conjecturing and feels that things are in order for the Christian world, he cannot now do enough to please Turner as he sets about showing her the best products he carries, describing the benefits of each at length. He may have a profit in mind but it appears more that his main intent is just to please her and make her smile. I roll up my papers and look out at the horses, their breath rising up and away from them, their heads nodding slowly, and then at people walking across the road. We are here. It is as if you could stand in the middle of the main street at noon on a quiet and bright Sunday and scream the name of Billy the Kid and have no one take no notice of you for anything other than the fact that you were disturbing the quiet of peace of a day in its course.

"Joseph!"

I turn around quickly, expecting somehow to see my brother alive again but it is me that Turner is addressing.

"Raisins and dried peaches!"

She is burning like a campfire. Light doesn't fall on her as much as it shines from right out of her.

Standing. Asking. Staring. Wanting. Reaching out for everything she has not yet touched.

And myself all of a sudden her husband.

ꙮ 79 ꙮ

The place looks to me as good as griddle cakes and molasses on a cold morning. The cabin sits atop a hill overlooking a stream and pine and birch trees cover it up from an approach at any angle. You would have to know it is here to know it is here and that suits me right down to the bottoms of my pockets. There is a stable for the horses and an outhouse for the shit and inside it is really just one big room with a pot-bellied stove and not much else, but the walls and floors are good thick planks and the rafters are made of full tree trunks with the bark still on them and Turner seems well-pleased with everything. She moves from window to window exclaiming her thoughts while I study the sightlines for shooting out of each of them and I say very little but I smile when she says, "Look at the trees from here!" and "You can see the stream from this one!"

We get settled as best we can by bringing in the provisions and our belongings. Turner stocks the shelves while I get a fire going so strong that the sides of the stove are soon red like a fat man's cheeks. I have a Saturday-night kind of a sweat on me now but it is not Saturday night and it is neither dancing nor lovemaking that is the cause of it, just the wood stove. There will be a big snow rolling in soon because the sky already has the steady grey cold roll of snow in it.

When she has everything organized just the way that she wants it, and some candles lit and some rice and beans on the stove, she turns and says: "I'm going to have a baby, Billy."

Well, shit.

✄ **80** ✇

No, it's not mine. What the fuck are you thinking right now?
You think that it is mine? Fuck you. I told you this already.
That it is not like that with the two of us. And it is not.
What the fuck do you think I am?
Have you not been listening to me all this time?

✆ 81 ◆

"You are what?"

"I am going to—"

"What?"

"—have a baby, Billy. I'm going to have a baby. Well, that is why I called you my husband in the town. People are going to need for me to be married, you see. I thought you should know."

The longer I live, the less I know anything about anything at all. Well, you reap what you sow. So what the hell am I doing with a baby on the way? I have not sown anything. And here I am doing the reaping.

"You're what?"

✺ 82 ✺

"What are you thinking now, Billy?"
I am thinking that now there'll be two people to visit my grave.
And also that I don't know what to say to Turner or what
to do.

❧ **83** ❧

"What will you name it?"

"The name is Billy." She says it real quick, just like that, before my question is out of me and into the air. Like she's been waiting for just that question, which I guess she has.

"Well, what if it's a girl?"

"Billy."

"Well, it might—"

"I mean that her name would still be Billy. The name serves fine for a girl too, I think."

Well, hell. Climb on up in the stagecoach and let's go for a ride. A baby. And by the name of Billy.

ᑫᕋ **84** ᕐᕗ

"You're not mad, Billy?"

My heart is broke a bit.

"Why would I be mad?"

"I don't know."

Just a bit is all.

"Babies get born every day, Miss Turner."

Probably get past that dark part of it pretty quick, I expect. Well, things happen. No sense pretending they don't or in getting yourself upset over it when they do.

ᕲᕲ 85 ᕲᕲ

I wait until morning to ask what I have to ask. All night long I
have told myself that I do not have to ask it, but it seems that I
was lying to myself the whole time.

"Who... I mean...well, who's—"

"He's dead."

"I—"

"Chance. The kid, I mean. He was real sweet to me that one
night, Billy, when we were with the wagons, and he was so scared.
I think he was scared of what was going to happen, Billy, and—"

"You want some eggs?"

"Billy, I—"

"We're gonna make us some eggs, Turner. And then we'll
have our breakfast. And there's nothing else we have to do for
today." I'm running out of things to say. "Nothing at all. And
we'll have some biscuits. And we'll watch the snow come in.
It's going to be a big snow, I can feel that."

These days the way days begin is the way they end too—
quiet. And I mean to keep it that way.

"You get yourself wrapped up into a blanket, Turner, and
you stay warm."

"It's already hot enough in here to stew a cat, Billy."

"Well. Never you mind that."

"Billy?"

What.

"Billy."

The way she says it.

ᴄ✿ **86** ✿ᴏ

There's not a lot of *"What if this had happened?"* or *"What if that had happened?"* in my life. There's just what was and what is and maybe what might happen next.

"I'll get the eggs." I put the skillet on the stove and push some butter into it. "We belong. Turner. And I guess now that all of us, the three of us, well, we are stuck with each other."

And I think that is a good thing to say. She doesn't say anything. But I think maybe that was the right thing for me to say.

✑ 87 ✑

The land in this county is just one hill, one valley, one tree after another. In a couple of months the trees on this hill will be so full that walking through them will be like parting a curtain before you. For now though they are like ink strokes against the remaining snow, it is mostly pine and birch in here with some walnut down in the hollow by the river, which before too long will spill over its banks with the spring run-off. At first this terrain unsettled me as I am used to being able to see people coming at me clear from all directions but I have started now to become accustomed to the fact that no one is coming here at all and we are well and truly and finally alone. At first, I would not let the fire burn through the night and we huddled tight in blankets wrapped well over our heads to keep from freezing, but after enough of Turner's complaining I relented. I had not wanted the sound of the cracking and hissing wood of the fire to drown out any sounds of strangers approaching us in the dark while we slept, but no stranger has approached and eventually I grew tired of chipping through the ice in the water basin in the mornings. And Turner stated that sleeping in a snowbank was not the suggested procedure for a woman with a child on the way.

Turner busies herself these days with the things that were her domain when she was a child herself—blankets and bonnets and soft gowns. There are still months before this baby will come but she is prepared for its arrival like a young girl is ready for Christmas in October. I busy myself with the chopping of wood and the shooting of squirrels, an activity as unlike shooting a man as any that I have tried. Squirrels are not much interested in confrontation and they do not move in any predictable way. They don't even much care if you do shoot them, it seems, but this lack of caring works to their advantage, not in the favour of the one doing the shooting, and it takes some time to put together enough for a pie.

Rabbits are another story altogether. They often sit very still and just wait patiently for the bullet. When shot they leap up tremendously into the air as if on springs and you think you have lost them but no, that is their last hop, they die both majestically and comically, as if they could leap away from death. And so we eat more rabbit stew than we do squirrel pie. Deer have been plentiful, and we no longer care much for the flavour and texture of dried meat and have all but given it up. We are spoiled both by the bounty of the hunt and the closeness of a town. Spoiled too by the power of the little wood stove carried up from the store by a strong team and I suppose we are spoiled also by the presence of each other. I would have been quite contented here even just with Joseph for company, which was the original plan if you'll recall. I think we would have fought less and worried at each other less than we ever did on the trail once we were well settled in here. We would have become two creased-up and worn-out old bachelors living here on a hill who everyone in town enjoyed both steering clear of and talking about in hushed tones. Though I am certain there are ample hushed tones expended in town and the farmhouses about the old man and the young—very young—woman living now up the Third Line and how do you suppose they ended up married when he looks well old enough to be her father? Their faces a florid red by what their tongues are playing with.

Turner has not been to town since her belly grew out and I can imagine what will be said of her and of the both of us when she shows herself in the summer with a child on her hip.

What will be said of her then? There will be very few church-supper invitations for us, I think.

Fine. I will play up the role of the doting father then, although I think that no amount of baby bouncing will stay the local goodly Presbyterian tongues from their activity. But in time they will accept us as the lovely young bride and her crusty old husband and they will turn their minds and gossip to matters such as *"How can she stand to be with him?"* and eventually to other topics such as the weather and the price of dried peas. Perhaps they will grow to think of us as something noble and biblical. Noah and his good wife. Perhaps church suppers will not be so bad after all.

There were stories told about my grandmother, that she would sit up late and lonely into the dark nights with a loaded .22 across her lap, occasionally firing it off into the darkness and nobody knew what at.

And nobody asked.

No one wanted to get shot.

You'd want a good pair of boots so you could run far and fast.

From this hill we are on with the trees bare at present you can see about five miles in any direction: down to the river valley, the lowlands, and the forested rises and slanted fields beyond them to the south. The nights are full of noise, from the worrying of the ice to the rustle of the dead leaves on the crusted snow to the scurry of small animals and the calls of the birds and the coyotes. But somehow it remains peaceful and what I hear most now in the dark is the sound of Turner's soft breathing in a quiet room with the wood of the walls opening and then closing in the heat and in the cold. Heat on one side, cold on the other. Light and dark and the movement in the spaces in between and the little house breathing.

At times I feel my mind drifting away from me with not a thought to be found in it. If God is pissed at me for anything I have done or not done he's keeping real quiet about it of late or I'm just not listening and that could be the problem, I suppose. I once knew a man named HaHa Orley. I never knew what his real first name was, everyone just called him HaHa. He was a happy sort of fella, you see, all the time, and that is how he got his name. Men could be sitting around complaining about the lack of food and being hungry and old Orly he'd just up and say, "Well, ain't it lucky for us we won't have too much shittin' to do tomorrow?" Locusts could fall from the sky and he'd say, "Makes a nice change from the rain, now don't it?" I never could figure out if he was happy or if he was just simple. And maybe they are the same thing. There's a lot we don't need in this life but we set our hearts on gathering all of it up for ourselves anyway, we spend all our time chasin' after it and it ends up being more than we can carry. The water in that river down there don't need a thing, not one. We want, want, want and I am certain it is because we know we are here on limited time. If all that a fox or a racoon wants is for its children to be safe and for there to be enough food for the day then that is not because its brain is smaller than ours, it is because its soul is larger, at least that is what I have come to believe. At any rate it is better off. Maybe it's just me that's simple or maybe I have become simple-minded over time. I ain't got no problem with being simple, not one thing against it, and I never have, you hear me, Joseph? Which one of us knows more words than the other, that is what it always came down to and I am here to say it don't matter and it never did. And listen to me talkin' away to a dead man. Anyway. It's quiet and there was not enough breeze this morning to hold a cloud up in the sky. I want absolutely nothing that I do not already have.

I knew a man from the Dakota territory and this one time we were doing some ranch work down there and I'm standing on the porch in the early morning rolling myself up a smoke and he walks out buck-ass naked with a tin cup full of hot coffee and he stands there looking out over all the nothing in front of us and he says, "I do wish I had me some dynamite."

And then he just drinks his coffee. I don't recall what happened after that, probably nothing. It doesn't matter much, he was a bit of a monkey anyway and used to clean out all the dirt from under his fingernails with his knife, then just wipe it there on the table where we ate all our meals. You'd be having your breakfast and there'd be a little mountain of dark earth next to your plate like a tiny grave. I think somebody shot him. It is likely to be the case. Edward his name was. Now Edward is just a word someone has carved into a stone or a plank of wood somewhere or a long-gone memory from someone's head who once knew him. Someone like me.

Turner has made little curtains for the windows that she likes for the way they catch the light in the morning and I like for the way they block the view of the inside of the cabin to anyone approaching it, but I do not tell her this, I just tell her they look real pretty and the child will be lucky to have a mother like her to look after all the little things such as that, and she smiles. To let her know that in spite of all this quiet we have here I still worry some about just about everything would be as pointless as a sack of harmonicas.

There is a woman in town who will come up here when Turner's time is near, and I have already seen to this. And I have on order the best-made cradle that can be had, and it is on delivery up from a place called Montreal and I am told it should arrive within the month. That will get the local chin-wagging teams in full operation. Some nights I think about the kid but I do not mention this to Turner. I suppose it is very likely wrong in some way for me to be a little thankful that he is dead and gone but I have no care for that if it is. I mean, depending on who's looking at the thing it is likely for the best, that is how I see it. Some would think that is a wrong way for me to think about it but I do not. Spending any time at all thinking it is a shame that he is dead would not lift the dirt from his eyes nor give him one more second with them open. The fire that melted them inside his skull like two eggs in an oven was not set by me and I could not put it out and, like I've said before, I have never missed anyone in my life and cannot see the advantage in doing so now. Sometimes I do something that is not smart and when I do make such a mistake I hear Joseph's voice in my head, but having a voice in your head is not missing someone, in this case it is just recalling that they were an enormous pain in the ass when they were still around on this earth. Some nights I think that voice is like the woman's voice I heard in the desert or like Mr. Samuels on my bed when I was a kid. The dead trying to get us to hear them. And some nights I just listen to the sounds of the forest and the river below us. And some nights I think about nothing at all and I have never done that before.

"Billy, you're going to have to buy a Bible next time you're in town."

Never done that neither, there was always one around whatever camp I was in.

"What for?"

"We need a Bible to write the baby's name in, for our family tree."

A baby. Something brand-new in this world.

↶ **88** ↷

Sometimes the worst things happen to us with no warning at all.

And blizzards too, I have learned in my first months of experiencing them to feel them coming in my bones, but not this time. This one arrives like an unexpected preacher on the doorstep. But snowstorms here are about as remarkable as horses at a rodeo so in the morning I pay the beginnings of it no heed and I head into town to see if any packages have arrived. Boyd Caldwell seems to be of a particular inquisitive nature this morning.

"What is it that you're looking for?" he wants to know.

There is a native tribe in which the punishment for a wife committing adultery is to cut off her nose. And just where has your pecker been is my question and what should we cut off if that pecker has maybe ended up where it should not be? That is just one tribe, mind you, no better and no worse than any other, including my own. Everybody everywhere is all too ready to punch their neighbour when they ought to be running themselves into a post. You ask me what I am looking for? A place that isn't completely and entirely fucked up. But don't we all think we are somehow deserving of just such a place when we have in no way qualified ourselves for it? I think but do not say any of this to Caldwell, mostly because he seems to own half this town all on his own and his family owns the rest of it and I do not need enemies anymore so instead I just say: "A box."

I have ordered the crib through the mail and not through

Caldwell's store and though it will come to him as postmaster when it arrives in its crate, I see no reason for him to know what it is. Let him find out about the baby like everyone else when it shows up in town in the spring. Everyone thinks they need to know things they do not need to know at all.

"Well, I'll send word if any boxes show up then."

"Any word of big weather coming our way?" I ask him.

"There's always weather coming," he says, "In about three months there ought to be a general thaw is what I expect."

"You're a regular weathervane. You got any cigars?"

"Nope. You smoke 'em? I can order some in."

"Not usual. Just felt like one is all."

"Be here in three days' time."

"Won't want one by then."

"Might be you could find some at the hotel, I wouldn't know for certain."

I stand by the window awhile and watch two men taking firewood off a wagon. Three men hitching their horses outside the tavern. "Shaw and McKerracher Tremendous Sale Bargains To Be Had." A woman is walking toward the mill with a child in tow, the child wrapped so tight against the cold that I can't tell if it's a boy or a girl. Snow seems to me an unnecessary thing. I do not see the good that it does for anyone.

"You see many strangers pass through here normally?"

"Nope. Not too many places for 'em to be going to from here. And here is not a place everyone wants to be. Not me, mind you, I like it just fine, so does everyone who settles here, I believe. It is quiet and prosperous and it is away from most people. An excellent combination of traits. How are you and your fine wife getting along out there?"

I turn from the window. The pine boards of the floor are smoothed to white like ground flour where people have walked. I cannot tell if there is anything in the way he says "your fine wife." "Tolerable. You got anything I could take her back?"

"Such as?"

"Oh, I don't know. Something to surprise her and maybe make it seem a little less like it is February."

"Well, I got some new cheddar up from Balderson. Fresh and soft as cow's milk."

"Slice me off some of that."

"And I got this…" he says, opening a drawer behind the counter and taking out some red ribbon, holding it up to the light from the window. "I just got this, as a matter of fact, it come in just yesterday. You are not the most immediate person that came to mind as a potential customer for it, mind you…"

"I'll take some."

"How much?"

"How the hell do I know how much? How much ribbon does a woman usual want?"

"In my experience? A young woman's appetite for such things is near inexhaustible."

Now I know there is something in the way he says "young" but I let it be. "Fair point. Then I'll take all of it. You got any other colours?"

"I got a rainbow. Red's just the last one to come in. I got green, yellow, pink, blue… I even got some gold and silver in here…" He keeps on pulling out ribbon like he's performing a magic trick.

"Just slice off some of each, I'm sure she'll find something to do with it all."

"Many seem to like a little bit of it in their hair."

"No doubt."

"That not a custom where you're from?"

"Not that I particular noticed."

Caldwell nods and begins to wrap lengths of cut ribbon

around something, I think it's called a bobbin, or some word like that. Joseph would know, or claim to.

"Well, a young woman likes something to make them feel special, I think. They seem to forget."

"Forget what?"

He pauses. "That special is what they already are." He finishes what he's doing and smiles and wraps the ribbon up in some brown paper. "And you wanted some cheese?"

Jesus Christ, people have got something to say on every single topic under the sun, don't they? Just because something is on your mind does not mean I got any extra room for it on mine is what I want to tell him. But I don't say this to Caldwell, you see? Just because it is in my head, I don't feel the need to spit it out toward anyone. Or maybe it is just that I get softer as I age. Either way I don't shoot him either.

On my way back home the wind picks up from the west with the feel of more snow for certain and by late afternoon it has begun to come down heavy, rolling in like a grey wool blanket resting over the tops of the trees and silencing everything in its path.

We light lanterns early and Turner opens up the ribbons and laughs and then smiles and then she says, "Thank you, Billy."

And it seems like she'll know just fine what to do with it all, so I get up to trim the fire as there is to be some slapjack and brown gravy to eat and she won't want too much heat in the stove so as for the gravy not to stick itself to the pot.

She is placing the ribbons onto her lap.

She is slowly smoothing them out with both hands.

You wake in the middle of the night from a dream you can't fully recall and you have to piss and you live in a house now and in a country that is half buried in snow and ice so you have to go outside to piss because you're not already there and also because you live with a woman so you can't just do it out the window because she doesn't like it much when you do. I don't piss in a chamber pot; I never have taken to it and I am not starting now. Something about it is wrong, like pissing into a gravy boat at the dining room table in a hotel. Those little pink flowers painted onto each of them. That is no proper place for a man to piss. So I would rather throw on my coat and boots and piss off the porch and freeze yellow into the ice and snow. This storm has become like a wall of white now and the wind is louder than a cat stuck in a clothes wringer.

Turner stirs in her blankets. "Billy…"

"Just going outside."

The dream was about Joseph. I guess it was about Joseph, at least he was there, but not at first. At first it was just me and my heart. I knew my heart was there because it was beating and I could hear it. I was worried that people in the next room or in buildings down the street could hear it, though I did not know where I was. Suddenly he was there, so close that I could see the pores in his face. He sat across a small table from me and poured out some whisky into two small glasses, two fingers each.

"Joseph—"

"No."

And that meant for me to not speak, you know how you know certain things in dreams without being told. So I sat there and looked ahead of me up at a painting on the wall of a man standing next to what looked like a prize horse. And then without any time passing in between we were on a green lawn, we were younger now and in front of a big white house, running and playing something or other the way young boys do. Well, some young boys, not us. There was never no big white house. And nothing like that ever really happened.

"Hey." Joseph handed me my drink across the table. "Pay attention," he said.

And then we raised our glasses to each other.

"You're dead," I said.

"No."

And then I woke up.

The wind takes the breath right out of you when it is this cold and the snow and the ice are a bright slap to the face. It is lucky that sleep has made me hard because otherwise my pecker would be trying to seek shelter inside my body and I'd be standing here trying to coax it out into the cold. No thanks, it would say...I am just fine tucked right up in here. It makes you dizzy looking out into all this snow whipping past. Goddammit, now I have to shit. That means a goddamned kneecap-deep walk out to the shithouse because Turner is not going to want a froze-up turd on the front porch in the morning and I'll be goddamned if I'm squatting over the gravy boat, blizzard or no blizzard. I may be a more peaceful man these days regarding the big things of life, but the small things get me more angry than ever before and I can curse a blue streak over not knowing where the matches are. Turner says that will have to stop once the baby comes, but it seems to me the baby is not going to hit the ground knowing how to talk anyway and by the time it learns, well, it'll be time to know a cuss word or two anyway. Can't go off to school not knowing how to swear and to fight.

"Your mother married an old man."

"Yeah? Well, fuck you!"

You tell 'em that right out loud, Billy, be you a boy or a girl, and you tell 'em first thing. Just because the sorry buggers who shoved themselves into those children's mothers are still alive or not the same age as Moses, that don't make those kids any special gift to the world and you best believe that. And if the schoolteacher and the trustees don't like that information they can just come on up here and talk to me about it and we'll all sit around and have ourselves a little chat.

Two stray dogs! They have been on the property for more than a week so now they think they belong here and Turner has been feeding them, so I guess they do. One big and black and the other smaller and brown. Who knows what kind they are. The hungry kind. Turner puts out meals for them each morning like we are running a rooming house for dogs. Two more things to put a name to.

Goddammit, my knees do not work the way they used to down south in the warmer weather. Each step I take sounds like the breaking of the breech of a rifle. If not for the howl of the wind it would sound just like someone was out here busting up branches for kindling. No matter. It's just bones. A life cooks down like gravy. Eventually the bones don't matter much and it's the sauce that's left and the sauce is the good part anyway. But that thought doesn't help you any when you're fighting your way through snow and ice to the crap house. Though it does help to see the whole arc and throw of a life while you're still living it and can stand apart from it a little bit and hold it in some regard. And when you are dead, things are, well, they are just simpler, that is my belief about it anyway. Maybe you come back as a crow or a fox after you die and no one knows your name because it's not yours anymore and you don't have anything and nothing has you. Nothing wrong with being a crow or a fox. I just don't think that death is how we see it to be, that's all, and I don't see how it could be. I do not know how it is, mind you, but we see most things in life pretty dark and wrong so I don't imagine we have the right fix on death either. Most people are easier to live with when they are dead, think about that. Joseph, for instance. He is easier to make shut up now that he is dead and the things he does manage to say seem a lot smarter than most of what he said when he was living so there must be some advantage to being dead.

"You look after that girl...that is your thing to do now," he says.

Well, hell yes, Joseph, and what the fuck is it you think I have been doing? That is what I'd have told him when he was face to face with me but now that his face is under the dirt somewhere or now that he is a crow...circling overhead...I just say to him, "Yes. Yes, I will."

Just to silence him because there is no advantage to be earned in arguing with a dead man, particularly when that dead man is Joseph. When he was alive he'd have rather died than lose a fight so now that he's dead I don't see the point in even trying. You win, Joseph. Crows don't take off unless there's a good reason to. In that they are unlike people. They are smarter.

Nothing is happening here in the shithouse so maybe the moment has passed me by. I'll be damned though if I'm going to track my ass back through the snow and get under a blanket just to have that roll of shit decide it is time for it to be born after all, so I'll just sit here and wait, I have lots of time and I am starting to lose the feeling in my toes so they are not as cold as they were and it is not so uncomfortable now that I am seated in the dark in this little wooden box and out of the wind. Maybe I will light the candle. Like visiting a church in the night. Seems a waste of a match but I light it anyway. I should have brought some tobacco with me, I was not expecting such a long expedition. A man sitting and having a quiet smoke by candlelight in a tight little wooden box in the middle of a midnight storm.

Tomorrow is Saturday. Maybe we can—

And it happens. A shot.

Happens fast.

Always does. Another shot. In the house.

Gun.

I don't have it. Don't have it. Fuck.

ᦉ 90 ᧕

"Fuck."

There are openings between the slats of the shithouse and I can see the bright gunshot flashes through the window of the cabin. They are shooting.

"Fuck."

I'm scrambling at the belt around my ankles and they're killing her.

"Fuck!"

And then the door of the shitter rips open and one of the biggest men I have ever seen is standing there with a shotgun levelled off at my chest.

If he moves his finger I'll be through the thin wall behind me and dead before I even hit the snow.

"Well hello, Billy," he says. And then he smiles.

An instant. That's what it comes down to.

And surprise. Sometimes it just comes down to surprise. The top of his head comes off with a shot from behind him and parts of his skull and face land right on my chest as if I have dropped a fresh-baked biscuit covered with jelly. It seems as his head explodes that his eyes take on a quizzical look but that could be my imagination. Things happened too quickly for that to actually be the case. Surely there is a moment though where he is confused. Just a short one, an instant. And then the rest of him falls away and there Turner is behind him, her legs spread wide in a steady stance and her shotgun ready for anything that might be coming next. Thin white nightgown in the snow. Big belly. Nothing comes next. What comes next is silence.

And then: "These bastards picked the wrong mommy to fuck with tonight." And she reloads. And she spits. And that's the way it is with her. She sums things up very good.

I brush and wipe the rest of the big man off of my chest like crumbs and sauce and—

"I, uh…"

"Oh. Right."

—hitch up my pants, then I step out of the commode.

"I got one in the house. One got away," she says.

"Mm."

"He said he was after money."

"He get it?"

"How could he?"

"It was right there in the room."

"No." She breaks the gun and slides in two more shells. "You were sitting on it."

"What?"

"I moved it two days ago. Take a look," and she gestures with the shotgun toward the hole behind me. I take the candle and lean in.

And I don't know if you've ever seen almost fifty thousand dollars looking back at you from down in a dark shithole, but it is something to see.

"Well, how—"

"There's a rope tied to it, so we can just pull it up when we need it. And when I say we pull it up I mean you, Billy. I ain't touching it now."

"We're back in the funeral business now, I guess."

"Not on this hill. You'll have to find somewhere else for these men to be dead."

"Right."

"Well, that's that for now. You comin' in?"

"You know I'm not."

She bites her lip. "Time's passed and he's already gone a ways, Billy. And there's a lot of weather."

"Not far enough. And not enough weather. So he ain't goin' very much further."

"Could just let him go."

"Could."

"You're gonna need another coat then."

"Give me the gun."

"You only got the two shells in it, Billy."

"That's one more than I'm going to need."

ᥫ᭡ **91** ᥫ᭡

Tracking a man is different than tracking an animal but the process is the same and the end too. The snow keeps up. It drives on into my face and it's all that I can see, which is not good when there's someone out there in the middle of it all who only wants to see me long enough to shoot me. Just long enough to say he's the man who killed Billy the Kid and then live off the fat of that story for the rest of his life and pick his teeth with my bones. The slanting white reminds me of sitting waiting for breakfast one morning in a kitchen in Montana country, the yellow light and the many dust specks on the air caught just there in the slant of it, these little floating worlds. Joseph said once that most of the dust we see is just the skin of dead people who have passed before us and of the living too, the dead skin that has come off them—and what we are seeing is death floating in front of us. I just wanted some bacon. Joseph said a lot of things...he said he read a lot of things too but I only saw him with a book one or two times in my whole life so I believe it is easily the case that he just made half that shit up on the spot.

"How does the world keep spinnin' around, Joseph?"

"Leopards."

"What?"

"There's a shitpile of leopards over there on the African continent, William, so many that the weight of all of them leopards throws the world right off its balance, so it keeps spinning around on its axis, and that's why we have night and day."

"Bullshit."

"Suit yourself. You're the one asked the question. I'm guessing you got no better answer than that."

Fucked if I don't. World keeps spinning 'cause it's got nothing better to do, that's all. It ain't a matter of choice. It sure as hell ain't a matter of leopards. You end up living the life you do and that is all. You shoot your first animal when you're a kid and you feel a little sad.

You should. That animal was more disappointed in the outcome of that shot than you ever were, I can tell you that.

This man is like to be the only one left in the world who knows where Billy the Kid is or that there even *is* a Billy the Kid left in this world to know the whereabouts of and if he gets to where he thinks he's going now, that news of his is just going to spread like smallpox like it always does. And with him knowing there is money at the top of this hill, he will be back and it's not just me now who'll get wrapped up in that either, it is Turner now and now it is Turner's baby too. There's a baby to think about, and I do. And so he is going to need to be dealt with, that man who is walking now but who don't realize he is already a dead man. He is just a moving set of clothes and he had better start to run. Or not. Really it don't matter at all what speed he sets himself at because all he's ever done will come to a trailing and to a burning end on him—a burning end and this will happen this night and not at some other time. We do not know, maybe it is the same for all of us the way we end, no matter what the cause, but for him that end is certain and it is soon. A very certain thing now. He will be broken and a pale thing with no more purpose in this life. His story is past due and I will see to its ending for him right now. There is no other way for him, he has made his decision, and I have made mine.

There is one thing about tracking a man through bush at night that is best not to forget though and that is the fact that you may not be the only one in that bush waiting to kill someone. If you are not careful about what you're looking at and listening for all of the time, a .45 slug to the back of your head can lessen your enjoyment of your evening considerable. In spite of the driving snow it is not completely black out here, the moon is slipping out from the clouds from time to time and when it appears it is like a magician with a deck of cards. The moon has a silver band around of it like a halo I saw once in a painting.

"Who was the painter?"

"Now how the hell do I know that, Joseph?"

"Usual they sign their names…signed just at the bottom right, did you not read it?"

"Jack. His name was Jack."

"Jack who?"

"Jack the fucking painter, that's who."

So what you're looking for mostly is broken branches and any things that should not be the way they are, particularly when you run out of tracks to follow due to the snow and the wind and the dark and what you do is you look for the things that shouldn't be there. I am learning all about snow. As I have said, I much prefer sand. I prefer dirt even more because it keeps a better record. Mud is what you really want. Mud is like a map that tells you where someone is going. I do not like snow at all, but so far the tracks have held because the wind and the snow are not so persuasive here under the cover of the trees. The sound of everything is close in here. He is concerned about being followed or he would be out in the open, making better time for himself. With no horse or provisions, he is making for Lanark for there is nowhere else for him to go and I will need to put two large holes into him before he reaches there for in that town I am not a gunfighter and I do not kill people in the street. I buy provisions and I discuss the weather with the shop-keepers in pleasant tones. I seldom even spit. Little Billy will go to school here. I do not want her showing a Wanted poster to her friends at the school or bringing in letters from her daddy in the jailhouse. She will have to say that I am her daddy, that is a clear fact and just the way of things plain and simple and the way that things will be. If I am not her daddy, there is only one thing for her mother to be in the view of the folks around here and that leaves only the one thing for little Billy to be too. No, she will need a daddy, and one who is not dead.

"You keep your mind on your business, William."

Speaking of dead.

"That child *is* my business, Joseph."

"Yes, of course, yes...but so is staying alive and first comes shooting this bastard candy ass in his head."

"How do you know he's a candy ass?"

"He's running, ain't he?"

He's right. My brother is right. A man would have stayed and finished things one way or the other. The fact that he's the last of the three makes him the weakest of all of them. Seeing as the other two were taken by surprise and shot by a pregnant woman, well, that don't make him worth much in the first place. What is wrong with being shot by a pregnant woman? Maybe nothing at all, come to think of it. Especially this one. I guess if I was going to be shot by a pregnant woman, this is the one I would want doing the shooting, but I have managed to avoid that so far and that is something to take pride in at least.

"The Lord God opposes the proud, William."

"Oh for fuck's sake."

"Listen to me: book of James, chapter four, verse six."

"You're a Bible expert now?"

"There's lots of time to read where I am."

"And just the one book, I suppose?"

"Many rooms, Ish, but just the one book."

Well, there is another reason to not get myself shot. I don't mind reading and I like sometimes to read myself an adventure story. But one without angels or whales in it. Sometimes I even like to be in one and I have been in several but there's been no book wrote yet about my adventures that's worth a bent nickel.

Either a man or a deer or a bear has grabbed that branch in climbing up that hillock recently and I do not believe that deers and bears make pulling on branches for leverage a habit. But men do. The new wood of the split in it winks to me in the dark. It is split almost through and the split is fresh. It is split along the length and not cut clean as a deer would do. The top of a hillock is just about the perfect place to stop and wait and see if anyone is after you.

Just past that rise. Right there.

Of a sudden I am running fast to my left just as quick as I can in the heavy drifts and I am being fired on and I am hit. I am a foolish man talking to ghosts in the dark and making plans for the future. If there were not so many trees I would already be dead. He has missed my chest and the bullet has gone through my shoulder and he has not been able to get off a second killing shot. I am a foolish man, but I am not a dead one. Not yet.

ᥴᕲ **92** ᕲᥲ

*T*hey both walk in laughing, you see, Turner, like they have just told some fine joke to each other. The fat one and the little one with the sloping eye. They are happy to have found each other now and they think they are starting fresh on some big, crooked adventure. This place has been made up to look like a saloon and they walk in just as if they are expecting to have a drink, their boots sounding confident on the hard wood floor.

But there will be no drink.

They know they are dead yet they think they have somehow beaten the game, you see. Well, they have been well tricked into this belief. They have been allowed to think it, to think they are now ready for a cheerful round two, another crack at everything. A clean start. They walk up to the bar in this tavern that is not a tavern, Turner, and it is only then that they realize there is no bartender, they look up and down the place and see that there is no one else there at all.

"Well hell, pour us out a drink anyway, Semples. We must have a drink. A measure of spirits now that we are spirits ourselves!"

This is what the fat one says.

And the little one he is still laughing as he reaches up to the bottles and one by one finds each of them empty.

"Caleb..."

And it is as he turns confused from the bottles toward his companion that the whole place turns to desert, just one big everlasting fucking desert for them.

That is when I enter, Turner.

It is difficult to explain for you what happens next, especially as you are blinded by being alive still and deaf too, but by the time they realize where they are now, they are staked to the ground with heavy rope that cannot be broken and I am standing over them with the hammer that drove those stakes into the dirt. It is like a dream to them in short pictures, but then time slows and it is real. It quickly becomes very, very real.

"What in the name of God is going on here?" the big one yells out.

He is terrified, you see, you can see that he is terrified.

And the little one he pisses himself.

The urine spreading like spilled ink across his lap.

And by the fourth day the sun has turned into a pair of hands pulling out their eyes. That is the fourth day.

On the fifth day they begin to putrefy inside of themselves like soup left for too long on the stove.

On the sixth day they both become silent but it is not because of any ending to them, for there is to be no ending to them. And no end to this. It is merely because their voices have fried in their papery dried throats. The sun peels back each layer of their skin, ivory bones poking through. Still they turn and they writhe. They will turn this way for always.

On the seventh day I tire of their theatrics, Turner, and I take my leave but not before standing over and spitting onto each of them.

The last water they will ever taste.

∾ 93 ∾

There is a part of me that wants not to get up from here. I do not mean from the snow here where I am bleeding out. I am thinking of an early morning in the cabin with Turner still asleep in her white sheets and me up and stumbling to make coffee on the stove and trying to stay quiet enough but failing and so up she is and while I make the coffee she puts a record onto the Victrola, which she has ordered all the way up from Detroit, and we listen without speaking. I do not speak because it is my belief that the man singing sounds as if someone is holding his nose together for him with pliers and at the same time twisting his balls with a gelding tool, but she is standing by the window and looking out into the morning and my opinion is of no importance. Women are better than men.

And all men know this.

They just react to it different.

The snow is so heavy now that it is hard to see anything at all. The kind of a storm that can get a man all turned around and lost and even dead if he is foolish enough to get himself stuck in it. That is if he's not already slowly bleeding to death on the ground as I am.

"My dick was always bigger than yours."

Speaking of death.

"Joseph, for Christ's sake there's a man here trying to kill me and I think I may already be obliging him by way of cooperation. This is no time for rulers."

"A man trying to kill you is nothing new."

"And from the place where you are, all you can think to say is that your dick was bigger than mine?"

"It's not all I can think to say, Ish. It's just what I'm saying now."

"It's not even true."

"You can see things from where I am."

"You got some kind of celestial tape measure? 'Cause right now my dick is frozen to the side of my leg like a curled-up centipede so I don't think now is a good time to be judging anything."

"Good a time as any."

"Is that what Jesus told you? Because from what I heard I don't believe he was much in favour of folks judging other folks."

"He's right here next to me, why don't you ask him?"

Just because you're dead don't mean you know everything. He thought he knew everything when he was alive too, so nothing has changed about him. You didn't know enough to keep from drowning, did you, Joseph? You did not know much about swimming, did you? Should have learned when you had the chance. He always was one sanctimonious bastard my brother. *Sanctimonious*. I have been saving that one up, Joseph.

"Might as well use it now, William, doesn't appear that you have too much time left."

"Bullshit. You know all and see all so tell me where is this bastard?"

"It does seem odd that he has not found you and shot you again."

"I am glad my predicament tickles your curiosity."

"Well, there's surprisingly not much to do here where I am."

"Apparently. Well, that don't worry me, I'm staying down here."

"Down is the wrong word, it's more as if—"

"I don't give a fuck."

"And you don't actually have control over when—"

"The fuck I don't."

And I'm up now and I'm moving. Which is the wrong thing to do. I would rather that he had come down here to me to finish me off. I should have waited for him and then I could have played dead and shot his fool head off for him when he did. But if he has not come down, he's up on that ridge and he is waiting for me. And with the snow this heavy maybe he's got some of the same troubles as I do, such as not being able to see a fucking thing. Likely he is even less familiar with snow than I am. And maybe he is afraid. Men who are afraid to die are the easiest ones to kill. That has been my experience.

"Those three were following us ever since New Mexico territory. You know that?"

"What?"

"Remember? We saw them in New Mexico just before we found Missouri murdered and then we saw them again in Texas from the saloon. You saw them again just today with their horses right here in this town while you were standing in the store worried about ribbon. Just too busy with being alive then to notice or do anything about it."

"Goddammit, Joseph, one of us is still fairly busy with life right now."

"For the moment is all, William. Like I said, you saw them again just today in town but you were too busy thinking about ribbons and a cigar to go out and see who they were. Plain as day who they were, the same men we saw before just as large as life and just as ugly. Anyone could have seen it."

"Anyone who is dead, you mean. Maybe you could have mentioned this fact this morning instead of now when it don't make a lick of difference. Easy to see shit when you got a magic telescope, ain't it? I thought you were just a goddamn voice in my head."

"Well, if that is the case then that would mean you're hallucinating from blood loss…and will die soon anyway, so it does not matter much."

"You are a piss-poor excuse for heavenly help from above, you know that, Joseph?"

"You'd best get yourself on up that ridge."

"You think so?"

"I do."

How carefully do you listen to a dead man? Well, getting up on that ridge is what I was going to do anyway. So fuck him. What I need to do is to get my ass up this hill without getting it shot off on the way there. There's always a chance that with all the time I've wasted already this corncob is down in the tavern in Lanark right now tellin' stories about him shooting Billy the Kid. I can just about imagine this mutt in the tavern in Lanark shooting his mouth off.

"You mean you didn't know that's who you had up there in those woods? Sure and that's Calamity Jane's daughter who's up there with him too. That's what I said. She's still there and she is somethin' to see, a pretty girl, a very pretty girl. And there's about five thousand dollars up there too. Five thousand dollars in cash in an iron box. Who's comin' back with me to get them some of that money and who knows what else they can get while they're up there? I told you she's a pretty girl, didn't I? Now who's goin' back up there with me?"

I am becoming delusional from the snow and the loss of blood. I am fully expecting to get on up that ridge top and find a whole lot of nothing but snow and more snow and I am also figuring that by the time I do get there he's gone or maybe he's already on his way back up here with half the town following him, but no—he is right there.

Well, there he is. Right there.

The damned fool has got himself turned around in the storm and now he is pointing down the other side of the hill. He's crouching and moving around now like he's trying to spot where I went. Well, friend, I am right here behind you.

And with the wind like it is, I can get up right close without him hearing a thing.

And so I do.

"Well hello, friend," I say.

He spins around but it doesn't take much to kick the rifle right out of his hands and away from him and without that gun holding him up there's not much to him, you can see that right easy. He's a scarecrow. He is the least of the three of them and that is for certain. Face like an unbaked biscuit and he's looking at me like there might be something he can say that will help him out.

There ain't.

I know this man. He was in the customs house at the border.

"You know who I am?" I ask him.

"Sure I do. You're Bill—"

When a twelve-gauge shotgun goes off twice in your face your conversational abilities are cut right down considerable. It was just the wrong thing for him to say. Or even to start to say. The thing now is that I have used up a lot of my own blood getting up this hill and it is more than I thought by the way my head suddenly feels heavy now that he is dead and the way that everything is going to white from the edges on in. That's not the snow doing that. That's my… Damn. I believe that I am going to pa—

"Billy?"

Goddammit, not again.

"I told you this girl was one to watch out for, Ish."

"You said no such thing to me, Joseph. At no point in your earthly life did you ever say, 'Watch out for this girl,' not once."

"Words to that effect then."

"Shit."

"She's trying to wake you up, William."

"I can hear that, Joseph."

"Well."

"Well, why ain't I waking up?"

"You're not exactly asleep."

"Goddammit, Joseph, don't you tell me that I am dead."

"You're not exactly that either."

"Well, what am I then?"

"You're the biggest ass in three counties, William. I know I mentioned that to you some time ago."

"Well, is she going to wake me up or is she not?"

"She is dragging you down the hill."

"What, now?"

"Right now, yes. And now she is pushing you up onto her horse."

"She's a strong one."

"William, what did you mean 'not again'?"

"What?"

"A minute ago when you said, 'Goddammit, not again.'"

"I mean she's already saved my life once tonight and now she's doing it again."

"I see."

"She is saving my life...ain't she, Joseph?"

"I expect so. Though you are still here close to where I am... so nothing is certain yet."

"Well hell, get me back to there, can't you? Of what use are you? There's a pregnant woman trying to save my ass and what are you doing to help? Don't you care nothing at all about your future niece? That maybe she should have a father who's not dead?"

"What makes you think it's going to be a girl?"

"I don't know. I have a feeling is all. I have had it for a while now."

"I see."

"You see so goddamn much, tell me what's going on now."

"Well, she's got you up on the back of the horse...and she's got your wound all packed up for you."

"My head hurts."

"She should probably lift it up. You're drooling down the back of that horse's ass."

"It's undignified."

"It's just spit."

"I mean being saved by a pregnant woman is undignified, Joseph. Once is bad enough, but twice? In one night? I'm god-damned Billy the Kid."

"Not anymore, William. No, you're not. There is no one left alive to know that now. Not anymore. Just her. She's the only one."

I do not enjoy my brother being right so much.

"Billy?"

Goddammit, so Joseph did get me to that safe place he talked about.

"Billy, *wake up now.*"

I'm trying to, Turner, I am trying to.

He said that he would.

"C'mon, Billy."

That place where nobody knows who Billy the Kid is. There's only one left who did and now there's not much left of him to speak of and now there's just…

Turner.

"Billy…"

And she's crying.

She's crying.

"What the hell are you crying for, goddammit?"

"I'm not."

But she is.

No point in arguing about it.

✌ **94** ✍

After it becomes well established that I am not going to die after all we have us some coffee and whisky and then the sun comes up and the snow stops falling. I am sitting up in bed all bandaged together and she is sitting in the rocking chair she bought for when the baby comes.

"Billy."

"You keep saying that."

"I like saying it."

I am hoping she will decide soon to cook up some bacon for us.

"Billy, this is the first time I have ever been somewhere that I wanted to be."

Is what she says.

ᥰ **95** ᥲ

Well hell, nobody expects a baby in the middle of the day, do they? These things are supposed to happen at night or maybe early in the morning, aren't they?

"Says who?"

"I suppose you know all about babies too now, Joseph?"

"I know they can arrive whenever they see fit to, Ish."

"That somethin' you learned with all your baby-makin' experience?"

"I may have made one or two."

"Well, not that you know of for certain, so I doubt very much that you were around when they arrived into the world to make a note of the time of day that it happened."

Then he's gone off again, which is exactly what he does when he's got nothing else to say, and I'm standing looking down at the wet on the floorboards.

"It's time now, Billy, it's time."

It's time.

✤ 96 ✤

I don't know a thing about babies. The only time I was ever close to a baby being born into this world was in a whore-house. It was the middle of a late August desert morning and it was hot. This Chinese girl they had working there, she wasn't one of the whores, she did the cooking and the washing, and her time came to have the child and I—this was not something you would know if you were just a customer, you understand—I was living there at the time and I knew all the girls pretty good and me and Charlie Bowdre sometimes we would just sit there in the kitchen and talk and drink coffee, and Sally, which is what she was called but that was not her name, she would make us the coffee and we would talk to her too and if she wasn't too busy with her chores she might just sit down with us but not for too long or she'd get into trouble. She had this little scar right under her left eye, I don't know what from, it looked like it had been there a long time.

Charlie and I were in the next room and a lady in there with her was supposed to know all about these things and helped hundreds of babies to get born and I don't know how we know as we sit there but we know that things are not going the way they ought to in that room with the girls going in and out all the time and little Sally yelling like she was. And sheets stained with blood. And Charlie and I we kind of want to go but we don't want to leave, if you know what I mean, so we put the bottle we are drinking out of to one side and ask can we help but nobody takes the time to even answer us, they just keep going in and out of that room and every time one of them

[390]

comes out she looks worse than when she went in. There's a Regulator clock swinging back and forth on the wall and Charlie and I we start watching that because there is nothing else for us to do and then Charlie takes out his Bowie knife and starts in to sharpening it and I wish I had one so I could do the same. I think that maybe I will take out my gun and clean it but I don't have any rags and all the towels in the house are in use so I make some coffee. There is nothing else to do.

"Do you think we oughta—"

"No," I tell Charlie, and I don't even know what he was going to say but I know there's nothing we oughta do now except maybe not be there but it is too late for us to not be there because we are there already.

"She'll do alright," I say. And I have no idea why I say this. I know she will not be alright. Sure enough she and the little baby both end up dead and they bring the baby out in a green blanket wrapped up real tight and Charlie and I we both know it's the baby but we don't know yet that Sally is dead too and we can't figure what to say because there is nothing to say or what to do because there is nothing for us to do.

"Maybe now?" Charlie says, looking at the door like the house is on fire.

"Yeah," I say. "Yeah, sure, let's go."

So we leave and it is the next day that we find out about Sally. I remember that one time she told us her parents lived all the way out in California and old Charlie he asked her is that near China? Charlie was never in a school in his life nor never read a book neither and she just laughed at him and then he laughed too and I remember that because I had seen Charlie strike a woman before for laughing at him like that once and also seen him kill a man for less. That was something about Sally—she was such a sweet girl, I guess he didn't mind that she laughed at him, and she just poured him some more coffee and he drank it down.

When we found out she had died he said, "That is a very sad thing, Billy."

And I agreed with him that it was.

We both went to her little funeral and we stood there in the wind and looked at the pine board stuck into the ground with her name on it and we found out that her name was really Hua instead of Sally and we also found out from one of the girls that her real name meant flower.

Charlie and I we paid to get that pine board changed up for a nice stone with her name carved on it and we never told anyone that. Probably about the only good and secret thing Charlie Bowdre ever did in his life, and me too.

We never knew what happened to her baby, probably down there with her, I suppose, I don't know where else they would have put it. Hua. Flower.

At the funeral one of the girls hands out little pieces of white paper folded and inside is a penny and a candy, and she says the candy is to sweeten the loss, and the money is to buy more sweets. It is what they do in China, she says, when someone dies. She says Sally—Hua—she told her about it one time. I kept the paper for over a year in my pocket along with that penny. I do not know where those things are now.

↶ **97** ↷

So you see that I am still uneasy in my mind even with Mrs. Kitley the baby lady here in the house now and everything peaceful and Turner telling me, "Don't carry on so...Joseph... people have babies every day."

"Not you."

"Well, thank the Lord for that—we don't have enough room."

Mrs. Kitley seems capable enough and has organized the room and the sheets and put some basins around the place as if she intends to catch rainwater in them but I am uneasy every time Turner shifts her position and makes noises that for certain do not indicate any kind of comfort.

"Please do relax yourself, Mr. Bonney, all this nervous energy of yours is doing no good to the situation at all, just be calm, just be happy that soon you're going to be a father."

Which is a few dollars short of the truth, but never mind.

"You'd be a great deal more use to us if you just had yourself a comfortable seat on the porch and drank yourself a whisky."

It does not seem to me that would be of any use at all and I suppose that is her point. Well, I am not a drinking man.

"Just do as she says, Joseph...and have a smoke and put your feet up on the railing or take your rifle with you and look for rabbits, just do something, instead of walking around in here like it's a train station and the 4:05 to Houston is late..."

"I don't know."

"Then just let those who do know worry about it on your behalf, Mr. Bonney, and you take your rifle or your tobacco or you take both and just go outside now and take the measure of the air. Even if it does you no good at all, it might do a world of good for your wife."

So I look toward Turner and she nods at me with some force so I take my rifle down from the wall and I go outside. I have no intention of hunting so I just sit down on the bench.

"You're about as much use as tits on a bull."

"I never understood that expression, Joseph."

"What is there to understand, Ish? Bulls don't have tits."

"Might as well have, what difference does it make to the calf? Be just as much use to the calf..."

And I haven't seen a rabbit in days.

"Well, I suppose that's a fact, Ish. I never considered it."

"Milk's milk."

"Seems like it would be unnatural though."

"About as unnatural as bein' tossed out here like wet garbage just to sit here with a dead man." I point up toward the ridge with the rifle. "I shot seven turkeys up on that ridge last month."

"That so?"

"Seven in one afternoon, they just kept on comin' like they was hungry for the lead."

"Turner will make a fine mother."

"Course she will. Can't you see I'm trying to change the topic of the conversation?"

"What for?"

"You're just as plug-headed dead as you were alive, you know that?"

"Well, I died, I didn't go off to college, what'd you expect?"

"I thought you said you were smarter now. I just figured dead folks'd know more about stuff than the living, that's all."

"Well, that shows how much you don't know."

"Ain't my fault. I ain't never been dead yet."

"Turkeys put up an awful fuss when they get shot?"

"Well, they don't like it much."

"I never shot any. I think fatherhood will sit well with you, William."

"What makes you say that?"

"Nothing really. It just seemed like the thing to say. To tell the truth, there's absolutely nothing in your life to date that would indicate you being even an adequate father."

"Cheers." And I have another pull from the bottle. You sure you don't want some?" I ask him.

"Fuck you."

"Alright. And you remember to say hey to God for me when you see him. Say, 'Billy sends his regards.' You listening to me?"

But Joseph is gone now and that is fine with me, that's enough of Joseph for a while. I don't see the point to him really. At least I am assured that I am not losing my mind. He is as painfully real dead as he was alive. Seems to me he should have more to do where he is now than he ever did when he was here and maybe that would prevent him from hunkering down here and bending my ear off like the long-winded fool that he is. I guess maybe there is not that much to do up there. Count the clouds. I suppose it's not for me to be wondering about the great mysteries of life and death. Maybe when we're a little family of our own we can start attending a church and some preacher can explain it all to me. Shit, I don't even know who I am anymore. Listen to me. Ol' Billy the Kid off to Sunday service with the family in tow.

Fresh-baked bread and clean clothes and a cut flower in a jar.

✧ 98 ✧

Riding into a sea of grass, grass high enough that a man riding into it could lose himself or pull it up and tie it across the horn of his saddle. The tops of the blades shimmer and shift in the sun. A lone melancholy rests down onto me now like an affliction, but as I ride, it lifts into something more akin to comfort. Somehow the sun on the grass and the few clouds in the sky reconcile me to the day and to whatever it will hold for me and for us. Whatever it is that normally rages inside of me is tamed for the moment and all that matters now is the gentle movement of the good horse beneath me and the aimless shifting of the breeze. Then I wake up from the daydream and still have that same feeling. There's nobody to tell me what I should do or not do. No neighbour. No lawman. No preacher. No do-gooder and no wrongdoer. No woman and no man. Not even myself. Just riding and brushing the tops of the grass with my right hand. Most of my days my life has contained something of a rodeo or a travelling carnival, or maybe a penny shooting gallery. But not this day and not anymore. This day the only things I have to do are to keep right on and see where I end up. I am not accustomed to things being of a gentle nature but I believe I could be, I could tailor myself to this suit of clothes just fine.

"You got any tobacco?"

"Dammit, Joseph, how are you gonna smoke when you're dead?"

"Doesn't matter. I suppose I have lost the taste for tobacco anyway."

"Fine."

"The way you say fine makes it sound like you know things, Ish."

"Fine."

"You don't know shit."

"I know more shit than I care to know, I know that."

"You think this is gonna take much longer?"

"Is what gonna take much longer?"

"What? Turner pushin' out a baby. That's what. Last I heard that's the main event that's goin' on here."

"Is that why you settled down here from the clouds again?"

"I told you, there ain't no clouds."

"Up from the fire then."

"There's no fire neither."

I have nothing to say to him now so I just sit and look out at the snow and the trees. I am listening to see what I can hear from the inside of the cabin but there is no sound from there.

"You ever know a man without sin?" Joseph asks.

"I don't even know what that means."

"It means a man that just did good for his whole life and he never did a wrong thing. You ever met a man like that?"

"I don't know that I'd care to."

"So no?"

"So of course no. There's no such man."

"How about a woman then?"

I go back to looking at the trees and the snow.

"Harder to answer that one, ain't it, Ish?"

I can't argue with him on that.

"You never can tell just what they're up to, that's how I always found it," he says.

I don't have to tell him anything to tell him that I agree with him on that, so I just stay quiet. Maybe they're not any better than we are. But it sure as hell don't seem that way much of the time. I sit some and listen to a woodpecker high up in a pine tree and I try to find it by squinting at the sun through the high branches.

"She'll be alright, William. They both will. So you can stop worrying."

The dead are always with us. They don't go anywhere.

But then he's gone. Again.

And I'm still worrying.

ᥟ **99** ᥦ

Goodness and light, my friends, goodness and light and all things are well.

I decide just to burn up the sheets as there is more blood on them than after a dirty gunfight and I do not suppose Turner will want to wash them or clean them so I set a fire out by the tree line. The smoke rises into the air and scares the crows from the trees. There is an expression and it goes that if you give a woman an acorn you'll soon be up to your ass in oak trees and I think it is true enough. Doesn't say anything about babies though. I do not intend to be up to my ass in babies. I never intended to be up to my ass in this country in anything other than whisky and snow, but here I am. Turner is sleeping now and so it is just me and Little Billy here now. Billy is also sleeping though. So it is just me really. Just me and a baby right here in my lap. William and Billy. I do not know.

Joseph knew his business, that I will say. Although this is not what he intended, it is still, by all measures, a vast improvement on my former situation. I am sorry, Joseph, both for having doubted you about coming here in the first place and for saying that things have worked out better overall without you around, but that does indeed seem to be the case. She is more even-tempered than you ever were and she is much more pleasant to look at and I am not going anywhere. I intend to stay here with this girl and her baby, I do.

Last night I dreamt I was in a train station somewhere out in the middle of some endless yellow fields. There was no one else there, and no trains coming that I could see. Nothing but .

yellow fields and blue sky, but I was waiting for a train though I had no idea why. That is not quite correct: I knew why, but I was keeping it a secret, if that makes any sense at all...a secret from myself. I don't think it was intentional—the part of me that was in the dream knew why he was there, and the part of me that was watching the man in the dream did not, and they weren't talking to each other is I guess how it was. The man in the dream sat alone on one of the long wooden benches and looked out at the expanses of dry wheat and then down at his boots. He sat like that for a long time and then he reached down and rubbed the dust from one of his boots and spat on them and wiped at them with a gloved hand. How can I describe to you how this felt for me to see? The yellow stalks below and the bright blue sky above and both of them going on forever and there was nothing else but the quiet breeze and the train station and the man who was me and his shiny boots. Now and then he would rise and step out onto the platform and peer down the tracks, then step back from the edge and straighten his hat. He was certainly waiting for something. He'd look out at the fields again and then return into the station though there are no clearly defined walls to this station, you understand, just the inside and the outside of it. He would stand there and regard the large white-and-black wall clock but somehow he did not seem to care at all what time it was. The clock was just something for him to look at. The fact of the matter was that the train was either here or it was not, the actual time of its arrival made no difference to him. He walked over to a wooden box on the wall that held schedules and reached for one to consult it. In a dream like this you cannot see what the schedule said. It is blurred and indistinct, not part of the dream. He does nothing else so you just start to get the feeling that he is in no rush about anything so you just watch him sit there and he straightens his collar, pulls at his tie. You feel he has some sense of occasion. Imagine yourself having this dream. You notice now the stillness of the wheat in the fields. How the breeze has died. He looks down the tracks. And then he turns and looks directly into your eyes.

Like he knows you've been there all along.

And you wake up.

You wake up and a girl you love—it is the day she has her baby. And then the both of them, girl and baby, they live through the day and then right through the night too and so there you are, the three of you, in a cabin in the woods where in the early mornings you drink a coffee and you rest your feet by the fire and the sunlight streams in through the windows and the days go by.

❧ 100 ❧

This place that Joseph found for us is finally a safe place to be. All the bodies of the past are buried good and deep and are no trouble now to anyone. I'll write whatever I want to write now, it is the time for that. Billy the Kid is well and truly dead now and it does not matter to a soul, least of all to William McCarty, and I am glad to see the end of him. People will believe what they see written down because they always have. Billy the Kid died a long time ago and that is in the history books they have written and in the ones still left to write. Cold drops of water hitting the back of my head in the summer heat with a storm approaching and the sky a dull metal grey. Riding a horse hell-bent across the New Mexico desert. Turner in her bath ordered all the way from Michigan and carried here by two strong horses, her yellow hair and her blue eyes. I put a book down on the table at night and I trim down the lantern to darkness and sleep better than I ever have and better than I have any right to. There is a rocking chair in that corner. There is a teacup on the windowsill there. She likes that cup because there is a picture on it of a little girl in a swing. So you take your boots off and when the sun goes down you go to bed, and the night pushes against the window glass, and you just let it.

I'm not a fool. You don't ever push someone to the point where they don't give a damn anymore. And when someone does decide to give a damn about you, well, you stick with that person and hope they stick with you and you try to give them reasons to do so. That's a lesson well learned and I pass it on to you now. You can keep these things that I've told you about here in this book close to you or not. It's up to you now. One person can't have that much effect on another's thinking anyway. Unless you love them. Or unless they shoot you. That's another thing I have learned and you can keep that or you can leave it alone also. The wooden frame of the fireplace is whitewashed. You see how that white paint there is charred with the darkness of the soot? And the wood there in the corner fresh split with a good axe? We don't leave much behind, that is all I am saying. We are dust.

I am Billy the Kid.

You ask me if I am sorry for the things I have done.

Are you?

I wasn't the leader of any gang.

I was for Billy all the time.

So just don't come sneaking up behind me because I don't need no more friends than I got right here in this room. And I sure don't need any more enemies than I have already had, although perhaps the truth is that I am out of enemies at last, perhaps that is finally so. And I don't care what you think about what I do or about what I did. I don't care what you think about me. I don't think about you at all so you may think about me whatever you please.

I am Billy the Kid.

Just go ahead and read the books that you have not read. Drink the wine that has not been drunk and play the music that you have not yet played. Life goes on by itself, it does not need you, and it does not need me. So just love it. Ring a bell. Dance. We are the only living creatures who know that we will end and who choose to forget about that fact every single morning when we rise—even on our last morning on the planet, still, we will be thinking of plans for tomorrow. I am broken down now and my knees don't work and my hand is slow but that is alright with me, I am now a peaceful man. This dream I'm living now comes in short sections and frozen pictures. Turner's hand on the table in the sun. The ice breaking up in the dark river. I am happy they come at all. In one picture Turner walks toward me through a summer field and the sun is behind her and she is smiling. On my deathbed I will think of her and I will start to float slowly up off the bed and into the air. In a room full of sunlight. It will be a miracle. And no one else will see it.

But that won't matter. And somewhere out in the fields somewhere in this world there's a man with a gun. There will always be such a man. Somewhere else a girl in a thin coat pokes at the ice on a pond with a stick, and she likes the way the ice sounds when it breaks, and a dog, somewhere else, many fields away, howls and howls.

In the very early morning before first light I get up and I see her bed empty and the baby gone too.

For a moment I'm alone in the dark but then I find her sitting there on the porch with the sun breaking out low through the tree line and the two dogs sniffing around her looking for food, wondering why it is that she is up so early. I sit myself down beside her, my old knees complaining, and neither of us says anything for a while and we just sit and look up at the lowering white moon as it sinks and as the slow sun rises, the sky turning now from black to blue and then to pink and finally to blue again, the dogs wagging at the unexpected company and the baby wrapped up tight and snug against the cold, her little head held tight against her mother.

We both sit here, looking out at the fresh snow, still not saying anything, and then we stand and we turn back through the half-open door and on into the cabin. She takes my hand. And if you listen close you will hear the three of us breathing.

There is no other sound.

Photograph of school class at Lanark, Ontario, about 1916. The only students identified on the back of the photo are Roy Reston Evans, third from the right, with pen marks above his head, and Wilhelmina "Billy" Bonney, seventh from left, front.

In the 1916 census of Lanark (North) Dist. 30, Sub-Dist. f-3, Ont. Archives Microfilm: T-6477, is found:

			Age:
Evans Danill R.M	Head	Jan 24, 1863	37
Evans Eliza J.F	Wife	Nov 29, 1866	35
Evans Nina G. F	Daughter	Feb 18, 1891	10
Evans Clifford	Son	Aug 17, 1892	8
Evans Clarence	Son	Aug 15, 1893	7
Evans Herbert E.	Son	May 28, 1895	5
Evans Roy R.	Son	July 9, 1897	8
Bonney Joseph	Head	Jun 22, 1859	58
Bonney Turner	Wife	Oct 17, 1887	29
Bonney Wilhelmina	Daughter	Feb 11, 1910	6
Bonney Josephine	Daughter	July 7, 1914	2

Based on this census entry, the estimated photo date is about 1916–17.

"I have no wish to fight any more."

—Billy the Kid, in a letter to Gov. Lew Wallace,
dated March 12, 1879

Acknowledgements:

The line "Don't call me Ishmael" was suggested by Broderick McRae. It is worth more than the agreed upon payment of a bottle of wine.

The transition on pages 370 and 371 was suggested by Kaylyn Kluever.

The smokehouse description is an adaptation from *Let Us Now Praise Famous Men* by James Agee.

The thrown-milk sequence is inspired in part by a sequence in *Coming Through Slaughter* by Michael Ondaatje.

The author would like to acknowledge funding support from the Ontario Arts Council.

With thanks to:

Hilary McMahon for being the sort of agent who will believe in a writer and his words even when he has begun to doubt them himself, and for being such a staunch and dedicated supporter of Billy.

My family for putting up with my time away in the desert. Tara, my ICU nurse in a time of plague, for always thinking that her dad would get this book done and published. Michaela, my front-line fighter for rights, for always asking how the battle was going. Taylor, the fixer and crafter of many things, for the many hours in the blind and on the range, talking of guns and of deserts and of manhood.

Deborah, for not giving up on me.

Susie Osler for running Fieldwork and for hosting Framework, which supported the writing of an initial draft of this novel.

Chris Osler and Christine Earnshaw for the use of their remote cabin where the last pages of this story were composed.

Carolyn R. Parsons, for managing to get my previous novel, *Skin House*, to the surface of the moon.

The Canada Council for the Arts and the Ontario Arts Council.

Phil Hall, Stan Bevington, Alana Wilcox, Beth Follett, bill bissett, Hazel and Jay Millar, and most particularly Brian Kaufman (a straight shooter).

And Mary Newberry, as always.

This book took some time to write, and was written in:
Kemptville, Ontario
Las Vegas, Nevada
Old Brooke Road, Perth, Ontario
New Orleans, Louisiana
Hurricane, Utah
Bennett Lake, Lanark County, Ontario
And on the unceded territory of the Anishnabek, Huron-Wendat, Oneida, and Haudenosaunee peoples.

ABOUT THE AUTHOR

Michael Blouin has been a finalist for the Amazon First Novel Award, the bpNichol Award, the CBC Literary Award and his first novel won the 2009 ReLit Award. He has been the recipient of the Lilian I. Found Award, the Diana Brebner Award and the Lampman Award. His 2019 novel *Skin House* won the 2020 ReLit Award for Best Novel and has been included on the NASA/Astrobotics Peregrine Mission to the Moon as well as the upcoming SpaceX lunar landing.

michaelblouinwriter.com

iambillythekid.com